The Fight
For
Lizzie Flowers

Carol Rivers, whose family comes from the Isle of
Dogs, East London, now lives in Dorset. Visit
www.carolrivers.com and follow her on Facebook
and Twitter @carol_rivers

Also by Carol Rivers

Lizzie of Langley Street
Bella of Bow Street
Lily of Love Lane
Eve of the Isle
East End Angel
In the Bleak Midwinter
East End Jubilee (*previously* Rose of Ruby Street)
A Sister's Shame
Cockney Orphan (*previously* Connie of Kettle Street)
A Wartime Christmas
Together for Christmas

The Fight
For
Lizzie Flowers

CAROL RIVERS

**SIMON &
SCHUSTER**

London · New York · Sydney · Toronto · New Delhi

A CBS COMPANY

First published in Great Britain by Simon & Schuster UK Ltd, 2015
A CBS COMPANY

1 3 5 7 9 10 8 6 4 2

Simon & Schuster UK Ltd
1st Floor
222 Gray's Inn Road
London WC1X 8HB

www.simonandschuster.co.uk

Simon & Schuster Australia, Sydney
Simon & Schuster India, New Delhi

A CIP catalogue record for this book is available from the British Library

Paperback ISBN: 978-1-4711-3133-2
eBook ISBN: 978-1-4711-3134-9

Typeset by Hewer Text UK Limited, Edinburgh
Printed and bound in Great Britain by CPI Group (UK) Ltd, Croydon, CR0 4YY

The Fight for Lizzie Flowers was written for *you*, my readers.

Acknowledgements

Once again, my thanks go to Simon & Schuster for whom I'm currently writing my thirteenth book. I still can't believe it! To Jo Dickinson, my awesome editor, and to the editorial, art and production teams, whose skill and ingenuity bring to life the very small germ of an idea in my head. To Judith Murdoch, agent extraordinaire, who has encouraged me to dig deep from the very start. With her help and support I've gained a new insight into my writing goals.

Finally, my thanks go to all the friends I have made on social media and Amazon, to those who have read the books, both in paperback, electronic and audio, and to those who have reviewed. I was able to reach more readers than ever this year, and felt honoured to learn about your lives and families in a very special way. In return, I published my first newsletter in 2015, expressing my thoughts on a more personal level. A big thank-you here to the talented Rik Ubhi, who made my newsletter possible.

Lastly, a nod to him indoors – Chris, who, a bit like a

police artist, creates sketches of my characters as I describe them, until suddenly they jump off the canvas and into my arms. Well, almost!

So, thank you everyone. I am truly grateful.

Carol Rivers

www.carolrivers.com

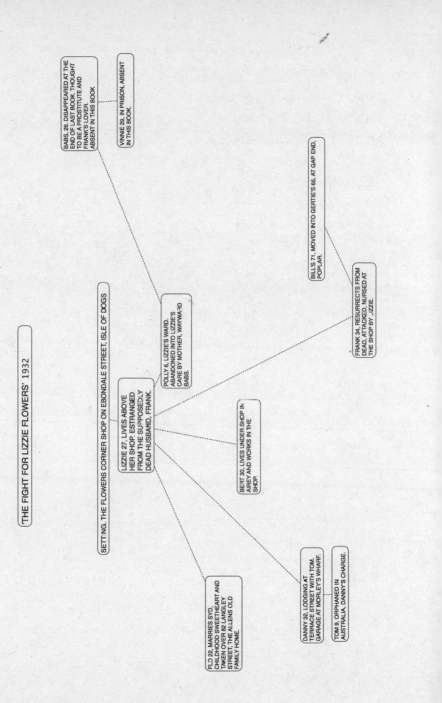

'THE FIGHT FOR LIZZIE FLOWERS' 1932

SETTING. THE FLOWERS CORNER SHOP ON EBONDALE STREET, ISLE OF DOGS

BABS, 26. DISAPPEARED AT THE END OF LAST BOOK. THOUGHT TO BE A PROSTITUTE AND FRANK'S LOVER. ABSENT IN THIS BOOK

VINNIE 29, IN PRISON, ABSENT IN THIS BOOK.

BILL'S 71, MOVED INTO GERTIE'S 65, AT GAP END, POPLAR.

FRANK, 34, RESURRECTS FROM DEAD, ATTACKED, NURSED AT THE SHOP BY LIZZIE.

POLLY 6, LIZZIE'S WARD, ABANDONED INTO LIZZIE'S CARE BY MOTHER, WAYWARD BABS.

LIZZIE 27, LIVES ABOVE HER SHOP. ESTRANGED FROM THE SUPPOSEDLY DEAD HUSBAND, FRANK.

BERT 30, LIVES UNDER SHOP IN AIREY AND WORKS IN THE SHOP.

DANNY 32, LODGING AT TERRACE STREET WITH TOM. GARAGE AT MORLEY'S WHARF.

TOM 9, ORPHANED IN AUSTRALIA, DANNY'S CHARGE.

FLO 22, MARRIES SYD, CHILDHOOD SWEETHEART AND TAKEN OVER 82 LANGLEY STREET, THE ALLENS OLD FAMILY HOME.

December 1932

It was a sunny winter's morning and ladders of gold streamed in through the registry office windows. It was also the last Wednesday before Christmas and Lizzie rejoiced in the fact that, at last, in her twenty-seventh year, she would be married to the love of her life, Danny Flowers.

The scene was set – low-key, no frills, just as she had wanted. Beside Danny stood Bert, her brother and best man. The ring was poised carefully between his great clumsy fingers, ready to pass to the groom. Bert's towering six-foot-four frame strained every stitch of his ill-fitting wedding suit, his presence giving her a feeling of reassurance. As did her good friends Lil and Doug Sharpe, seated in the row behind, the only witnesses to today's brief civil ceremony.

Lizzie looked into Danny's clear blue eyes, spaced evenly in his handsome, weather-beaten face. A jagged scar on his forehead was still visible, the handiwork of her late husband, Frank, Danny's older brother. Thankfully, nature had healed the vertical slash of smooth, pale skin and Danny's blond hair fell lightly across it, disguising any unsightliness. But the thought of Frank and the violence he had been capable of still made her shiver.

Uncannily, a door ground open at the back of the room and her mother's words flashed into mind. *'Someone's just walked over my grave, Lizzie, girl. The hairs on my neck are standing on end.'*

But why had she thought of that now? Lizzie wondered as Danny took her hand in his. Frank was dead and buried; a swollen, almost unrecognizable corpse dragged from the River Thames seven months ago, now laid to rest in East London Cemetery.

She and Danny were to be man and wife today. Nothing could spoil this moment. Not even those painful memories she had buried, sealed and locked away, and hoped would fade completely as the years passed.

Danny moved closer. His tall, powerful figure was dressed impeccably in a hand-finished black suit and silk tie. Thick blond waves parted on his crown and a smile curved over his even white teeth.

Lizzie's heart lifted in anticipation. This was the moment she had dreamed of since Danny had sailed out of her life to seek his fortune in Australia almost twelve years ago. She had loved him then. She loved him now. It was as if she had never lost him, never taken his brother for her husband.

And lived to regret it.

Chapter One

'I love you,' Danny whispered, tracing his thumb gently over her fingers. 'Always and forever this time.'

Her heart raced, missing yet another beat. 'Always and forever,' she repeated, her voice lost as the registrar, pasty-faced and squat, cleared his throat noisily.

The door rattled again.

Danny held her gaze, as though forbidding her to turn round. She saw Bert pass Danny the ring and the golden band gleamed, poised to glide effortlessly over her finger.

But it was as if her eyes couldn't help themselves. As if in slow motion, she turned, the minute details of the room imprinting themselves on her mind. The shabby wallpaper, the well-thumbed reference books on the shelves, a vase of white chrysanthcmums placed on a small table and a sprig of holly pinned precariously above the handwritten notice wishing the public at large a Festive Christmas and Happy New Year.

'Oh Christ, it can't be,' she heard Lil gasp behind her.

In that moment, Lizzie's world began to crumble. The feeling of unreality she had been trying so hard to suppress all day now fully encompassed her. The man – the *intruder* – was walking towards them. A dark fedora shaded his eyes. A camel-coloured coat was buttoned over his chest. But it was the two-tone brown-and-white brogues that sent real fear throughout her body. Shoes that were her late husband's trademark in life.

And so – Danny had told her – in death.

Lizzie shook her head, refusing to believe what she saw. If this was a ghost, then everyone else was seeing it too. Lil and Doug stood open-mouthed, staring at the figure in the aisle. The registrar frowned, a look of annoyance on his face at the interruption. But it was Danny who stepped forward and squared his shoulders, confronting the apparition. 'Frank? But you're supposed to be—'

'Brown bread,' Frank acknowledged, his pale blue eyes moving uncertainly in their red-rimmed sockets.

Lizzie felt fingers of ice on her neck. Frank, her dead husband, was here, in this room. The same man Danny had identified in Limehouse morgue, back in May.

'But it can't be you,' Danny said. 'I saw you. Fished out of the river—'

'Not me,' Frank replied softly. 'Sorry to disappoint.'

'Is this some sick joke?' Danny demanded. 'What are you playing at, Frank?'

'This ain't no game, Danny. I'm flesh and blood stand-ing here. Same as you.'

'But I saw what I saw,' Danny insisted. 'It was you—'

'Floaters are ten a penny in the docks,' Frank

interrupted with a slight shrug. 'You should have took a closer gander.'

Before Danny could reply, the registrar spoke. 'Who are you, sir? This is a private ceremony, with invited guests only.'

'You'd better ask her.' Frank nodded at Lizzie.

But she was speechless; like Danny she couldn't believe this was Frank. He was thinner and paler than he used to be, his cheeks sunken under his eyes. But he was still wearing his trademark stacked-shoulders overcoat and ridiculous two-tone brogues.

'Mrs Flowers?' the registrar prompted. But Lizzie could only shake her head as she tried to speak.

'I . . . I . . . don't know . . .' she mumbled at last, her voice a distant echo in her ears. 'He was – he is—'

'Alive and kicking,' Frank said quietly. 'Last time I saw you, gel, I was on my way out of this world. And no one is more surprised than me to be standing here in one piece. But this time, you have my word I ain't here to make trouble.'

'Your *word*?' Danny repeated incredulously. 'Why the hell should anyone take your word? You're nothing but bad news, Frank. And though you are family and in all conscience I should be relieved that it wasn't a brother of mine they fished out of the river, I am truly gutted.'

As the two men faced each other, all Lizzie could think was why in God's name had she married a man like Frank Flowers? She could still smell his drunken breath on their wedding night. Feel his hands ripping at her clothes. The dream had turned to a nightmare. She had been blind. Naive. And worst of all, she had lost Danny.

'Get out of here,' Danny continued with quiet menace. 'You ain't welcome, Frank. This is my and Lizzie's day. We are going to finish what we came here for.'

'Problem is,' Frank said, slowly raising his eyes, 'the law thinks different.'

Suddenly Lizzie understood what was truly happening. It didn't matter where Frank had been or why he was here. The sad truth was there wouldn't be – couldn't be – any marriage today. No blushing bride or wedding kiss after Danny had slipped the ring on her finger, no congratulations and confetti on the registry office steps. No wedding breakfast. Gone was the planned knees-up, the tinkling of ivories and serious drinking until dawn. Frank had robbed her of happiness once again.

'Come, come!' the registrar exclaimed impatiently. 'Please either leave or be seated, Mr— ?'

'Flowers,' Frank provided. 'This lady here is my wife.'

The silence in the small room was deafening; Lizzie could hear her own heartbeat. No one moved, or drew a breath.

'It's true, ain't it, Lizzie?' Frank insisted. 'You and me tied the knot – when was it? Must be all of seven years back.'

'Wife?' the little man repeated as he turned to Lizzie. 'But you have applied as a widow to be married here today.'

Lizzie felt her face flush. She stared at Frank and into

his expectant gaze. 'Y-yes . . . I was,' she faltered. 'But there's been some kind of mistake—'

'Obviously,' the official replied, and taking the ledger in front of him, he snapped it closed, pushing it to one side of the desk with an expression of undisguised anger.

Chapter Two

A bead of sweat rolled down Lizzie's back. Her two-piece suit, the perfect shade of green that she loved and only a shade lighter than her deep, sea-green eyes, was clinging uncomfortably to her skin. Her jaunty, narrow-brimmed hat of the same shade, with a delicate three inches of embroidered veil, felt a mockery now.

She heard Danny breathing hard, watching Frank as he stepped towards her. 'You're the one good thing that's happened to me, Lizzie. And I'd cut off my right arm if I could change what I did. I've seen the error of me ways and I reckon, if we gave it a shot, you and me could make a go of it. It's never too late to change.'

Lizzie glared in disbelief at the man who had cheated on her from day one of their marriage. Not caring how much he hurt her or how deeply she had been humiliated. Staring into his face, she felt the breath leave her lungs as she shook her head. 'Listen to you, Frank! Listen to what you are saying! After all that's happened do you really believe there could be a future for us? Look at me, look at Danny, we're here to begin a new life. A life that, until you walked into this room, we had intended to make together.'

'But you can't leave me now, Lizzie,' Frank pleaded, opening his arms and gazing into her eyes. 'Not now. Not now I've sorted myself out. And I have, honest to God, I have. On my life, Lizzie, they only just unlocked the door. Can't you see I'm gen this time?'

Lizzie's head started to reel. 'What door?'

'I've been ill, gel. Really bad. But they cured me. They knocked the shit out of me in the hospital and it worked.'

For one moment Lizzie wanted to laugh. She wanted to laugh long and deeply at the irony of such a statement. If only she could laugh! If only she could see the funny side of the ruination of her wedding day.

'You have got some nerve,' Danny burst out, pulling his brother round to face him. 'You turn up at the very minute we're about to get wed and give us some sob story about being in hospital?'

'It's true,' Frank said with a nod. 'I was in a loony bin. Mad as the proverbial hatter.'

'What's new? You've never been the full shilling,' Danny replied, pushing his brother away from Lizzie. 'It takes a nutter to try and blow up his family and think he can get away with it.'

'I swear it's the truth,' Frank insisted as he shrank back. 'That day I set the bomb off in Lizzie's shop, I was out of me mind. I didn't know what I was doing. All I can remember is I heard these voices in my head. Voices saying I had to get rid of you to get my wife back. Then Ferreter turned up and it's all a blank from there, till I woke up, ranting and raving, in this hospital. I was out of my mind. I didn't even know my own moniker. The shrinks put me behind bars with all these crazies. I thought I'd died and landed up in hell. It's been the worst six months of my life.'

Danny drew a breath and shook his head fiercely. 'Pull the other one, Frank. Can't you think up something more convincing?'

'It's the truth, Danny. I swear it.'

'Enough!' Danny shouted, pushing his brother's shoulder again, until he stumbled back and almost fell against a chair. 'You are nuts, Frank. That's old news. But listen to me and listen good. Stay away from us. Stay away from Lizzie. Somehow you've managed to cling on to life. But enough is enough. You've had all your chances and blown them. If I ever see you round here again I'll personally put right what Ferreter failed to do.'

Frank looked at Lizzie. He said quietly, 'Is that what you want too? Don't you believe me, gel?'

Lizzie felt the tears very close as she stared at the man whom she had married and promised to love, honour and obey. Whose child she had adopted as her own. It wasn't enough that Frank had put her sister in the family way and out of it had come their one blessing in Polly, an innocent child whom Babs and Frank had heartlessly chosen to abandon. Now he was claiming that madness had driven him to lie and cheat and almost kill his family.

She shook her head slowly and whispered, 'Danny's right, Frank. You've used up all your chances.'

'One more,' Frank implored huskily, reaching out. 'I can do it now. I can look after you and Polly like I should have. And Babs too. I can make things right—'

'Get out, Frank!' Danny shouted. 'Get out before I lose my temper. You are on borrowed time, chum, do you hear me?'

Lizzie saw the understanding slowly settle on Frank's face. His eyes were moist and suddenly devoid of expression. He swallowed, his breath flowing out of him as he pleadingly searched the faces turned towards him. No one spoke; Lizzie knew they were all in shock and Frank's shoulders slumped in resignation. Finally he turned, making his way slowly to the back of the room.

The door ground noisily on its hinges. Lizzie found herself staring at the empty space where a few seconds ago her dead husband had stood, alive and breathing and telling her he wanted her back. 'The law is very strict about remarriage.' The registrar's voice broke into her tangled thoughts. 'The law also frowns on threats and violence of any sort. This is a most reprehensible state of affairs.'

Danny ignored him and pulled Lizzie gently into his arms. 'Looks like we have to think again,' he said in a choked whisper. 'I don't know what to say to you, except, I'm sorry. Heart sorry he's back in our lives again.'

'Can you believe it?' Lil demanded, finding her voice. 'It's the Franks of this world that get away with murder,' she told the registrar angrily. 'Including his own. These two were marrying in good faith today. That toerag was supposed to be dead and none of us gives a rat's arse about what the law thinks. It's these two people standing here that matter. So you can stop looking so po-faced and get on with the service.'

The registrar pulled himself up and tugged at his waistcoat. 'I'm sorry, madam, there is nothing further I can do. The office is now closed.'

'He's right, this changes everything,' Doug said, taking hold of his wife's arm. 'Nothing for it, but to get back to the house and try to sort something out.'

'But it just ain't fair,' Lil objected again, her eyes filled with angry tears. 'That cow son is like bloody Lazarus!'

Lizzie felt Danny slip his hand around her waist. 'Let's get out of here,' he said, acknowledging Doug. As if in a dream, Lizzie found herself walking out of the room and into the cheerless winter's day.

Chapter Three

'You're kidding me,' Ethel protested, after she had listened to what Lil and Lizzie had had to say. 'Frank is alive?'

'And twice as ugly,' said Lil.

Lizzie leaned against the sink in Lil's kitchen and stared at all the food that Lil had prepared. What would the guests think when they arrived and were told there was no wedding? Would it all be wasted? But it was Danny who was really worrying her. He'd not said more than a couple of words on their drive from the registry office.

'Danny's taking it badly,' Lizzie admitted. 'He was so sure it was Frank in the morgue.'

'Danny did his best,' Ethel replied. 'That body had been in the river a long time and must have looked like Frank.'

'I should have made the identification,' Lizzie said wearily. 'But at the time I couldn't face it.'

'No wonder, after what you went through,' Lil replied as she lit up a cigarette.

'So what else did Frank say?' Ethel enquired as she poured herself and Lizzie a sherry.

'He wants me to take him back.'

'No wonder Danny is gutted.' Lil jerked her head angrily towards the front room where Danny, Bert and Doug were commiserating over a glass or six of beer. 'Danny was a breath away from slipping the ring on your finger. Another ten minutes and Frank couldn't have done nothing.'

Ethel sipped from her glass thoughtfully. 'I can't believe Frank would have the nerve to come to the registry office.'

'Exactly!' exclaimed Lil as she threw a gin and lime down her throat. Licking her lips she banged the empty glass down on the draining board. 'How come he walks in on your wedding at the very moment you're to be wed? I mean, that's one heck of a coincidence, by anyone's standards. And then all that rubbish he spouted about being in hospital. He's lying, of course he is. Porky pies is what your old man does best. You of all people, Lizzie, should know that by now.'

'Yes, I do. But why make up such an unbelievable story?'

'I reckon he's done six months in the nick.'

Ethel removed her apron and pressed her hands over her slim-fitting blue dress. 'So why not admit it?' she asked as she slipped a loose strand of honey-coloured hair back into place. 'You're not going to take Frank's nonsense seriously are you, Lizzie?'

'No, but what does it matter what's true or not? The fact is, I can't marry Danny. We'll have to drop all our plans.'

'It's just not fair,' Lil grumbled. 'Polly ain't stopped talking about Christmas and how you was all going to be together.'

Lizzie glanced out of the window to where Polly, her niece, and young Tom, Danny's adopted son, were mucking around with a ball. Timothy and Rosie, Ethel's teenage children, were sitting on the wall, watching them. They all had big smiles on their faces. Those smiles would soon disappear when she broke the news to Tom and Polly.

'Here, watch out!' Lil rushed to the window as the ball banged against the glass. She yanked open the kitchen door. 'Keep that ball away from me window, if you don't want your ears boxed. Timmy, you're the oldest. Give an eye to the youngsters, won't you?'

All four heads nodded. 'Sorry, Gran,' Timothy shouted.

'That's all right, love. But breakages don't come cheap.'

Lizzie smiled as Lil closed the door, a grin on her face. 'Your Timmy is a card, ain't he?' Lil chuckled.

'Remember, Mum, it's Timothy now,' Ethel corrected. 'Timmy's a thing of the past.'

'It's bit of a mouthful when you've known him as Timmy since the day he was born.' Lil rolled her eyes.

'Yes, but he's fifteen now. And just started work.'

Lil scoffed loudly. 'I'll bet it was his other gran who made him change his moniker.'

'No, it wasn't,' Ethel said quietly.

Lizzie knew Ethel had a hard time with her mother-in-law. After Mr Ryde had died a few years back, Richard Ryde began to divide his life between his mother's house in Lewisham and his own at Blackheath. It was a sore point for Ethel and Lizzie knew that Lil was only too eager to prove it.

'He's a looker, your lad,' Lil said with an affectionate smile as she studied her grandson through the window.

Lizzie nodded. Timothy was tall and lanky like his father, but he had Ethel's fair skin and blue eyes.

'Your Rosie will turn out a cracker, too.' Lil took a sly glance at Ethel. 'You'll have to watch out for the boys.'

'Give us a break, Mum, she's only just turned fourteen.'

'Wait till she starts stopping out late, like you used to. Then we'll see sparks fly.'

Ethel laughed. 'I liked to enjoy myself when you weren't watching.' She paused, frowning at Lizzie. 'Amazing, isn't it? They grow up so quickly. Only a year or two ago, she was playing with dolls like Polly.'

Lizzie smiled, staring wistfully at her six-year-old niece as she followed Tom around the yard. At nine years old Danny's adopted son was the spit of Danny. All blond hair and big blue eyes. While Polly was auburn with pretty blue eyes just like her mother, Babs.

At the thought of her absent sister, Lizzie felt a pang of sadness. Babs, a year younger than herself, had left the East End over a year ago, preferring a life on the streets to caring for Polly. Would she ever come back to the East End, she wondered sadly?

'Your ex is a cunning sod,' Lil warned, taking a long puff. 'He knows how much you think of Pol. He also knows he stands a good chance of being her father.'

'Not that it's ever been proved,' Ethel said quickly. 'Babs kept tight-lipped about that one.'

'We all took it for granted when Babs was up the spout that Frank was responsible,' Lil said with a shrug. 'They was going at it like rabbits behind Lizzie's back all the time she was married.'

'Mum!'

'Well, it's true, Ethel.'

'Yes, but Lizzie doesn't need to hear it again, does she?'

'Doesn't bother me,' Lizzie said, although this wasn't strictly true. It still hurt somewhere deep down when she let herself think about Frank cheating on her. 'Babs wasn't the only one, anyway. Frank had plenty of affairs. But if Polly is his, one day she'll have to know it. I don't want her to think the worst of her father.'

'So what you going to tell her?' Lil said archly.

'I'll cross that bridge when I come to it.'

'And if Frank comes to the shop?' Lil asked. 'Chucks his weight around like he used to? The kid ain't daft. She'll see him in his true light then.'

'Let him try,' Lizzie said firmly. 'Bert wouldn't have that.'

'True, Mum. It'd be a brave man who'd argue with Bert,' Ethel agreed and all three nodded.

Lil sniffed and cuffed her long nose with the back of her wrist. 'Poor Pol. She don't deserve a father like him, a two-bit crook with a knack for bashing women. Or a mother like Babs on the game.'

'I don't want to think about all that, Lil.'

'I only speak the truth, love. When Frank appears again, as he will, he'll come out with all the soft soap. You'll have to remember that he got Babs in the family way. And Polly was just a couple of weeks old when she decided she'd had enough of motherhood. The silly cow couldn't wait to go back to her life as one of Ferreter's trollops. Aided and abetted by Frank, needless to say. Christ, Lizzie, you've been to hell and back with that scoundrel!'

All three women were silent for a moment. Lizzie knew deep in her heart that Lil was right on all scores. But Polly meant more to Lizzie than the sins of the past. And even though Frank had been and done all Lil said he had, and worse, it was Polly who counted now.

'Look on the bright side,' Lil continued, gulping down smoke, 'at least Babs ain't shacked up with Frank still. She don't give a damn about Pol. Where is a mother's love in all that?'

Ethel crossed her legs, glancing at Lizzie. 'Have you ever thought of adopting Polly?'

'Yeah,' interrupted Lil eagerly, unable to stay quiet. 'Good idea. Tell them how your husband knocked off your sister, and how when Polly was born they abandoned her, leaving you to do the honours. And how, six years on, you're the closest to a mother that Polly has ever had.' Lil pointed the cigarette and the ash spilled on the table. 'Oh, yes, and there's the small matter of your old man trying to blow up your shop and you and your family with it. They'll put up no argument then!'

Lizzie shook her head. 'The welfare won't help the likes of me. I'm married to Polly's father, they'd say, and tell me to get on with it. And without Babs's consent there's nothing more I can do.'

'Your Babs was always flighty,' Lil said bitterly as she ground her dog-end into the metal ashtray. 'What with her and your brother Vinnie, who was always a sod, your mum had a tough job on her hands. If she couldn't keep them on the straight and narrow, what hope is there for you?'

But no matter what anyone said, Lizzie still felt she had failed to keep her older brother Vinnie out of prison and Babs from the streets. And though she looked on Polly as her own, Babs was Polly's birth-mother.

'You look all in, gel.' Lil placed a hand on Lizzie's arm. 'Why don't you go next door? Have a chat with your sister. She's got her drawers in a twist about not being able to get the morning off work for your wedding. As it stands, she didn't miss nothing.'

Lizzie had put off going in to see Flo, her younger sister. She knew she would be very upset. Flo hated Frank with a vengeance and had cause to.

'Better get it over with,' Lil urged. 'Remember, your little sister has stuck by you through thick and thin, whereas Babs and Vinnie buggered off. Flo had Frank taped right from when she was a kid and had the scarlet fever. He took you to visit her at the sanatorium and turned on the charm. But Flo wouldn't have none of it.'

Lizzie recognized the truth, even though it was painful to hear. What a fool she had been to fall for that charm. And it had been Flo who had tried to warn her.

Ethel touched Lizzie's shoulder. 'Chin up, love. Flo's bark is worse than her bite.'

Lizzie looked fondly at her good friend. They had grown close over the years; close enough to know what each other was thinking. And now the glance that passed between them spoke volumes.

Polly ran into Lizzie's arms as she walked into the yard. The little girl was a picture of Babs at her age. All coppery hair and big smiles. Lizzie felt the familiar pang of guilt that somehow along the way she had failed Babs. How could she not want to share in her daughter's life? Was it something that Lizzie had done?

'Did you marry Uncle Danny?' Polly asked breathlessly. 'Did they throw the confetti?'

'Uncle Danny and me decided to wait a while.'

'Are we still having a party?'

'Course we are.'

'What about Christmas? I thought we was all going to live over the shop and get a big Christmas tree and stay up late.'

'We'll still have a party.' Lizzie touched Polly's beautiful hair. 'And lots of nice things to eat.'

Polly giggled. 'That's all right then. Can I tell Tom and Rosie and Timothy?'

'Yes, but mind that ball on Auntie Lil's window.'

Polly scampered off. Relieved that Polly didn't seem too disappointed, Lizzie made her way over the broken fence to her sister's house. Somehow she had to deliver the news to Flo without more eruptions, then try to get through the rest of the day.

Chapter Four

Danny Flowers sat in the decked-out front room of No. 84 Langley Street, his beer untouched beside him. The clock on the mantelpiece showed almost an hour to go before the guests arrived. An hour in which to steady his nerves. He had a suspicion the news of Frank's return would already have circulated. The sympathy, the hand-shakes, the winks and nods were all coming his way. And he had no choice but to take them on the chin.

Danny lifted his glass and, for the first time that day, enjoyed the bite of the alcohol. Not that it would douse the fire in his chest that still raged. Anger and bitter disap-pointment fanned the flames of his resentment towards Frank. Yet, he asked himself, where was his compassion for the brother who'd cheated death and returned to life? Even if Frank was the devil incarnate, he hadn't deserved to die by Ferreter's hand. Frank was his brother, his only kith and kin other than Dad. They were family and blood-linked. But he didn't trust Frank further than he could throw him. And now, it seemed, history was about to repeat itself.

'Cheer up, lad. It might never happen.' Doug Sharpe, nursing his ale, glanced at Danny with a frown of concern.

'I'm angry at myself, Doug. How could I have been so mistaken about Frank? I saw him on that marble slab – or what was left of him.'

'Not your fault,' his old friend insisted. 'You were ninety-nine per cent certain it was Frank the coppers dragged out of the water.'

'And the one per cent manages to turn up on our wedding day.' Danny sat forward, gazing into Doug's fatherly face with its calm expression. At sixty-seven, Doug had been a white-collar worker at the docks, and had always provided for his family. But after the loss of his two sons in the war, he'd aged dramatically. Danny admired him for the way he'd pulled through the nightmare and somehow got on with his life. He was wise and steady and had been in all their lives since forever, standing by Lizzie through the mess of her marriage to Frank. For that, Danny would be eternally grateful. They were good people and Danny loved them for it.

Doug's smooth forehead wrinkled under his thinning grey hair. 'Stop beating yourself up, cocker. We all know you did your best.'

'I saw a body wearing Frank's clothes and shoes, and half a face. I didn't hang around to find out I was wrong.'

'Any one of us would have given the nod,' Bert agreed in his deep, lumbering voice. A voice, Danny reflected, that could only have come from a man who weighed over nineteen stone and stood almost with his head in the clouds. Bert sat squashed in an armchair, his tie removed and the buttons of his shirt undone. 'You wasn't going to get any help from Old Bill.'

'I've got a nasty feeling it don't end here.' Danny stretched his broad shoulders, uncomfortable under the restrictive tailoring of his wedding suit. He was more accustomed to his overalls, the ones he wore at the garage. He wore them with pride, knowing the business was his own little kingdom. He'd thought he was on the way to a happy life now, with the garage on its feet and Lizzie as his wife. How wrong could a man be?

He stared desolately at Doug. 'The point being, who did I identify as Frank?'

A knock at the front door prevented anyone from venturing an opinion. Danny stood up. 'That'll be Cal. I asked him to go by the pub and see if there was word on the grapevine. If there is, the landlord will know.'

'Y'all right, Danny?' Cal Bronga, Danny's mechanic, best friend and only employee, stepped in. Black-bearded, with ebony shoulder-length hair, Cal was the agile bush-man Danny had first met in the gold mines of Australia. No one had been more pleased than Danny when Cal had eventually followed him to England last summer.

'Find out anything?' Danny kept his voice low.

'No, boss. Not a breath.' Cal shook his dark head. 'Like you told me, I checked at the Quarry and the Ship, then drove past your old man's drum. Quiet as a dingo's fart.'

'I can't see Frank visiting Dad.' Danny felt the swell of anger again in his chest. Their father was entitled to some peace in his twilight years. Frank had never given Bill Flowers the respect he was due. Despite all the effort Bill had put in to compensate for the early death of their mother, Frank had still turned out the bad apple.

Cal followed Danny in, grinning broadly at the two men seated in the chairs. Bert stood, dwarfing Cal momentarily as he clasped his hand.

Doug said after a while, 'Frank don't have any friends on the island. Without Ferreter's muscle behind him, I can't see him making waves.'

'Well, he managed more than a ripple today.' Irritably, Danny flicked undone the top button of his shirt and slid out his tie, stuffing it in his pocket. 'Five minutes later me and Lizzie would have been wed with an official signature to prove it.'

Cal moved closer to the window and nodded to the street. 'Looks like we've got company.'

Danny joined him, to see their guests approaching. He knew without a shade of doubt that not one of the invited stepping into the house this day would welcome Frank's return.

Chapter Five

'Calm down, Flo, don't upset yourself.' Sydney Miller reached out for his girlfriend.

'Don't tell me to calm down, Syd.' Flo Allen pushed him away. 'Frank has screwed up our lives again. Why couldn't he stay dead, like most people do when they stop breathing?'

Lizzie gazed at her sister. Flo had to get her annoyance off her chest. Flo, although five years younger than Lizzie, was protective, loyal to the last. More to the point, she could not forgive Frank for the unhappiness he had brought to their lives.

'You don't believe his bullshit, do you?' Flo thrust back her short, shiny brown hair and raised her black eyebrows challengingly.

'No, course I don't,' Lizzie assured her. 'The registrar had no choice but to call off the wedding.'

'Lizzie ain't at fault,' Syd agreed. 'But we know who is.'

Lizzie liked Sydney Miller a lot. He was officially Flo's lodger, but Lizzie knew he had shared Flo's bed since moving into Langley Street. Syd had been Flo's first boyfriend and Lizzie had disapproved of him. But somehow he had managed to distance himself from the influence of his notoriously troubled family.

Lizzie sighed deeply as she sat on the well-worn fireside chair. This was the house she and her brothers and sisters had been brought up in. Passed now to Flo, it still held the memories of their childhood and she loved it.

'Well, someone's got to eat all the food,' Flo said with half a smile as she stuck out her ample bust under the soft material of her damson chiffon blouse. The colour was flattering but was currently at odds with the scarlet blush of anger flooding into her cheeks. 'I'll just get me bag and we'll go next door.'

'Where the hell has Frank been?' Syd asked Lizzie when they were alone.

'In hospital, so he says. A mental institution.'

'In that case, why don't you and Danny just move in together?'

'What would it be like for Polly and Tom if we did? The gossip was bad enough after Frank bombed the shop. The kids at school wouldn't go near Polly. They were afraid Frank would come after them too. I can't let that happen again.'

'Yeah, I get your meaning.' Syd pulled a white square of crumpled cloth from his trouser pocket and blew his nose. He was wearing a white shirt and armbands and a smart grey waistcoat. Standing only five foot seven tall, he was a pocket Hercules. He made up for his lack of height with his strength and bulging biceps. With his close-cropped light brown hair, square jaw and fresh-faced complexion, he looked every inch the Billingsgate porter. 'How's Danny taken it?' he asked in concern.

Lizzie looked away as her insides tightened. There wasn't a bad bone in Danny's body, but Frank had pushed him to his limit today. Even when Danny had returned to England last year and learned of Frank's treachery, he'd still refused to believe that Frank had deliberately deceived him. Even now, it was hard to believe that she'd fallen for Frank's twisted version of Danny's married life in Australia. Who could blame Danny, after discovering the truth, for hardening his heart?

'I've got five brothers,' Syd continued in a whisper, turning to glance over his shoulder. 'I've only got to say the word and your problem will be sorted. You won't see Frank for dust.'

Lizzie lifted her eyes to the man who would soon be her sister's husband. Syd was tough and kind and he would love Flo until his last breath. But he was also a Miller. And their name in the East End was legendary. It was a known fact that each brother had spent more time in custody than at liberty. Lizzie always marvelled that her soon-to-be-brother-in-law was the only Miller to be born with an instinct for goodness.

'No, Syd,' she refused. 'Thanks all the same.'

'I'd stick my neck out for you and Danny.'

'Better we sort it ourselves.'

Syd nodded, flushing slightly. 'Just as long as you and Danny know I've got your backs.'

Flo walked into the parlour, pulling on her coat, and Syd was beside her in seconds. 'You all right now, love?'

'As right as I'll ever be with that cheapskate about still.'

No more was said as they all trooped out through the kitchen door and made their way into Lil's over the broken fence.

Chapter Six

Lizzie was relieved to find that their friends and neighbours were enjoying the occasion even if there was no wedding to celebrate. But it was Danny she was concerned about.

Going over to where he stood she reached down to run her fingers gently across his hand. His glance met hers and she smiled. Since their hurried departure from the registry office, they had only had time to exchange a few words. Their wedding day had been turned on its head. Neither of them had found the sentiments to soften the blow.

'So what do we do now?' he said, frowning slightly, a question in his deep blue eyes. 'I still want us to be together. Do you?'

'Yes, that goes without saying.'

'Then let's go ahead. Move into March Street.'

Lizzie looked up at him and tried to think of the right words to say. 'We'll talk about it later,' she said. And knew they were the wrong ones, as Danny stiffened and pulled away.

'There never will be a later, will there?' he said, his voice filled with raw emotion. 'Not as long as Frank's around. You're still tied to him by a damned piece of paper!'

'Give me time, Danny, please—'

Suddenly he left her, his broad shoulders disappearing into the crowd. Lizzie felt as though the earth was opening up and pulling her down into it. The happy future she had thought was beginning as from today had gone and Frank had driven a wedge between them. She stared ahead sightlessly, then realized someone was talking to her. Putting on a brave face, she smiled and managed to get through the pleasantries. Then as soon as she could, she left the room and made her way to the kitchen.

She opened the door and to her surprise found Ethel and Cal standing together. They moved apart quickly, but not before Lizzie had seen the guilty expression on Ethel's face.

'Cal was just describing Australia,' Ethel said nervously. 'How big it is and how warm, even in winter.' She paused, glancing up at Cal, and blushed.

Cal tore his gaze away and smiled at Lizzie. 'I'd better be off. We've got a few motors in for repair at the garage. The owners will want them for Christmas.'

'Thanks for calling by,' Lizzie said as he left by the back door.

'Did I interrupt something?' Lizzie asked her friend mildly.

'No, course not. Why?'

'You look like a girl of sixteen again.'

'Oh Christ!' Ethel blushed, much deeper this time. 'Lizzie, I never wanted this to happen. But I knew the moment I saw him. It was as if we were old friends. Yet he's lived on one side of the world and me on the other.'

'You're seeing him?' Lizzie rolled her eyes. 'When did this start?'

'The day he came over to your shop. Danny sent him to help us with the decorating, remember?'

Lizzie nodded. She had never thought Ethel would be telling her this.

'We just sort of clicked. Not that I don't feel guilty. I do. Me and Richard were so young when we got married. Everyone expected us to wed, so we did. But when the babies came along Richard just seemed to go his own way. It was as if he resented my attention going elsewhere.' Ethel's face clouded. 'His mum was always there to provide the looking-after he wanted. Sounds silly, but me and the kids never really came into the picture. Richard is the golden boy, always was, always will be. And now it's like we lead separate lives. Funny, I've played the part of a good wife. I tried to do my best but I always knew something was missing. I didn't know what it was till I met Cal.' Ethel took a long breath. 'But you guessed that, didn't you?'

'I just didn't know how unhappy you were,' Lizzie admitted. 'Does Richard know anything?'

'Don't think so. He never tells me he loves me. That stopped a long time ago.'

'What about the kids?'

'They're fourteen and fifteen. Teenagers. Off enjoying themselves.'

'But how do you find time to see Cal?'

'I was given the sack at Rickard's. The depression hit them badly. But Cal seemed to make things better. We talk and laugh and I forget all my troubles.'

'So what are you going to do?'

Ethel shrugged. 'I might ask you the same question.'

Lizzie raised her dark eyebrows and sighed. 'Danny wants us to move in together.'

'Will you?'

'I don't know what to do.'

Ethel smiled. 'Looks like we're in the same boat.'

Lizzie's heart went out to her friend. She had never known Ethel to look at another man and it was her who kept the family together. Richard seemed to spend more time with his mum than his family.

'What are you thinking?' Ethel asked anxiously. 'Do you think I'm a bad person?'

'No, but I wish you'd told me before.'

'You've had a wedding to plan. The happiest time of your life.'

'Yes,' agreed Lizzie ruefully, 'though it ain't turned out quite that way.'

'I know. And all the more reason I shouldn't be bothering you with my worries. I'm cheating on Richard and the guilt keeps me awake at night. But in the morning, I need to see Cal again.'

Lizzie sighed softly. 'When Danny came back from

Australia last year, I was still a married woman. Frank was my husband, for all that was said and done. But Danny was on my mind all the time.'

'You never cheated on Frank, I know that for a fact.'

'Not until Frank was supposedly found dead. And then—' Now it was Lizzie's turn to blush. 'We thought we were free to be together.'

'You'd waited a long time.'

Lizzie nodded. 'I've loved Danny for the best part of my life. But I'm another man's wife. Where does that leave me now?' Lizzie asked, knowing Ethel couldn't provide an answer. At least one that she wanted to hear.

Chapter Seven

All the guests had left and it was almost dusk. Flo and Syd were washing up in the kitchen and Lizzie was helping Lil and Ethel to clear up the leftovers and dirty glasses and plates strewn about the front room.

Just then a loud screeching noise outside made Lizzie turn to the window. Lil joined her and they peered out into the murky evening. A car drew up and a man wearing a raincoat climbed out of the vehicle's passenger seat. Walking over to Danny and Bert who were smoking in the street, the man reached inside his coat. At the same time a uniformed police officer emerged. Lizzie gasped aloud as she saw Danny being pushed roughly inside the car. At this, Bert leaped forward, only to be confronted by the smaller man who barred his way.

'Oh God, Lil, it's the coppers!' Lizzie ran from the window and into the passage where she collided with Flo and Syd and the children. 'Danny's being taken away,' she blurted as they all scrambled to open the front door.

'Danny!' Lizzie ran outside, coming face to face with the stranger.

'Where are you taking Danny?' she demanded. 'Who are you? What do you want with him?'

'I'm Detective Inspector Bray from the Limehouse Constabulary,' the officer told her, his voice thick and low. 'We think that Mr Flowers will be able to help us with our enquiries.'

'Enquiries?' she repeated foolishly. 'What sort of enquiries?' She looked round for Bert who stood staring at the car. 'Bert, do you know anything about this?'

Bert shook his head. 'We was just having a smoke and this motor drives up.'

'What the hell do you think you're doing?' Flo interrupted, rushing to stand beside Lizzie. 'You can't just take someone away like that.'

'I'm afraid I can,' the detective replied, sliding his trilby hat over his greasy brown hair. 'Now, I advise you all to go—'

'Where are you taking my dad?' Tom slipped by the policeman and pulled on the handle of the car.

'Your dad is coming with us for a while, son. Now, off you go, there's a good lad.' The detective turned and climbed into the front of the car. Lizzie and Flo jumped back as the vehicle roared off, turning the corner of the street with a squeal of its tyres.

'The swines,' Flo cursed as they all stood staring after it. 'What makes them think Danny can help them? And how did they know where to find him?'

'It's ridiculous,' Lil muttered bewilderedly. 'Downright ridiculous!'

'Yeah, but did you clock what the geezer said?' Bert pushed his big hand over his face. 'He's from the Limehouse nick. And that was where Danny went to identify the stiff.'

'Of course,' Flo groaned, nodding fiercely. 'This is to do with Frank. Think about it. For the past seven months we've had peace and quiet. Now, on the very day Frank shows up, all hell is let loose.'

'You're right there, gel,' Syd agreed angrily. 'It's Frank they should be questioning. Not putting Danny through the wringer.'

Lizzie looked at Tom and Polly. Tom's cheeks were wet with dirty tears and he rubbed them with his knuckles.

'Is the policeman taking Uncle Danny to prison?' Polly asked with a sniff.

'No, of course not.' Lizzie opened her arms. 'Come here for a cuddle, you two.' She hugged Polly and Tom. 'Everything's going to be all right, I promise.'

'Look, we won't solve anything by freezing out here on the street,' Lil decided as the cold darkness settled around them. 'Let's have a cuppa and put our heads together. When Doug comes back from taking Ethel home, I'll cook a fry-up. We need a good meal to put a lining in our stomachs. By the time we've eaten, I reckon they'll have brought Danny back.'

'They better, or else me and my brothers will be paying them a visit,' Syd muttered as everyone trooped indoors. A comment that Lizzie dearly hoped was made in the heat of the moment.

*   *   *

'You're welcome to kip in the spare room,' Flo said as the clock on the mantel struck ten. 'I've got plenty of blankets to go round.'

'Tom could sleep here, in the boys' room,' Lil suggested, looking across to the couch where Tom had fallen asleep in the crook of Doug's arm. 'The poor kid is knackered.' Though Greg and Neil, the Sharpes' two sons, had perished in the Great War, they still called the room they used as a spare the boys' room.

'Bert can kip on the put-you-up,' Doug agreed quietly.

Lizzie stroked the top of Polly's auburn head. Curled against her, Polly was also fast asleep. 'Thanks, but I'd like to go home.'

'You think they'll keep Danny in?' asked Syd, and not waiting for an answer continued, 'I reckon it's not too late for me and Bert to drive over and have it out with Old Bill.'

Lizzie knew Syd was eager to take action. But common sense told her that frayed tempers could make things worse for Danny.

'I'd prefer to go myself, Syd, thanks. It's been a long day and I want to get the children home to bed. If Danny isn't back by morning, I'll have Bert take me to Limehouse.'

'The coppers are out of order,' said Doug with a nod, 'but Lizzie's right, far better a good night's kip for every-one. Tomorrow's a new day.'

Lizzie disentangled herself gently from Polly. She placed her in Bert's arms. Doug roused Tom and when the two children were settled in the van, Bert coaxed the engine into life.

Lizzie hugged Flo and Lil. 'Thanks for everything.'

'Take care, now,' Lil said, shivering.

'Don't worry,' Flo told her. 'Danny will be back in no time.'

Sinking down on the damp leather of the passenger seat, Lizzie watched as the small group of figures melted away in the darkness. Bert cursed softly as the rattling vehicle moved forward. Lizzie's thoughts swept back to the events of the day.

Frank was alive. Her dead husband was not the corpse Danny had identified at Limehouse in May. How had that happened? She had believed Frank to have been drowned and her tears had been few after the life Frank had led her. But she hadn't wished him dead. And despite all he had done, he was still, as far as she knew, father to Polly.

Sighing softly, Lizzie stared from the window that was streaked with dust and pigeon fouling. The interior of the van reeked of vegetables together with a sour whiff from its previous owner, a fishmonger. A small, brown metal box with three oblong windows and a flat front, it clattered noisily along the road. Finally Lizzie glimpsed the deep blue sky. The moon was a slim silver crescent pushing its way between the stars and into the Christmas night. She yearned for Danny and the future they had hoped for. A future now out of reach.

Silently she wiped a tear from the corner of her eye. Bert cursed again, grinding the gear with such force that every bone in her body jarred.

*　　*　　*

'What baffles me,' said the policeman as he lit himself another cigarette and narrowed his eyes at Danny, 'you've got your only kith and kin, a man as I understand it who has well and truly shafted you. And you're looking down on him – he's a bit worse for wear, granted – and you give us the thumbs-up that this drowned package is your brother.'

Danny shifted uncomfortably on the hard wooden chair. His arm still throbbed from the rough handling. He couldn't begin to understand why he was here, other than the copper's continual reference to the day, seven months ago, when he was faced with the sight of a corpse and asked to identify it. But, Danny wondered, why collar him like this?

Danny froze as he looked up at the plain-clothes policeman. Did they suspect he had something to do with the dead man's drowning? 'How do you know Frank shafted me?'

Bray smiled as he leaned back on the chair positioned at the table. He threw the packet of cigarettes on its filthy surface. 'I know all about you. I know everything there is to know. I know because I've done my homework. The man you identified as your brother turns out to be one Duncan King, late of Whitechapel. Thief, bookie's runner, grass, small-time black marketeer, you name it, King tried it. Now, a week or so after you'd given us the nod in the morgue, King's missus paid us a visit. She was complaining her other half hadn't shown up for a while. But King was a fly-by-night, a shape-shifter – even she admitted that – so we dismissed it. Then, a couple of months later, she pays us another visit. This time she slaps a tatty black book on my desk, claiming it was her old man's bible and he never left the house without it. I ask her why she hadn't found it before. She says it was hidden, that she'd torn up every floorboard in her search for a few bob. King kept his swag well hidden, especially from her. The book, she insists, was his bible with all his punters' names and how much they owed him. So the good lady is convinced her husband is deep in the shit. And after going through this new evidence, we are convinced too. The man has enemies. Lots of them. He lost more on the gee-gees than he ever made from his life of crime.'

Danny studied the policeman's face. The unkempt greasy brown hair, flaky skin and unhealthy pallor of a hard-drinking, hard-living copper who was after a collar. Without lowering his gaze, Danny scraped back his chair and leaned his elbows on his knees. He frowned slightly as he said, 'I didn't know the man.'

Bray nodded slowly. 'In the week we brought up the body from the river we had five deaths in six days. Four didn't match our lad. But the fifth, in appearance, height and stature, did.' Bray grinned showing uneven browned teeth. 'So we dug him up. And guess what?'

'What?' Danny steeled himself.

'Our soon-to-be grieving widow identified a birth-mark on her husband's backside. It was the size of a half-crown, the closest our thief ever got to the monarchy's boat race.' He paused. 'So here we are, you and me, having this nice little chat.'

'I was wrong, I'll admit,' Danny said.

'That's good of you,' Bray sneered sarcastically.

'I don't know King. I wasn't his friend or his enemy. I believed the dead man was my brother. It was a simple mistake.'

'A simple mistake to you. Might be the answer for us.'

Danny nodded understandingly. 'So I'm up for the frame, am I? You've got hassle from your superiors and want to tie up the loose ends. I'm nothing to you, so you ask around and there's plenty of punters who'll tell you what you want for a couple of bob.'

'Your brother is alive, as you well know.'

'I didn't,' Danny objected. 'Until this morning. But I have an idea you know about Frank turning up at my wedding.'

Bray raised his eyebrows speculatively. 'So how do you feel about that?'

'How do you think?'

Bray smirked unpleasantly as he stood up and ambled round the table in his crumpled suit. He stubbed his dog-end slowly in the ashtray. 'So tell me, why shouldn't I book you for the murder of Duncan King? I say you knew him, owed him, fell out, smashed his face in, ditched him in the river. And when he surfaced, identified him as your brother. Problem solved. Two birds with one stone.'

'Except, you'll never find my name in that black book.'

Bray's eyebrow twitched. 'Maybe your name didn't get written down.'

'You just told me Duncan King kept a bible. If I'm not in it, what interest did he have in me?'

Bray meandered to the door, stuck his hands on his hips and stared at the floor. 'You think on your feet, Mr Flowers.'

'It's the truth.'

Bray looked up. 'Why should I believe you?'

Danny leaned back on the hard chair and licked his lips. His mouth was dry and his arm was really aching. 'Why would I deliberately misidentify Frank? If I knew it wasn't my brother, and Frank was to walk back into my life the very next day, I'd have some explaining to do.'

'You might be a gambler, Mr Flowers. One of King's punters. Being pressed himself, perhaps he came after you for payment. Wanted what was his. And you didn't have it.'

Danny swallowed hard. 'I'm not a betting man, Detective. I'm a businessman. I don't have a fondness for throwing away hard-earned cash.'

'Ah, yes. You make a few bob on the motors. What kind of business is that?'

'A legitimate one,' Danny replied coldly.

The policeman paused. 'So how much did it cost you to set up this so-called legit business?'

'That's none of your business, squire,' Danny answered shortly. 'But I can tell you that there was a *For Sale* board on the land and it came down when I bought the freehold. I have papers to prove it and you are welcome to inspect them whenever you like.'

'You must have been desperate,' Bray commented rudely. 'Morley's Wharf ain't been used in years.'

'That's right, it's old marshland and gone to the dogs. The water breaks through the wall in winter and in summer it's as dry as a bone with no irrigation. But for my purposes it suits.'

Bray looked at him curiously. 'So let's talk about your brother. Did he have any connection to King? And what have you to say to his untimely return from the dead? After all, he's responsible for making it all go tits up for you today.'

Danny forced himself to keep calm. Bray was looking to needle him, get a result. And it was almost working. 'I've nothing to say about Frank,' Danny replied stubbornly.

'You hated him for taking your girl, isn't that right? And wouldn't any man get the hump over that? But you swanned off to Australia. It was odds on your brother went after her in your absence.' Bray glanced slyly at Danny, adding, 'And had her.'

Danny could remain seated no longer. Without realizing what he was doing, he sprang from the chair and landed on the surprised policeman. Thrusting Bray against the wall of the interview room, he pushed his face into the copper's. At the same time two uniformed policemen ran in and caught him by his arms. They dragged him back and pinned him over the table; a fist landed in his side and a boot in the back of his leg. Danny tried to resist, but was landed a punch square in the mouth. Blood trickled warmly from his lips.

'Sit him down.' Bray's voice was soft, menacing. 'Touched a nerve, did I, son?' He jerked his dirty jacket back into place.

'Leave Lizzie out of this.'

Bray leaned his palms on the table. 'Why should I?'

Danny looked up angrily. 'Because you think you know it all, but you don't know anything.'

Once again Bray's dark eyebrows lifted. 'Well why don't you enlighten me, then? That's all I'm asking, my friend. A little information and you can be on your way.'

Danny stared silently at the copper. Short of Bray opening him up with a knife and spilling his guts, Bray wasn't going to achieve anything. Danny was no grass and even if he had had dealings with King, which he hadn't, Bray wouldn't have got another word out of him.

The detective seemed to recognize this. He irritably snatched the packet of cigarettes and struck a match. He inhaled deeply, blowing the smoke into Danny's eyes. 'Bang him up,' he told his officers. 'A night in the cells might take the bastard's smile off his face.'

Danny watched helplessly as Bray turned and left the room.

Chapter Eight

Lizzie pulled back the bedroom curtains and gazed out onto Ebondale Street leading north from the shop to Poplar and east into the greyer, drabber areas of Cubitt Town. The Isle of Dogs opened out like a patchwork quilt of dusty, uneven roofs and back yards, a horseshoe of land jutting out into the Thames, pockmarked by factories and warehouses. The river itself was hidden from view, but not the bridges, every one of them alive with early morning traffic, the gateway to the glittering, flotsam-covered docks and wharfs of the island.

The chimneys of the smoke-blackened houses were belching grey clouds. The day was even greyer. She thought at once of Danny and the long evening she and Bert had spent anticipating his release. But by midnight they had turned in, giving up hope.

Lizzie shivered in the cold. She wondered if the children were still fast asleep, Polly in her bedroom and Tom in the small box room next to it. The upper floor was silent as she listened for signs of their waking, and heard instead the guttural rumble of Bert's snoring downstairs in the storeroom at the back of the shop.

She turned slowly, slid on her dressing gown and trod softly along the landing. Leaning over the banisters she could hear sounds resembling a distant steam train. Bert was sleeping on the battered old couch, just a few feet away from the open door leading up the narrow staircase to Lizzie's quarters. Quietly she looked in on the children. She was relieved to see each of them snuggled down in their beds. Yesterday had been long and exhausting for a six- and nine-year-old. Tom had tried to hold back the tears when she'd put him to bed. He missed Danny, and the lodgings that he and Danny had moved into on Terrace Street. And though he tried to be brave, he'd fallen asleep in Lizzie's arms, his cheeks still wet and sticky. As they might have been when he was a baby.

It was some while later when Lizzie was busy in the long narrow galley kitchen, preparing breakfast, when she heard Bert on the stairs.

She broke the eggs into a pan, and turned up the gas. Bert would be ravenous as he usually was on waking. Her brother occupied the airey below the shop. Damp basement rooms which many years before had been home to Bill Flowers and his two boys. But Bert was not a cook and often joined her for a meal, together with Danny and Tom. Polly adored her Uncle Bert despite his tremendous size and startling appearance. They made an odd-looking pair, Lizzie often reflected. A giant and a child, peas in a pod.

'Kids still sleeping?' Bert grunted as he made his

entrance. Filling the kitchen almost, he sniffed at the air. 'Got a thirst on me an' all, after yesterday.'

'Sit down in the front room and pour the brew.' Lizzie indicated the large room to the right along the landing. A hatch had been carved out in the wall and through it the dining table could be viewed. A shiny brown teapot stood on its surface, together with china and cutlery, a loaf of bread and a bowl of dripping.

'No news, then. What do you think they're doing with Danny?' Bert stood where he was, his clothes unchanged from the previous day. He scratched his head and blinked his sleepy eyes.

'Don't know. But I'm going to find out.'

'What you gonna do, gel?'

'Go over to the station, of course. On the way there, we'll call at Gertie's. Find out if they're all right.'

'You reckon one of 'em took bad?'

Lizzie nodded as she fried the bacon. 'I hope not. But it seems the only explanation.'

'Are you gonna say about Frank?'

'Danny would want me to. Frank is Bill's son, after all. It's going to be a shock for him to be told Frank is alive. And I need to tell him first before some other well-meaning soul springs it on him.'

Bert shrugged. 'Frank ain't been nothing but bad news since the day he was born. Bill always reckons Frank lost his marbles when Daisy died. But you'd think a little kid wouldn't hold a grievance against his own dad for his mother's passing.'

Lizzie sighed softly. 'And against Danny too.'

Bert mumbled and pushed his hands over his tieless, crumpled white shirt. He licked his lips. 'I could do justice to that breakfast, kid.'

Lizzie smiled. 'Wake the kids first, will you? Then after we've eaten, we'll be on our way.'

'What if Danny turns up and we ain't here?'

'I'll leave a note, tell him we called by his dad's.'

'His motor's still at Lil's, don't forget.'

'Well, my bike's round the side of the shop.'

Bert gave a roar of laughter. 'Danny on a bike? You've got to be joking.'

Lizzie forked the crisp brown bacon onto the plates. 'It'll have to be Shanks's pony, then.' Smiling ruefully, she couldn't imagine Danny on a bike either. Two wheels had never been Danny's style.

The knot of anxiety in her stomach that she had woken with eased a little as she thought of going to Limehouse. Taking action was better than doing nothing. Danny was an innocent man. What could the policeman want with him?

Danny wasn't a law-breaker. He had worked hard all his life and learned a skill in Australia. He'd come back to this country to put his talents to use in the garage. There were few men who would have taken an orphaned boy under their wing, as Danny had. And made a new start for them both on the other side of the world.

Her smile softened as she thought of Polly's fifth birth-day a year ago. Danny had turned up and it was as if nothing had changed between them. A decade hadn't altered the way she felt about him. At his side was Tom who she'd at first thought was Danny's son. Blond and blue-eyed, he certainly could have been.

The sound of Bert's laughter as he woke the children brought her sharply out of her thoughts and back to the moment.

'Lord, girl, I'm relieved to see you.' Gertie Spooner opened the door and stared at them. 'I was wondering how I could get a message to you. I'm sorry we didn't turn up yesterday.'

'What happened?' Lizzie smiled anxiously as she looked at Gertie who stood in her uniform, the one she had worn all her life. A badly knitted navy-blue jumper, its sides tucked into an apron tied around her thin waist. Lizzie had seen the same skirt many times before. Old but not grubby, the hem of which dangled above her laced-up brown shoes.

'Come in and I'll tell you.' Now in her mid-sixties, she looked it. Lizzie knew Gertie had always been strong as an ox. But this morning her eyes were tired and her grey hair hurriedly pinned away from her lined face. Lizzie knew Gertie had not had an easy life. She had been Bill's right-hand man at the shop, and had helped to raise Frank and Danny after Daisy Flowers's death.

'Hello, rascals.' Gertie took each child's forehead and kissed it. 'You two are growing by the minute.' She pushed the two children into the narrow passage thick with the smells of camphor and cabbage. 'Granda is upstairs, Pol.

Take Tom with you to say hello and cheer him up.' Gertie shooed the children up the roughly boarded staircase. Turning back to Lizzie and Bert, she asked at once, 'Where's Danny?'

'Can we go in the front room and I'll tell you?'

'Course. I ain't had time to tidy, but sit yourselves down.'

Lizzie and Bert made their way into the house; a three-storey Poplar terrace left to Gertie by her parents. It seemed a large and lonely house to Lizzie, but Gertie loved it. And had finally persuaded Bill to move from Ebondale Street to live with her at Gap End.

The smells of cooking coming from the downstairs kitchen were blown along the passage together with a trace of Sunlight soap.

'Don't trouble to take off your boots, Bert,' Gertie threw over her shoulder. 'I ain't house-proud, as you well know.'

Lizzie had to adjust her eyes in the dim, cluttered front room that was always darkened by heavy drapes. There was just enough space on the button-backed leather sofa stuffed with cushions to sit down.

Gertie took her place on the armchair by the black-leaded grate. The mantel was filled with small china knick-knacks. A dusty gooseberry-green curtain hung from the dark wood in front of the fireplace. Gertie folded her hands in her lap. 'I'll make no bones about it, Lizzie,' Gertie began before Lizzie could explain about Danny. 'I'm heartsore sorry to hear you and Danny aren't wed.'

'You know about that?' Lizzie said in surprise.

'A visitor landed on the doorstep yesterday.' Gertie shifted uncomfortably. 'Just as we were about to leave for Lil's. Needless to say, it was a shock to match no other.'

Lizzie took a sharp breath. 'Was it Frank?'

Gertie nodded. 'It took the wind from Bill's sails.'

'If Frank laid a finger on him—' Bert began, jumping to his feet.

Gertie was already shaking her head. 'Sit down, Bert. Frank never touched him.'

'But how did he know Bill was here?' Lizzie asked.

Gertie shrugged. 'He worked it out. Knew his dad was moving in with me once he retired.'

'So what sob story did he give you?' Bert boomed, still angry.

'He said he's been in a hospital.'

'Do you believe him?'

'Dunno. But if Frank thought that tale up, it's an unlikely one.'

Bert nodded. 'That's what we all think.'

'But on the other hand,' said Gertie, raising a palm as Bert was going to speak, 'he came with an apology. And saying sorry ain't in Frank's nature. Nor is the fact that he freely admits to all the wrong he done you, Lizzie. And his father.'

Lizzie wanted to say that, wherever Frank had been, apologies had come too late, but she didn't want to upset Gertie. She knew that Gertie had a soft spot for Frank, always had. And the bond between them had never broken. 'What else did he say?' Lizzie asked.

'That he wants to make amends.'

'A bit late for that, on Lizzie's wedding day, ain't it?' Bert demanded.

Gertie ignored this. 'Bill heard him out, listened to every word Frank said, but then he took poorly. And Frank went for the doctor.'

'The doctor?' Lizzie sat up. 'What's wrong?'

'Nothing that don't happen to someone who's led the hard life Bill has. The old workhorse is wearing out. Doctor told him to rest. But will he? Your father-in-law don't know the meaning of the word, Lizzie. He's still up at the crack of dawn. Works like a navvy in the back yard, digging up all me garden. Insists he needs the exercise. That his legs won't work if he don't move 'em.'

Bert thumped his hands on his knees. 'Frank should know better than to give the old man such a fright.'

Gertie fixed Bert with a sharp stare. 'What else was the boy supposed to do?' she asked. 'I ain't defending Frank, no. But when all is said and done, he is Daisy's boy. And when he was said to have drowned, Bill grieved more than his pride would allow him to show. Why do you think Bill gave in to moving here from the shop? It was the memories of his sons and the life they had shared, for better or worse, that tore him apart.'

'But he wants to live with you, Gertie,' Bert said innocently. 'All them years slogging at the shop. Now this is your time together.'

'Don't you believe it!' Gertie waved her hand dismiss-ively. 'And don't look at me like that, my lad. Me and Bill are good friends, but living under the same roof ain't paradise.'

Lizzie stared at this tiny, frail-looking lady who had been the backbone of the Flowers family, yet had never taken the name. She was Gertie Spooner, always had been and probably always would be. She equalled Bill in his efforts to raise two motherless boys and run a business. The shop had seen them all through the lean and hungry years of the depression. They had always planned to end their days together. But was she was telling them that Bill wasn't happy?

'So where is our Danny?' Gertie said in a hard voice.

'The law came for him last night,' Bert told her. 'We was standing in the road having a smoke and they just drove up. Said something about him helping them with their enquiries.'

'What enquiries?' Gertie frowned.

'Dunno. But we reckon it's to do with Frank turning up.'

'They've taken him to Limehouse where Danny iden-tified the corpse,' Lizzie explained. 'Me and Bert are driving over there now. But I wanted to call here first. Can we go up and see Bill?'

'Course.' Gertie stood up. 'You know I am sorry, love, don't you? About the wedding.'

'Yes, I know, Gertie. Did Frank say what he was going to do now?'

'You know the score there, girl. More than I do.'

Lizzie knew she wouldn't get more out of Gertie. Though Frank didn't have any friends on the island and certainly had more than enough enemies, he did have Gertie to turn to.

Lizzie guessed, as she and Bert climbed the stairs, that for all the unhappiness Frank had caused in the family, he knew that he'd be forgiven here.

'Shh. Granda's asleep,' Polly whispered as Lizzie walked into the bedroom.

Lizzie sat down on the wicker chair beside the large double bed where the two children stood. She took hold of Polly's cold hand. Bill seemed to be sleeping peacefully under the eiderdown. Two thin pillows supported his white head and Lizzie thought of the man who had worked tirelessly all his years as a costermonger. Bill had supported her throughout her turbulent marriage to Frank. And now as she looked at him, she saw the toll that the worry had taken.

She couldn't help wondering if things would have turned out differently if Danny had followed his dad into the business. Frank would never have had the chance to bully Bill, not while Danny was around. And the shop would have thrived under Danny's care and become the expanding business Bill had worked so hard for it to be.

Lizzie leaned forward, touching Bill's cheek. He took a breath and she let her hand drop away. She didn't recognize this man. He seemed to have shrunk in the few weeks since she'd last seen him. Was it Frank's bombing of his beloved shop that had broken Bill's spirit? Or was the discovery of that Limehouse corpse to blame? Or perhaps, Lizzie wondered, it was as Gertie suggested: Bill was just getting old.

'Is Granda going to wake up soon?' Polly asked.

'I hope so.'

'Yer, he'll be back on his feet in no time,' Bert agreed, turning his cap in his hands.

A movement from the doorway caused them all to turn round. Gertie motioned to the children. 'Go downstairs, you kids, and we'll get out the cards.'

'Can we play patience, Grandma?' Polly asked excitedly.

'We'll play whatever you like, ducks. You two know where the cards are. Then later, after we've had tea, your Granda will be awake.'

When Tom and Polly had gone, Gertie looked at Lizzie. 'The doctor gave Bill something to make him rest. Looks like it's doing the job.'

Lizzie sniffed. 'He's going to be all right, isn't he?'

'As right as rain.' Gertie patted her shoulder.

'We'd better go. You sure you want the kids to stay?'

Lizzie gazed down at her father-in-law. She bent to kiss him. The skin of his cheek felt very thin.

'Off you go now,' Gertie told her. 'And tell the bobbies from me, they'll have Gertie Spooner to answer to if they don't send Danny back to his father.'

Lizzie smiled. She knew Gertie loved Daisy's boys as her own and meant every word she said.

Chapter Nine

'Take a closer look, Mrs Flowers,' said the policeman as he placed the dog-eared black-and-white photograph in front of her. He bore a faint resemblance to Frank as he stood in the sleazy type of clothes that Frank liked to wear. 'Have you ever seen him before?'

Lizzie knew he was studying her closely. The same plain-clothes copper who had arrived at the house last night and bundled Danny in the car now wanted her help. She raised her eyes slowly and shook her head. 'I told you. The answer is no.'

'Would you like to know who he is?'

'No. Why should I? Where's Danny?' She pushed the photograph away, towards the filthy ashtray.

'This is the late Duncan King,' Bray continued, drawing the photograph back with nicotine-stained fingers. 'He's a South London crook and the man your brother-in-law identified as your husband at the morgue in May.' He looked at Bert. 'And you, Mr Allen. Do you recognize this man?'

Lizzie glanced at Bert who had refused to cooperate

from the moment they had walked into the station. After a scuffle with two of the policemen who had intended to lead Lizzie away from him and into an interview room, the senior policeman had called off his watchdogs. Lizzie had taken Bert's arm and they had been led along the sour-smelling corridor to a dim, windowless room. It was no bigger than the storeroom at home. From that moment on, Bert had glared belligerently ahead and refused to speak.

'I advise you to answer,' the policeman threatened. 'Unless you have no objection to occupying that chair for the foreseeable future. I am sure Mrs Flowers has better things to do with her time.'

'Don't know him,' Bert grunted. 'Never seen him before in my life.'

Detective Inspector Bray smoothed his thumbs together. 'The burning question in my mind is how come your husband walked large as life into Poplar registry office yesterday morning, when he was supposed to be six foot under?'

Lizzie's jaw dropped. How did he know about that?

'Yes, I can see you're wondering how we got the information.' He smiled, showing uneven brown teeth. 'We had a telephone call from the registrar. Not often he finds himself compromised, having almost aided and abetted bigamy.'

'It wasn't bigamy.' Lizzie stared into the sunken eyes of the man questioning her. 'I believed I was a widow.'

'A widow?'

'Yes. I thought Frank was dead.'

'Because the man you wanted to marry told you so?'

She looked up at him. 'What do you mean by that?'

'True, isn't it?'

'Danny thought it was Frank in the morgue.'

'So he led us all to believe. But you see my problem, don't you?' The policeman's foul breath on her face made her wince. 'I am left with Duncan King's missus giving me grief over the disappearance of her dear departed who was identified as none other than Frank Flowers before he was sunk down six feet and buried.'

Lizzie studied the image that the policeman refused to take away. 'I don't have any idea who Duncan King is. But this man does look a bit like Frank, and I expect it was an easy mistake to make.'

'So you're saying your brother-in-law genuinely made a cock-up?'

'Yes, of course it was a mistake.'

'But a man must know his own brother.'

'He was in the water a long time.' Lizzie refused to be browbeaten even though she knew the policeman, for some reason, was trying to get her to admit that Danny had deliberately misidentified Frank.

Bray smiled without humour. 'The body wasn't a pleasant sight, that's true. Although you didn't see it, did you? Why not, Mrs Flowers?'

'I . . . I didn't want to.'

'I'll ask again, why not?'

'Because it would be upsetting, of course.'

'A puzzling sentiment . . .' The policeman crooked an eyebrow. 'Since you hated the sight of him.'

Lizzie sat up. 'Who told you that?'

He tapped the side of his nose. 'It's my job to know these things.'

'Well, you're wrong. I didn't hate Frank. I was frightened of him. Of what he might do.'

'If he found out you were carrying on with another man?'

'No!' Lizzie was about to jump to her feet. But Bert was there before her.

'You ain't talking to my sister like that—'

'Sit down, or else I'll have you removed,' the detective growled as Bert loomed over him.

'Do as he says, Bert.' Lizzie tugged her brother's arm.

'My version is,' continued Bray as Bert slumped back to the chair, 'you and your boyfriend cooked up a scheme to get rid of him. With your husband out of the way, there was nothing to stop you tying the knot.'

'That's not true.' Lizzie tried to respond calmly. 'As you know Frank isn't dead.'

'So your plan went adrift.' Bray shrugged. 'And when a body conveniently washed up, you hit on plan B.'

Lizzie felt her stomach turn. 'That's ridiculous. Danny and me weren't doing anything wrong when we decided to get married.'

'Well, it now seems you were.' Bray gazed at her with hard eyes. 'Let's go over this again. There's you and there's your – *estranged* – husband. Then there's you and

Danny Flowers, his brother and your intended. I have a floater from the other side of the river, with no clue as to why he met his end. If we'd looked into his demise a few months earlier you might not be sitting here now.' He paused, scratching the side of his unshaven jaw. 'I have more questions than I have answers. Though Duncan King won't be much lamented, his end is still unaccounted for.'

Lizzie felt the sweat on her top lip as the policeman stared accusingly at her. 'I'm telling you everything I know.'

'And you were not aware your husband was alive until yesterday morning?'

'No, of course not.'

The detective narrowed his eyes and, in silence, slipped an arm over the back of his chair. He lit a cigarette and crossed one leg over the other. He nodded to the papers on the table, a file of well-worn documents. 'Me being a recent addition to this constabulary, I've done a little research. Your family has enjoyed a chequered history, Mrs Flowers. One brother, Vincent, doing time for aggravated assault. One sister, Barbara, arrested and cautioned on a number of occasions for soliciting. And your business premises infiltrated not long ago by Commie agitators.'

'Commies didn't wreck my shop. It was Frank, as you well know.'

Bray tilted his head. 'There's no report of that.'

'I told the police at the time.'

'Did you give statements to that effect?'

'Yes. So did my sister Flo and Danny, of course.'

The policeman blew out a cloud of smoke. 'Then I appear to be missing some information.'

'Why don't you ask Mik Ferreter about the dead man?' Lizzie said angrily. 'He was the last person to see Frank before he disappeared. Or is it safer for you to go along with what villains want and label me and Danny as liars?'

Unruffled, the detective pushed back his greasy brown hair. He slewed round on the chair and folded his arms. 'Perhaps you'd like to tell me your side of the story then? Since the villain you're naming is holidaying in Wandsworth.'

Lizzie felt the sting of frustrated tears in her eyes. Like many of the police who were in the pay of the under-world, Bray preferred to take the easy way out rather than investigate Frank's involvement with his one-time boss, Mik Ferreter.

'I've nothing to say,' Lizzie said stubbornly. 'You can't keep me and Bert or Danny here. We've done nothing wrong.'

Bray looked at her coldly. In the silence that followed, Lizzie's heart pounded. Bray stared at her, sizing her up. She looked at Bert, telling him with her eyes not to say anything.

'Thank you for your time, Mrs Flowers,' Bray said suddenly, folding the papers and standing up. 'Mr Flowers is outside, waiting for you. Tell him he'd better stay local. I might need to pull him back in again. And it's highly likely that I will.'

Shocked at their dismissal, Lizzie took Bert's arm and pulled him past the detective. Outside the door a uniformed officer stood on guard. He made no move to stop them as they walked to the desk.

'Danny!' She hurried to where he stood.

He held her gently. 'What did they want with you and Bert?'

'We came to find you. Why didn't they let you go last night?' Lizzie asked as they walked into the bright light of the day. She lifted her fingers to touch the black and blue skin around his eye.

'Bray's sidekicks were a bit handy.'

'They wanted me to say we had a plan to get rid of Frank,' Lizzie said as they walked across the road to the van.

Danny nodded. 'Me too.'

'They're after a collar,' Bert grumbled. 'Come on, let's get out of here.'

'Is Tom all right?' Danny asked when they were squashed safely in the van's front seats and Bert was driving.

'The kids are over at your dad's. Danny, Frank's been round there.'

'What?'

'That's why they didn't come to Lil's yesterday. Bill had a turn and Frank went for the doctor.'

Danny's unshaven face was grey. 'Is Dad all right?'

'The doctor gave him something to make him rest.'

Danny drew his hand over his forehead and rubbed his temple. 'Seeing Frank back from the grave must have done it.'

'Gertie said he had a shock, but Frank didn't cause no trouble.'

Danny laughed mirthlessly. 'As if he hasn't caused enough already.'

For a few seconds Danny closed his eyes. Then, shaking his head, he turned to stare out of the window, trying to hide the fury that filled his face.

Lizzie sat silently as Bert drove them towards Poplar. She hoped Bill would be awake and able to talk to Danny. Bill had looked so old and frail in that bed. It was a fact Danny was sure to put down to Frank's visit yesterday.

Chapter Ten

Danny sat at his father's bed, saddened by the sight of the sick man. Sitting propped by the pillows, Bill looked pale and gaunt. The collar of his striped pyjamas hung loosely around his scrawny neck. His dad had always been his hero. A man who was the business, literally. He had been a coster all his life. Great-grandfather Flowers had sold fruit and veg from his barrow and invested his profits in bricks and mortar. The result of which was Ebondale Street. Danny was proud of his heritage; pioneers of business since the days when the East End was all marshy land and windmills. Great-grandfather Flowers had been a wise Jew. He'd listened to the Rabbi's advice. And as the island had flourished, so too had the Flowerses. That was, until Danny's two uncles had absconded. He couldn't help smiling at the story he'd been told of the two men, leaving the country with pockets full of gold sovereigns. Bill and his father had been left penniless. But that hadn't stopped them building up the business again.

Staring at his dad, Danny thought of the young man his father had been. Slightly built but strong, agile. He'd met and married Daisy Owen when they were both sixteen. Danny didn't know if they had wed for love, or if it was just the comfortable arrangement of tough, hard-working islanders, with enough nous to get themselves known as honest, decent folk who sold from shelves marked at bargain prices. Danny had seen the family album many times. He'd recognized in himself the young, hardy-looking coster who could balance a crate of cauliflowers on his head and heave it with gusto onto the back of a horse-drawn wagon.

That was how tough his dad was. Yet Bill was a man of soul. He didn't attend the synagogue, but he'd never forgotten what his father had taught him. Look after your customers and the customers will look after you. And Danny knew that Bill had followed this to the letter.

Bill's lips parted in a wan smile. But the smile was slow to reach his rheumy eyes. 'You all right, son?' Bill put a hand to his ear. 'Speak up, you know I'm a bit mutton.'

'Never been better, Dad.' Danny grinned. 'It's you I'm worried about.'

'I'm as fit as a flea, Gawd help us.' He made a face. 'What rubbish has Gertie been telling you?'

'Gertie's all right. She says you had a turn.' Danny didn't want to speak of Frank – not yet. He felt it was up to his father to say. As much as Danny had convinced himself that his brother was to blame for the old man's condition, instinct told him to keep quiet.

'A dizzy spell, that's all. You don't want to listen to Gertie. Women takes things to heart. The doctor says

I'll be as right as rain in a couple of days. But I can't lie here all that time, done up like a kipper. Help me put my slippers on, son.' He took hold of the sheet and threw it back.

'No way, Dad.' Danny replaced the sheet. 'No use you arguing. You gave us all a fright. And now you have to take your medicine, or else.'

Bill looked his son in the eye and chuckled. 'You're throwing your weight around, young Daniel.'

Danny's heart contracted; the familiar term that he hadn't heard in years, perhaps even back to his childhood, rendered him silent for a moment. He loved his father but had never known how much until this moment.

'And you're staying put,' Danny replied, forcing humour into his voice.

A quick chuckle came from the old man's throat. Danny saw how tightly his father's pale skin moulded to his cheekbones. There was a razor cut on his chin that had bled and congealed under his grey whiskers. Danny wanted to clean it away and offer to shave him. Instead he enquired, 'Did the two kids behave themselves?'

Bill's smile stretched over his crooked teeth. 'You have a fine boy in Tom. He was here, not a minute ago, with Pol. They'll make young blood for the shop, but perhaps not in my time.'

Danny knew the business was everything to Bill, which was why, after his retirement, Bill had given the shop to Lizzie. They were like father and daughter, had suffered Frank's abuse, and taken comfort over the years from each other. They also both had the coster's touch for making money.

Danny reached for his father's hand. He squeezed the lean fingers gently, fearful of cracking them. 'Dad, you are going to get well and strong. You know that, don't you?'

'I've had a good life, Daniel.'

'And you'll have more.'

'A man has always got hope.'

When had this happened? Danny asked himself. This man who had seemed blessed with eternal life, the father who had encouraged him to leave for the other side of the world and seek his fortune, the coster who even at sixty years of age had hauled potato sacks on his back as if he were only twenty.

Bill drew his hand away roughly. 'I don't like this business of staying home. And it ain't my home, it's Gertie's.'

'It's as good as. You've always said you'd move in with her.'

'Yes, but not yet.'

Danny laughed. 'When, then?'

'I don't intend seizing up like a rusting old bike.'

Danny shook his head wearily. 'But you always said you wanted to enjoy your time with Gertie.'

Bill nodded. 'Yes, but on me two feet.'

'You make a lousy patient.'

Bill laughed. 'Don't I?' He chuckled and Danny rejoiced at the familiar sound.

'Listen, do you reckon we should get away after

Christmas? A holiday. You and Gertie, me and Lizzie and the kids. A week at Margate or Southend. In one of them nice boarding houses, where you can look over the sea to the piers and beyond. Like you showed me and Frank when we was kids.'

Bill smiled. 'And your brother was the reprobate he always was.'

Danny smiled too, and in his father's eyes he could see only love and affection. He knew in that moment that what Bert had once said was true. Bill was a father first and foremost and always would be.

'After Christmas, we'll take that holiday,' Bill agreed.

'Speaking of Christmas, me and Lizzie will come over. Cook the dinner. You and Gertie can put your feet up. Take it easy like the doc said.'

Bill waved this away. He looked into Danny's eyes. 'I'm sorry you didn't get hitched, lad.'

Danny nodded. 'So am I.'

Bill gave a throaty cough. 'I saw your brother.'

'Yes, I know.'

'I suppose Gertie told you.'

Danny gave a soft sigh and looked down. 'I'm sorry I made that mistake. I thought it was Frank they'd found in the river.'

'None of us is perfect.'

Danny found his chest tightening. Hiding the emotion that swirled inside him, he nodded.

'You and Lizzie. You'll be wed one day.'

Danny held himself tightly in check and watched his

father's eyes slowly close. No more was said as Bill's head fell peacefully back against the pillow.

From the back seat of the van, Lizzie watched Danny step out onto the darkened pavement of Terrace Street. Tom joined him, shivering in the cold night air. The shadows were long in the reflection of the gas lamps outside the rows of cramped, sooty houses, one of them Danny's lodgings. Danny had moved there in the summer, into the care of a kindly landlady, a young widow who was happy to look after Tom when the need arose. Lizzie was warmed by the sight of the parted curtains. The light shed a seasonal cheer onto the cobbled road. The glass was strung with home-made decorations and a candle or two burned inside, reflecting a welcome.

'Why can't Tom come home with us?' Polly asked as she leaned out of the van window. 'You could too, Uncle Danny, if you want.'

Danny smiled, leaning forward to ruffle her hair. 'This is our gaff, sweetheart, and I reckon we all need a good kip.'

'You could have a good kip at our place.'

Lizzie took Polly's shoulders. 'Danny and Tom will be over on Christmas Day and we'll all go up to Granda's.'

Danny signalled to Bert. 'Thanks for the lift, mate. We'll walk over to Lil's tomorrow for the car.' He bent low and looked at Lizzie. 'Make sure you lock up tonight. I know Bert's kipping in the storeroom. But it'll ease my mind if I know you've taken care.'

Lizzie didn't want to leave Danny and Tom. But what

other choice did they have? They were not man and wife, they were friends, and in the months since Frank had supposedly died they had become lovers. Now she wanted to hold Danny close, have his arms tightly around her. She wanted to feel his body against hers, strong and reassuring. She wanted him to make love to her and to sleep with him the whole night through as they had planned for their wedding night. To wake up in the morning and turn over on the pillow to see one another. If their plans had worked out, they would all have been together as a family. They would have spent the day in celebration with the kids, a visit up West, taking Pol and Tom to Oxford Street to see the Christmas decorations.

Danny had planned a meal at a corner house. He would have driven them to the Embankment and a supper of hot roasted chestnuts. Finally the kids would have fallen fast asleep in their rooms and Danny would have shared her big double bed, their arms, at last, locked around one another, legitimately. But Frank walking into the registry office yesterday morning had put an end to their dreams.

Bert revved the engine. 'See you on Sunday, Danny.'

'Happy Christmas, Uncle Danny, Happy Christmas, Tom.' Polly waved.

Lizzie looked into Danny's eyes as the van moved off. His tall figure and Tom's smaller one disappeared into the gloom. Polly yawned, slipping down on the old leather of the seat, and Lizzie drew the child into her arms. 'Do you think me mum will come to visit at Christmas, Auntie Lizzie?'

'I don't know, love.'

'Where is she?'

'I wish I knew.'

Polly stuck her thumb in her mouth. 'She might bring me a present. She could put it under the tree in the shop.'

'Father Christmas will bring you a present.'

'How many?' Polly looked up at Lizzie, her blue eyes dancing under her fringe of auburn hair.

'You'll have to wait and see.'

'Tell me about the Christmas when Uncle Danny drove you and all the Allens to Granda's for a party.'

Lizzie smiled as Polly's head fell against her shoulder. 'You've heard the story dozens of times.'

'Tell it again, Auntie Lizzie.'

'Well, it was Christmas afternoon as I've told you, a long time before you were born. Uncle Danny arrived at Langley Street where the Allen family lived and where Auntie Flo and Uncle Syd now live.'

'I've got a lot of uncles and aunties, ain't I?'

Lizzie laughed. 'Yes, the Allens are a big family. Now, it was the end of 1920 and Uncle Danny was about to leave England to seek his fortune in Australia. But before he left, your Granda gave a big party at Ebondale Street, where he lived in the airey below our shop. All the market traders turned up and some of Granda's friends and neighbours—'

'And you all had a knees-up.'

Lizzie laughed again. 'You know this story as well as I do.'

'You taught me the words to the song you sang.'

'Do you remember them?'

'Yes, but you sing it better than me.'

Lizzie stroked Polly's hair. "'If those lips could only speak, if those eyes could only see,'" Lizzie sang softly and Polly's little voice joined in. As they sang together, the memory of happier times warmed her. The years before Danny had sailed out of her life and the Allens were all still living at Langley Street.

'Was my mum beautiful, Auntie Lizzie?' Polly asked when they'd finished singing.

'Yes, very. As beautiful as you.'

'I wouldn't mind if she took me to the park again,' Polly mumbled sleepily, 'but she'd have to promise to bring me home. I don't want to go back to that funny house and sit with them ladies in their drawers again.'

Lizzie wrapped her arms tighter around Polly. This was a memory, thank God, that was growing vague in Polly's mind. A drunken escapade, down to Babs and Vinnie, an event that Lizzie hoped would dull with time. Polly's stay at the brothel had been brief, but alarming. The hazardous ride afterwards in Vinnie's car had only been brought to an end by Danny's quick thinking. Lizzie felt her skin grow clammy as she remembered how close Polly had come to disaster.

She listened to the sound of Polly's soft snore lost in the rattling of the vehicle. What did the future hold for this child? How was she to protect her?

Chapter Eleven

Three months later

Danny surveyed his kingdom: the garage and the fore-court that backed onto Morley's Wharf. Beyond this, the eyesore of a derelict factory, occupied by a group of river men. Danny liked to see the ragged children playing on the mudflats. He often threw them a tanner as they scamp-ered over the dock walls. Sometimes, after he shut shop, there would be an accordion playing or a mouth organ and he and Tom would join the community at their fire. They'd take bread and cheese and pickled onions with them. And in return, enjoy a mugful of hot broth, stewed in a pot over the brazier. Tom enjoyed the freedom of being away from his lessons and playing on the wharf with the rag-tag children. Very soon friendships had been forged. The poignant strains of the music would rise up under the deep blue sky and Danny would think of his youth as he gazed into the hot embers of the brazier. His life as a barrow boy had not been so different to this. The law had moved him on more times than he'd had hot dinners. He'd been jeered at and ridiculed for his lowly trade. He'd had Bill pushing him one way and the coppers the other. But he'd always kept his dream safe in his heart of one day making good.

And now that day had come. It had taken every penny of his capital to buy this pitch and make it his own. But he'd seen the potential and knew this land had been marked out for him. Business was booming. He'd won a contract with the Port of London Authority and was making a name for himself.

He breathed in deeply, savouring the sights and smells of his turf. His patch. He'd spent ten years of his life in the dark of the mines, waiting for this. Not that he'd ever guessed he was destined to own a scrubby patch of water-side land back in England!

Now on this late March morning, he couldn't help thinking back to the events of Christmas last year. His brother returning to life. Their father's sudden illness. And the distance that had grown between him and Lizzie since.

And the law was still breathing down his neck. Bobbies passing his way and taking ganders at his vehicles. But what could Bray prove that wasn't true? Nevertheless, the taste in his mouth was bitter.

Danny's eyes roamed over the scene before him. His ears caught the harmonies of the river; the hoots of the boats and barges and the grind and rattle of the cranes and factories. He felt like a king here. It was only when he remembered his separation from Lizzie and Pol that his spirits sank.

'Looks like a bonza day, mate.' Cal Bronga approached,

having parked his vehicle beside the garage. Cal grinned, showing his even white teeth. 'And the ockers told me it always rained on the other side of the world.'

'The East End is the best of British, Cal. Anyone who denies it is a fool,' Danny agreed. He gestured to the towering vehicle he had just parked on the forecourt. 'Let me introduce you to London Transport's S-type double-decker. Open top, bit of a wreck. She needs new tyres and a full service.'

'We taking the whole fleet?'

Danny laughed. 'We'd be set up for life if we did. No, this old girl is out of action for the general public. We're to fit her up before they use her to mend the trolleybus over-head wires. Her bosses may even turn her into a canteen.'

'Why choose us?' Cal asked with a frown.

'I gave the omnibus company a quote. We came out the cheapest. And we have the facilities.'

'First bus I've worked on. I hope we know what we're doing.' Cal gave a low chuckle. 'Cos I don't know one end of her from the other.'

Danny clapped his friend on the back. 'We'll soon find out. And hopefully, she'll be the first of many. Come on, we'll get changed into our togs and sort her out.'

Cal looked at Danny as they walked across the gravel to the doors of the workshop. 'You heard from your old man?'

Danny's face clouded. 'In the pink since Frank's been visiting.'

Danny regretted the dismay in his voice, but it was hard

to disguise. They walked into the interior of the ware-house and towards the wooden staircase that led up to the office. Danny jumped two stairs at a time, hoping Cal wouldn't press the subject. He knew Cal's interest in Bill was genuine. But after Christmas things had headed rapidly downhill. The long-lost son had returned, reformed in every way.

Danny reached up for the key to the office, balanced on the ledge above the door, and let them in. He peeled off his donkey jacket and shirt. He knew Cal was staring at him curiously, so he turned, heaving a sigh of resignation. 'I reckon Gertie bungs Frank a few quid. She says he's got rooms in Poplar.'

'Ain't that asking for trouble?' Cal remarked.

Danny grunted his agreement. 'As long as Frank stays out of my way, I'm happy.'

Cal put the kettle on to boil and placed two chipped enamel mugs side by side on the shelf. 'You should move in with your girl.'

'I would, if it was down to me.'

Cal placed two steaming mugs of tea on the desk between the overflowing piles of paper. 'You seen that copper's motor again?'

Danny nodded. 'Once or twice.'

'He couldn't make the frame stick as much as he tried.'

'Yeah, but he's done enough damage,' Danny pointed out. 'Me and Lizzie ain't been the same since. It's like he put the mockers on us. Saying we was out to get Frank and planned it all.'

'Give her time, mate.'

'Yeah, but how much?'

'What's your dad's take on all this?'

Danny gave a low sigh as he shook his head. 'He's rewriting history. Convinced Frank's a changed man. In Lizzie's eyes it makes me look as though it's me in the wrong.'

'She knows better than to believe that.'

Danny shrugged. 'Does she? I don't know any more.'

'Man, you're letting this get to you.'

Danny looked up under his pleated blond eyebrows. 'You might be right. But I can't get Lizzie to talk to me. Not about things that matter. When I ask her what she wants to do, she says we'll wait. See how things work out. Well, I know how they'll work out if we don't do something to change the situation. Lizzie and Pol will live over the shop. Me and Tom will stay at Terrace Street. I asked her to come away with us next month so we could spend some time together. But she says she can't afford to leave the business.' He shook his head in puzzlement.

'She's not had hassle from Frank, has she?'

'Not that I know of.' Danny took a heavy breath. 'Anyway. Enough of my troubles. Let's get down to business. Move the motors around downstairs.' He gave a rueful smile. 'We've still got the bills to pay.'

Cal reached for the vehicle keys that were hanging on the row of nails driven into the office wall. Running back down the wooden stairs, Danny heard his friend start up the first vehicle parked over the inspection pit.

Danny took a deep breath, searched in his pocket for his cigarettes and remembered he hadn't stopped to buy any. Going to the small cupboard on the wall, he pulled out his tobacco tin and papers. As he rolled himself a smoke his thoughts went to Lizzie again. Then his dad and inevitably to Frank. They chased round in his head until they collided in one big cloud of anxiety. He didn't believe a leopard could change its spots. No more than an evil man could become a saint overnight. Judas had proved that point and he had been Jesus's best mate. But his dad believed the story Frank had concocted about a stint in an asylum. The miracle cause of his redemption. The old man now insisted that, given time, Frank would turn into the son he had always believed Frank could be. But in Danny's book, it was some rare form of electrocution that could cause a man to repent and change his lifelong characteristics.

He placed a thin roll-up between his lips, lit up and closed his eyes as he inhaled. Frank had always been lazy, dishonest and two-faced. But Danny had accepted this as a kid. He'd tried to steer Frank away from the trouble he courted. Why in heaven's name then, Danny thought for the hundredth time, had he believed Frank would do the right thing by Lizzie while he was in Australia? Madness, that's what it was. Or perhaps – and more honestly – he had deliberately turned a blind eye to Frank's potential for mischief.

Just then, Danny heard a shout from downstairs.

He moved quickly to the interior window. Below, Cal

had driven the two motors parked over the pit to the rear of the garage. The timber boards covering the cellar had been lifted away. A dull light gleamed.

'What's up?' Danny yelled as he left the office to lean over the balustrade of the wooden stairs.

Cal emerged slowly from the cellar. 'Our tools have gone walkabout. Someone's cleaned us out!'

Danny's jaw fell open as he stood in the musty-smelling cellar they used as a workshop. It was empty. From the smallest of items fitted to the shelves lining the surface of the bench to the floor. His lathes, drills, braces and vices were gone. His entire booty from Aussie. His hard-earned investment. His wherewithal to perform his work. Every tool, freshly coated with oil and grease, had disappeared. Down to the last screw. To the last tack. Even the engine hoist, its chains and couplings.

'They've nicked everything,' Cal said unnecessarily, his voice full of incredulity. 'I couldn't believe my own eyes.'

Danny stared at the naked walls, the oily sawdust on the floor. The sight was unbelievable. They had been robbed, overnight, of everything vital to the business. It was as if someone had sucked up every item and replaced the thick timber boards overhead, leaving no indication of a wholesale robbery.

'It's not some chancer,' Danny decided. 'Whoever it was, they planned it. They had to move the two vans to get down to the cellar. How the hell did they do that?'

Cal shook his dark head. 'The keys were locked in the office. You saw me take them just now.'

'Whoever they are, they're clever.'

'And found the key on the ledge above the door.'

'Yeah, but they'd have had to get in the garage first. And only me and you can unlock the big doors.'

Danny was trying to think rationally, but he was consumed with anger. There had to be a motive, other than thievery. 'An amateur would have used a crowbar to get in, smashed the motor windows and pushed them off the boards. This job was so neat and tidy it looks as if they've swept up behind them. Why bother to put the timbers back and reverse the motors into place?'

'You're right,' Cal agreed after some thought. 'It's like someone's sending a message.'

'This has Ferreter's trademark.'

'But he's banged up,' nodded Cal.

'Must have been a few of them,' Danny murmured. 'The engine hoist alone needs muscle.'

'Have you checked on the store out back?'

'Jesus, no!'

Danny leaped the steps of the cellar, his head and heart banging like drums. He was drowning in sweat. The thought of someone getting into his store was almost more than he could bear.

Chapter Twelve

They reached the rear of the garage together but it was Danny who was first to climb through the small opening to the store. He'd locked the Nissen hut with a heavy chain that secured the iron bar. But something looked wrong. It was as if there was one small detail of the picture that he didn't see. A detail that sent a message to his brain and forced adrenalin through his veins.

The muscles in his legs felt like wood. His stomach turned with force as Cal paused breathlessly beside him.

'Something's wrong,' Danny said, narrowing his eyes.

'The lock's *in situ*,' Cal replied with clear relief. 'No one's got in there.'

'It's wrong,' Danny insisted, staring at the chain that he himself had padlocked the night before. 'It looks wrong.'

'Nah, mate, don't worry, they couldn't get past the shackle. Only you've got a key. And nothing, other than dynamite, would bust open that baby.'

Danny tried to move, but his instincts were alight with foreboding. He knew what his friend was telling him was true; the bar and padlock were a round cross-section of steel and could tether a battleship. Danny had brought in a locksmith to make certain the store was impenetrable. He had secured the roof and the walls with cast iron. He was confident of every inch of it. He had to be. Inside were the engine parts for his repairs. More valuable even than his tools. The latest horsepower engines for heavy-duty vehicles, camshafts, chassis and gearboxes. Every item of his stock was an earner. He'd seen to that personally.

Now he just stared at the solid door, no more than his height and width. There was more chain and lock than there was wood. To the unsuspecting eye, it was exactly as he had left it last night.

Danny forced himself forward, his heart pounding. Cal followed, his breath heavy in Danny's ear. Danny reached out and drew his fingers over the smooth metal of the shackle. The mechanism slid instantly from his touch. A glistening, spinning, hissing metal snake unravelled before his eyes.

He almost jumped back with fright. The coil of chain wound into the dust at his feet. They gazed down at the padlock, apparently untouched, sheared neatly across its diameter.

Lizzie was about to cash up; the Friday had ended on a high with customers enjoying the fine weather. She had sent Bert to buy the unsold fruit and veg from the market. A practice that Bill had started years ago, and as successful today as ever it was. Knock-down Friday prices brought in the bargain hunters before the weekend. Once they were in the shop, their purses opened.

Lizzie knew she could have had no better teacher than Bill Flowers. He knew every trick of the trade. The years of working at his side, and making contacts, had given her coster knowledge. The traders of Cox Street market were her biggest rivals second only to Chrisp Street. But they were also her friends and saw to it that she was looked after.

At teatime today the women had flocked in, eager to grab their spoils. The smart ones had managed to rifle their men's wage packets before the Friday night's booze-up. Unless the odd shilling or half-crown was set aside by the discerning housewife, Lizzie knew, all the weekly wage would be tipped down the ale-house drain.

She also knew that word went round. And like Bill, Lizzie never failed to meet her customers' needs. The small change burned holes in their pockets and she was there to help them choose wisely.

'There ain't much left now,' Bert told her as he humped the last of the carrots on his back. 'But I'll weigh up what's left and make penny bags for tomorrow.'

'Put in a few nice extras, Bert. Some of those Brussels will do. And maybe a spud or two.'

'Right you are.'

'Is Pol playing in the yard?'

'Yer. With two of them kids from across the road.'

Satisfied Polly was close by, Lizzie continued to write up the day's takings. Business was good all round. Her glass display cabinet was an eye-catcher. Well worth the money she'd spent on buying it. Cakes, pastries, bread, toffee apples and bags of sweets were the most popular. The idea had come from Lil Sharpe last year and it was a cracker. Lizzie didn't need to take stock. Everything was gone before the next morning. She knew if she had more suppliers to buy from, she could make a real go of it. A kind of cooperative for women. She liked that idea. She liked the idea even more of opening another shop. With the addition of groceries like bottled onions, gherkins and pickles, all-time favourites, there was bound to be a rapid turnover.

Lizzie rang up the last figure in the brass till. She was thinking about her idea when she heard the tinkle of the bell over the shop door. Danny strode towards her. He looked dirty but handsome in his overalls and her heart lifted at the sight of him. Until she remembered that things between them were very different to how they had been before Christmas. Their dreams of a happy family had all been shattered the moment Frank had walked into that registry office.

And yet, was Frank to blame for cheating death? she asked herself as Danny approached.

Now, as she smiled at Danny, she wondered how he could have been so mistaken in the identification of the corpse. Fragments from the interview with Bray were like pinpricks of doubt. 'A brother would know his own brother,' the policeman had suggested.

Danny bent, and with gentle affection kissed her cheek. 'How's trade, kid?'

'We've had a good day.'

He glanced at the empty glass cabinet. 'I can see that.' He looked over his shoulder and out of the window. 'You got any late customers?'

At this suggestion she laughed. 'Business is over for the day.'

'I've got some bad news.'

Lizzie looked at him uncertainly. 'What's wrong?'

'Have you seen Frank?'

'No, why should I have?' She hesitated, frowning. 'You know he won't turn up here.'

'That's exactly what he might do. Someone's cleaned out the workshop.'

'What!'

He smiled without humour. 'A puzzle, ain't it? Coincidence, Frank showing up and all my stuff is nicked. Everything down in the workshop.'

'And you think it's Frank?'

'Well, it ain't Ferreter. He's in the jug.'

'But what proof have you?' Lizzie asked in confusion. 'Did anyone see him?'

'No, but who else has it in for me?'

'Danny, it don't sound to me as if Frank would do that. Your dad says he's done with his bent days—'

'How would Dad know – *really* know – what Frank's intentions are?' Danny broke in. 'Frank will have told him what he wants to hear.'

'Bill is no fool,' Lizzie protested. 'He's forgiven but not forgotten the punishment Frank put him through.' She saw the fear now in Danny's face and the changed man he was becoming. It was as if Frank's return to life had drained Danny of his own. 'Danny, I can't keep living in fear of the past. And neither should you. Who else would want to burgle the garage?'

'That's just it. There ain't no one.'

'There must be.'

'It sounds like you're defending Frank.'

'No, why should I?'

'That's what I'd like to know.' His eyes were full of reproach.

'Danny, we can't go on like this.'

'Then move in with me.' Danny took hold of her, drawing her close. 'Let's do as we planned. Set up home together. I'll sell up, if I have to. We'll have enough behind us to go somewhere we ain't known. Start afresh as Mr and Mrs. We'll leave the memories – and Frank – behind us. You'll have all the time in the world to sit back and enjoy yourself. Be a real mum, look after Polly and Tom.'

'You want us to run away?'

'I'd call it making a fresh start.'

'But I've worked hard for this shop. As hard as you have for the garage. You don't want to sell up, no more than I do.'

'I'd give it all up if you asked me.'

'I would never do that.' Lizzie looked into his unshaven face. A face she loved so much and yet he felt like a stranger. 'Running won't help,' she whispered. 'Mud sticks wherever you go.'

'So you're going to stay married to Frank forever?'

'I'm not saying that.'

Danny threw back his head. 'I'm supposed to kick my heels in the meantime?' He stared at her, adding in a low voice, 'For twelve long years I dreamed of you and me, from back in the day, when I asked you to go with me to Aussie. I lost you then and I'm losing you now.'

Lizzie was silent, her thoughts in turmoil. As much as she loved him, she had carved a life out of her misery and won her right to live the way she wanted with Polly. There wasn't anywhere they could run to. Frank or no Frank, this was her and Pol's life and she cherished it. If only Danny could understand that.

There was resignation in his face now. He shrugged and, turning, walked to the shop door. 'I'll see you around.'

'What are you going to do now?' She followed him.

'Find myself some tools. Whoever cleaned me out won't stop me from running my business.'

The bell tinkled and Danny's tall figure strode across the street. He climbed in the parked truck and drove away.

Was losing Danny the price of Frank's return? Lizzie wondered sadly. She hadn't meant to defend Frank, but why would Frank steal from the garage? If what Bill said was true about Frank's change of heart, his making an enemy of Danny just didn't add up. Frank needed all the friends he could get, including his brother.

So what was she to believe?

Chapter Thirteen

It was the last Sunday in March and Lizzie was sitting with Flo on the bench in Island Gardens. Polly was with her Uncle Syd and Lil, back at Langley Street, and she and Flo had snatched an hour to themselves.

'Well, you're the first to know,' Flo announced with a wry smile, as she settled herself on the hard wooden slats. 'I'm in the family way.'

'You're expecting?' Lizzie gasped.

'The doctor examined me.'

'Are you sure?'

'Yes, course. I'm feeling sick as a dog, can't face breakfast and I'm having to force down dinner.'

'Flo. A baby! Come here and give me a hug.' Lizzie pulled her sister into her arms.

'Dunno what the neighbours will think.' Flo grimaced. 'It won't take long to get round the street.'

As they sat in the pale spring sunshine, Lizzie's glance went to her sister's full breasts. Her well-proportioned figure was hidden under her herringbone wool wrapover coat. Flo had always been well-endowed and she looked no different today. But her deep brown hair seemed thicker and glossier and her cheeks had the fresh blush of health. 'I'm three months gone already.'

'What does Syd have to say?'

'Oh, he's talking names already.' Flo rolled her eyes. 'You'd think we'd won a fortune on the gee-gees. He don't seem to be bothered I'll have to pack in work as soon as I start showing. Lucky enough I'm on the big side anyway and no one has said anything yet. My boss won't like it, of course. I only just had the promotion at Christmas. And there goes our posh honeymoon. All our pennies will have to be spent on the baby.'

'Yes, but you're having the family you always wanted.'

'It wasn't supposed to happen so quickly.'

Lizzie smiled. 'That's what comes of having a lodger.'

Flo blushed hotly. 'Syd wanted us to get married last year. I should have taken him up on his offer.'

'You can still be married in white if you do it soon.'

'Yes, provided me dress covers the bump.'

'You should be celebrating. I'm sure Syd can't wait for the day when he can slip that ring on your finger.'

'Nor can his mum.'

Lizzie took in a breath. 'Have you told her?'

'I went to meet the family last Sunday. Syd said it was time I did. As you know I've been keeping my distance as the Millers have got a bit of a rep in the East End. But this baby changes everything. They will be its only grandparents.'

'What are they like?'

'Syd's mum, the Missus, has worked all her life as a char

but three of his brothers are doing time. Syd's old man lives for the gee-gees and his tipple. Walter and Clifford run a scrapyard when they're not on their holidays. How my Syd ever turned out the sound sod he is, I'll never know. The family live in a three-up, two down over Mile End. Sons, wives, girlfriends and the grandkids.'

'A bit crowded then. Do they know you're in the family way?'

'Not likely. I found myself mute after listening to the accounts the women gave of each birth.'

Lizzie laughed. 'At least you've broken the ice.'

'Yes, a day with the Millers is memorable.'

'You'll soon be the Missus's daughter-in-law.'

'I just hope Syd can steer clear of Walter and Clifford. They kept trying to talk him into the family business.'

'What does Syd have to say about all this?'

'Oh, you know Syd.' Flo wrinkled her nose under her fringe. 'He sees a redeeming feature in each one of his brothers. And only puts distance between them and us because he knows I won't go along with any old hanky-panky. But the baby coming along means that not only will we have to get spliced, but I'll have to swallow my pride too.'

'If you love a man, then you love his family.'

Flo's curved dark eyebrows arched sharply. 'Like that, is it? Love one, love 'em all?'

Lizzie frowned at her sister. 'What do you mean?'

'From what you've told me today you sound as if it's all happy families with Frank again.'

Lizzie knew that Flo was not going to let her off lightly. She'd tried to tell Flo in as few details as possible about Frank's return to the fold. But Flo was like a dog with a bone. 'Bill has given him another chance is all I said.'

'And you're siding with Bill?'

'I didn't say that. Bill's made up his own mind.'

'You know you're asking for trouble, don't you?' Flo's look of disgust was plain.

'After what you've told me about the Millers, I'd say the pot was calling the kettle black.'

'Syd is a good bloke, unlike your husband. Do you really believe this cock and bull story about a loony bin?'

'I don't know what to believe. But Bill has been like a father to me. And he's happier than he's been in a long while. When he calls in the shop, it's just like old times. He cracks a joke and talks to the customers as if he was still running the business. Gertie is willing to believe what Frank says, because he is having a healthy influence on his dad.'

'Do you want my opinion?' Flo asked impatiently.

Lizzie thought she knew Flo's opinion but she wasn't prepared for what her sister said next.

'I think you're still Mrs Frank Flowers at heart. Frank is a shrewd operator. Always was. I remember how even I was taken in as a kid. Until the night of Bill's Christmas party before Danny went away. And then I saw what you didn't see. Or perhaps you didn't want to see. I saw him looking at Babs in a way that he never looked at you. Unlike you, our Babs was easy but she was lazy. Whereas

Frank saw the potential in you, a hard worker and good earner. Now he appears again like the Angel Gabriel, his debauched and villainous nature having undergone a miraculous change. He'll have polished his fallen halo until it blinds you and you forgive him everything.'

'That's not true, Flo. I'll never take him back.'

'You're a soft touch when it comes to family,' Flo replied with a shrug. 'Oh, you told that thug Ferreter to sling his hook, never flinched as you faced him down. But closer to home you're easily fooled. After Mum and Dad left us it was the end of the Allens. The end of an era. You should have married Danny and left the East End behind you.' Flo stopped, adding accusingly, 'God knows you and Danny are entitled to some happiness after all these years.'

'I want that happiness too.'

'Then take it. The sooner the better.'

'I have to work this out in my own way.'

'By which time Danny will have finally decided to bugger off.'

At this, Lizzie looked away.

'I'm sorry.' Flo touched her shoulder. 'I shouldn't have said that.'

Lizzie swallowed, taken aback at the pain she felt as Flo's words struck home. 'I saw Danny on Friday. There was a burglary at the workshop.'

'Who did that?'

'Danny thinks it was Frank.'

'You can't blame him,' Flo replied unhelpfully. 'But really, gel, what about you two?'

'What about us?'

'You know what I mean.'

Lizzie looked hard at her sister. 'Danny wants me to move in, start afresh somewhere else. But that's not for me.'

'Christ, Lizzie, are you sure?'

Lizzie nodded. 'So I'm to have a niece or nephew soon,' she said, changing the subject quickly.

'Yes, late September if me dates are right.'

'So there will be the patter of little feet again in our old house.'

Flo's cheeks flushed red as she nodded. 'I hope our ma's pleased, wherever she is. And Pa too.'

The silence stretched between them as Lizzie looked across the park, remembering the days of their childhood. The Allens had come here many years before; Vinnie and Bert had played on the foreshore, searching for treasures in the mud. Flo and Babs had enjoyed the sandpit, their faces and hands caked with more dirt than sand by the time they made their way home. The gardens were full of memories and, as she looked back at Flo, she wondered if Flo would bring her children to play here too.

Flo grinned. 'I'll be knackered lugging all that weight around in hot weather.'

'You're as strong as a brewery horse.'

'I'll look like one an' all.'

They laughed, both relieved the tension was broken. 'Don't worry,' Lizzie chuckled, 'me and Pol will come round and make sure you're resting. I'll bring you one of Lil's Victoria sponges.'

Flo groaned. 'I feel sick at the thought of food.'

'You won't be sick forever.' Although it had been a shock to hear about the baby, Lizzie wasn't surprised. After all, Flo and Syd had lived together, albeit as land-lady and lodger, for some while. It would be lovely to have a baby in the family again. Polly had been such a dear little mite. So pretty with her tufts of copper coloured hair and big blue eyes. As she thought of Polly lying in the cot, Lizzie had a warm feeling inside. From the start, Polly had revelled in the love of her close family. Flo and Syd and Bert never failed to provide what was lacking from Babs. They loved Polly as their own. And as the years had gone by, Polly had accepted and not questioned the gap that Babs had left in her young life.

What had become of Babs? Lizzie wondered yet again. Where had she gone and what was she doing? Did she miss her child and the love that Polly would eagerly give her?

Only Babs could answer that.

Chapter Fourteen

It was a mild April afternoon, and the cloudy sky had given way to occasional showers. Lizzie had left Bert to cover the exposed greengrocery with an old tarpaulin. She had managed to dodge the showers on her way to the school.

Now as she stood at the school gate, she craned her neck to see if Polly was in the playground. A light spring breeze blew the stray strands of her dark hair away from her face. Polly's teacher, Mrs Price, saw to it that every child was out of class by five minutes past four. Today Polly was late. There were only a few children left on the weed-speckled square of asphalt in front of the old Victorian building. Polly had loved West India Road School from the moment she had begun there just after her fourth birthday. She was a bright little girl and learned her three 'R's quickly. Lizzie knew that Polly was an achiever. Waiting for her niece to appear, she felt a familiar curl of anticipation. She never tired of the pride she felt when Polly appeared in her school beret, her navy-blue drill slip, green blouse and jersey. Over her shoulder would be strung her shoe bag, and her hair would have come loose from her plaits. Somewhere on her face would be an ink smudge.

Lizzie pushed open the iron gate. As she walked across the playground, Polly appeared at the school door.

'Auntie Lizzie!' Polly ran into her arms.

'You're late today, monkey!' She hugged Polly, catching a whiff of the inks and papers of the classroom on her niece's clothes.

'I'm a monitor now. I have to help Mrs Price clear away.'

'How did you get to be a monitor?'

Polly looked serious. 'You have to be good to get a badge.'

'And are you good?'

Polly giggled as she skipped along. 'A bit.'

'Well, I'm very proud of you.'

Polly stopped suddenly. 'There was a man outside the gates today. I think it was Uncle Frank.'

Lizzie froze. 'Uncle Frank? Are you sure?'

'Dunno. I forgot what he looks like. But he said he was.'

'What did he want?'

'He just said hello.'

'Was that all?'

'The whistle went so I had to go in.'

Lizzie drew Polly close. 'Are you sure that's all he said?'

Polly nodded solemnly as she stared at Lizzie. 'I was a bit frightened. Is he gonna blow up the shop again?'

Lizzie shook her head quickly. 'No, course not.'

'Billy Roper said he was.'

'Well Billy Roper's wrong.' Lizzie drew her hands over Polly's narrow shoulders. The children at school had been very cruel last year after the word went round that Polly's home had been bombed. When the police had reported the shop was a target in the spate of East End uprisings, Polly's friends had deserted her. Rumours had quickly spread. The parents suspected the Flowers family were involved with political activists. And it seemed Frank appearing had started them off again.

'Did you tell Mrs Price what Billy said?'

Polly shook her head.

'Why not?'

'I didn't want me badge taken away.'

'But why would she do that?'

'Because all the Flowerses are Commies.' Polly blushed.

'Who told you that?'

Polly looked down. 'Billy.'

Lizzie lifted her chin. 'Billy is just a little boy repeating a bad word. He doesn't even know what it means. He should mind his manners if he doesn't want to get into trouble.'

'So we ain't—'

'No we're not. And if Billy says that word again, tell Mrs Price. She won't stop you being a monitor. But she will stop Billy from being foul-mouthed.'

Polly grinned. She slid her hand in Lizzie's. 'What have we got for tea?'

'Your favourite. Pie and mash with lots of gravy.'

As they walked home, Lizzie talked to Polly, hiding her

growing anger. Billy Roper didn't know what he was saying. He was only repeating what he'd heard from an adult. But if Frank hadn't turned up at school, Polly wouldn't have been upset.

She decided that, after Polly was in bed that evening, she would cycle up to Poplar and make her feelings clear to Bill.

Chapter Fifteen

'Come in, love, you sound out of breath.' Gertie indicated a vacant spot by the wall where Lizzie could leave her bike. 'What brings you out this time of night?'

'Is Bill up?'

'Yes. He's in the parlour. I'll make a cuppa.'

Lizzie caught Gertie's arm. 'Don't trouble, Gertie. I can't stay long. I've left Polly with Bert.'

Pulling her cardigan round her, Gertie led the way to the front room. 'Bill, it's Lizzie.'

'Hello, gel.' Bill lowered his feet from the pouffe. Lizzie was pleased to see he looked well.

Lizzie sat on the sofa. The parlour was stuffy and the coal fire was still burning, even in April. Bill and Gertie had certainly changed their ways, Lizzie thought. Once upon a time, they were hardy mortals. But with ill health, Lizzie supposed, all that had changed.

'Everything all right?' Bill asked.

'Well, yes and no.'

'Don't like the sound of that.'

'Polly told me Frank went to the school today.'

Bill scratched his whiskers. 'He said he'd walked by. He only stopped to say hello.'

'One of the kids told Polly he was going to put a bomb in the shop again.'

'Did you put her right?'

'Yes, but she was frightened.'

'It was a one-off,' Gertie interrupted, glancing at Bill. 'Frank was only passing. Didn't cause no trouble.'

'I don't want it happening again.'

'Look, love,' Bill said, sitting forward. 'Ain't this all a bit daft? She is his kid after all.'

'We don't know for sure.'

'You only have to look at her to see. The colour of her hair is your Babs's. But the blue of them mince pies is Frank's. She should be told he's her dad.'

Lizzie had made a bargain with Bill but he seemed to have forgotten it. Besides which, the decision to tell Polly about her father was Babs's and Babs's alone.

'By the time we see your sister again, Polly could be sixteen, not six,' Bill replied light-heartedly.

'When the time comes I'll tell Polly the same as I told you. It's only her mother who can answer her questions.'

'And what about Frank?' Gertie asked shortly. 'He's doing his best to do right by you and Pol. After all, your sister hasn't shown up in almost a year. Didn't even say where she was going. She might never return. Have you considered that?'

'Yes, but I'm hoping she'll be back some day. Until then, I'll look after Polly, same as I always have.'

'And Frank?' Bill asked. 'If you won't let him see the child, then what has he to strive for?'

'He never cared for her before.'

'A changed man is my son, Lizzie. You understand he's trying to make amends.'

'Have you heard about Danny's garage?'

'No.' Bill looked up sharply.

'He had a burglary. All his tools were stolen.'

'He ain't blaming Frank for that, is he?' Gertie demanded.

'You'll have to ask Danny about that.'

'We would. But he don't come round.'

Lizzie stood up. 'Please ask Frank not to go to the school again.'

'Don't cut him off without hope,' Bill pleaded, trying to get up from the chair. He reached out in an effort to stop Lizzie from leaving. For a few seconds he swayed, then, as Lizzie rushed to his aid, he slumped back. His head fell against the cushion and Gertie quickly took a small brown bottle from the mantel. Pouring a thimbleful of its contents into a tumbler, she handed the glass to Bill.

'What's that?'

'For the ticker,' Gertie said quietly.

'I didn't think he still had these turns.'

'Only when he gets agitated.'

'Bill, I'm sorry. I've upset you.' Lizzie sat down again. Once more she saw it was the old man sitting there, frail and feeble. The man who had supported her through thick and thin in the years when Frank had bullied and threatened her, draining the money from the business and wasting it.

'No, my dear. I'm just a little lacking in breath.' Bill forced a smile and took her hand. 'What do they say? It's always the creaking gate that lasts longest.'

'Is there anything I can get you?'

'Just your attention for a few minutes longer.'

'Bill, I know you believe Frank when he says he's changed,' Lizzie said soothingly. 'I want to believe that too. And I trust your judgement more than I trust anyone's. But I can never allow Frank back into my life. Too much has happened between us.'

'Yes, but what if he could win your respect? Just that. Nothing more.'

'My respect?' she repeated doubtfully.

Bill gave a laboured intake of breath. After a few seconds, he said in a heavy voice, 'He wants to prove his worth to you and to the world. It's not in his interests to nick from his brother or upset his kid. It's his family he's trying to win back. Think about it, Lizzie. He's been a fool. But he ain't that much of a mug to say one thing and do another. Not in the East End where everyone knows each other's business.'

'So what are you saying, Bill?'

'Let him see Polly every so often. With your blessing. It'll help keep him on the straight and narrow.'

'But Polly was afraid today,' she protested, feeling Bill's argument drawing her in. 'Billy Roper called the Flowers family Commies. Even if Frank's intentions were innocent, children can be very cruel.'

'Then she should hear the truth for herself.'

'Please, Lizzie,' Gertie said and came to sit on the sofa. 'Polly will hear things, it's on the cards. Frank ain't invisible and people will point the finger. If Polly sees for herself that he means no harm, it don't matter what any kid says.' Gertie smiled encouragingly.

Lizzie shook her head. 'I don't know.'

'There's just a couple of weeks till Easter. Bring Pol round. An hour, that's all. We'll have something nice for tea. She knows no harm will come to her at her Granda's house. Frank will make an appearance, be on his best behaviour, and that's a promise.'

Lizzie looked into Bill's anxious face. The lines were deepening around his eyes and his hair was almost silver white. She loved him deeply and admired his sense of loyalty to Frank. But this was asking too much.

'Ain't it worth a try?' Bill persisted. 'Better the child don't live in fear and can answer up for herself at school. Frank's back on the island with a view to staying, Lizzie. He was born and bred here and is as much part of the Smoke as we are.'

'As is Danny,' Lizzie said pointedly. 'This ain't easy for him, Bill.'

The old man nodded patiently. 'Danny should speak to his brother. Know his brother wouldn't cross him.'

Lizzie sat with a heavy heart. Bill wanted the best for both his sons, but had too much happened in the past? Danny was in no mood to forgive and forget.

'Frank don't mean no harm, I swear it,' Gertie said.

'But then you've only got our word, ducks, and it ain't going to be easy proving he's no threat. He was a sod once and is tarred by that brush.'

Lizzie stared pityingly at the old costermonger and his faithful partner. Her soft heart twisted as she listened to their words and saw the hope in their eyes. They were genuine in their attempts to reunite this broken family. It was a last attempt, she knew. The years were no longer plentiful for Bill and Gertie. They were desperate for a result.

But was she?

Chapter Sixteen

Seated at the dressing table in Cal's lodgings, a large, shabby room above a Cubitt Town café, Ethel lifted her fair hair from her bare shoulders and twirled it into a knot at the back of her head. She had no need to pinch her pale cheeks or add mascara to the lashes of her blue eyes. Here in this funny little room, she was happy. Content to be with a man who was Richard's exact opposite.

She smiled at Cal as he stood behind her, meeting his gaze in the mirror. A lean, supple figure, he watched her with an animal's wary eyes as she pinned her hair. The more she had of Cal, the more she wanted him. His black hair fell to his shoulders, his beard had been shaved off but had grown again quickly. She loved its rough texture. Sometimes at nights when she lay by Richard, she would think of Cal's body and pretend it was him sleeping only a few inches away.

But why was she so excited by this quiet man? she wondered. She knew so little about him. But that didn't seem to matter to either of them.

She leaned forward, placing her chin on her elbows,

her eyes trailing up to a browned illustration on the wall. 'What's that?' she asked curiously. 'A dragon?'

Cal laughed as he strolled casually across the room. Wearing only his white pants, he stretched his brown body. 'He's the bunyip, a devil who lives in the rivers and billabongs. The poor old fella's blessed with a croc's head and dog's face. He's got flippers and tusks and he'll leap out of the swamp and eat you up.' Cal caught hold of her shoulders and she jumped.

'Cal, don't do that.'

'He ain't real.' Cal kissed her gently on the neck.

'Is that to kill the bunyip with?' Ethel pointed to the long wooden shaft hung prominently on the wall above the mirror. She shivered at the sight of the vicious-looking blade driven into the top.

'It was my grandfather's tribal club,' Cal replied. 'My ancestors used it in battle.'

'Did he give it to you?' Ethel asked, curious now.

'Grandfather raised me and my sister.'

'Where were your parents?'

Cal shrugged. 'Dad went off in the bush one day and never came back. My mum and sister . . . they died of the grog.'

'Cal, that must have been awful.'

'My grandfather was a good man. He looked after us and taught us the old traditions. Tried to keep us from going to the drink.' His black eyes flickered as he stared into the mirror.

Ethel shivered as she looked at this man. There was so

much she didn't know about him. 'This is the first time you've told me about your family.'

'It's the first time you've asked.'

Ethel looked down. 'It didn't seem to matter before.'

'Does it now?'

She nodded silently.

'Can I ask you a question?'

'Yes, but that doesn't mean I'll answer.'

'You're a good-looking Sheila,' Cal said quietly. 'You could have anyone. Why me?'

Ethel blushed. 'How many Sheilas do you know?'

'None like you.' Slowly he began to slide down the straps of her slip. In a rush of embarrassment, Ethel stopped him.

'Cal, don't. I've got to go.'

'Why? You said you had all day.'

'Yes, and the day's almost over.'

'What's all the rush? Your kids are with their gran.'

Ethel rolled her eyes as she slipped her straps back over her shoulders. 'Yes, but Timothy's too old to stay the night now. And if he won't stay, neither will Rosie. My mother-in-law don't let them listen to the radio or go into Lewisham. She thinks they'll get up to something.'

'Like their mother.' Cal grinned.

Ethel frowned. 'Don't rub it in, Cal. I feel guilty enough as it is.'

'You shouldn't, you're entitled. I'll run you home in the car. What's an hour as the crow flies?'

'I don't want you anywhere near me house,' Ethel

threatened as she leaned her head to one side. 'Not in that hearse you're driving.'

'It's a damn fine Studebaker, imported from the US of A,' Cal replied with amusement. 'You appreciated it enough the other day when—'

'All right, all right!' Ethel blushed as she thought of the last afternoon they'd spent together. Cal had driven her out Bromley way and they'd parked in a secluded spot. She couldn't believe that she'd let him make love to her in broad daylight on the big leather seats. Anyone could have caught them. Yet it had been their recklessness she'd found exciting.

'Good memories,' he whispered in her ear and Ethel shivered.

Ethel smiled sweetly as she reached for her blouse. But Cal dragged her back into his arms. 'I don't give up easy. You're a little cracker, Ethel.'

'Now you've messed up my hair.'

'I'm gonna mess it up some more.'

Ethel knew this was wrong, but she couldn't stop herself.

'Kiss me again, girl,' Cal whispered as he ran his hands over her, 'or I'll set the bunyip on you.'

'You wouldn't dare,' she murmured, grateful for the fact that she had never been wanted like this before.

Soon Ethel had forgotten she had a home to go back to and only heard the sounds coming from outside; the gulls flying over the smoke-blackened boarding house above the café. The smell of the rope works and the pickle factory drifting in through the window. The shouts of the noisy kids in the street. She forgot about getting home for Richard's tea. Another few minutes wouldn't matter.

But Ethel regretted her decision as, several hours later, she flew off the bus and rounded the corner only to see Richard standing at the door of the house. He was dressed in the same suit he wore to the office every day of his working life, his angular face set in a scowl and the late afternoon sunshine reflected in the lenses of his spectacles.

'Where have you been?' he demanded as Ethel hurried up.

'I thought you were at your mother's tonight.'

'She has a church meeting. I asked you, where have you been?'

Ethel shrugged, trying to push past. 'Shopping, that's all.'

'What have you been buying this time?' Richard's pale hazel eyes narrowed spitefully. 'Obviously something too big to bring home with you.' He followed her in. 'I told you, we have a perfectly comfortable suite.'

In panic, Ethel turned to face him. 'That doesn't stop me looking,' she improvised, trying to look offended. 'As a matter of fact I've seen a nice one at Harper's in the High Street.'

'Harper's?' Richard exploded, his sallow complexion turning red. 'They charge a fortune for their furniture. I hope you don't expect me to ask Mother for the money.'

'Your mother again!' Ethel exclaimed fiercely. 'I might have known you'd bring her into this.'

'And why not?' Richard argued. 'She bought our

present sofa and chairs, which are still in perfectly good working order.'

'They were our wedding gift, Richard,' Ethel said helplessly, 'well over fifteen years ago.'

'And they'll do for another fifteen in my opinion.' Richard nodded and folded his arms across his chest.

'Oh – oh, damn you and your mother, you're both impossible!' Ethel wailed, tears spilling over as she turned and ran up the stairs. Banging the bedroom door behind her, she threw herself on the bed.

The tears that fell on the bedcover were tears of guilt, frustration, disappointment and self-pity. Her self-centred, penny-pinching husband hadn't given a single thought to the idea she might be having an affair. But rather, he chose to believe that she would happily waste time trawling around the shops with the intention of buying a three-piece suite that they couldn't possibly afford.

She didn't know who she despised more.

Herself, or bloody Mrs Ryde.

Chapter Seventeen

Easter had come and gone with record profits. Now they were at the end of April, and trade was still brisk. Lizzie was thinking about the new shop as she opened the books. It was time to invest her profits. What would Bert think of her plans, she wondered, as she watched him drag the sacks of vegetables across the shop floor.

'Lil and Doug should be here soon,' she said as she placed the price paddle in the sack of potatoes. 'We could do with three times as many cakes from Lil.'

Bert straightened and rubbed his stomach. 'Not half.'

'Bert, what do you think of opening a new shop?'

'What, like this one?'

Lizzie nodded. 'Have you seen that shop near the school in Ripon Street? The empty one Mr James ran as a hardware store?'

Sweating, Bert nodded, his boot pushing a sack into position beside its neighbour. 'Bit run down. Been empty a long time.'

'Could do with a coat of paint. But it would scrub up well.'

Bert drew his forearm over his wet forehead. He blinked his bulging eyes free of moisture and took hold of the broom. Leaning his elbow on the handle he frowned. 'What you driving at, gel?'

'I wrote to the landlord and made an enquiry. I'm going there to have a look round.'

'What for?' Bert asked with an air of confusion.

'If the rent is reasonable, I'd like to run it as a greengrocer's, bakery and confectionery store.'

'Blimey, are you serious?'

'Why not?'

'No one's done that before.'

'I know. But there must be other women like Lil who can cook as well as she can. We'll ask around for home bakers. For those who can't bring their stuff in, we'll use the van to collect. We'll order jam sponges, buns, toffee apples, fruit scones and individual apple pies like we do from Lil. And anything else that strikes a chord. Cheap enough for the factory workers and labourers on their way to the docks.'

'We'll have to keep the cakes out of the dust.'

'Mr James's shop is big enough.'

'So what's this shop gonna be called?'

'It would be a sort of women's cooperative.'

'Would it make money, though?'

'This shop is. We'd run it on the same lines. There must be lots of women who want to work from home.'

'Yeah, but it's usually washing and sewing, ain't it?'

'Yes, but why not something different?'

'Dunno. Never give it a thought.'

'Well, I have.'

'Blimey, gel, you don't let the grass grow under your feet! But who's gonna run the new shop if you and me are here?'

Lizzie grinned. 'I've already asked Ethel if she'd like to join the firm.'

'Don't she work at Rickard's?'

'She's not there any more. Well, what do you think?'

Bert frowned at the worn handle of the broom, as if making a serious decision. 'Sounds like you've already made up your mind.'

'You're in this business too.'

Bert looked pleased. 'Whatever you say goes, Lizzie.'

Lizzie smiled with pleasure. She put on her leather apron and slid off the cover of the glass shelves. Their surfaces had to be kept clean for the stock that Lil and Doug were delivering.

When the door opened ten minutes later, she expected to see their first customers. Instead three strangers stood there.

'Good morning, my dear,' said the first, a short, well-built man wearing a fedora. He slid it off and ran a pudgy hand over his shiny, hairless skull. He was, Lizzie decided, in his late thirties. He wore a shoulder-padded overcoat that at once reminded her of Frank. The two taller men, similarly dressed, stood with their backs to the closed shop door.

Lizzie said nothing as he held out his hand. 'Mrs Flowers?'

'Yes?'

'I'm Leonard Savage.'

Lizzie didn't like the look of him or his pals. They had walked in her shop as if they owned the place.

'What do you want?'

'Just a word, that's all.'

'What kind of word? We're not open till eight.'

Leonard Savage dropped his hand. 'This won't take a moment. You wouldn't want us bothering you in working hours. I mean, this establishment is all nice and tidy. Shame to mess it up.'

'No one's messing up this shop, mister,' Bert growled, stepping forward.

'Did Frank send you?' Lizzie demanded.

'No one sent me,' the man replied calmly, his lips turning up in his fleshy, round face. His light brown eyes were watching her carefully under their hairless eyebrows. 'Certainly not your husband.'

Lizzie started. 'How do you know Frank's my husband?'

'I know everything, my dear.' The bald stranger walked slowly to the cabinet. Glancing over his shoulder, he nodded to the big man on his right. 'Nice bit of tat this, Albert.'

The man grunted in reply.

'Glass can break, unfortunately.'

Bert pushed Lizzie to one side. He raised the broom and pushed the handle into Leonard Savage's chest. 'Get your mitts off there, pal.'

Before Lizzie could speak the man called Albert put his hand under his overcoat. 'Get back,' he ordered, pointing a gun.

Lizzie froze. The gun was aimed straight at her. She knew Bert was staring at it too.

'You call that a weapon?' mocked Savage, snatching the broom from Bert. 'You'll need more than a stick if you're to insure your premises against damage, Mrs Flowers.' He broke the broom in two across his knee and threw it at Bert's feet.

Lizzie felt an ice-cold chill on her back. She was being threatened and there was nothing she or Bert could do about it.

'That's better.' Leonard Savage tilted his head. 'You can't always be a winner in this life, my man. There are the leaders and the followers. Brooms are not for the major players in business.' He jerked his hand to the gun. 'As you can see.'

Lizzie felt her heart beating so fast it hurt. How dare this thug walk into her shop and threaten her!

'This is my card.' Savage reached into his pocket. 'I'm in security and credit brokering. My offices are in Aldgate as you will read. Leonard Savage is the answer to all your problems, your guardian angel, Mrs Flowers. I help keep the streets clean and safe for hard-working shopkeepers like you. The East End being what it is, a lady like you is vulnerable. As you found out last year when someone decided to blow out your windows.'

'So you do know Frank?' Lizzie felt the blood drain from her face.

'I answer to no one but myself, dear lady,' Savage repeated. 'You are looking at the main man. I'm visiting your drum personally, so we can become acquainted. The money you'll be weighing out will be for legit reasons. Isn't that right, Albert?'

The big man holding the gun nodded.

'So, my dear, you'll be relieved to know that after my initial inspection I accept your custom. It's obvious these premises . . .' he looked around slowly, 'earn a good wedge. There are bad people in the world today. Hungry bastards. And it could be seen as a weakness that a woman on her own is running the show. Yes, you have one man here, but does he earn the respect of three, when he is equipped with only a *broom*?' Leonard Savage turned round laughing. He indicated to his men that they should laugh too. They did so accordingly, until the bald man put up his hand and they stopped. 'My heart bleeds for you, madam. I am a perceptive man, having great respect for the fair sex. I see your problem. More, I can rectify it. As of this moment, you are under the care and protection of Leonard Savage.'

'I don't want your so-called protection.' Lizzie stared at the man who held the gun. 'Do you intend to shoot me in front of all me customers?' She nodded to the road where Doug's green Singer had just drawn up. Lil was climbing out.

'The lady's got a point,' Savage said, waving his hand. 'Put it away for now, Albert.' He moved to join his men. 'Business for today is concluded. Mrs Flowers has sensibly agreed to the contract terms. If you value your nice glass shelves and new windows, then next time we meet, I'm sure our conversation will be more cordial. And we can settle the terms in hard cash.' He stared into Lizzie's eyes. 'Give my regards to the *other* Mr Flowers, won't you?'

Lizzie's heart jumped again. 'I don't know who you mean.'

'Just pass on this message,' Savage muttered. 'Tell Danny Flowers a sensible man like him should seek my protection too. After all, he don't want no more of his Crown Jewels lifted, does he?'

'What do you know about that?' Bert burst out. His fists were clenched as he pushed past Lizzie.

'Bert, no!' Lizzie pulled him back.

There was a grin of triumph on Leonard Savage's face. 'Well, we must be on our way. Nice doing business with you, my dear.' Savage politely raised his hat as Lil walked in the shop.

'Who was that?' Lil asked as they watched the three men make their way past Doug and cross the road to their large green-and-black car.

'A man called Leonard Savage.' Lizzie felt her knees shake. She sat down on the stool.

'Are you all right, love?'

'I will be in a minute.'

'They was slime-ball villains,' Bert growled as he craned his neck to peer at the departing vehicle. 'Protection, my arse.' He stood at Lizzie's side. 'You all right, gel?'

Lizzie nodded, but she wasn't.

'What did they want here?' Lil demanded, frowning in concern at Lizzie's anguished expression.

'He's after money, just like Ferreter was,' Lizzie said bleakly.

'And we thought we'd seen the last of the gangs,' Doug said as he stood by Lil. 'Didn't they think twice when they saw Bert?'

'They broke me broom and pulled a gun,' Bert growled angrily.

'A gun?' Lil repeated, an incredulous look on her face. Lizzie just nodded.

'They had the drop on us,' Bert complained, pacing the floor and glancing out of the window.

'Christ, that's worrying,' Doug said, putting his hand on Lizzie's shoulder. 'No wonder you're shaken up.'

'What exactly did he say?' Lil asked.

'He said he was my guardian angel.'

'More like Satan if you ask me,' Lil burst out. 'Ain't it time to call in the coppers?'

'Like Charlie Bray, you mean?' Lizzie replied with scorn. 'A bent copper, out to prove me and Danny are troublemakers.'

'Danny has to know about this,' Doug said firmly.

Lizzie agreed. 'Savage threatened Danny too. And he knew about the robbery.'

'How did he know about that?' Lil looked puzzled.

'He said he knows everything. And by the way he talked about Frank and Danny, I don't doubt he's done his homework.'

'What are we going to do?' Lil said, looking from one to the other.

Lizzie picked up the card. 'This is what Savage left.'

Lil read aloud. '*Leonard Savage & Co. Security and Credit Brokers.*' She frowned. 'What does that mean?'

'Posh words for extortion and money-lending,' said Doug on a sigh.

'*Chancel Lane, Aldgate*,' Lil continued. 'Never heard of it.'

'So what else did he say?' Doug asked.

'He said Danny should get his advice if he didn't want any more burglaries.'

'What!' Lil screamed. 'So that means it was Savage who did the burglary.'

'Looks like it,' Lizzie agreed.

'And we all thought it was Frank,' Lil said, a shocked expression on her face.

'I'll drive over to the garage now.' Bert fumbled in his pocket for the van keys. 'Give Danny the nudge.'

'No, Bert, you'd better stay here,' Doug said thoughtfully. 'Not that it's likely, but Savage might turn up again.' Doug looked at his wife. 'Let's unload the cakes. Then we'll drive over to Danny's and put him in the picture.'

'Don't like to leave Lizzie,' Lil said with concern.

Lizzie stood up and smiled at her friend. 'Doug's right, Lil. Danny needs to know what's happened. Leonard Savage won't call while me customers are about.'

'Yeah,' said Bert. 'I'll have to buy another broom.'

Everyone managed to smile. But Lizzie knew that a broom wasn't going to be of any use if Leonard Savage did show up again.

Chapter Eighteen

Danny listened to what Lil and Doug had to say, then, looking at Cal, who had joined them in the office, he said, 'This sounds like a new crew moving in.'

Cal nodded. 'But who is this Leonard Savage?'

'Whoever he is,' Lil said, glancing at Doug who sat beside her, 'pulling a gun like that he put the wind up Lizzie and Bert.'

Doug nodded. 'Only to be expected.'

'You've got to give it to the girl,' Lil added with a grin. 'She told him what she thought of him and his so-called protection.'

'But why the shop?' Cal questioned, leaning against the wall and scratching his head. 'And the garage?'

'He has to start somewhere,' Doug said quietly. 'Maybe he's taking over where Ferreter left off.'

Danny nodded. He'd been convinced the robbery was down to Frank. But now he wasn't so sure.

'He's not local,' Doug confirmed. 'I've not seen him before.'

'Sounds like he's the geezer who nicked our tools, though,' Cal said angrily.

Lil took out her cigarettes. 'It gave Lizzie a real turn, seeing that gun.'

'But he's in no hurry to move in on the shop,' Danny said, frowning. 'Or else he'd have emptied the till there and then.'

'Seeing as he seems to know so much, wouldn't mind betting he's been waiting to make a move,' Cal said slowly.

Danny hit the side of his head with his hand. 'Course, Cal. You're right. He said he knew everything. So it's likely he's been sniffing around after us for some time.'

'Might be worth a look outside. See if anyone's there.' Cal was already on the landing. Danny heard him go lightly down the stairs and then the click of the front door.

'You mean we've been followed?' Lil said in a startled voice.

'Dunno, Lil. But this geezer knows too much about us.'

'He's putting the squeeze on,' said Doug, standing up, and like Danny walking around the office. 'And seeing what happens.'

'Jesus, you two. Sit down.' Lil lit up and took a deep breath, picking a speck of tobacco from her bottom lip. 'You're giving me the creeps.'

'Lil, this is serious. One of them had a gun,' Doug impressed on his wife. 'He could have killed Lizzie or Bert or even us.'

Lil put her cigarette nervously between her lips. 'It might not have been loaded.'

'It was,' Danny said, which made Lil sit upright.

'How do you know?'

'Villains don't walk around waving empty shooters. They ain't toys, Lil.'

Cal came back up the stairs and walked slowly into the office. He glanced at Doug and Lil.

'Well?' demanded Lil, her ash spilling on the wooden floor.

'A motor went off by the dock wall.'

'A big one with white-walled tyres?' Doug asked in alarm.

Cal nodded. 'A Daimler. They was in no rush either. As if they wanted me to see them.'

Everyone was silent. Lil stared at her husband. 'Now I really have got the wind up.'

Danny nodded. 'It's called intimidation. That's what villains do.'

'Intimidation, protection, whatever you call it,' Doug said on a heavy breath, 'it's poison to all of us.'

'That's about it,' agreed Danny. He pushed his dirty hands down the front of his overalls and walked out onto the landing. He looked down on the garage beneath. He had two of the buses ready to move on and a smaller vehicle waiting for repair. They were managing with the tools he'd bought up Mile End, but life would have been a lot easier with his old kit. Still, no time to think about that now. He'd find out sooner or later who took his stuff and they would live to regret it, he'd make sure of that. As for what they were to do now, there was only one course of action. But no one was going to like it.

Taking a moment to compose himself, he breathed in the fumes of his workshop below and the oil and grease odours that hung like an invisible cloud from the rafters. Then pulling back his shoulders he returned to the office and three expectant faces.

'Doug, you'd better keep your eyes pinned over the next week,' he said and received a nod from his friend. 'Lil, there's no reason to think they'll bother you at all. Today was just a bit of ruffling of feathers.'

'I'll give 'em ruffling me bleeding feathers!' Lil tried to joke.

Danny smiled. 'But I'd like you to tell Lizzie that Bert needs back-up.'

'What?'

'Savage is right. A broom is no match for guns.'

'Christ, you're not thinking of—' Doug began, but Danny was shaking his head.

'No shooters yet. Lizzie wouldn't hear of it.'

Once again there was silence. If safety measures had been up to him, Danny would have kept a shotgun at least in the storeroom, even if it wasn't loaded. But he knew Lizzie's take on that and he'd have to work round it.

'What you going to do then, son?' asked Doug calmly.

'I'm going to sort out a crew.'

'Crew?' Lil and Doug said together.

'Hired muscle. Enough for the shop anyway. Cal and

me can take care of the garage. But Lizzie will need cover.' Danny flexed his tight shoulders. He knew no one, least of all Lizzie, would like the idea. But if he could find the right calibre of hired help, then Savage wasn't going to move in on any of them. At least, not without a fight.

'Do you know of anyone?' asked Doug in surprise. 'I mean, anyone suitable?'

'It'll take me a few days,' Danny said evenly, 'but I've a fair idea.'

Danny knew that it had to be done. He didn't like it, and it went against the grain. He'd hoped that here on the island he could carve out a living on the right side of the law. But that was easier said than done as he'd found out with Bray.

If he was going to jump in at the deep end, he'd have to be sure he was the strongest swimmer.

'At least we're on neutral turf,' Danny remarked to Cal as they entered the public house. He looked around the smoke-filled bar and studied the faces. The Quarry, back in the day, was a traders' ale house, filled with budding entrepreneurs and market stallholders. They were a bright lot, and honest in their own way. But that was in his dad's time. Things had changed since then.

'Clock anyone?' Cal asked as they made their way to the bar. It was a warm Saturday night in May and still light outside. Danny thought how a tavern never seemed to be as welcoming at this time of year. The hearth was missing the roaring fire. Despite the fine day, the atmosphere was gloomy. The beer smelled stale, the spittoons were full and the bare boards creaked under their footsteps.

'Not yet. I owe Michael O'Grady a favour for tonight.' Danny smiled at the landlord who gave him a nod. There wasn't a great friendship between them. But when Danny had explained his need, O'Grady had understood.

Danny and Cal moved to a stall at the rear of the big, noisy room. Danny glanced round as they tried to make themselves comfortable on the hard wooden benches.

He saw the usual faces, clusters of twos and threes, hugging their tankards and glasses. None of them had looked round at their entrance. But Danny knew that each one of them had ears cocked. The Quarry might not be a gentlemen's club, but everyone here tonight knew each other's business. And he wouldn't be surprised if they knew his, too.

'Did O'Grady give a time?' Cal asked, his black eyes trawling the figures at the bar.

'We were to be here after nine.' Danny shrugged, his hand slipping to the claw-tooth hammer in his jacket pocket. He didn't expect trouble. Not at this stage. But he was now in uncharted waters.

'Do we have a name?'

'No,' Danny replied. 'They're from across the water. That's all O'Grady would say.'

'Can we trust him?'

Danny sipped his ale. 'No way. But we can trust our

money and what it will buy. Sides, these characters were once shafted by Savage, so I'm told.'

Cal sat tensely nevertheless and Danny wondered what was going through his mind. This wasn't really his call. He was just the hired help. Yet to Danny, Cal had become the closest of all his friends. Not that he had many. But Cal had been with him from the bad days. Deep in those stinking Aussie pits, where Cal's skin was invisible against the blackened walls. And he'd had to fight for his life, just as Danny had. The black bushman and the Pom. Danny smiled at the memory.

A figure walked in the door. Danny came sharply back to the present. He narrowed his eyes, felt Cal tense beside him. But it was just a young lad, barely legal enough to stick his nose inside an ale house.

Cal met Danny's eyes and they settled back again on the benches. Cal took out his tobacco pouch and rolled his own, but still with his gaze fixed on the doors. Danny sat watching the pimps and prostitutes and the sprinkling of bookies and runners that mixed with the cabbies and small-time villains. He wondered what Bill would say about the pub now. Knowing Bill, he'd probably go right over and talk his way into a drink.

That was his dad. Fearless. Everyone's mate. Danny gave a long sigh of reflection. The night he'd walked in here a year ago, he'd been Frank Flowers's brother. The kid who'd run a barrow in the early days, then scarpered halfway across the world. Well, he'd had to face that down. He was back. And he intended to stay. He'd made his point all right, the night some loudmouth had taken a swipe at him. Danny had ducked that one and landed his own. He'd done the same the following week and the next. Eventually his baptism of fire was over. He'd even gained one or two customers. And now there were winks and nods rather than abuse.

But it was not the regulars Danny was here to meet. It was the shadier element who, so far, he'd had no truck with. Now, it seemed, all that was about to change.

'Mister?'

Danny looked up. The boy stood there. He was even younger up close than Danny had first thought. Thirteen? Fourteen? He smelled and it drifted over the table as he rubbed his dirty hands over his torn trousers.

Danny nodded. 'What do you want?'

'A bob.'

'What for?'

'For fetching yer.' A filthy palm shot out.

Danny stared at it. 'Who sent you?'

'Dunno. Some geezer.'

'Where is he?'

'You gonna give me the money?'

Danny dug in his pocket and handed over a shilling. The youngster cuffed his nose again, then said, 'Down the alley.' Before Danny had climbed to his feet, the boy had spun away and disappeared.

'What was all that about?' Cal asked, leaning forward.

'Seems like our man is the nervous type.'

'Yeah, well, so am I. Which one is he?'

Danny shook his head imperceptibly. 'Not here. Outside.'

'I don't like the sound of this,' Cal muttered.

Danny frowned as he stood up. Neither did he.

Chapter Nineteen

Danny stared into the dark alley that ran down the side of the Quarry.

'I don't like it,' Cal said again.

'Neither do I.'

'Where does it lead?'

Danny shrugged. 'Down to the dock walls.'

Cal peered into the darkness that seemed to have fallen quickly. 'Anyone could be up there.'

'We ain't got much choice.' Danny turned briefly to his friend. 'Scrub that. I mean, this is my shout, Cal, not yours.'

'Yeah, right,' Cal dismissed. 'So I clear out and leave you to it.'

'My interests are at stake, not yours.'

'You reckon?' Cal said with amusement. 'Hell's bells, Danny, I haven't had a good scrap since Adelaide.'

Danny grinned, but the smile soon fell from his face when a shadow appeared, not ten feet away. It was too dark to see who he was, but Danny gauged he was a few inches smaller than either him or Cal.

'Danny Flowers?' The voice was deep, with an accent.

'That's me.'

'Who's with you?'

'My partner.' Danny stepped a pace forward. 'You got a problem with that, chum? If you have, the deal's off.' Danny knew this could be a trap. Cal was right, it didn't feel good. 'Listen, I'm after a straight trade. Your men for my cash.'

Danny narrowed his eyes at the lean figure. He could see the man was roughly five ten, wearing a leather waistcoat like a smithy might. His arms were bare and muscular, his feet planted apart in working boots. By the light of the moon, Danny caught a glimpse of his face. Not one that instilled confidence, Danny thought as he studied the penetrating eyes that hadn't left his for a second.

Suddenly four more figures appeared. They stood barring the alley, with no way past.

'I'll take the two on the left,' Cal breathed softly. And Danny nodded, sensing their gut instincts had been right. But before he had time to move one of the figures fell on him. The heavy weight was unexpected and Danny toppled back. A pair of arms encircled his chest and emptied the breath from his lungs. He looked into the man's eyes, hidden under his tangled hair. A twisted smile stretched across his face.

Danny gasped for air, his arms pinned to his side. He knew all that was left to him was his head. He brought it down hard on the bridge of the man's nose. The bruiser let go and staggered back. Danny took the advantage and his first punch landed square on his opponent's left eye.

Danny knew he was lighter and quicker, and he ducked the clumsy return, stepping sideways, sending his boot hard into the man's groin.

'Behind you, Danny!' Cal shouted from the darkness. But it was too late. An agonizing pain in the small of Danny's back sent him sprawling. With no time to recover, he was hauled up by his collar and thrown the length of the alley. He spat blood as he looked up, the world going round in circles.

He could hear Cal, but he couldn't see him. Sweat was pouring into his eyes. There were grunts and groans and dull thuds all around him. Danny blinked hard and caught a movement in the corner of his eye. Somehow he managed to grab hold of an ankle and pull hard. The man fell, with a whoosh of air from his lungs. Danny climbed on top of him, punching and hoping he was doing some damage.

'You all right, mate?' Cal asked, breathing hard as Danny climbed shakily to his feet.

'Yeah, just about.' He saw a figure coming out of the shadows. Danny took out his hammer. The man screamed as the metal claws found his knuckles. He swung again, giving Cal time to recover.

They fought then, any tactic they could dream up. Danny knew the odds were against them but he didn't care now. It would be a fight to the last.

'That's enough,' a voice said suddenly.

Danny looked round. Out of the darkness walked one slim figure as the others melted into the night.

Cal was panting hard beside him, his fists still raised.

'Who are you?' Danny demanded breathlessly. He spat the blood from his lips.

'Just a man taking care of business.'

'What kind of business is it when you beat up your own customer?'

The man in the leather waistcoat laughed. 'Sure, you've just had a sample of the merchandise. You know what you're buying. Now we can deal.'

Danny shook back his damp, bloodied hair. 'Not until I have a name.'

The figure shrugged. 'How will Murphy do?'

Danny pulled his jacket back into shape. 'It's a start.'

'You don't need to know any more.'

'You're Irish?'

'And would you be having a problem with that?'

'I don't like being set up.'

'What else did you expect?' the man who called himself Murphy demanded. 'Were you intending to inspect my soldiers like market heifers? No, fair's fair, Mr Flowers. You know my men's worth now. Your terms have been met. The goods tried and tested.' Murphy cocked his head to one side.

Danny studied what he could see of Murphy. Compact and upright, with short-cropped hair and a challenge in the way he held himself. He wasn't a bruiser, nor did he sound an ignorant man. But one thing Danny knew for sure. Murphy had a fearsome reputation south of the river. If they were to cut a deal tonight, it was up to Danny to call the shots before Murphy did.

'Let me look at them,' Danny said. 'I want to see what I'm buying.'

Murphy laughed . 'Haven't you had enough of my boys?'

'Do you want to trade or not?'

'Have you brought the money?'

Danny patted his pocket. 'It's here. And that's where it's going to stay until I'm satisfied.'

Murphy lifted his hand and beckoned without looking back. The four men appeared and Danny glanced at Cal. A grin spread wide on Cal's face as one of them, cupping his ear, wiped away the blood running down his neck.

Danny made no pretence of enjoying the next few minutes. He would have liked to show his appreciation of being half crushed to death in a manner that befitted the occasion. But he was pleased to see the result of his and Cal's handiwork. The four sweating, bruised faces glared back at him resentfully. He gave an unimpressed shrug and turned to Murphy. 'Are these the best you have?'

Again the Irishman laughed. 'You won't find better.'

Now it was Danny's turn to scoff. 'You'd better be right about that.'

Murphy stared at him. 'Ah so, the man has balls.'

'You didn't come out of it so well yourself with Savage, I hear,' Danny said and the Irishman was suddenly silent. 'I need a crew that's not going to duck out at the first sign of trouble.'

Still the man said nothing. His swarthy skin and dark stubble, together with his penetrating gaze, gave him a presence. As Danny drew in a breath, Murphy stepped up to him. 'Don't be talking to me about Savage. The man is scum.'

'Agreed.'

'Be careful, Danny boy. You may be out of your depth.'

'Were you?' Danny felt the man's breath on his face.

Murphy said in a threatening whisper, 'Stay out of my business. And I'll stay out of yours.'

'Suits me.' Danny made him wait before he took out the money, drawing the wad of notes from his inside pocket with slow deliberation. Danny smiled to himself as the sound of hard cash rustled in the air.

'I see you're a man of your word,' said Murphy agreeably.

As Danny handed over the payment, he wondered if Murphy was.

Chapter Twenty

Ten days later and the shop was as secure as a fortress. Even Flo, who arrived on her bicycle on the bright May morning, had to agree that Lizzie, in the circumstances, had made the wisest decision.

The week before, Lizzie had been shocked to find four burly young men on her doorstep. Danny introduced them as her new porters. He told her they would work in shifts. Two by night and two in the day.

'You'll have twenty-four-hour cover,' he had explained. 'Don't ask them any questions. If there's trouble, you and Pol get in the van and drive over to me. Leave them and Bert to sort out a problem.'

'I can't afford four extra wages,' she'd protested, but Danny had shrugged this away.

'They're paid for.'

'What?'

'It's settled, Lizzie. Don't ask no more.'

'They're dodgy, ain't they?'

'They're what you need right now.'

She had reluctantly agreed and forced herself to watch

the men dressed in porter's clothes, cloth caps and boots acquaint themselves with her business. She hadn't liked it, but she'd had to accept it.

Lizzie smiled as she thought of Bert's indignation. That was, until Lizzie reminded him of Savage's visit. The ineffectiveness of a broom against a revolver.

Now as Flo and Lizzie watched two of the men heave the sacks of vegetables onto their shoulders, puffing and grunting like genuine porters, Lizzie couldn't resist a chuckle.

'You should have seen Bert when they first arrived,' Lizzie said as she and Flo walked out to their bicycles. 'He stood them in the yard and explained the difference between a King Edward and a cauli.'

Flo burst out laughing. 'What are they going to do if the opposition arrive? Clock 'em with ripe tomatoes?'

Lizzie's smile faded. 'I don't want no guns.'

'So what will they do?'

'Use their initiative, I hope.'

'Yes, but have they got any? Who is the one who ties back his long hair with a bit of string?'

'That's Fowler. The other is Elmo, with the red hair and beard. They work in the day and the other two come at night.'

'What do your customers think?'

'As big as they are, the men are good at the job.'

Flo laughed. 'What does Bert think of that?'

'He don't trust them an inch.'

'Good old Bert.'

Lizzie pushed her bike to the gutter and climbed on.

For modesty's sake, she was wearing trousers. She'd wound her long black hair into a knot at the back of her head. Flo was wearing a loose smock.

'I can't wait for you to see my dress,' Flo said as they began to cycle together.

'Is this your first fitting?'

'Yes, if I ever get there!' Flo was wobbling all over the road. Lizzie began to wish they'd taken the van. Poplar was a good twenty minutes' ride away. And Flo had put on a lot of weight.

'I need the exercise, as you can see,' said Flo, trying to cycle in a straight line. 'Don't worry, I'll get me breath in a minute.'

It was the end of the week and the roads were busy. They cycled in and out of horse-drawn carts and one or two motor cars. The docks lay baking in the sunshine and smelled of the waste and flotsam flowing into them.

Lizzie was worried about Flo. Her sister was fighting with the handlebars. The basket on the front bounced up and down. She was more than relieved when they finally arrived in Poplar. The dressmaker's shop was in the High Street, in between the fishmonger's and the bakery. Early morning bagels had already left the ovens and were on their way to the traders. The fishmonger was cooling his trays of fish with cold water and swatting away the flies.

Lizzie stepped to one side as the street sellers hurried by. The Indian sweet man with his box of candyfloss slung over his shoulders. The French onion seller in his striped Breton shirt.

Flo dismounted and stretched her back. 'Me bum's killing me.'

'We should have taken the van.'

'Yes, but it stinks in there.' Flo mopped her damp fore-head. 'All I need now is for me waters to break. That would really cheer Syd up. He's wearing a face like a slapped arse at the moment.'

'Why's that?' Lizzie asked as they leaned their bikes against the lamp-post.

'You'll only get upset if I say.'

'Now you've said that, you'll have to tell me.'

Flo brushed her wet fringe from her eyes. Blowing out air, she shrugged. 'He's got the hump, cos of Danny find-ing those blokes.'

'Why should Syd care about them?'

'When I told him Danny was hiring, he wanted to know why Danny hadn't come to him. He said he offered you help on the day Frank turned up.'

'Yes, but I didn't want to involve Syd's family.'

'What's wrong with them?' Flo asked indignantly. 'Aren't they good enough for you?'

'I didn't mean that. You've always wanted Syd to steer clear of his family.'

'It's different now,' Flo reasoned with a shrug. 'I'll be a Miller on the 1st of July. So will this.' She pointed to her bump.

Flo's tune had definitely changed, Lizzie thought with alarm. She had always kept her distance from Syd's family. And with good reason. Syd was the only one of the

Missus's sons without a criminal record. A fact, the Missus boasted, not due to his good character but because he had escaped detection.

But with the baby on the way and marriage not far off, what else was Flo to do? Lizzie reflected anxiously. Syd's family were now to be hers.

'The Millers have cleaned up their act,' Flo said in defence of her soon-to-be-in-laws. 'Walter and Clifford are legit.'

'So why was Syd offering their help?'

'To keep things in the family,' Flo said hurriedly, blushing.

'So, if they're as straight as you say, why would they want to lock horns with someone like Leonard Savage?'

'They ain't angels,' Flo said heatedly. 'But they know how to take care of themselves. You've got to in a world like this.'

'Flo, granted you're nearly a Miller,' Lizzie replied carefully, 'but you're also an Allen. Don't try to fit in with views you don't hold with.'

'And what do you mean by that?'

'Well . . .' Lizzie hesitated. 'You sound different. Don't change from the person you are.'

'So I suppose you didn't change when you married Frank?' Flo accused angrily as they stood on the hot, crowded pavement. 'Well, you did. I can vouch for that. If Babs was here, she would agree.'

'This isn't to do with Babs. I'm surprised at you, Flo, going on about guns and things. If Ma heard you talking that way she'd turn in her grave.'

'Our mother is dead, Lizzie. And our father,' Flo said, tears welling in her eyes. 'And anyway, Ma wasn't slow to take our brother's dirty money. She knew Vinnie worked for Ferreter, but she still took it. Without Vinnie to provide for us, we'd have all starved.' Flo added spitefully, 'Beggars can't be choosers.'

Lizzie stood open-mouthed as she listened to her sister. This was a darker side to Flo. Was it all bravado?

'Flo, do you love Syd?' Lizzie asked curiously.

'What do you mean?'

'You ain't getting married because of the baby, are you?'

'Christ almighty!' Flo almost stamped on the ground. Her cheeks went scarlet. 'Syd was right about you. You act the Lady Muck. But really you're just the same as any of us.'

'Flo, don't swear like that.'

'Don't tell me what to do. I wish I'd never asked you to come with me today.'

Lizzie stared in bewilderment at her sister. Flo might have a temper but she never said cruel things. Lady Muck? Was that really what Syd had called her? Lizzie felt the sting of tears in her own eyes.

Suddenly Flo clasped her stomach. 'Ouch!'

'What is it?'

Flo gasped. 'Don't know. Must be that bloody bike ride. I've got the stitch.'

'Let's go inside. You'll feel better if you sit down.'

Lizzie led Flo inside the dark, stuffy shop filled with

racks of clothes hanging in every available space. There was a long white gown on display at the far end and a pair of white shoes beneath it.

'That's me dress,' Flo groaned, still clutching her stomach. 'I told Mrs Davies to make it on the large side as I'd put on weight.'

Lizzie led Flo to the chair at the counter.

'Is something wrong?' asked a grey-haired lady emerging from another room. 'Oh Miss Allen, it's you. Have you come for your fitting?'

'Can my sister sit down, Mrs Davies?' Lizzie asked, holding tightly to Flo's arm. 'She's not feeling well.'

'Oh dear! Yes, of course. I'll fetch a glass of water.'

'Don't say I'm expecting,' Flo warned when they were alone. She leaned forward on the chair, her legs apart.

'Flo, is it the baby, do you think?'

There was no answer as Flo wriggled around.

Lizzie waited anxiously as Mrs Davies returned with a glass of water. She put it to Flo's lips.

'It's very hot today,' said Mrs Davies. 'You may have a touch of the vapours.'

But Flo barely had taken a sip before she twisted and turned with her arms wrapped tightly around her belly.

Lizzie had a feeling something was very wrong. Flo's skin was grey. Her eyes were beginning to roll in their sockets.

'I'm going for help,' Lizzie decided as Flo seemed to go into a world of her own. 'Stay with her, please.'

Looking startled, Mrs Davies nodded. 'I'll do my best, dear. But I think you'd better hurry.'

Outside in the street, Lizzie looked around. There wasn't a policeman in sight. Was the baby in distress? Would Flo be all right? These thoughts filled her mind as she waved her arms at a passing vehicle, trying to make it stop. But the motor car chugged steadily on its way.

What was she to do? Panic filled her. There was no sign of the law when she wanted it.

She saw a horse and cart making its way in the other direction. She tried to run after it, but it was soon lost in the busy traffic.

Lizzie stood on the hot pavement trying to catch her breath. She cried out to the people milling around her. 'Please help me!'

But it was as if they were deaf, staring at her suspiciously. Then, just as she was about to run back to the shop, a hand fell on her shoulder.

'Are you all right?' a voice asked.

She turned quickly on her heel. But the sudden, small hope was dashed when she saw who it was.

Chapter Twenty-One

'What are you doing here?' she demanded as she gazed at Frank.

'I might ask you the same. Running up and down the pavement like you was on fire.'

'Get out of my way, Frank.'

'Well, that's a nice greeting, I'm sure.'

'Trust you to turn up like a bad penny.' Lizzie knew she had to get back to Flo. But Frank was in her way.

There was the sound of someone shouting. Lizzie saw Mrs Davies outside the shop, waving her arms. She left Frank and ran as fast as she could to the dressmaker. 'What's the matter? What's happened?'

'Miss Allen's collapsed,' Mrs Davies told her. 'I couldn't do anything – she just fell off the chair.'

Lizzie hurried inside and went on her knees beside Flo. 'Oh, Flo, Flo! What's the matter?' But Flo was out cold.

'Has she fainted?' Mrs Davies asked anxiously.

'I don't know,' Lizzie shrieked. 'Flo, wake up!'

'Can I help?' Frank was standing there.

Lizzie looked up; she didn't care who it was that she pleaded with. 'Please go and fetch an ambulance.'

'That'd take time. I've got me car parked just down the road. Give me a minute and I'll bring it up and drive you to hospital.'

Lizzie watched Frank, her disaster of a husband who would not normally lift a finger to help anyone but himself, run out of the shop. Could she trust him to help? But what else could she do?

Flo suddenly moaned. 'Oh Flo, please come back to us.' Her eyelids flickered. Lizzie stroked her hot forehead. Her sister was trying to say something. Was she delirious?

The next few minutes went very slowly as she cradled Flo in her arms. But Frank soon returned and, drawing Lizzie gently aside, he lifted Flo into his arms. He carried her outside to the dark blue car parked by the shop. Lizzie helped him to lay Flo on the back seat.

'Take this for her head, dear.' Mrs Davies gave Lizzie a cushion.

'Thank you.' Lizzie climbed in and sat on the edge of the seat. 'Hurry, Frank, please.'

As the car sped along, Lizzie saw a red stain seeping through Flo's dress. Was Flo losing the baby? She heard Frank use the horn as the car swayed from side to side, going fast. Flo opened her eyes, but they rolled up in their sockets again. Lizzie kept talking, but she didn't think Flo could hear her.

Lizzie looked anxiously out of the window. Frank was

driving them into one of the side entrances of the hospital.

'Are we in the right place?'

'Yes,' Frank shouted as he jumped out of the car. 'I'll get someone.'

Within a few seconds a blue-uniformed nurse and two porters arrived. Lizzie watched, heart in mouth, as they laid Flo on a stretcher. 'My sister is expecting,' she told the nurse as they took Flo through the entrance and into a room smelling strongly of disinfectant. 'Her name is Flo Allen. We were just visiting the dressmaker's when she felt unwell.'

'Do you know why she was unwell?' asked the nurse calmly.

'It could be because we rode our bicycles. There's blood on her dress.'

'Yes, I can see that.'

'Can I stay with her?' Lizzie asked.

'The doctor will examine her first. Take a seat in the waiting room. I'll keep you informed.' The nurse was about to walk away when she glanced at the figure behind Lizzie. 'Frank, please put your car around the back. You know the rules. Only ambulances are allowed there.'

As the nurse hurried after Flo, Lizzie turned back to Frank. Before she could speak he dashed away. The waiting room was crowded so Lizzie found a space in the passage. She walked up and down, wondering when she would be told what was wrong with Flo. And how did the nurse know Frank?

'Sorry. This is a very busy time of day for the hospital,' Frank said as he hurried back.

'How do you know that?'

'I work here as a porter.'

'You're a porter – *here* at the hospital?' Lizzie asked incredulously.

'Mostly on night shifts.' He smiled hesitantly. 'It was being in hospital meself that did it. I saw a lot of illness and it scared me into doing something that wasn't crooked.'

'But how did you get a job in this hospital?' Lizzie blurted, her mouth falling open.

'I was given a letter of reference from the asylum.'

'Is that allowed?'

'Dunno. But it started me off on the road to redemption.' He laughed at himself, then added seriously, 'It's never too late to change, so they say.'

'I find that hard to believe in your case. And what were you doing by the dressmaker's shop?'

'I'd just finished my shift.'

'And happened to be walking along the road when me and Flo turned up?' Lizzie was beginning to think that somehow he'd followed them.

'My lodgings are in the next street.'

'You mean you ain't at the brothel?'

'No. All that's over with, gel,' he assured her. 'I've got decent rooms and a shared lav. It will tide me over till I can find something better.'

'So it was just a coincidence you saw me?'

He nodded. 'Well, heard you first. You was too busy yelling and screaming to notice me.'

If someone had told her that her lying, cheating, lazy, good-for-nothing husband had got a job and digs, she would have laughed in their face. She looked closely at the man who always wore gangster-style suits and coats. But the padded shoulders and fedora were now gone. So too were his trademark two-tone shoes. His blond hair was cut short and combed smartly into place. The navy-blue shirt and black trousers looked very much like the uniform the porters were wearing under their brown coats.

Lizzie suddenly felt her head swim. At the same time her legs began to tremble. She knew the after-effects of shock.

'You don't look too good.' Frank guided her to one of the chairs by an open window. 'Take the weight off your feet. Then stick your head between your knees.'

She did as he told her. She couldn't allow herself to faint. Not when Flo needed her.

'Take deep breaths,' Frank said quietly, still steadying her, as she tried to fight off the dizzy spell.

'I suppose now you're going to tell me you're a doctor in your spare time,' she couldn't help saying as she slowly sat up.

Frank grinned, seeming to take no offence. 'I ain't so keen on the sight of blood meself.'

She pulled her arm away. 'You can let go of me now.'

He sat beside her, staring down at the floor.

'I suppose I should thank you,' she managed to say as she felt more like herself.

'You don't need to.'

'I hope Flo didn't recognize you.' Realizing what she'd said she added, 'You know how she feels about you.'

'Yes, I know,' Frank agreed lamely. 'But I've always had a soft spot for the girl. I couldn't help overhearing what you said about a baby.'

Lizzie flushed. 'Please don't repeat what you heard.'

'I've forgotten it already.'

When a nurse came along, Lizzie jumped up. But the young girl hurried past. Lizzie slumped down again.

'Don't worry,' Frank said, 'they're a good bunch here. They'll look after her.'

'I hope so.'

Frank clasped his hands together. With a lurch of her stomach Lizzie saw he was wearing his wedding ring. 'I remember a time like this all them years ago,' he said to the floor, 'when Flo had scarlet fever. She was in a bad way. We took her on the cart to the isolation hospital.'

Lizzie turned away. 'Your good deed was only to impress me.'

'I thought a lot of you both.'

'You mean you thought a lot of number one.' She stood up. 'Please go, Frank.'

He slowly got to his feet. 'You sure you'll be all right?'

'I said so, didn't I?'

He was about to turn away when he stopped. 'I know

what I was, Lizzie,' he whispered sadly, 'a good-for-nothing phoney. I left you and Dad to fend for yourselves and then expected a cut of the profits. All I want to repeat is, I'm not the shyster I used to be. No reason for you to believe me of course, which is why I appreciate you letting me see Pol at Gertie's. I tell you, gel, she's the light of my life; I love that kid and I promise you, I'll always do my best for her, and be there if she wants me.'

Lizzie stared at her husband coldly. 'Words are cheap, Frank. And you're a class act with the charm.'

'I promise—'

'Don't waste your breath,' she interrupted. 'I've heard too many of your promises only for them to be broken.' She walked to the door Flo's stretcher had gone through.

What was happening to Flo? She had to find out.

'I'll go then,' he called.

'Don't try to see Flo,' she warned over her shoulder.

Lizzie's mind was in turmoil. He'd said he was making his way home to his digs when he saw her. Did she believe him? He had thanked her for letting him see Pol. Was he genuine? Polly had said she didn't mind seeing her Uncle Frank. They played dominoes with her Granda and Polly liked that. But would Frank soon tire of his better self? He hadn't been there for the first six years of Polly's life. Yet now he was claiming he loved her.

Lizzie didn't know what to think. Her heart wanted to believe that good had triumphed over bad. But her head was warning the opposite.

Chapter Twenty-Two

'Your sister had a narrow escape,' Dr Shaw told Lizzie as she stood in the small office. The nurse who had been with Flo was writing in a book.

'Is the baby all right?'

'Yes, so far. But it was a close call. Had you delayed any longer getting here, she may have miscarried.'

Had Flo told the doctor she was unmarried? She wasn't wearing a ring. 'It was a long journey on the bikes,' she said.

'The bleeding may have nothing to do with exercise,' the doctor explained. 'Your sister is carrying her first child. Not all women have straightforward pregnancies. From now on she will need plenty of bed rest. She tells me she's given up work, is that right?'

Lizzie nodded, although it wasn't quite true. Flo had taken her annual two weeks' holiday. She was going to give in her notice when she returned.

'Good.' Dr Shaw, a tall, stern-looking man in his fifties, gave Lizzie a brisk smile. 'We're going to keep her in of course, under observation. Tomorrow I'll examine her again. We'll know more then.'

'Can I see her now?'

'Yes, but only for a short while. And please try to keep her calm. She has a tendency to get overexcited. At the mention of remaining under my care, she protested loudly.'

Lizzie smiled. She knew the news of a hospital stay, however brief, would distress Flo. 'When she was a child, Flo had scarlet fever,' she explained. 'And had to stay in a hospital for infectious diseases. Then she went to a convalescent home. She was away for months and hated it. Since then, she don't like hospitals.'

To Lizzie's surprise, the doctor nodded understandingly. 'I see. Well, perhaps you can reassure her that we are not monsters here, rather medical staff who try very hard to put our patients at ease.'

Lizzie warmed to the soft chink in the doctor's armour.

The nurse took Lizzie to see Flo who was now awake as she lay in the bed. Lizzie put her arms around her tenderly. 'How are you feeling?' she whispered.

'Rotten.'

'The baby's all right though.'

'Yes. So they tell me.' A tear rolled down Flo's hot cheek. Lizzie brushed her untidy dark hair into place with her fingers, and plumped up her pillow. 'Lizzie, I don't like it here.'

'You're in the best place. Remember, you have the baby to think of. And all the staff seem very kind.'

'How did I get here?' Flo mumbled.

Lizzie felt her face go red. She couldn't tell Flo it was

Frank who brought them in the car. Dr Shaw wanted her to be kept calm. 'I found someone to drive us.'

'I don't remember anything. Only falling on the floor in the shop.'

'You were delirious, saying something about the Missus and your wedding dress.'

'I didn't feel well before I left home this morning.'

'And yet you still rode your bike.'

Flo smiled weakly. 'I thought it would do me good. I've been eating too much lately and put on too much weight.'

'Did the doctor tell you that from now on you must rest?'

Flo wrinkled her nose in distaste. 'He won't see what I'm getting up to when I'm home.'

'You'll do as you're told if you want to keep your baby.'

Flo sighed and dropped her head to the pillow. 'Will they let me home tomorrow?'

'We'll have to see.'

'Christ, this reminds me of when I was in—' She stopped and screwed up her eyes. Another little tear escaped.

Lizzie leaned forward and wiped the tear away. 'You're a big girl now and responsible for two. Don't worry, you'll be home very soon. This isn't anything like the sanatorium.'

'I hope not. Will you tell Syd?'

'Yes, of course.'

'What about our bikes? Someone might pinch them.'

'I'll see to it, don't worry.'

'Time is up, I'm afraid,' said the nurse, tapping Lizzie's shoulder.

Lizzie kissed Flo's cheek and smiled. But they were both tearful when she left. Lizzie caught the bus home. She sat quietly in the rear seat, deciding what to do. First she would send Bert over to the dressmaker's for the bicycles. Then he could drive over to the garage and tell Danny what had happened. She knew Danny would be very angry that Frank had appeared to turn up in the nick of time. But, when all was said and done, it was Flo who mattered the most.

Lizzie thought about what Frank had said. He was grateful for seeing Polly. He'd assured her that Polly meant a lot to him, but should she have to believe what could be just more lies?

Then there was Syd to tell but he wouldn't be home until after six. She would have to go over and break the news.

It wasn't something she was looking forward to doing.

'Whenever your husband turns up on the scene it's bad news,' Syd said, predictably angry.

'I know. But Flo and the baby are all right.' The more Lizzie tried to explain, the more Syd was getting distraught.

'He's working there – at the hospital, you say?' Syd demanded.

'Don't worry. I've told him to stay away from Flo.'

Syd clenched his fists. 'He'd better or else.'

'I'll drive you to the hospital, if you like.' She hoped Syd would calm down before he saw Flo.

'No, Doug will do the honours.' Syd dragged on his coat.

They walked outside and stood on the pavement. 'I didn't tell Flo who took her to the hospital,' Lizzie explained hesitantly.

'Do you think I would upset me own missus?' Syd snapped at her as he banged on the Sharpes' door.

After Lizzie had explained everything to Lil and Doug, the men drove off to the hospital. 'Come in,' Lil said, raising her eyebrows, 'and tell me what really happened.'

'It's true, every word,' Lizzie said as she sat down on the couch in the front room. 'Frank just appeared out of the blue.'

'I don't believe that.'

'No, I don't expect anyone would. But he said he was on his way to his digs.'

'Working at the hospital?' Lil muttered as she searched for her cigarettes and found them on the mantelpiece. 'What's his game? Pinching stuff and selling it on to the black market?'

Lizzie hadn't thought of that. She shrugged.

'Why would a big hospital like that employ the likes of him?'

'He said he was given a letter of reference by the place he was in.'

'Do you believe him?' Lil said scornfully as she lit up.

'I don't see how else he could have got the job. Anyway, I was so worried about Flo I didn't care who helped us.'

'Does Danny know about this?' Lil asked, blowing smoke through her teeth.

'Yes, I sent Bert over to tell him.'

'You know what I think?' Lil arched her thin eyebrows. 'It wasn't a coincidence he turned up out of thin air. I think he was following you. Stepped in to make himself look good.'

'How would he know that Flo and me would be in Poplar High Street this morning? I didn't even know myself till Flo came over and asked me to cycle with her.'

'He must have found out somehow.'

'Can't see that, myself, Lil. His answer was, when I asked him, that he's got lodgings round the corner.'

Lil smirked. 'He's got you believing his patter again.'

Lizzie didn't want to argue. She knew Lil's dislike of Frank would never change. 'I'll have to get back to Polly now.'

'Did the poor kid see Frank at Gertie's?' Lil asked as Lizzie got up and went to the hall.

'Yes. But he behaved himself.'

'I should hope so.'

As she drove back to Ebondale Street, Lizzie thought about her conversation with Lil who had insisted Frank was playing more devious games. But Lizzie didn't see how he could have known or even guessed that she and Flo would be cycling to Poplar that morning. The more she thought about it, the more she knew it wasn't possible.

Her thoughts came to an abrupt end as the van turned into Ebondale Street. A group of children were playing in the road. One of them was Polly who was kicking a ball to Georgie March, a scruffy kid who lived in the next street. Bert was sitting on an upturned crate outside the shop, smoking.

Lizzie climbed out of the van and called to Polly. 'Why are you playing in the street, Pol?'

Polly smiled breathlessly. 'Our yard's too small. And it stinks.'

'They're only vegetables. And there's enough room to kick a ball.'

Polly's mouth trembled. 'I ain't ever allowed outside. It's not fair.'

Lizzie tried to take her hand but she snatched it away and ran back to her friend.

Lizzie walked over to Bert. 'You know I don't like Polly playing out here.'

'I was watching out for her,' Bert said with a shrug.

'What if Savage turned up?' Lizzie felt herself growing angry.

'Elmo's inside. The two of us would have seen him off,' Bert replied, unconcerned. He stood up and put a large hand on her shoulder. 'Take it easy, gel.'

'How can I, with everything going wrong?'

'That's not like you.'

Tears threatened as Lizzie blinked. 'Polly means everything to me, Bert.'

'Yer, I know. I'll get her in. Did you have a rough time with Syd?'

'You could say that. No one believes Frank's on the level.'

Bert raised his heavy eyebrows. 'Do you?'

'All I know is, we got Flo to hospital in time to save the baby.' Up until this moment, she had believed the same as everyone; Frank Flowers's priority was himself. And that would never change. But this afternoon, in the hospital, she had begun to wonder.

Lizzie called to Polly. 'It's time for tea.'

'I want to play with Georgie,' Polly called back.

Lizzie walked over to the little boy with a mop of curly dark hair and a runny nose. He took a step away and she smiled. 'Do you want to come in for some tea, Georgie?'

'What about them Commies?' Georgie said, pushing back his untidy curls.

'Do you know what that means?' Lizzie asked him.

'No, but me mum says to stay away from them.'

'There's no Communists in Polly's home, Georgie. We just sell fruit and veg. And very nice cakes, of course.'

'You got some for tea?' Georgie licked his lips.

'Yes, do you like apple pie and custard?'

Lizzie smiled as the two children ran into the shop. Though Georgie made sure he gave Elmo a wide berth.

Chapter Twenty-Three

Sydney Miller's dander was up. Over the week he'd been visiting Flo, he'd come to the conclusion their troubles were all down to Frank Flowers. The lunatic, and yes, he truly believed Flowers was one, had the gall to lay his filthy hands on his missus under the pretence of taking her to hospital.

Syd was furious. He himself had never learned to drive. Yet, there was this scum, Flowers, acting like flaming Prince Charming. You'd think Lizzie had never undergone seven years of misery as his wife, the way she had told it. 'And all I can do is ride a bike,' Syd muttered to himself as he left the female ward in which Flo was recuperating.

He stood in the empty passage, trying to console himself. The visitors had gone a quarter of an hour ago. Flo had wept as he left her. She was a strong woman but she hated hospitals.

Were his two brothers outside as arranged? he wondered nervously. Clifford and Walter were not known for their punctuality. Syd was breaking a sweat under his collar.

Despite his hatred of Flowers, the thought of what they were about to do was playing havoc with his guts.

Syd sighed heavily, walking slowly to the big doors. The trouble had started two nights ago when Flo had insisted he told her how she'd come to be at the hospital.

He'd evaded it for as long as he could. But Syd knew he wasn't a good liar. And so did Flo. Sitting up in the bed, with the colour back in her cheeks, she'd said, 'What's going on, Syd?'

'What do you mean?' he'd replied innocently.

'You ain't been right all week.'

'I miss you.' He'd tried to flatter her but Flo was having none of it.

'Come on, Syd, spit it out.'

'It ain't nothing, honest,' he'd lied again and badly.

'I'm getting the hump,' Flo had said. 'No one will tell me the truth. I asked Lizzie when she visited, but got the same story. This someone did the deed. Like a ghost he must have been for the invisible part he played. Then I remembered something. Going fast in this car. And the driver shouting out to hold on. I recognized the voice. It was like a bad dream.'

Syd knew he had been rumbled. When he'd finally admitted the name of Frank Flowers, Flo had erupted. The doctor had been called and he'd given her a jab. It was late and when he'd gone back to her bedside she just had this sad look on her face.

'Why weren't you there when I needed you?' she'd asked him.

'I ain't got a car, love.'

'No, but that imbecile had.'

The insult had hurt to the quick. Why did it have to be Frank Flowers of all people who demeaned him? Any other bloke and he could have taken it on the chin.

As far as Syd could understand it, Flowers was responsible for all the aggro in the family. And that was when he'd made up his mind to talk to his brother. Walter would know how to help him. And even if their relationship wasn't close, Walter was a businessman. Well, he ran the family scrapyard and had his head screwed on right.

After downing a few pints too many at the pub, Syd had cycled to Mile End. In the afterglow of the brew, he'd come to the decision that a fish porter like him would never amount to much in his wife's eyes. His standing in the family needed re-evaluation. And it was only Walter who could help him there.

'For a start, you've got to chuck in your job,' Walter advised. 'You're beginning to smell like a gorilla's armpit each night. I can even niff it now.'

'But I've portered since I left school.'

'Time for a change, boy. A clean shirt and a good barber.'

'Walter, we've got a kid on the way.'

'Yeah, but Billingsgate is dead-end,' joked Clifford, his younger brother, who had turned up at the meeting.

'Not many blokes have a licence,' Syd had argued mildly.

'And look where it's got you.' Walter wagged his fat

finger as he polished off his chaser. 'Come into the firm, Sydney. I'm on the lookout for a driver.'

'I can't drive,' Syd admitted guiltily. 'That's the problem.'

'Driving's a doddle,' Clifford had assured him. 'Even for you.'

'Come on,' chivvied Walter, smiling that smile of his that caused his sweating round face to look faintly agreeable. 'If you don't make the jump now, you'll be wiping the scales from your mitts by the time you get to Dad's age.'

Syd thought fleetingly of his father. Walter Miller senior was rarely present at family conferences. The Missus usually headed the table. A potent mixture of brown ale and gout took their dad off to his bed. At sixty he was an eighty-year-old, thought Syd sadly. Was Walter insinuating that he was to turn out the same?

'We'll teach you to drive,' Clifford assured him. 'There ain't nothing to it. You'll be ducking and diving round the East End like an old-timer. We'll take you out in the scrapyard lorry, right? There's just two gears, forward and reverse. Well, nearly. After a couple of weeks you'll be flying, right?'

'Dunno,' he'd resisted for all of ten seconds.

'Your old lady will respect you,' Walter had concurred. 'Especially when you tuck a twenty in her palm for the kid.'

'A twenty?' Syd had repeated. Twenty quid was more than he earned in a month.

'Sovs,' added Clifford with a nod.

'Your old lady has a right to be gutted,' continued Walter in an intimate tone. 'I wouldn't want Flowers's filthy hands all over me when I was out of it. That's taking a liberty, that is.'

'All the more reason to give her a nice surprise when she comes out,' Clifford insisted.

'Look, take this.' Walter had squeezed two notes into his hand and they weren't pounds. 'This is up front. You've earned this, mate.'

'I ain't done nothing.'

'You've come to us. You done the right thing.'

'You're our brother, right?' said Clifford, smiling the same smile as Walter. 'You're a Miller. People should know you're not to be messed with.'

Clifford patted him hard on the back. 'My old lady lost a kid last year. Nearly full term she was, an' all. And it was only me bunging her a few bob extra that put a smile back on her face.'

As he drew his mind back to the moment Syd reflected on the plan of action his brothers had devised. They, as in the three of them, were to put the fear of God up Flowers. He'd be out of the East End within the week. Syd and Flo and Danny and Lizzie would be rid of the lying, shit-stirring clown that Flowers was, thanks to the Millers.

Now, as Syd hurried to the rear of the building, he was half hoping his brothers wouldn't be there. But to his surprise and also alarm they were.

'One for the road at the local?' Walter suggested. 'Night staff don't clock on for another hour.'

Syd nodded, eager for a reversal of plan. They walked to the Queen's and downed as many ales as they could before chuck-out.

'No boots, no dusters, right?' Syd said as they made their way back to the hospital. 'No knives or razors.'

'Would we?' replied Walter with an innocent expression as he turned up the collar of his overcoat over his outsized Miller ears.

It was a warm May night and Syd could smell the antiseptic drifting out from the hospital. Together with the scent from the apple trees on the green, it caused Syd's stomach to revolt.

Hidden by the trees, Walter said, 'We'll nab the git as he walks in, bring him over here. We've got good cover.'

Syd nodded. He had to keep reminding himself they were only going to warn Flowers off. Then he'd be able to guarantee Flo that her brother-in-law was history. And it was down to him.

'Then we'll sort out this Savage,' Walter assured him.

'What?' Syd brought himself fuzzily back from the vision of himself earning respect from his wife.

'You was saying about the shop,' Clifford reminded him.

'Did I?' Syd recalled the endless pints he downed on his visit to Mile End. What else had he blabbed?

'How some idiots have put the squeeze on Lizzie,' Walter urged.

'Yes, but she's taking care of that.'

'She's hired goons,' Walter said dismissively, 'who, by all accounts, don't add up to much of a lump.'

'Yeah, morons,' agreed Clifford, stroking back his greasy brown hair with fingers the size of rolling pins.

'How do you know that?' Syd mumbled.

Walter tapped the side of his big nose.

'The girl needs heavyweights to do the job. Like us.'

Syd stared at his two brothers in shock. What were they going on about? They were his kith and kin and he forgave them their faults. Yet his instincts were shouting he was well out of his depth.

'Is this the geezer?' Walter nodded to a tall figure strolling across the hospital grounds.

Syd's legs went to jelly. He peered into the gloom. 'N-no, don't think so,' he lied.

'Got to be, ain't it?'

Clifford grinned. 'Yeah, course it has.' He rubbed his big hands together.

'What are we waiting for?' Walter belched beer and drew the back of his hand across his mouth. 'Let's do the deed. Give lover boy the recognition he deserves.'

Chapter Twenty-Four

It was the end of May when Lizzie took Polly to Gertie's again. Polly had been out of sorts and off school. But now, as Lizzie and Ethel walked towards Poplar with Polly skipping ahead in her school uniform, they talked about their visit to Mr James's empty shop.

'The notice in the window says it's still for rent,' Lizzie said as she slipped her hand through Ethel's arm. 'But with Flo being in hospital, I haven't given it much thought.'

'Mum says Flo is happy now she's home. The hospital was getting her down. I just hope she puts her feet up.'

'Syd will keep an eye on her,' Lizzie replied. 'He's packed in his job at Billingsgate.'

'That was a surprise.'

'The family firm beckoned, I hear. Syd's brother Clifford is teaching him to drive the lorry for the scrapyard.'

'Dad thinks he was daft to leave a steady job.'

'Syd always wanted to drive.'

'What does Flo think of that?' Ethel asked curiously.

Lizzie grinned. 'She wants a car too.'

Ethel nudged her elbow. 'Everyone's trying to keep up with the Joneses. Or should it be the Flowerses?'

'I don't know about that.'

They walked on a little way. 'Did you see there was lots of space inside Mr James's shop? Plenty of space for a display cabinet.'

'Yes,' Ethel agreed enthusiastically. 'It was all very nice.'

'We could buy a second-hand one from the rag and bone man. Even an old oven for the room out back.'

'Do you think there would be enough interest from the locals?'

'Yes,' Lizzie replied confidently. 'I'd like to call the shop "The Bring and Buy Shop".'

'Don't you want your name on the sign?'

'Not yet. I want women to know the shop is for everyone.'

'That's a nice idea.'

'Would you take it on?'

'Do you think I could?'

'You won't have much time to spare when business gets cracking.'

Ethel grinned. 'I should get back to a routine.'

Lizzie asked the all-important question. 'How are you managing without your pay packet from Rickard's?'

'Money's tight. As you know, Richard's careful with the housekeeping.'

Lizzie stopped and looked at her friend. 'You won't have to ask him for any if we pull the shop off.'

'Yes . . .' Ethel hesitated.

'It might be tricky at first,' Lizzie conceded. 'A new business needs a lot of attention. How will the kids and Richard feel about that?'

'Timothy and Rosie won't mind. They're older now and I wouldn't have to ask Mrs Ryde to look after them.' Again Ethel paused. 'Richard will have other ideas. But he never did like me working anyway.'

'This shop will be a bit different, Ethel. Once we get it off its feet, with home-made goods coming in on a regular basis, and fresh fruit and vegetables at knock-down prices, we'll take on more staff. Perhaps Rosie would like a Saturday job and a few hours after school?'

'She'd be happy with that.'

'You'll have Bert for deliveries.'

'What about Ebondale Street?'

Lizzie shrugged. 'I've got Fowler and Elmo now.'

'Do you like them?'

'They ain't too bad.'

Ethel's face was pensive.

'What's wrong?'

Ethel looked up from under her fair lashes. 'I was wondering, have you seen anything of Savage?'

'No. Why?'

'Would he be likely to take an interest in the new shop?'

Lizzie suddenly understood Ethel's hesitation. 'I wouldn't think so. He won't know I'm involved.'

'It's just that – well, what if he came round and demanded money?'

Lizzie nodded slowly. 'I can't say it wouldn't ever happen. But I don't want you to worry either.'

Ethel looked down. 'Richard would be hopeless in a tight squeeze.'

Lizzie knew Ethel's enthusiasm had taken a big dip and she understood why. 'Let's wait and see how things go, shall we?'

'Do you mind?'

'Course not.'

They stood on the corner of Gap End as Polly ran down it. 'How is the romance?' Lizzie asked, and saw Ethel's face brighten.

'We meet at the garage when Danny's not there.' She blushed. 'I never realized how hard those bus seats are.'

They both laughed, but Ethel took Lizzie's arm. 'Are you sure you don't mind waiting a bit? About the shop, I mean. What if it goes to someone else?'

'There will always be another one.'

'I'm not as brave as you.'

Lizzie smiled, even though she was disappointed. Ethel would make the perfect manageress. It would also give her the chance to make a new life for herself as the kids, inevitably, left home. 'I wouldn't say that,' Lizzie teased. 'Not with a mother-in-law like yours.'

Ethel laughed . She glanced down the rows of crooked terraces that led up to an old railway yard, now in disrepair. 'Is Frank seeing Polly today?'

Lizzie nodded. 'We were to visit every Thursday. But Polly had a cold last week.'

'He really does want to see her, then?'

'So he says.'

Ethel smiled. 'So miracles do happen.'

'No one wants to believe that.' Lizzie raised her eyebrows. 'Including your mum who's dead certain he's faking it.'

Ethel grinned. 'That's Mum.'

'What do you think?' Lizzie asked of her friend.

'Of the new Frank?' Ethel raised her shoulders. 'I don't know. But like you, I think it's worth a go.'

'You're definitely in the minority.'

Again Ethel shrugged. 'Only time will tell.'

'Thanks for being such a good mate.' Lizzie hugged her friend.

'I ain't much of one, if I'm such a scaredy-cat.'

'Stop that. You're always there for me.'

After they'd said goodbye, Lizzie was left with mixed feelings. Would she go ahead with the new shop without Ethel? She had always pictured Ethel there, in a smart uniform like Ethel had worn at Rickard's, with that lovely smile of hers welcoming the customers.

Ethel had a good brain, was honest as the day was long, and had a talent for knowing what sold. She had been the backbone of Rickard's haberdashery for many years. But Mr James's shop wouldn't be vacant forever. It was spacious, clean and had an outsized back yard. Mr James had kept all his timber and rope in the store there. It was also going cheap.

If she didn't take it, someone else soon would.

★   ★   ★

'Am I gonna have tea with Uncle Frank today?' Polly asked Lizzie as they stood outside the green-painted door.

'I should think so.'

'We played dominoes last time.'

Lizzie smiled. 'Did you win?'

'No, it was Granda. But Uncle Frank said I'm a good player as I can add up quicker than him.'

'What else did he tell you?'

'He said Gertie used to cook boiled beef and carrots for him and Uncle Danny. They was only little like me. It was the best stew in the East End and made them grow up big and strong. Can I have some of Gertie's boiled beef one day?'

Lizzie nodded, surprised that Frank had talked so openly about his childhood. And in a positive way too. She only wanted Polly to hear the good things for now. 'Knock again, Polly. They couldn't have heard us.'

Polly giggled as she took hold of the brass horseshoe. 'Granda's a bit mutton, Gertie says.'

'Who's taking me name in vain?' Gertie said as she opened the door. 'Oh it's only you, mischief. That's all right, then.' Wearing a flowered apron and a scarf around her head, Gertie bent to kiss Polly. 'Run along to the parlour. Your Granda's there.'

'How is he?' Lizzie asked as she stepped inside. She knew by the look on Gertie's face something was wrong.

'Could be better. I was wondering if you'd turn up.'

'Sorry we ain't been. Polly had a cold. She was off school.' Lizzie smelled the air, thick with camphor and cabbage.

Gertie drew Lizzie close and, glancing over her shoulder, whispered, 'I've got something to tell you.'

'What?'

'It's about Frank.'

'Frank?' Lizzie repeated, her tummy beginning to churn.

'Yer. He was attacked.'

'Frank? Attacked?' Lizzie said in a shocked voice. 'When?'

'About the time Flo was in hospital. He was going to his night shift when these thugs set on him.'

'Who were they? Why would they do that?'

'Dunno.' Gertie pulled her scarf tighter. 'It was too dark to see.'

'Did they hurt him?'

'You could say that. He put up a good fight, though.'

Lizzie felt her head swim. There was always something with Frank. If he wasn't in trouble, trouble wasn't far behind. Danny was right about that. 'So what happened?'

'The coppers were called to the hospital. But let's face it, Frank Flowers ain't gonna come top of their list for attention.'

'Frank was in hospital?'

'Until they decided to offload him.' Gertie reached out for the banister to lean on. 'Brought him in an ambulance and took him upstairs. The poor sod can't walk. As if a trouncing wasn't bad enough they put a knife in his shoulder.'

'Oh God, Gertie!'

'A few inches lower and he'd have had his chips.'

Lizzie stood in silence. Had Frank upset someone so much they wanted to kill him? Secretly, she had begun to believe he was trying to go straight.

'Does Danny know?' she whispered to Gertie.

'He ain't been round.'

'I'll get Bert to tell him.'

'He should come and see his brother.'

'Yes,' Lizzie agreed when she saw that Gertie was so exhausted that even standing up was an effort. 'Looking after an invalid must be very tiring.'

'I'm doing my best. But he's as weak as a kitten from loss of blood. The doctor gave him some pills, but they don't help much with the pain. You'd better go upstairs and see for yourself. Second door along the landing. I'll get some tea on for Polly.' She made her way slowly back to the kitchen.

Lizzie went reluctantly up the stairs to the bedroom. She was dreading what she would find when she got there.

Chapter Twenty-Five

Frank didn't stir when she walked into the bedroom. He was lying on his back with his arms at his sides. Bandages covered his bare chest and as she drew closer she saw the sockets of his eyes were a sickly yellow and swollen.

'Frank?' She stood at the bed.

His gaze found her. Flicking out his tongue he licked his dry lips. 'Blimey, if it isn't an angel.'

'Frank, what happened?'

He swallowed, making a strangled noise. 'Got done over, didn't I?' His eyes rolled to the wooden chair beside the bed. 'Sit down, gel.'

'I can't stay long.'

'Don't matter. It's nice to see someone.'

She sat on the chair. 'You look terrible.'

'Thanks.'

'Are you in trouble again?'

'No, I told you, I'm going straight.' His voice was a hoarse whisper as he put his hand to the bandages on his chest. Closing his eyes, he made a choking sound. As he moved, Lizzie saw the dressings were stained.

'So who did this and why?'

'Gawd knows.'

'I don't believe you.'

'No, I suppose you don't,' he mumbled, 'but it's the truth.'

'Gertie said you were knifed.'

'Yeah, too right I was.'

'So you're lucky to be alive.'

He blinked his puffed eyes.

'Did they rob you?'

'Yeah, one of them grabbed Dad's watch,' Frank said hoarsely. 'He gave it to me when I started my job. So's I'd never be late.'

'Was it the one he wore in the shop?' Lizzie remembered Bill's watch. He'd worn it for years. The clock face was extra large with big, bold figures.

'Yeah. Wasn't gold or nothing. But it had a nice leather strap. When I told the law this, they was quick to put it down as thievery. Tidied up their books nicely.'

'Are they still looking into it?'

A faint smile touched his cracked lips. 'Yeah, in the other direction.'

Lizzie sighed. 'Gertie says you can't walk.'

He rolled his eyes. 'My back is done in. I've got a sore arse from lying in bed and Dad has to help me when I pee. I'm about as much use as a pork pie at a Jewish wedding.' Frank stopped talking as Polly's laughter drifted up from downstairs. 'How is the kid? I've missed seeing her.'

'She's had a cold. Or else we'd have been round sooner.'

'You'd have had a fright if you'd seen me last week.' Frank managed to turn his head. 'Did Flo's baby make it?'

Lizzie nodded. 'The doctor said she has to keep her feet up.'

'She won't like that, knowing Flo.'

For a moment they were silent until Lizzie spoke again. 'Do you have any idea at all who your attackers could be?'

Frank's pale eyes stared back at her. 'There was three of them. Two big 'uns and one smaller than me.'

'And you didn't see their faces.'

'They jumped out and surprised me.'

'Have you made any enemies recently?'

Frank tried to laugh, but coughed instead. 'I've got plenty to choose from.'

'I mean, someone who might pay someone else to do this?'

Frank lay quietly until he rasped, 'There was something about one of the voices.'

'Did you recognize it?'

'No, I was too busy trying to get me oar in.'

Lizzie sat back and sighed. Frank brought so much on himself. Was this the other side of his repentant coin? she wondered. 'I'm sorry to find you like this, but I've got to go now.' She went to stand up but he lifted his hand.

'Stay a bit longer,' he pleaded. 'There's something I need to say.'

She sat on the edge of the chair. 'What is it?'

'Could you get a message to Danny?'

She stiffened. 'Gertie already asked.'

'I want Danny to know I'm sorry.'

'You've said all that before.'

'I've never given him cause to be proud of his brother,' Frank said, catching his breath. 'Not even as a kid. I was never in Danny's league. He was good at everything, shone like the Bethlehem Star. He was the barrow boy that everyone loved. I was the dimwit in the shop, shovelling the spuds.'

'That's how it seemed to you.'

'That's how it was.'

'You could have made good. Same as Danny if you'd tried.'

'I know, I'm just saying, I wouldn't blame Danny if he didn't call over. But I'd like him to.'

'I'll get Bert to pass on the message.'

Frank turned and flinched. 'Don't you see him?'

'I'm too busy trying to make a living. There's a crook trying to muscle into Ferreter's shoes.'

Frank stared at her. 'What's his name?'

'Leonard Savage. Do you know him? He seems to know you.'

'No, honest to God, I don't. What's he want?'

'Protection money, of course.' Lizzie wondered if Frank was telling the truth. Could it be Savage's men who'd attacked him? Had Frank done some running again and not paid his debts?

'Lizzie, I swear I don't know him.'

'Have you done jobs on the side while you've been at the hospital?'

'On my life, I haven't.'

'I've got to go now.' Lizzie had heard all this before.

'Don't leave,' Frank croaked, trying to sit up.

'Why should I stay?'

'Because I think a lot of you and want you to know I'm on the level.'

'That's not funny, Frank.'

'The God's truth is I knew you were special from the moment I saw you at the market. You didn't see me. I'd just helped Danny fill up the barra and was on my way back to the shop. You was talking to Dickie Potts, the old bloke who sold newspapers. Danny told me who you were and I thought, that's the girl I'm going to marry. But Danny got there first. I knew you'd never look at me. Not while Danny was in the picture. I—'

'So you persuaded Babs to destroy Danny's letters,' Lizzie interrupted angrily. 'How could you do such a thing? You told me he was marrying someone else.'

Frank licked his lips. 'I know, I'm sorry.'

'What good is sorry now?'

He dropped his head back on the pillow. His eyes still held hers. 'I ain't even told Dad this. But there's something else. You see, I'd hear these voices inside me head. And I'd try my best not to listen to them. But they always won in the end. It wasn't till I was in the nut house that they stopped.'

Lizzie frowned. 'What sort of voices?'

'Bad ones, telling me to do things . . .' He stopped, his eyes staring vacantly. 'That's what the electric shock did.

They shoved this needle in my arm and put an electric current through me. For months the torture went on. In the end I didn't struggle. I let 'em do it. And I took the pills. And now there's no voices any more.'

'So you're saying these voices told you to hurt people?'

'That's why I drank. To cover 'em up.'

'So you're claiming the liar, cheat and villain in you has disappeared? You ain't the same man who waited in my shop to light a fuse – and if it hadn't misfired the blast would have blown your own family to pieces?' She hadn't realized she was trembling as she gave vent to her feelings. 'You robbed us of a life that might not have been perfect, Frank, but we could have made a home together. We could have had our own babies. Children to give our love to, as you now say you love Polly. If you'd got off your backside we could have made the shop turn a profit and Bill could have taken it easy. But you went your own way. A bookie's runner was better than being a husband and father. When we got married, Frank, I put the past behind me and my feelings for Danny. You and me, we took vows. I kept them, because you were my husband. You forgot you had a wife.'

Lizzie stood up, marvelling at the fact he had so much pity for himself and had not a drop to give her.

'Christ, Lizzie, what can I say?' He tried to reach out.

'I'm going now.'

'Tell Danny, will you?'

She looked into his eyes. Then turning quickly she walked out of the room. Her legs were heavy, drained of strength. Why did Frank keep putting her through all this? Why did she allow him to get to her? Why hadn't she walked out of the room before he'd started with all his excuses?

Slowly she made her way along the passage. For all her anger at Frank, there was Gertie and Bill to consider. They were trying to look after an invalid when neither of them was in good health.

Frank was like the proverbial cuckoo. He had come back to the only nest that would have him. And filled it.

Chapter Twenty-Six

'What's wrong with Uncle Frank?' Polly asked when Lizzie walked into the parlour. Polly was sitting with Bill, playing dominoes. A currant bun was half-eaten on the table beside the small wooden bricks.

'He's not very well.'

'Has he got a cold like I had?'

'Something like that.'

'Can I go and see him?'

'Next time,' said Bill before Lizzie could reply. Looking into her eyes the old man asked, 'Did he tell you anything?'

'Not really.' Lizzie took the plate with the bun and gave it to Polly. 'We have to go soon. Ask Gertie to put this in a bag for you.'

'We ain't finished our game.'

'Granda will keep the dominoes on the tray for you.'

Polly did as she was told and, when Lizzie was alone with Bill, she said quietly, 'Are you all right, Bill?'

'Not so bad, thanks.'

'And Gertie?'

He sat back with a sigh. 'She's up and down them stairs all bleedin' day.'

'Bill, do you have any idea who could have done it?'

'Do you know they left him for dead?' Bill said, breathing hard.

'Frank says he's legit, but can that be true? Does he owe money? Is he back in the rackets again?'

Bill shook his head fiercely. 'He's shook off his past, but look what's happened to him. It just ain't right, it—'

'Don't upset yourself.'

'Can't help it. The cowards.'

'What can I do for you and Gertie?' Lizzie asked.

'This ain't your lookout, gel.'

'He's still my husband, whether I like it or not.'

For a while the old man was silent, chewing on his false teeth. Then pushing the tray of dominoes across the table, he heaved a sigh. 'You know, when the two boys was young they were solid. But as they grew older, I knew something was wrong. Up here.' Bill tapped the side of his head. 'My father would have said Frank was a schlepper. That bad blood ran in the family as it had with my uncles when they scarpered with the family fortune. And for a while, as you well know, Frank proved him right. You and me both suffered at Frank's hands. And perhaps we can never forget. But if it's within my power to forgive before I leave this mortal coil, then I must try. For the sake of my own soul. As well as his.' Rubbing the cuff of his woollen cardigan against his cheek he said in a pained whisper, 'Not that I ask it of you, my dear.'

Lizzie heard voices in the passage. 'I ate all me bun,' Polly called as she bounced into the room.

Lizzie kissed Bill's cheek. 'We'd better be going.'

He looked up at her with sad eyes.

As they walked home, Lizzie was listening with one ear to Polly. But Bill's words were going round and round in her mind. They wouldn't go away. Bill had confided he was trying to forgive Frank for the sake of his own soul as well as his son's.

But was true forgiveness possible?

'Tell me you're kidding,' Bert spluttered that evening as Lizzie served up his meal. 'This is a joke, right?'

The shop was closed, Polly was asleep and Lizzie had come to a decision. 'There's nowhere else for him to go.'

Bert pushed away his plate and took a long gulp of his ale. 'Why should we have him?'

'Because Bill and Gertie can't manage.'

'Frank wouldn't lift a finger to help you if you was in trouble.'

'I know.'

'Don't do it, gel. You'll regret it.'

'It will only be until he's back on his feet.'

But Bert was shaking his head firmly. 'You ever seen a pig fly?'

'I need your help to bring him over.'

Bert's shocked brown eyes rolled up to the ceiling. 'And how we gonna do that?'

'In the van.'

'But you said he was flat on his back.'

'He is. But you and Danny will manage it.'

Bert gawped at her. 'Danny? Now I am laughing, Lizzie.'

She took Bert's hand. 'Can I count on you?'

Bert stared out from his hang-dog eyes. 'Dunno what Danny will have to say about all this.'

'Frank claims he was set up. He swears he's on the level. Something ain't right here, Bert.'

'Yeah and it's Frank.'

'Danny should hear him out.'

Bert looked at his supper on the table before him. 'I'll think about it,' he grumbled as he stuck his knife into the cold chicken pie. He began to eat ravenously and Lizzie smiled as she hurried downstairs. She knew that with a little more persuasion Bert would help her.

She found Fowler sprawled out on the settee in the storeroom, snoring loudly.

'Wake up, Fowler.'

'What?' The big man blinked. He grabbed the iron bar beside him. 'Is it the opposition?'

Lizzie shook her head. 'No, but where are the night shift?'

'Elmo's gone for 'em.'

Lizzie watched Fowler as he pulled on his jacket. 'Where do you know Danny from?' she asked.

He looked startled, peering out from his long hair. 'Why's that?'

'I'd just like to know, that's all.'

Fowler stared at her slyly. 'We have a drink together now and then.'

'Is that all?'

'Yeah. What's on your mind?'

Lizzie walked round the storeroom thoughtfully. She stopped and turned slowly towards him. 'From now on, I'll pay your wages.'

'They're taken care of,' he protested at once.

'Tell Danny you're on my books. And if he has any complaints he can talk to me. You see, Fowler, I don't want anyone else giving you orders.'

Fowler looked at her apprehensively. 'I'll have to see about that.'

'When you come in tomorrow, I want to know that you and Elmo are working for me. That you'll do what I say, *when* I say. If the arrangement doesn't suit you, I'll understand. But I can offer you permanent employment. Not just a casual back-hander down the pub. That goes for Elmo too.' Lizzie watched him thinking, looking her up and down as if he'd never been spoken to like this by a woman before.

'What about the night shift?' he asked after a few moments.

'I don't need them. Bert can take care of that. So, Fowler, I'm either your boss or not. Which is it to be?'

'Danny won't like this.'

Lizzie nodded. 'You're not wrong there. He ain't going to like much about the next few days.' She took six pounds from the till, her week's takings, and counted it out under his nose. 'Two pounds severance pay for your pals. Four pounds between you and Elmo for starters. I don't know how much Danny is paying you, but I'll match every penny.'

The big man just stared at her. She kept her eyes on him, wondering what he would do. The money had caught his attention but was it enough to make him see that she was serious?

After a few seconds he shrugged. Pushing the money into his hip pocket, he nodded.

Lizzie held out her hand. 'Agreed?'

Once again, he hesitated. Reluctantly he took her small hand in his. She gripped it as hard as she could. If trouble followed Frank here, she would be ready for it. But she had to be sure she could trust the people around her. Even if she couldn't trust Frank. This was her way of doing things. She was tired of people telling her she would live to regret her decisions. The choices in her life were hers to make. And good or bad, she would make them.

That was how it was going to be.

Chapter Twenty-Seven

It was early in June when Lizzie next took Polly to see Flo. Lizzie knew telling Flo that Danny and Bert were going to move Frank to Ebondale Street would be the hardest part of all.

'Can I go in to Auntie Lil's?' Polly asked as they arrived in Langley Street. 'Rosie might be there.'

'Yes, play in the yard. I'll call you when Auntie Flo makes tea.'

Rather than knock on the door, Polly dashed round to the lane to climb over Lil's wall. Lizzie saw Flo's front door was open, so she went in. 'Anyone home?'

'Come in, stranger,' a voice shouted. 'We're in the parlour.'

Lizzie was welcomed by smiles from Flo who sat in the armchair with her feet up on the pouffe. Syd stood at her side. A flush of red was on his round face as he drank his beer.

'I'm glad to see you're following doctor's orders,' Lizzie said as she bent to kiss her sister's cheek. 'How are you feeling?'

'Fed up,' sighed Flo, waving to the chair. 'Sit down and make yourself comfortable. Where's our Pol?'

'She's gone to see if Rosie's next door.' Lizzie took the chair nearest the window.

'I was wondering when you'd call round.'

Lizzie was reluctant to explain about Frank so she looked up at Syd and asked lightly, 'Is the patient behaving herself?'

Syd nodded, giving Lizzie a nervous smile.

'Syd's been a real tonic,' Flo said hurriedly, 'turning his hand to the cooking and all sorts. He's even got the wedding service sorted at the Friends' Hall up Mile End, near his mum's. It's booked for the 1st at eleven o'clock; the minister don't mind that we're not religious. He says he marries all sorts.'

'Does he know about the baby?'

'He will on the day.' Flo giggled as she looked down at her bump. 'Syd's paid him up front for his trouble. A generous handshake that will keep him sweet as a nut.' Flo laughed, catching Syd's glance, and he laughed quickly too.

'Have you sent out any invitations?'

'I'm not bothering,' Flo replied with a shrug. 'After all, there's only our families coming. The Missus says not to waste our money and save up for a party to wet the baby's head.' Flo looked up at Syd again. 'We've been given a crib by Clifford. And Walter's wife, Gladys, turned out all her old baby clothes, as after their last kid, the sixth, the doctor told her it's unlikely she'll have any more.'

'Is there anything else you need for the baby?'

'Only a pram. But that will have to wait till I can go out shopping.'

'Mum says we can have hers,' Syd said quietly. 'It did for all of us and me brothers' kids too.'

'That's why I want a new one,' Flo told him shortly.

'But we could save—'

'Mrs Davies delivered my wedding dress.' Flo gave Syd a black look. 'She made a big fuss of me and put an extra bit of lace trimming on the veil.'

'She was very worried when you passed out in the shop,' Lizzie said, wondering if this was the time to mention Frank. But as she was about to speak, Flo rushed on.

'Do you think Danny will give us a car for the day?'

'I'm sure he will. Flo, there's—' Lizzie began but Flo was into her stride.

'Does Pol still want to be my bridesmaid? If so, she'll have to have a dress and, as I can't get out to buy one, I'll have to leave that to you. Pink or yellow would be nice. Whatever you can buy at the market. Then there's the ring. Have you still got Danny's?'

This took Lizzie by surprise. 'No. Of course not.'

'Do you think he'll need it?'

Lizzie shrugged. 'I don't know.'

'It's a shame to waste it.'

Lizzie looked at her sister in dismay. Flo could be very tactless when she wanted something. 'The ring won't be wasted.'

'Oh, so you two are still on?'

'What do you mean?'

'Well,' Flo said calculatingly, 'a little bird told us your old man was moving back in again.'

'Who told you that?'

'Syd was up the market doing the shopping and bumped into Gertie's next-door neighbour.'

'What did she say?'

'Only that Frank had an accident, was off his feet and that Gertie had been looking after him. But you was going to take over the job.'

'News travels quick.' Lizzie didn't like the way Flo was speaking. Her tone had become aggressive as it always did when she had something to say and hadn't yet said it.

'I was hoping you'd tell me yourself,' Flo said grudgingly.

'This is the first chance I've had.'

'Or was you going to do the deed and tell me after?'

'No,' Lizzie said, glancing at Syd and hoping for his help, but he ignored her. 'I wanted to talk about your wedding first.'

'What's Frank got to do with my wedding?'

'Nothing. But you mentioned Frank—'

'I was talking about the ring,' Flo interrupted. 'Not him.'

'Did the neighbour also tell you that Frank nearly died?'

'What do you mean *nearly*?' Flo said sarcastically.

'Some thugs gave him a vicious beating then knifed him in the shoulder.'

'A pity it wasn't his heart.'

'Flo, I don't like hearing you talk that way.'

'What do you expect?' Flo demanded, sitting forward and going red in the face. 'To hear third-hand my sister is going to take back her lying, fornicating, thieving criminal of a husband was a shock.'

'For a start I'm not taking Frank back,' Lizzie said patiently, afraid that Flo was getting distressed. 'I'm only trying to help out Bill and Gertie. And second, I'm here today, aren't I? I'm not trying to keep anything from you.'

'Haven't you enough to keep you busy with the shop to run and Polly to look after? Frank is dead-weight. A time-consuming liability. Why should you care if he lives or dies?'

'Flo, be reasonable,' Lizzie pleaded. 'The arrangement is only for a short while, just until he can go back to his rooms.'

'He's fooled you again,' Flo accused. 'Syd, tell her. She mustn't do it.'

'It ain't the best idea you've ever had,' Syd agreed.

Flo blew noisily through her lips. 'You must guess what's happened, Lizzie. Frank's landed himself in trouble, that's what.'

Lizzie shook her head. 'He doesn't even know who did it.'

'Of course he does,' Flo argued. 'The truth is that your nearest and dearest owes money to some bookie and this is pay-back time.' Flo banged her hands on the wooden arms of her chair. 'All I can say is, the blokes who duffed him up made their biggest mistake when they didn't finish the job.'

'Flo, love, don't take on so,' Syd interrupted, placing a hand on her shoulder. 'Remember the baby . . .'

'How can I forget it?' Flo burst out. 'Just look at me. I'm the size of Blackwall Tunnel and expanding.' She jerked her head towards Lizzie. 'Just don't expect me to come visiting you while that son of a bitch is living under your roof. I wish he'd never turned up that day at Mrs Davies's. I hate to think he touched me. I would rather have had the baby there and then. Now, give us your arm, Syd, and help me up.'

Quickly Syd put down his beer. Sliding his hand around Flo's waist, he helped her to her feet. Flo shook down her flowing dress. 'In case you've forgotten, me and Syd still have a wedding to plan. I wouldn't mind a bit of help if you can spare the time off from all your good works.'

'I hadn't forgotten,' Lizzie said. 'I'll order the flowers from the market, if you like. Just tell me what you want.'

'That's very good of you, I'm sure.' Flo scowled.

'Is there anything else?'

'Syd will give you the list. Do you want some tea?'

'Yes, please.' Lizzie didn't dare refuse, though if she'd had an appetite before it was now gone. She didn't want Flo to get any more upset and risk the baby's health. 'Can I help you in the kitchen?'

'No, thanks. And don't scold me for being on my feet because I'll scream if you do.'

After Flo had gone Lizzie looked up at Syd. 'Can I have that list?'

He went to the mantel clock and slid out the paper.

'Would you like red or white roses for the button-holes?' she asked as she read down the list.

'White will do.'

'Syd, I won't mention Frank again—'

'Good.'

'But there's just one more thing. Did you see anyone lurking at the hospital when you visited Flo?'

'No, why should I have?'

'It seems Frank lost his watch when he was attacked. It was Bill's and not worth much. But it was of senti-mental value.'

Syd stared at her, suddenly angry. 'What do you expect me to do about it?'

'Nothing. But if you did see anyone suspicious—'

'Then good luck to them, that's what I'd say,' Syd inter-rupted her, taking another gulp of ale. 'Frank ain't nothing to me. He's a parasite, a low-life, and you're bonkers to take him back. Flo's right, he's got you where he wants you. In my opinion you should have given him short shrift the moment you saw him outside Mrs Davies's.'

'Flo could have lost the baby,' Lizzie protested, surprised at Syd's reaction. 'She needed help and I didn't care who gave it.'

'You should have sent for an ambulance.'

'That would have taken time.'

'I offered you my help on the day Frank showed up,'

Syd said accusingly, swiping the froth from his lips with the back of his sleeve. 'My brothers and me would have put an end to all his malarkey. Done everyone a favour. Just like we'd have dealt with that villain, Savage, if you'd asked, instead of running to Danny who would have done better to have stayed out of the picture seeing as you're now back with your old man. But it seems to me the Millers just ain't good enough for you.'

Lizzie's mouth fell open. 'That's not true, Syd, and you know it.'

He snatched the list from her hands. 'For Christ's sake, Lizzie, me and Flo, we're having a kid. Our wedding is on the horizon and Flo's in a delicate state. She don't need all this aggro with Frank.'

'I don't want to upset her.'

'You might as well be kipping with him the way you're acting.'

Lizzie sat there open-mouthed as he walked past her to the kitchen. She had never heard Syd talk like this before. A conversation she'd had with Flo came back to her mind. Did Syd really think of her as Lady Muck, as Flo had made out?

Was he turning against her too?

Chapter Twenty-Eight

Danny took two steps down the rickety wooden staircase and stopped dead. From where he stood he could not only hear voices but if he craned his neck he could just see, over the top of the roof of the parked lorry downstairs, three figures standing at the entrance to the workshop.

Cal stood, blocking the way of three men. He'd shunted the wooden trolley used for horizontal repairs to one side. Now he stood with his shoulders tensed under his oily overalls. The man facing him was short and squat, not your normal type of punter, but easily recognizable as trouble. The two apes accompanying him were squaring up, flexing muscle and silently eyeballing the opposition.

Danny knew that, if push came to shove, neither would stand a flying fart's chance. Cal had the instincts of a swamp croc: movement so fast and lethal they wouldn't see the spanner appear from his pocket before it connected with skin and bone. Danny knew Cal of old. His friend could absorb provocation like a sponge. Insults rolled off him as easy as bush rain. Men down the mines had mistaken his silence for weakness. But there would be one word, one action, and the party would start.

The soft menace of the stranger's voice droned in the warm afternoon air. Danny couldn't hear what was being said. But at the bottom of the staircase, he paused, reached out to the nearby workbench and snatched the claw hammer. Sliding it through his belt, he strolled casually around the parked vehicle and stood at Cal's side.

'Ah, Mr Flowers! I've been looking forward to meeting you.' The smallest of the three men held out his hand. 'The name's Leonard – Leonard Savage.'

This came as no surprise to Danny. From Lizzie's description, they fitted. Three goons with cheap suits and hats and the stink of even cheaper brilliantine.

'What took you so long?' Danny said.

'So Mrs Flowers passed on the message?' Savage pushed aside the flap of his suit. Danny knew the action was meant to intimidate. Hinting at the weapon that may or may not have been waiting within easy reach.

'I don't take kindly to threats,' Danny replied, nodding to the two men behind Savage. 'If you want to talk, talk. But it's just us. Tweedledum and Tweedledee aren't invited.'

The smaller man laughed. 'You have a sense of humour, Mr Flowers.'

'I wasn't joking. Get rid of them.'

'They're my insurance, naturally.'

'Your choice,' Danny said dismissively.

Savage jerked his head at Cal. 'What about him?'

Turning to Cal, Danny gave a brief nod.

'That's better,' Savage said as Cal drifted into the work-shop and the two heavies shambled off towards the flash green-and-black Daimler parked nearby.

'If you're carrying hardware,' Danny said shortly.

Savage opened his jacket. Sneering, he murmured, 'Relax, Mr Flowers, I've no quarrel with you.'

'Wrong,' Danny replied coldly. 'You upset a close friend of mine. When you did that, you upset me.'

Savage's face darkened. 'I simply put a proposition to Mrs Flowers—'

'Forget it,' Danny barked. 'I'm not interested in your bent services. Neither is she.'

'You're a hard man to deal with.'

'I don't like racketeers.'

'I come here as a potential buyer,' Savage said, opening his arms innocently.

Danny laughed. 'The motors here won't interest you.'

Savage took a white handkerchief from his top pocket and patted his forehead. 'I'm not after your stock. It's your garage I like. Plenty of room and a nice, comforta-ble cellar for servicing my vehicles.'

'How do you know there's a cellar?' Danny took in a sharp breath.

'Just a guess, that's all.'

Danny's stomach dropped. Could this be the thief? Savage was staring at him as if he knew what he was thinking.

'You're the animal who did the job,' Danny accused in a hoarse whisper.

'Careful, now, Mr Flowers.'

Danny tried to keep calm. But his blood felt as though it was boiling. Savage was taunting him. And the more he taunted, the more Danny felt himself losing control. But even if he managed to get his hands around Savage's throat, there would be no time to wring a confession out of him. How many more men were in that vehicle? Were they carrying weapons?

It was a trap and Danny knew he was about to walk right into it.

'What are a few tools when the chips are down?' Savage goaded. 'To a businessman like me, they're worth practically nothing.'

'Then why nick them?' Danny said bitterly.

'Did I say I did?' Savage looked around him innocently. 'Look at the bigger picture. I'm offering you a generous wedge. Enough to buy yourself a smart little set-up in the city with spanking new motors. The most you'll have to do all day long is polish them. Seems to make a lot more sense to me than roughing it out here.'

'And why should you do that?'

'I told you. I'm a businessman.'

'So that's what you call yourself.'

'Don't stand in the way of progress, Mr Flowers. It could be dangerous.'

'Why do you really want my place?'

Savage smiled, his thick lips parting as he said softly, 'I'm taking over this turf, son, whether you like the idea or not.'

Danny braced himself and took a step forward. 'Get out and off my property.'

Savage stared at him, his face filling with anger. Suddenly he looked over his shoulder and signalled to his men.

'Think twice before you bring them into this,' Danny warned.

'And what are you going to do?' mocked Savage, laughing. 'Stamp your feet in a puddle of oil?'

'No, I'm going to have my mate drive that eight-ton Port of London Authority lorry behind me straight at you.' Danny raised his hand and heard Cal start up the engine. 'It can kick up quite a speed from the off and is as tough as a tank, and it will flatten anything in its path, including you, your boys and your motor.'

Savage took a step back as Danny heard Cal drive the lorry forward.

'You'll regret this,' Savage shouted, stumbling in his effort to join his men. 'I'm not finished with you or your poxy garage.'

'I'll be waiting,' Danny replied, enjoying the powerful rumble of the engine as the lorry crept nearer. Savage glared as he gathered his men and hurried towards their waiting car.

'Did we do the trick?' Cal called from the cab high above Danny's head.

'Yeah, for now, anyway.'

Danny watched the limousine glide away, its tyres crunching on the gravel.

'How much did he want?' Cal asked as he dropped down from the lorry.

'Not a penny.' Danny dragged his gaze back to his friend. 'He wants to buy us out.'

'This place?' Cal said in surprise. 'The *garage*?'

'We've got our thief,' Danny nodded. 'He more or less admitted to it.'

Cal gave a low oath. 'Bastard.'

'I couldn't agree more.'

'What are we going to do about it?'

'Wait.' Danny shrugged. 'Not much else we can do.'

'But why?' Cal walked with Danny back to the garage. 'What's he want this place for?'

'For servicing his vehicles, so he says.'

Cal laughed as they made their way around the lorry. 'He ain't a threat to you, mate. We've taken on bigger contenders in the mines.'

'I don't like being threatened, Cal.' Danny replaced the hammer on the workbench. 'He'll be back, and we'll be ready for him. I want to know where our tools are. And I want them back – with interest.'

Cal grinned and sliding his hand to Danny's shoulder, said, 'Sounds like a plan to me.'

Chapter Twenty-Nine

Bill Flowers winced at the strength of the pain. He knew it well, like a familiar tap at the front door. He sat perfectly still in his coms, allowing his legs to dangle over the side of the bed. He turned gingerly to glance at the empty space beside him left by Gertie and it was then the agony struck. He gasped, grabbing the glass of water balanced on the night table. It was spilled before he had time to suck it into his throat.

Bill felt the sweat break out like a rash all over him. He didn't dare to move lest he make the pain intolerable. His eyes grew wide in fear. The sides of his mouth stuck together, as though he'd trudged a week in the desert.

How long would this spasm last? Always his silent question. He had spent all his life a coster, proud of his strength and agility. Now he was counting the seconds to when he might stumble across the bedroom floor to call for help.

Yet he couldn't entertain putting on Gertie again; their night's sleep had already been disrupted. Frank had screamed out, and they'd rushed into his room, only to find him half out of bed. Eventually they'd settled him with the laudanum. But sleep was impossible after that.

Had Gertie managed to drift off again? he wondered. She must be downstairs or in the yard khazi, her first port of call in the mornings. With a gasp, he buckled forward, the breath leaving his body.

How would they find him? More accurately, how would Gertie find him? Sprawled out on the floor in his coms, the indignity of death revealing the pee stains on his flies.

Bill shook his head sadly. He'd never have believed it of himself; from a healthy young man into a helpless old fool. Almost overnight, it seemed. Through his sweat-laden lids, he saw the small round bottle of Mackenzie's. The smelling salts beckoned to him from the wash stand.

A yard's distance only. Maybe not even that. But it might as well be a mile. He could smell himself, his fear: a fresh, fearful odour from his armpits. The vice tightened. He would be rendered unconscious soon.

But he welcomed the end now. He'd had enough. This was where he ducked out.

'Take me, you hear! Get it over and done with!'

Then suddenly he could breathe again. His body fell limp, released from the tension. The attack ended so abruptly, he couldn't believe it was gone. He sat, perched like a wounded bird, ready to fly or flop. He stared at the bare boards beneath his feet. His gaze was fixed on them, wide still, but in surprise this time, not fear. Had the enemy withdrawn, he wondered? As if watching from a distance, he saw himself, an old man, skin and bone, the brittle skeleton beneath the dirty underwear. Alive still, would you believe!

He made a noise, just to see if he was still in the land of the living. He coughed and, hearing the strength in his lungs, he coughed again, encouraged. A drop of sweat from his forehead trickled to the end of his nose. He cautiously wiped it away.

Inching himself upright, he took a breath. 'The pain's gone,' he muttered in amazement as he gazed around the room. The furniture was in perspective; hard edges of the brown wood wardrobe, the eight-drawer tallboy, Daisy's nursing chair in the corner, the one she'd used to feed Frank. The green leaves of the aspidistra re-homed here from Frank's sick room. Life looked as clear as a bell again.

Closing his eyes, Bill nodded. The Grim Reaper would have to wait. And let's hope he has the patience of a saint, Bill added to his prayer.

Clutching hold of the bed end, he shuffled to the wash stand. Unscrewing the top of the sal volatile, he shoved the bottle under his nostrils. He gasped, as the reviver sped its way to his brain.

So far, so good, he thought, taking another shot for good measure. The light, the pale shimmer of dawn, flowed in through the windows.

Bill made his way to the chair. His trousers, shirt, collar and tie were folded over its back. He wouldn't bother with a strip wash this morning. He'd make things easy on himself. Savouring his second wind, he pulled back his shoulders, slyly waiting to see if his heart remained in his chest.

It did. No pain, no disturbance. Only a draining weakness. He paused for another breath and decided to sit down for ten minutes more.

Returning to the bed, he lowered himself slowly, exhaustion in every limb. Placing his palms on his knees, he dropped his head, staring at the boards once again.

His thoughts returned to Frank in the next room. He'd be suffering the effects of the sedative, no doubt. But they'd had little choice in the early hours when in his distress he'd knocked over his pee bottle.

He heard a movement downstairs. Was it Gertie? No. If he wasn't mistaken, he could hear the rattle of the front-door key on its string.

Bill hoisted himself to his feet. He stood uncertainly, trying to decipher the noises. Someone was coming upstairs. Too heavy a tread for Gertie. Bill stared at the bedroom door. Softly it creaked open. A figure appeared. He blinked to clear his vision.

'Danny?'

'It's me. Are you up yet?'

'Do I look as if I'm kipping?' Bill managed to chuckle.

Danny strode across the floor, surprising Bill as always as he stared at the reflection of himself as a young man. Frank was Daisy, had her nature too. But Danny was a Flowers all the way through. He seemed to have filled out, put muscle onto those fine broad shoulders. And the light in his eyes, as blue as his own once were, warmed Bill to his cockles.

'Taken to sleeping in, Dad?' Danny teased good-naturedly and Bill grinned.

'None of that, you cheeky blighter.'

'Where's Gertie?'

'Out in the lav, I expect.' He nodded to the wash stand. 'Pass me my choppers and you'll see what a beauty I am.'

Danny took the enamel mug containing the set of brown dentures and gave it to Bill. 'Give us your best smile, then.'

'Patience, my boy. A good thing is worth waiting for.' Bill smiled widely. 'How's this for good looks?'

'Blinding,' replied Danny, returning the mug, then sitting on the bed beside his father.

'So to what do we owe the honour?' Bill screwed up his eyes.

Danny chuckled. 'So your memory is slipping too?'

Suddenly Bill remembered. 'You've come for your brother.'

His son's face clouded. 'Aye. But this ain't my best day, Dad.'

'Then walk away now, son. I'm not asking for help.'

'Always the proud gaffer, eh?'

Bill lifted his weak arms. 'We'll manage. We always have.'

Danny looked away. 'Where is he?'

Reluctantly, Bill jerked his head. 'Next door.' Perhaps he should just refuse outright. Lizzie had meant well, the girl had good intentions. But the burden would be heavy. His two sons and her in the middle. What trouble would brew in that mix?

Danny nodded slowly, as if reading his father's thoughts.

'Listen, Dad, it's taken me a while to swallow on the wedding. I didn't want to come round here with ill feeling. It's not easy, losing what you've wanted all your life. But it was my mistake, leaving Lizzie. I should have stayed in the shop, built up the business. Seen that you was all right and put a ring on her finger.'

'You've not lost your Lizzie.' Bill cleared his dry throat. 'She's in your corner, son.'

'Not mine,' Danny said, stiffening his back.

'Now then, that's bitter talk.'

'It ain't settled with Frank,' Danny continued and Bill's heart squeezed to hear those words. 'It was you who raised me to fight fair. I'll admit there's been moments I've wanted to hurt Frank. But I'll square up to him when the time's right. And I know it ain't now.'

Bill nodded slowly. 'You'll have a fair wait, considering the state of him.'

'Frank's fooled us all before.'

'You think this is all to get your girl's sympathy?' Bill asked in surprise.

'Why not? He's tried every trick in the book so far.'

Bill was grateful that life had blessed him with two sons, but to see them at odds like this was a terrible thing.

After a while, Danny spoke again. 'Bert's bringing the van over. We'll take him in that.'

Bill placed a hand on his son's arm. 'You're a good man, Daniel. Take care of your brother.' He gave another deep sigh. With Danny's aid, he pulled himself to his feet. His arms went around his son in a grateful embrace.

Chapter Thirty

'Be a good girl for your teacher.' Lizzie kissed Polly at the school gate.

'Will Uncle Frank be there when I get home?'

'Yes. Like I told you last night, Uncle Danny and Bert are going to fetch him from Granda's.'

Polly frowned, looking thoughtful. 'Which bed is he going to sleep in?'

'Mine. And I'm going to share yours. That is, if you don't mind.'

Polly clapped her hands. 'I can stop up late, like you.'

'Cheeky!' Lizzie tucked Polly's long plait behind her shoulder. 'Now go along in.'

'Will I see Tom?'

'No, he'll be at school, like you.'

'Can he come over soon?'

'Polly, you're going to be late.' She gave her niece a gentle push. 'Now run in, the bell's gone.'

Polly skipped off in her blue cotton dress. As Lizzie began to walk home, she sighed. Polly, like Bill and Gertie, had accepted Frank's change in character. She had forgotten the frightening events of last year when Frank had tried to blow up the shop. The children at school had stopped teasing her. There were no more 'Commie' insults from Georgie March. But Polly was only a six-year-old. She saw everything with innocent eyes. If only Frank really had changed his ways, Lizzie thought, then, when Polly learned one day that she was his daughter, the truth wouldn't be so hard to take.

A customer was waiting outside the shop when she arrived back.

'Where's your men this morning?' the woman asked.

Lizzie unlocked the door. 'I gave them the morning off.'

'They're not bad blokes when you get to know them.'

Lizzie smiled as she weighed the vegetables and packed them in the shopping bag.

'Ah, your van's just arrived,' the woman said, glancing over her shoulder. 'Bert been out on a delivery, has he?'

Lizzie shut the till drawer. She wanted to close up while Danny and Bert brought Frank in. 'Is there anything else I can get you?'

'I wouldn't mind some cakes.'

'I'll have some tomorrow,' Lizzie replied, guessing her customer knew this already.

'See you tomorrow.'

'Ain't that Danny Flowers too?'

'Yes. I must help them unload.' Lizzie waited until the woman had gone, then signalled Bert.

He climbed out of the van and joined Danny. They

opened the back doors and pulled out a piece of wood. Lying on top of it was Frank.

Lizzie put the kettle on as Danny walked, tall and broad-shouldered, into her kitchen. Now that Frank was safely in bed, she had sent Bert downstairs to the shop.

It had taken a lot of huffing and puffing to carry the home-made stretcher up the stairs. 'When we tried to get him out of bed at Bill's he screamed like a stuck pig,' Bert had told her. 'So Bill gave us this old door to carry him on.'

Danny sat down at the table and took out his tobacco tin from his overall pocket. 'You were right. They did a good job on him.'

'So you believe me now?' she said, placing a steaming mug of tea on the table.

'What's he got himself into?' Danny asked.

Lizzie sat down. 'I told you, he said he was just going in to the hospital to start his shift.'

'Did he nick all those pills?' Danny drew on his cigarette, narrowing his eyes. 'You could sink a battleship with that lot.'

'Some are for the pain. Others are to stop the voices.'

Danny frowned. 'What voices?'

'The ones he heard in his head, telling him to do bad things.'

Danny raised his eyebrows as he smoked. 'So he's finally got you believing his tall story.'

'Danny, your brother is here because he's sick. If you have any other ideas on what we should do with him, then I'd be happy to hear them.' She felt the heat of anger in her face. 'If not, do me and yourself a favour and drop the subject.'

He ground his cigarette out in the ashtray. 'What's all this about Fowler and Elmo?'

'They're on the shop's books now.'

'So they tell me.'

'I don't expect you to pay my bills.'

'Same old Lizzie.' He smiled, throwing back his head. 'As stubborn as they come.'

'I want things done my way.'

'Are you sure you can handle this?'

'I pay their wages, that should be enough.'

Danny nodded slowly, turning the mug on the table. 'I had a visit from Savage.'

Lizzie's heart skipped a beat. 'What did he want?'

'He wants my pitch.'

Suddenly she felt afraid. 'What did you tell him?'

'You know the answer to that one.' He drank his tea and stood up. 'He's trying to move in on the island. He started with you, then lifted my tools. Little touches here and there. It's an old trick, and he thought he might get lucky. But so far he hasn't. I'm warning you, Lizzie, don't underestimate the enemy.'

She looked into his eyes and nodded. 'Thanks.'

'What for?' He came to stand close to her.

'Everything. Today—'

'You're right. I've damn well got no suggestions. I wish I had.'

She felt his warmth, his presence. Once they would have been in each other's arms, taking comfort from sharing. Once, before Frank, before Savage . . .

Bert called from downstairs and Danny touched her cheek. 'Take care of yourself.'

When he'd gone, she gazed at his empty mug, missing the closeness they had once shared.

Chapter Thirty-One

'Your Flo is solid child-bearing stock,' the Missus assured Lizzie as they watched Flo and Syd walk out of the Friends' Hall. 'You can see that a mile off. Me old mum used to say that wide hips birthed the best babies. She's carrying low, so it's guaranteed this one is a boy.'

Lizzie smiled at Syd's mother who was dressed in bright tangerine and a saucer-shaped navy hat. 'Ain't that an old wives' tale?'

'Yes, but with my brood, it's never been wrong so far.' Her large round face was wreathed in smiles as she waved to Flo and Syd with an orange glove. 'Come on, gel, let's get outside for a breather.'

Lizzie followed the impressive figure as the congregation filed out of the hall. Doug had volunteered to take photos and had assembled the family around the bride and groom.

The Missus, still glued to Lizzie's side, wiped a tear from her eye. 'Where's my old man gone? Down the boozer, I expect.' She gulped air. 'Your Pol looks lovely, don't she? Did you say she was your sister's kid?' The

Missus, who didn't seem to expect a reply, slapped a hand on her ample stomach. 'Where's the lav? I've got a touch of the collywobbles. Back in a tick, dear.'

Lizzie seized her chance to find a quiet corner. Moving to the edge of the crowd, she gazed across at the bride and groom. She wanted to remember this moment as Flo and Syd stood together as man and wife for the first time. Flo's long dress of white silk satin with its high-shaped waist was beautiful. Mrs Davies had sewn pearls over the delicate points of the sleeves and around the edges of the short white veil. Her smile was so joyful as she looked into Syd's eyes that Lizzie felt close to tears.

When Flo caught hold of Polly's hand, Lizzie's chest swelled with pride. If only Babs could see her daughter now! Polly wore an ankle-length dress of pale lemon silk and organdie. A white satin band was tied around her waist. Her white shoes and socks peeped out from under the hem of her skirt. That morning Lizzie had plaited her long auburn hair, pinning the plaits up onto her head with small lemon roses and matching lace.

Lizzie knew she would remember this day forever. Her little sister was a wife and expectant mother. Would they, as sisters, grow closer as the years passed? Through all the ups and downs of life? Would the baby be a girl? Or a boy, as the Missus predicted?

Just then, Danny's tall figure appeared. Dressed in a dark suit and pale grey tie, he was tying white ribbons to the windscreen of a car. Flo had told her that Danny had bought the beige four-seater roadster, intending to start a wedding car service. With its two wheels mounted at the rear, folded-down hood and long, low chassis it looked the part. A cheer went up as Syd led his wife towards it and Danny opened the vehicle's rear door. Flo shook away the confetti as she climbed in.

Lizzie smiled when she saw Bert. He was bending low, trying, unsuccessfully, to tie one of Syd's boots to the rear of the car.

'If there's one person who don't blend in with the scenery it's your Bert,' a familiar voice chuckled. Lizzie turned to find Ethel and Richard standing behind her. Her friend wore a pretty beige dress and choco-late-coloured cloche hat over her fair hair. Richard, whom Lizzie had only ever seen wearing a grey suit, was dressed in formal dark blue, a white, triangu-lar-shaped handkerchief poking out of his breast pocket. His light brown hair was parted on the crown and cut evenly around his ears. A pair of pale hazel eyes stared out from behind his spectacles. Lizzie went on her toes to kiss his cheek. 'It's lovely to see you, Richard. Did you enjoy the service?'

'I'm not one for this sort of thing.' He glanced quickly at Ethel. 'I hope you think I've done my bit.'

Ethel looked at Lizzie. 'Richard means he's not joining us at the reception. There's a lot to do at home.'

'The garden won't tidy itself,' Richard replied tartly, shoving his spectacles along the bridge of his nose. 'Or the house.' He threw Ethel a frown which Lizzie politely ignored.

'I'm sorry to hear that, Richard. Can't I twist your arm? The party might be fun.'

'Thank you, but no,' Richard answered dismissively. Frowning at the noisy crowds, he tightened his shoulders. 'I'll catch the bus back, Ethel. Have you left supper? I don't want to waste valuable time messing about in the kitchen. Not with the front flower beds needing weeding.'

Ethel bit her lip. 'There's cold meat and pickles. But if you want spuds, you'll have to fry yesterday's potatoes.'

Richard opened his mouth then, seeming to think better of it, he closed it. 'I'll be off then. Goodbye, Lizzie.'

'Goodbye, Richard.'

Without a word more, he turned and, deliberately avoiding the Missus who was engaged in conversation with the bride and groom, he disappeared.

Lizzie looked at Ethel, who suddenly burst into laughter. Soon Lizzie was laughing too, and although she felt sorry for Richard, clearly a fish out of water in unfamiliar company, she was relieved to see that Ethel was far from upset.

'That's my husband for you,' sighed Ethel as she composed herself, wiping a tear from the corner of her eye. 'The original action man.'

Lizzie chuckled. 'You do have a nice garden.'

'Yes,' agreed Ethel. 'But the weeds ain't going to grow that big in one day, are they?' She looked Lizzie up and down. 'Your outfit's stunning.' Ethel indicated Lizzie's pale green calf-length frock and new high-heeled shoes.

'Crêpe de Chine, is it? We used to stock that material in Rickard's.'

'Me and Pol went up to Aldgate as a special treat. I took an afternoon off and left Bert and Fowler in charge of the shop *and* Frank,' she added ruefully.

Ethel rolled her eyes. 'They didn't kill each other, then?'

'Not quite.'

Ethel looked down at her beige dress. 'I couldn't really afford this outfit either. Richard hasn't stopped complaining. He says I'm extravagant. And you'd think I'd asked for the Crown Jewels when I told him I wanted to buy this dress.'

'But he must have thought it looked nice.'

'Didn't say so. The kids did though, bless 'em. They said I only looked about thirty-five, which I am in a few weeks' time.'

They both smiled, but Ethel's happy expression vanished when Lizzie asked how things were at home.

'Same old story,' she answered wearily. 'Honestly, we had such a row about him coming today. Dunno how I managed to get him this far. Now I'm paying the penalty and have got this splitting headache.'

'Your mum will be disappointed he's not with you.'

'It seems mixing with my family and friends is a step too far for Richard.'

Suddenly Danny tooted the horn and the wedding car drove by. Flo waved excitedly and blew them a kiss.

'They look happy, don't they?' Lizzie sighed wistfully.

'Marriage, eh?' Ethel murmured. 'Wonderful on the day. It's just the thirty years after.'

Lizzie laughed, but she knew Ethel was serious. 'Don't tell Flo that when you see her.'

'I won't. But you know something? If Richard and me ever split up, I'd never marry again.'

'Not even Cal?' Lizzie asked.

'*Especially* Cal. I reckon real happiness is too good to last.'

'Is that what you really believe?'

Ethel looked away. 'Per'aps. I don't know.'

Lizzie linked her arm with her friend's. 'You and me, we ain't got normal marriages, it's true. But on the other hand, we do know what love is.'

'Yes, but not with our husbands. I miss that, Lizzie, don't you?'

'Ethel, it's not like you to be down.'

'It's weddings. They bring out the grumpy me.'

'Come on, grumpy. Let's move closer to the car.' Lizzie felt sad for her friend. Ethel wanted to be in love with Richard. The man she had married. The father of her children. But the reality was, Cal was the man who fulfilled her.

As the car passed, Flo threw her bouquet. Lizzie saw one of the young Miller girls run to catch it. She blushed as she looked proudly at her friends and family.

'The next bride,' Ethel remarked thoughtfully.

They watched the rumpus the bouquet-throwing had caused. Squeaks of delight from the girls and teasing from the men. 'One thing's for sure,' Lizzie decided, 'now Flo is a Miller, life will never be boring.'

'You can say that again.'

'The Missus told me she thinks Flo's first will be a boy.'

Ethel grinned. 'Another little scallywag to add to the clan. Talking of which, how's Frank?'

Lizzie knew that, unlike most people, Ethel was asking out of genuine concern.

'Bert's found him a walking stick. And though the pain of getting out of bed nearly kills him, he can hobble to the end of the landing.'

'Has Danny been to visit?'

'No and I'm not expecting it.'

'Poor Danny,' Ethel said softly. 'I mean, cripple or not, Frank is back in your life.'

'I can't help that.' Lizzie managed to add reasonably, 'It's not forever. I keep reminding myself of that.'

'Funny, those words have been in my head too,' Ethel mused. 'One day I'm going to finish with Cal. The next, I've changed my mind.'

'You can't switch off your feelings.'

'Goodness knows I've tried, but it don't work.'

Lizzie noticed the traffic had started to move again. 'Look, everyone seems to be leaving. Where's Rosie and Timothy?'

'Dad said he was driving them and Mum back home in the car. I told him I was going to walk as I've got this rotten headache.' Ethel paused. 'Tell you what, we could take the bus. The 59 goes past Mr James's shop. We can see if it's still empty. Think about what we could do with it when all our troubles are over.'

Although Ethel said this light-heartedly, Lizzie knew their business plan was still their guilty pleasure. Would they both be free enough one day to lead the lives they really wanted to?

'I should really call by the shop to see if Frank's all right,' Lizzie said as she thought of the invalid she had left struggling to dress himself that morning. 'I gave him some breakfast and left him a sandwich. I didn't want him messing around in me kitchen.' She knew they would be away all day. But neither she nor Bert had said they would be back to look in on him. Which now made her feel all the more conscience-stricken. If Frank had been Danny then she wouldn't have hesitated, would have hated to see him painfully trying to perform the simplest of actions, like buttoning up a shirt. But this was Frank. And Bert had insisted he must help himself. Bert still didn't trust Frank.

'Why did you want to keep him out of the kitchen?' Ethel asked.

'It's too dangerous with the gas and all. He might turn it on and forget to turn it off. I don't want another explosion like last year.'

'He wouldn't do that again, would he?'

'No, not deliberately. But he seems to have lapses in concentration. It's all them medicines he takes. Pills for this. Pills for that. What if he took too many?'

'You sound concerned.'

'Do I?' Lizzie realized she'd been talking non-stop about Frank.

Ethel nudged Lizzie. 'Tell you what, I'll look in on him for you. Then you can go to Mum's and see Flo. I need a bit of breathing space.'

'Are you sure?'

'Course. As long as Frank don't attack me,' Ethel teased.

'If he did, at least we'd know he was getting better.'

They both laughed.

Lizzie rummaged in her bag. 'Here's the key to the shop.'

Ethel pointed. 'Look, there's a bus! Let's run for it.'

Holding on to their hats they made a dash. Lizzie was excited as they climbed aboard. She would have time to enjoy the party now. And for one whole day, forget about Frank.

Chapter Thirty-Two

Lizzie sat next to Danny on Lil and Doug's yard wall, the only vacant space left now the party was under way. Her thoughts turned with affection towards the tufts of dried weeds that once were Doug's vegetable patch.

Before the war, her father and Doug had often passed time here. Two strong men, best friends and neighbours, admiring the spuds or carrots that Doug managed to encourage into life. As a small child she remembered the men enjoying an ale on a wooden bench by the shed while Kate and Lil gossiped in the kitchen. None of them, thank God, Lizzie thought with a pang of sadness, could have imagined in 1914 what was to befall them. Both the Sharpes' sons lost in the trenches, Kate's unexpected death and Tom Allen's fatal injuries – events that were mirrored in almost every family by the end of the conflict.

She sighed. Like Doug's small green oasis, family life as they had all known and enjoyed it had disappeared forever. And now she gazed with more than a little longing at the neglected oblong of turf and dilapidated wooden shed, its buckling tin roof leaning heavily against the outside lavatory.

Suddenly she was jolted back to the present. A group of young people came laughing and talking from the house; the Miller grandchildren and Timothy and Rosie among them. Lizzie watched Timothy as he picked up the wreck of Lil's old bike and sat astride it. His fair hair flopped over his face, as he gained the attention of one young girl. She was, Lizzie thought, very pretty and looked close to Timothy's age.

'Do those two remind you of anyone?' Danny asked as he followed her gaze. 'You was about her age when I plucked up the courage to ask you out.'

'To the Hammersmith Lyric, wasn't it?' Memories flooded back.

Danny grinned. 'Yeah. *The Beggar's Opera.* I'd been putting a few bob away to make an impression.'

Lizzie blushed. 'You never told me that before.'

'I've never told you a lot of things.' He sipped his ale then looked at her, his blue eyes teasing. 'I'd try to catch you alone at the market but your dad always kept a close eye on you.'

'I had to push his chair.'

'Course, but I found a way in the end.' He took another long swallow of his ale, licking his lips and grinning.

'What was that?'

'You remember that old geezer, the newspaper seller?'

'Dickie Potts. He was a nice old man.'

'I had a word with him. He used to keep your dad talking so we could have a minute to ourselves.'

'You never did!'

'It was worth a few bob.'

They laughed together and Lizzie realized how long it had been since they'd shared a joke. That's what she'd loved about him. He always used to be cheerful and a bit reckless. 'Devil-may-care' as her mum used to say. She wanted to say that things might have been different for them if he hadn't gone to Australia. Frank would never have got a look-in. But why rake up the past again? One thing they couldn't deny: the attraction was still strong between them. Now Danny was at ease, he had dropped his guard a little. She could feel it in the way he was looking at her. In the warm summer's air and in the husky depths of his voice.

Lizzie knew her feelings must be easy to read on her face. She said quietly, 'We're still young, Danny.'

He drew back his shoulders. 'Don't feel young when I think of you with Frank. I feel angry. And cheated.'

'Come and see your brother—'

Danny began to shake his head. 'It won't make no difference.' Just then a rumbling sound came from the lane and Danny stood up. 'Sounds like Cal's motor. He's dropping Tom off.'

Tom came racing across the lane. His first question as he climbed over the wall was, 'Where's Polly?'

Lizzie was surprised to see how quickly Tom was growing. He was almost as tall as her now. 'Polly's inside. She's been waiting for you.'

'I've got a job at the garage,' he told her. 'I have to sweep the forecourt and wash a car.'

'Did it come up shiny?' Danny asked, crooking an amused eyebrow.

'Yeah, I could see me face in the windows.'

'Are your hands clean?'

Tom turned up his palms for Danny to see. 'I washed 'em and changed my clothes an' all.'

'Off you go then and join the party.'

Cal had followed Tom across the lane. He was wearing a clean shirt and trousers and gave Lizzie a big grin. 'Flo tied the knot, did she?'

'Yes, well and truly.'

'Give her and Syd me best. Tell them to have a drink on me.'

Lizzie knew Cal hadn't been invited to the wedding. Ethel had confided that Lil had her suspicions about her daughter's affair. And even though Lil didn't care for Richard, she wouldn't entertain the thought of Ethel ever straying.

Cal glanced over Lizzie's shoulder. 'Ethel inside?'

'She's at the shop. We're supposed to be closed for the day. But Ethel called by for me, just to see if . . . if everything's all right.' She glanced quickly at Danny.

Cal grinned. 'I'll see if she wants a lift.'

'Thanks for driving Tom over,' Danny said, clapping Cal on the arm. 'You'd better scoot now before Lil sees you.'

'Right,' agreed Cal swiftly and, nodding at Lizzie, he hurried off.

Lizzie sighed. 'Lil will give Ethel hell if she finds out, for sure.'

Danny nodded. 'Cal's a good bloke but he's a loner. Always has been.'

Lizzie said thoughtfully, 'Perhaps Cal's never been in love before.'

Danny just shrugged. 'He's me best mate. But he was born and bred in the outback, never settled down in the mines and is a wanderer at heart. I don't want to see Ethel get hurt.'

'Neither do I.'

Just then, Lil poked her head out from the kitchen door. 'Lizzie, Danny, go in to Flo's, will you? Tell them it's time to stop gassing and come in here to cut the cake.'

Grinning, Danny took Lizzie's arm. 'Better jump to it. It'd be a braver man than me who challenged Lil Sharpe.'

'Christ, Frank, how did you get in this state?' Ethel stared at the figure lying on the kitchen floor. 'You wasn't supposed to come in here.'

'I thought I'd make meself a cuppa.'

'The place reeks of gas.'

'I managed to turn off the tap but lost me footing when I heard noises downstairs. I thought it was Lizzie and she'd give me a rollicking if she caught me.'

'You're not wrong there. You're a walking accident, you are. Now I'll try to lift you up. Grab hold of the table and I'll push.'

As Ethel assisted him, he let out a cry. 'Now what's the matter?' she demanded as he stood up shakily.

'It's my back.'

'I'll help you to the bedroom and you can sit down. You ain't safe around here. Then I'll make you a cuppa.'

She gave him his walking stick and helped him along the landing. Ethel was determined not to let her pity show. But it was difficult. The man who everyone hated was a shadow of his former devious, lying, villainous self. For a moment she could understand Lizzie's dilemma. Frank didn't deserve her goodness. He'd been a rogue all their marriage. And if it was only sickness that changed him, what would happen when he got well?

If he got well. Either way, Ethel couldn't see an easy way out for Lizzie. Her friend had a soft heart, no matter what she said to the contrary. The question to be asked was why hadn't Lizzie taken the opportunity to rid herself of a deadbeat husband?

The answer was clear to Ethel, if it wasn't to Lizzie herself. It was the way Lizzie had been raised. Lizzie's mother, Kate Allen, had stuck by her husband who had returned from war without his legs. Literally, half a man. Kate had never weakened, not for a moment. Even though Tom Allen himself was slowly dying of gangrene. Kate had instilled into her oldest daughter that marriage should last forever. Through thick and thin. Or, until one of them died. This was what kept Lizzie tied to Frank.

Ethel watched Frank collapse onto the bedroom armchair. The sweat poured from his face. His shirt was wet and his eyes were full of fear. Like Tom Allen, Frank was certainly half the man he once was.

'Ta, Ethel.' His face was screwed up in pain.

'Is it your back?'

'Yeah, gel. It's a bugger.'

Ethel sat down on the bed. 'You'd have thought the knife would have done you in.'

'If it had gone any deeper, it would have.'

Ethel raised an eyebrow. 'Some might have welcomed that outcome.'

'And I wouldn't blame them.'

A changed man, eh? Ethel thought to herself ruefully.

'I'll get you that cuppa.'

'Ethel?'

'What?'

'You know I think the world of her, don't you?'

Ethel frowned, tilting her head. 'No, I don't. You've given Lizzie hell and you've got no one to turn to now, so you're behaving yourself.'

Frank's thin face contorted. 'No, it's not like that.'

'It's what everyone thinks.'

'I know.'

'If you let Lizzie down, Frank Flowers, I'll find a knife and stick it in you myself. You can take that as a promise.'

He nodded, wiping the sweat from his face with the back of his sleeve.

In the kitchen, Ethel thought about what she'd said. She had just threatened Frank, but it had only been words.

She loved Lizzie like her own sister and she didn't want to see her hurt again.

Ethel picked up the carving knife that lay on the bread board. And turned it in her hands. She smiled. Frank was a lucky sod. He'd come through a knifing and a good kicking and survived. Perhaps people like him always did. So chewing his ear off a little with a few threats wouldn't do any harm.

She put the kettle on to boil.

Chapter Thirty-Three

'You've got to keep shtoom, Syd,' Clifford Miller instructed his younger brother. 'No one will find out who did it. It was only us and the bastard himself who was there.'

'You said it was just going to be a tickle,' Syd remonstrated weakly.

'He put up a struggle. Didn't reckon on that.'

'You said no knives or dusters.'

Clifford frowned and pointed a grubby finger in his brother's face. 'No, you said that, Syd. Now listen, mate, you are a Miller. Your birthright is to take what you want in life. So far, all you've done is ponce around with a load of fish on your uncle Ned. Well, those days are over. You're a scrapper now. You can drive. Well, almost. You arc in the firm. And rule number one is we take care of each other.'

Syd thought that comment was a bit ripe. Neither Clifford nor Walter had taken care of their other three brothers who were doing time for burglary and aggravated assault. They'd been nicked and sent down *because* they were Millers. So why should Cliff and Walter look down their noses at fish portering? It had been a steady job, a solid one. And though he'd had to kowtow to the fish buyers at the market, he'd worked his arse off since school to get his licence. Something none of his other brothers had achieved.

Syd's gaze slid across the front room to the women of his family stuffing their faces and knocking back the port wine. His mother was holding court, as usual. But none of the women was a patch on his Flo. He loved his family. But he was also ashamed of them. He'd tried to do as Flo wanted. Steer clear of their influence. It was just the one time in his life he'd slipped up. And it was Frank Flowers who'd been his undoing.

And somewhere along the line, he, Syd Miller, had not only lost his beloved job, but also was learning the age-old skills of shafting punters and flogging old tat.

Syd looked into his brothers' florid faces. They were sinking as much booze as they could lay their hands on. In their cheap suits, they thought they looked the bee's knees. They gave him hearty slaps on the back and knowing winks. Syd looked round to see if anyone was watching.

To his dismay, someone was. Syd offered Lizzie a weak smile. He regretted having spoken the way he did to her. Guilt had made him aggressive.

Syd tried another smile, deliberately tuning out Clifford and Walter's voices. He widened his eyes and raised his glass.

But Lizzie just stared at him.

★   ★   ★

Ethel finished making the tea and sandwiches, wondering just how quickly she could make her escape. She'd left the bowl and jug full of warm water, a flannel and soap on top of the bedside table. All Frank had to do was wash himself. That wasn't much to ask. She hadn't fancied helping him to do that. And to be honest, Frank had seemed happy enough to be left to his own devices.

She lifted the tray and made her way back to the bedroom. Frank was sitting where she had left him, but he'd still not finished with his ablutions.

'Come on, let's get you tidy.' Reluctantly Ethel put the tray on the bed.

'Don't trouble yourself. I can manage.'

Ethel saw he'd taken off his shirt and vest and loosened his braces. His movements were slow as he tried to put his shirt back on. Wincing, he pushed the cloth over his skinny chest. He wasn't complaining and, if he had, Ethel suspected she would have told him what to do with his aches and pains.

She found a clean shirt in one of the drawers. 'You'd better put this on.'

Ethel looked at his skinny chest and protruding ribs. There was a bandage around the top half of him which she realized must cover the wound.

'You're dead lucky,' she told him again as she took away the old shirt and helped him with the new.

'More dead than lucky, you mean.'

'Don't start that.'

'There was three of them. I could have handled one.'

'And you really don't know who it was?'

'No. Don't think so. But . . . maybe the voice. It rang a bell.'

'Did you tell Lizzie that?'

'No. I kept shtoom.'

She helped him to link his cuffs. 'Frightened to put a foot wrong, eh?'

'You could say that.'

'Listen, Frank, if you want my advice, get better quick.' She let him button up the front. 'Then leave Lizzie alone to get on with her own life. You'll stay friends a lot longer that way.'

At this, he stared up at her, his blue eyes pale and watery. 'I don't want to be friends. I want to make up for the past and—'

'Don't even go there,' Ethel cut in, quickly taking away the bowl. 'You have to make a new life for yourself. It's the jam you got yourself into. And let's face it, you're off your trolley half the time.'

Frank gazed up at her, like a dog, she thought, about to be whipped. 'I've got me tablets now. I'm not going crazy again. Look at me. This is what I am, a bleeding cripple. But I'm on the mend. And I want a chance to give her a better life—'

Ethel put the basin down on the dressing table. 'Listen, Frank, you've got to stop this.'

'If you was to tell her I've changed, she'd believe you.'

Ethel laughed. 'You crafty sod. That's what you're

after. Me on your side, cos you know Lizzie and me are best mates.'

'No, honest, Ethel—'

The shop bell tinkled and startled both of them.

'I must have forgotten to lock the door.' Ethel looked round. 'Someone thinks we're open. Now eat your sandwich. And when I come back I don't want to hear a word more from you. Lizzie's better off without you and you can take that as my confirmed opinion.'

Ethel hurried along the landing and down the stairs. She wasn't about to start serving spuds, not in this get-up. Whoever it was would have to catch the market before it closed. There was still time—

Ethel gasped as a tall figure loomed before her. 'Cal, my God! You gave me a fright!' She put her hand on her racing heart. 'What are you doing here?'

'What do you think?' He put his arms around her. 'I took Tom over to Flo's and Lizzie said you was here.'

'Did Mum see you?'

'No, course not.'

'Thank goodness for that. I couldn't stand more questions today. Not with this headache.'

'Come closer and let me get rid of it for you.'

'You're a cheeky sod, do you know that?' Ethel felt a shiver of delight as he rubbed her back.

'You seem to like it.'

Ethel grinned. 'You don't have a care in the world, do you?'

'I'll show you how much I care.' He put his lips down

hard over hers. 'Have I ever told you you're a beautiful Sheila?'

'Lots of times. Now stop this. You'd better come out the back.' She took his hand and led him through to the storeroom. But she was in his arms again almost before she could breathe. 'Cal, not here.'

'Where then?'

'I've got to go over to Mum's. They'll wonder what's happened to me. And I still haven't finished feeding the patient.'

Cal frowned at her. 'Is he giving you trouble?'

Ethel shook her head in amusement. 'Frank couldn't pick a fight with a paper bag. I found him on the kitchen floor unable to get up.'

'I'll help you.'

Ethel pushed him away. 'No you won't. You'll stay right here. And wait for me.'

'Just one kiss to keep me sweet, eh?' He drew her against him and Ethel's resolve disappeared. Cal was the best kisser she'd ever known in her life. Not that she'd tasted many men's kisses other than Richard's. She'd had a few boyfriends when she'd left school, but it was always more of a grope and a hurried one at that. Lil had watched her like a hawk even then. And seeing as her two brothers had died young men, Ethel had accepted Lil's reasoning. She had one child left from three. She knew the pain her mum had gone through.

'I want you, Ethel, you know that, don't you?' Cal began to unbutton the top of her dress.

'We can't. Not here.'

'Why not? It's the perfect place.'

'Someone might come in – and what about Frank?'

'He can wait. He'll have to.' Cal slid the soft material from her shoulders. Ethel knew resisting was useless. Her insides were pulling together, as if they were calling out for him. Her breasts were on fire.

She fumbled for his belt and loosened it as he kissed her. Neither of them heard the shop bell tinkle until it was too late.

'Christ, who's that?' Cal demanded as in the midst of their fumbling a louder noise followed.

'They must be nicking something!' Ethel hissed, quickly pulling down her skirt. 'Stay here, I'll see to it.' Cal struggled with his clothing and then took a silent step to the storeroom door.

Chapter Thirty-Four

Lizzie was talking to Flo, but her attention was on Walter Miller. He was talking to Syd and Clifford across the room. She couldn't take her eyes off Walter's arm as it went up and down, conveying the glass of ale to his mouth. Below the cuff of his jacket he wore a wristwatch.

She'd seen the same watch many times over the years, its unmistakably large face splattered by potato dust, or carrot tops. A family heirloom that had never left Bill Flowers's possession. Not until he'd decided to give it to Frank.

'Lizzie, are you listening to me?' Flo shook her shoulder.

Lizzie nodded. 'Yes, course.' She knew Flo had been talking but her sister's words weren't registering.

'You weren't thinking about *him*, were you?' It was an accusation. Lizzie saw the annoyance sparkle in Flo's dark eyes. Flo had changed into a pretty pale blue dress that she was going to wear for her honeymoon, two nights up West, bed and breakfast.

'If you mean Frank, then no.'

'Well, what's your answer?'

Lizzie tried to wrench her eyes back to Flo but they kept straying over to the men. 'About what?'

'There, you see, you ain't been listening. I was asking what name you liked best. It's a toss-up between Kate after Ma if it's a girl. Or Lillian after the Missus.'

'I didn't know Lillian was the Missus's name.'

'Everyone will shorten it to Lil.'

'What if it's a boy?'

Flo smiled proudly. 'Nelson Sydney after Syd's grandad. I don't fancy Walter or Clifford, the other names put forward.'

'Flo, does Syd see much of Walter and Clifford these days?'

Flo looked puzzled as she stared at Lizzie. 'That's a funny question to ask now Syd works at the scrapyard.'

'They seem to be getting on well,' Lizzie said quickly. She couldn't bring herself to ask outright where Walter had got the watch. Or could she? The fact Walter had Bill's watch on his wrist could only mean one thing. He'd taken it from Frank. And Frank hadn't given it away. It had been stolen in the attack. Lizzie's stomach did a roll as she thought of the possibility that Walter and perhaps Clifford – even Syd, had been Frank's attackers.

'The Millers have been very good to us,' Flo said defensively. 'We haven't gone short of a penny. But I can see on your face you disapprove of them.'

'No, it's not that.'

'What is it then?' Flo's dark eyes narrowed.

Lizzie knew that it was pointless to voice her

suspicions. Flo would get upset if she thought Syd was being criticized. And Walter and Clifford were now his best buddies. Flo wouldn't hear a bad word about the Millers. They were her family now and had gone from sinners to saints in Flo's mind. But nothing could change the fact that the leather-strapped watch on Walter's wrist once belonged to Bill who had given it to Frank.

'Come on, you two.' Danny came to stand at Flo's side. 'Lil's not got the patience of a saint as we all know.'

Flo looked across at Syd. 'You'd better fetch me husband too.'

Lizzie wanted to tell Danny about the watch. But how could she with Flo listening?

Flo took Lizzie's arm. 'What was you going to say?'

'Only that your honeymoon dress looks lovely.'

Flo grinned. 'I can't wait for our first night up West. It will be funny to do it legit as Mr and Mrs.'

Lizzie smiled. 'No worrying about the neighbours now.' She glanced back to Syd and his brothers. The only person she could confront about the watch was Syd. But after their last meeting, their relationship had been strained. He'd blow his top if he thought she was accusing his brother of stealing.

All Ethel could see as she stepped into the shop was two figures rolling about in the wooden crates. Fruit and vegetables were flying everywhere. The man who Cal was throwing punches at was dressed in a fawn overcoat.

There were already stains over it where they had rolled in the spilled tomatoes and oranges.

Ethel jumped back as they fell towards her. The next thing she saw was a tangle of arms and legs bouncing against the glass cabinet. Lizzie's neat rows of toffee apples fell from their shelves. A splintering noise came from the glass but neither of the men stopped fighting. Punching and struggling, they landed on the sacks of King Edwards that Bert stood by the shop door.

Ethel wanted to help Cal somehow; the other man, who towered above him, lifted a wooden box and brought it down on Cal's shoulder.

'Leave him alone!' Ethel shrieked and ran forward, pounding the man with her fists. Without even glancing at her, he pushed her aside. The blow sent her reeling and she ended up on the floor.

Before she could get up, Cal landed a punch on the man's nose, then another. The man fell to his knees, groaning loudly.

Wiping the blood from his mouth, Cal hurried over to her. He lifted her up gently. 'Are you hurt, Ethel?'

'No.' She pushed her hair from her eyes. Her legs felt like buckling. 'Who is he?'

'I caught him with his fingers in the till.'

Ethel gave a little moan as she rubbed her sore head.

'You sure he didn't hurt you?' Cal asked again as he took her shoulders.

'N—' 'No,' she had been about to say, but over his shoulder she saw a frightening sight. The man had recovered and was back on his feet. His fleshy round face was full of anger and pain.

'What the—' Cal began as he turned round.

'Think you're a big man, eh?' demanded the thief as he levelled the gun at them. 'Well, let's see how big you are when I pull this trigger.'

Ethel screamed. She knew there was no escape.

Cal pulled her behind him as a shot rang out. And Ethel slid to the floor.

The mantel clock in Lil's front room said it was a quarter to five and there was no sign of Ethel. Lizzie was worried. Had Frank caused trouble somehow? Had he fallen and Ethel been unable to pick him up? But Cal would have helped her. What if Ethel and Cal had decided to do some romancing on the way home? Where would they have gone? Back to the garage?

Lizzie tried to think. But the noise was deafening, what with the singing, dancing and merrymaking, something the Millers were expert at. Flo's friends from work had already left, politely making their excuses. It was clear the Miller clan had every intention of celebrating late into the night. The empty plates were piled up in the kitchen. Meanwhile the Missus had sent Clifford to the pub off-sales for more beer. Lil and Doug had driven to the East India Dock Road to buy fish and chips for an army.

Just as Lizzie was wondering if she should slip out to look for Ethel, there was a tap on her shoulder.

'Where's Ethel and Cal got to?' Danny asked, raising his voice above the racket.

'Perhaps they've gone to the garage.'

'No. Don't reckon they would.'

Lizzie shrugged. 'Then they must be at the shop.'

Danny's face darkened. 'It's got to be Frank. What else could it be?'

Lizzie knew that she had to find Ethel. 'I'd better go over there.'

'I'll drive you,' Danny said abruptly. 'Where are the kids?'

'They were making a racket and Lil sent them up the park. I was going to fetch them before Flo and Syd left.'

Danny nodded. 'We'll tell Timothy and Rosie to do that.'

'But what will Lil think when she finds us gone?'

Danny shrugged. 'Bert can tell her we've gone to get Ethel.'

'Won't that sound suspicious?'

Danny just raised his eyebrows. 'Lil will be suspicious anyway.'

Chapter Thirty-Five

Lizzie knew something was wrong the minute Danny drove up to the shop. The blinds were all down. She'd left them up, with the notice on the door clearly stating they were closed for the Saturday. She'd given Ethel the key to get in, which she must have used, as the blinds were down. But why were they?

'Danny, something's wrong.'

Danny brought the car to a halt. 'Why's that?'

'I was in a rush this morning and left the blinds up.'

'Ethel must have pulled them.'

'Yes, but why?' They sat in silence as Danny switched off the engine. He'd put the hood over them as the evening was closing in. The wedding car smelled of polish and oil. Some of the confetti had stuck to the dashboard. Lizzie looked at the shop again. At this time on a Saturday she and Bert would be just beginning to bring in the boxes from outside.

'Well, we can't sit here all night.' Danny pushed open his door.

Lizzie did the same. As she stood on the pavement,

there were a few people around, a cyclist or two and some noisy kids screaming along the street. The afternoon din had subsided. The sound of the river tugs' hooters drifted over the roofs of the houses.

Lizzie followed Danny up to the shop door. He tried the handle. 'It's locked.'

'Ethel must have done that in case any customers tried to get in. Here, I've got a spare key in my bag.'

Danny tried again. 'No joy.'

'Perhaps Ethel's left the key in the lock.'

'Or the bolt has been pulled.' Danny banged on the door. 'Ethel, Cal, are you there?'

There was no response and Lizzie's stomach churned over.

This time Danny used his fists. Lizzie looked round to see if anyone had heard the racket. But the street was now deserted.

Just as Danny was about to bang the door again, the blind moved. Lizzie saw Cal's dark face and heard the bolt slide back.

'What's up?' Danny asked as they stepped in and Cal closed the door quickly.

The shop was in semi-darkness.

'We've got trouble. Big trouble.'

'Where's Ethel?' Lizzie's eyes fell on the glass cabinet. Or what remained of it. 'Oh no!' She put her hand to her mouth as she saw the glass, cakes, toffee apples and vegetables littering the floor. It reminded of her of that fateful day the year before when the bomb had gone off.

'Sorry about the mess, Lizzie,' Cal said gruffly.

'Cal, what's wrong with your arm?' Danny said in a startled voice, pointing to the rag. A red stain was showing through.

'I was lucky. It's just a scratch.'

'Did Frank do it?' Danny demanded.

'No, mate, no. Look, we can't talk here. Ethel's waiting upstairs. She's been hoping you'd come over.'

Lizzie didn't ask any more questions. She wanted to see Ethel. They all hurried upstairs, past Frank's room where the door was shut.

'Ethel? Oh Gawd, are you all right?' Lizzie stopped when she saw Ethel sitting bolt upright on the couch, visibly shaking. Her face was white as a sheet. Her make-up had vanished and her hair had fallen messily around her shoulders.

Ethel burst into tears. 'Oh Lizzie!'

Lizzie hurried to sit beside her. She took Ethel's cold hands and rubbed them. 'I . . . I'm so glad you're here,' Ethel spluttered.

'Here, use my hanky.'

'Thanks.'

'I said to Cal you'd look for me when I didn't get back. I was just worried Mum would want to come with you.'

'No, she's busy with the food. We slipped out on the quiet.'

'Thank God you did,' Ethel sobbed, wiping her eyes and blowing her nose. She pushed her hair from her wet face. 'It was awful. I can't believe what happened.'

'What *did* happen?' Danny turned to Cal.

'Let's all sit down,' Cal said, touching Ethel's shoulder gently. 'Take it easy, Ethel. Everything's gonna be all right now.'

She nodded, looking up at him. Lizzie had never seen her friend so upset before.

'This'll take a bit of explaining,' Cal said as he and Danny sat on the wooden dining chairs.

'Take your time,' Danny said as he looked in concern at his friend. 'But first, should I get you a doctor?'

'No, as I said it's just a surface wound.' Cal frowned at Lizzie. 'Someone came in the shop. Me and Ethel – well, we were in the storeroom. We heard this noise and I went to see what it was. I saw this big sod pinching from the till.'

'Stealing from *my* till?' Lizzie repeated on a gasp.

'They had a fight,' Ethel interrupted breathlessly. 'And that's when your cabinet got broken.'

'Don't worry about that.'

'Then suddenly he was pointing a gun.'

'What!' Lizzie exclaimed. 'A gun? Was it the same man as before?'

'Could be. But as I wasn't here that day, I ain't sure.

'Lizzie, I never understood how it really felt when you told me about those men,' Ethel continued, 'the ones who came in your shop to threaten you. Not until today. I thought we was going to die.' A tear rolled down her cheek. 'But Cal pulled me behind him and I heard the gun go off. I'm ashamed to say I passed out.'

'The bullet only grazed the skin of my arm,' Cal said,

glancing at Ethel. 'But when I heard the next shot, I thought, I won't be so lucky this time. Then, to my surprise I realized I wasn't looking down the barrel of the gun. Instead I was still in one piece and our visitor was stretched out on the floor.'

Ethel nodded, sniffing away her tears. 'When I came round there was the man on the floor just a few feet away. His eyes were wide open. He was dead. There was blood all over the boards and bits of' – she put her hands up to her face – 'his chest.'

'He was dead?' Lizzie asked and Cal nodded.

'As a doornail.'

'But who shot him?' Danny asked.

There was silence then Ethel and Cal said together, 'Frank.'

'Frank?' Lizzie repeated. 'But how could he?'

'Somehow he got himself down the stairs,' Cal explained. 'When I turned to look where the noise was coming from, there was Frank, holding a shooter as old as the hills.'

'My brother had a gun?' Danny asked in a shocked whisper.

Cal nodded uneasily. 'It was your dad's old service revolver.'

'How did he get hold of that?'

'He said Bill gave it to him. Just in case he met with any trouble.'

'I can't believe Dad would do such a daft thing.' Danny shook his head in disbelief.

'Frank heard me scream and managed to drag himself along the landing and down the stairs. He saved us,' Ethel declared. 'He really did.'

'So where did Frank keep this gun?' Lizzie demanded as her relief that Ethel and Cal had not been injured soon turned to anger. 'He knows I wouldn't entertain the idea of having one here.'

'Dunno. But he didn't even know it worked,' Ethel replied. 'He said he was just going to scare them off.'

'Instead he killed someone,' Danny said in a bitter voice.

'Like Ethel said, it was him or us,' Cal said with a shrug.

'So where is he, the dead man?' Lizzie asked.

'In the storeroom. I hid him and his gun under the crates and cleared up the mess in the shop.'

At this Ethel gave another choked sob. 'I – I left Cal to do it all. I – I couldn't bring meself to help.'

Cal lifted his shoulders again. 'I had to get him out of the way, before someone saw. I lowered the blinds after.'

'I've never seen a dead person before,' Ethel whispered, staring into space. 'I feel ashamed of meself for being so weak. But he . . . the dead man . . . all that blood—'

'Then we got Frank back upstairs,' Cal interrupted, glancing anxiously at Ethel. 'He was in a bit of a state. So we gave him one of his knock-out pills.'

'And you've never seen this bloke before?' Danny stood up and began to pace the room.

'Well, yes, I have mate.'

Danny frowned. 'But you said —'

'It didn't dawn on me who he was, until I got him in the storeroom,' Cal explained. 'He was one of the heavies Savage brought with him to the workshop. But he was wearing a hat then.'

Danny rubbed his chin. 'So the chances are Savage sent him to the shop, knowing Lizzie was closed for the day.'

'How would he know that?' Lizzie asked doubtfully.

'You've had a notice on the door saying you were closed on July the 1st.'

'Savage is moving in on us again,' Cal said darkly.

'He finds out the shop will be closed,' Danny suggested, 'sees his opportunity and sends his man to do damage. Break the place up. Just as a reminder to Lizzie that he's in the picture. He knows word will get back to me and so he kills two birds with one stone.'

'What do we do now?' Cal said in a tight voice.

'Get rid of the evidence,' Danny said without hesitation.

'What, get rid of a dead body?' Ethel gasped. 'But shouldn't we tell the police or something?'

They all stared back at her. Lizzie took her hand again. 'We can't do that, Ethel.'

'Why not?'

'The law won't believe your story.'

'Why wouldn't they?' There was panic in Ethel's voice. 'It's the truth.'

'It might be,' Danny said quietly. 'But you have to ask yourself one question. What's in it for Lily Law? Now, I've no time for me brother, but the coppers will fit him up – and perhaps you and Cal – for whatever is best for them.'

'But Frank was only defending us.'

'Or, their argument might be, Savage's man was shot deliberately in cold blood.'

'But it wasn't like that.'

'I know,' Lizzie agreed patiently. 'But an investigation is the last thing any of us want. How are you going to explain being here with Cal? Think of the consequences. Do you want an investigation into your private affairs? Richard and your mum will have to know. And the kids.'

Ethel looked desperately at Cal. 'I don't want that.'

'Neither do any of us,' Danny said heavily.

Ethel stared around at her friends. 'But how do we . . . do we . . . get rid of a dead body?'

'You don't need to know, Ethel,' Danny replied. 'All you have to do is go back to your mum's and say nothing about coming here today.'

Ethel put her hands to her cheeks. 'But I can't face Mum like this.'

'You'll have to. It's the only way.'

'But what will I tell her?'

'Think up a story. Like you was out walking and you didn't feel too good. So you sat down somewhere, until me and Lizzie found you on the park bench.'

'I did have a headache.'

Lizzie squeezed her friend's hand. 'She'll believe me if I tell her that you was in a right state over your row with Richard.'

Danny nodded. 'Take the car and drive Ethel back. I'll show you the gears.'

'But Flo and Syd will be expecting you to drive them up West.'

'Tell them I've gone to get something at the garage first. That will give me time to clean up here. Send Bert back here with the van. I'll need it tonight.'

'What for?' Lizzie asked, feeling her stomach drop.

'It's best that you and the kids stay at Lil's for the night.' Ethel stood up. 'I only hope I can keep me nerve.'

'You will.' Danny smiled. 'Let Lizzie do the talking.'

Ethel nodded. But Lizzie knew it wouldn't be easy looking Lil in the eye and telling her a concocted story. She always seemed to get the truth out of Ethel. But this time, Ethel was going to have to act convincingly.

Chapter Thirty-Six

'Gawd, girl, where have you been all day?' Lil demanded as Lizzie and Ethel walked in the back door. The kitchen was smothered in dirty crocks. 'I'm up to me armpits in washing-up.'

'Sorry, Mum.'

'I should think so. I was relying on you to help me. Them Millers have eaten more grub than a plague of locusts.'

'Lil, we'll help you now.' Lizzie took off her jacket. 'Better late than never.'

'And to make matters worse,' Lil persisted, glaring at Ethel, 'some tone-deaf ape's been hammering the life out of the piano. Sounds as if he used his feet, not his fingers. If only you'd been here, you could have played us a decent tune. After all, what was the point of me and your dad forking out on all them expensive piano lessons if you never make use of them?'

Ethel gave a smothered groan. 'I said I was sorry, Mum.'

'It wasn't Ethel's fault. She didn't feel well, Lil,' Lizzie broke in, repeating the story that Danny had suggested.

But as she was talking Ethel reached out to hold on to a chair, her face draining of colour.

'Christ, you do look rough, my girl,' Lil said, her tone changing as she dropped the mop and hurried to her daughter's side.

Ethel took one look at her mother and burst into tears.

'What's the matter, love? What is it?'

'I don't know,' Ethel said through her sobs.

'Do you feel sick?'

'A bit.'

'You have been a moody cow lately.'

Ethel put her hands over her face.

'You ain't pregnant, are you?'

'I think she could do with a rest,' Lizzie said before Ethel could answer. 'Can she go up to the boys' room?'

'Course. Here, love, lean on me. We'll have to push our way through the mob. They're as drunk as lords, most of 'em.'

Lizzie took one of Ethel's arms and Lil the other. Lizzie felt Ethel's weight growing heavier. What if she was to faint again? Or ramble on about what happened at the shop?

But somehow they managed to steer her through the party-goers, who, as Lil remarked, had sunk enough booze to sink a battleship. Upstairs, Lil opened the door to Ethel's old room. Lizzie saw the big double bed that had been Ethel's for donkey's years.

'You poor cow,' Lil said as she helped Ethel undress down to her slip.

'I just need forty winks. Me headache might go then.'

'Do you want an aspirin?'

'I'll see what I feel like later.'

'Your dad's over at Flo's, clearing up the fish-and-chips papers,' Lil told Ethel as she drew the curtains. 'He'll pop his head round the door later and bring you a cuppa.'

Ethel buried her face in the pillow. 'Thanks.'

Lizzie squeezed Ethel's arm. 'See you a bit later.'

The din was even louder when Lil and Lizzie went downstairs. Lil had to shout above the noise as she stood at the sink. 'What's up with my girl?' she yelled at Lizzie. 'You know, don't you?'

'She had a tiff with Richard,' Lizzie explained over the singing and yelling. 'As you know, the upset gave her a headache.' Lizzie began to dry the wet china. 'She just wanted a bit of peace and quiet to sort out her thoughts.'

'She'd tell you if she was pregnant.'

'Well, she hasn't.'

'Is that why she and her drip of a husband had a row?' Lil continued as if she hadn't heard. 'Don't he want another kid?'

Lizzie just shrugged as she put away the plates.

'Another baby after fifteen years!' Lil said almost to herself. 'Christ, no wonder they was at each other's throats. Richard won't want the expense of another kid. He's a mean sod, I'm sorry to say, even if he is my son-in-law.'

Lizzie realized Lil had talked herself into the fact that her daughter was expecting. She had even forgotten to

ask about Danny and when he'd be back for Flo and Syd.
Well, who was she to contradict Lil at this moment ? The
suspicion that Ethel was having a baby was engaging all
Lil's attention. And for the moment, her wrong assump-
tion would serve a useful purpose.

As Lil swished the water around the sink, a line of
drunken dancers came falling into the kitchen. The men
and women were trying to hold on to each other's waists
and kick their legs in the right direction. But the conga
was more like a free-for-all, and the chairs, table and
crockery on top of it almost went over.

'Clear out, the lot of you!' Lil shrieked. 'Look at what
you've done.'

But no one took any notice. They were all laughing
and singing too loudly to pay any attention to Lil.

Just then a cheer went up and a man wearing someone's knickers on his head stumbled into the kitchen. He
shouted above the others, 'Got a cloth 'andy? Cyril's
brought up his dinner on the carpet.'

Lil's eyes flashed wide in horror. 'You Millers are dirty
bastards, the lot of you. Out you go in the street and take
your mess with you.'

But again no one took any notice. The laughter and
jeers followed Lil as she grabbed a rag and elbowed them
all out of her way.

Danny looked down at his brother who had woken with a
start as he walked into the room. He felt a moment's pity
for the slumbering figure, then pulled himself together.

Frank had got them into a whole lot of bother, no surprises there. But Danny had to admit that the day could have ended tragically, but for Frank's intervention.

'What's going on?' Frank mumbled as he tried to sit up. 'Who's there?'

'It's me.' Danny pulled a chair up to the bed. He looked hard at the man who lay slumped against the pillows. Frank was a mess. Unshaven and bleary-eyed, he could have been suffering a hangover from hell.

'Give me them, will you?' He didn't acknowledge Danny, but pointed a shaking finger to the bottles on the bedside cabinet.

'What are they?' Danny took a bottle and opened it. He tapped a brown tablet into the palm of his hand.

'They're for the pain. Me back's killing me.' Frank tipped back his head and without water, swallowed the pill.

'Talking of killing, thanks to you, we've got one of Savage's men enjoying a permanent rest in the storeroom.'

Frank's head fell against the pillow. 'It was a lucky shot, that's all.'

'Right through the heart. A bull's-eye.'

'Yeah, but look at me hands. I can't keep 'em still.' He held them out and Danny saw they were shaking. Was he putting it on?

The suspicion was there in Danny's mind, as it always was with Frank. 'Where's Dad's gun?' he asked, looking around.

Frank turned his head. 'In the drawer.'

'Why did Dad give it to you?'

'Just in case, that's all.'

'Just in case you wanted to kill someone?'

Frank groaned loudly. 'Course not. But you don't know what it feels like to be a sitting duck. How can I protect meself?'

'From your many enemies, you mean,' Danny said scornfully.

'Someone did this to me.'

Danny frowned. 'So you knew Dad's piece would fire?'

'No. Well, yes,' Frank hesitated, 'but Dad said it hadn't been used since he come home. It was just to scare someone off.'

'But you pulled the trigger anyway.'

'Christ, Danny. The bloke downstairs was aiming for Ethel and your mate.' Frank turned his head. 'Give us another one of them pills, will you?'

Danny picked up the bottle. Frank swallowed a pill noisily. Then letting himself sink back he said in a hoarse whisper, 'What're we going to do?'

'*We*?' Danny repeated, lifting his eyebrows. 'As usual, it will be me sorting things out.'

'Thanks, Danny.'

'I ain't doing it for you, as you well know.'

Frank was silent as he lay there.

'I'm going to clear up the shop. Then you'll be on your tod for a while.'

'You're gonna leave me?' Frank looked alarmed and tried to sit up. He fell back, fear in his eyes.

'Just stay where you are and keep out of trouble.' Danny stood up and opened the drawer. 'So this is it.' He stared down at the ancient hand gun. It was a wonder it fired at all. The mechanism looked rusty and the handle was broken. 'I'll take this and dump it.'

'No!' Frank objected as the sweat poured from his face. 'It's all I've got to defend myself with.'

'What if the cops find it? Your name's on the collar when the body turns up and they dig the bullet out of his head.'

'But what if someone tries to get to me? Like the bastards who did this.'

Danny shrugged. 'You'll have to throw your pills at them.'

'Strewth, Danny, have a heart.'

'Yeah, like you did on that day you and Vinnie paid me a visit?' Danny hurled at his brother. 'You did to me what someone'd done to you. What were you after, Frank? To get rid of me once and for all?'

Frank's head slumped back on the pillow. 'I was off me rocker.'

Danny pushed the gun into the waistband of his trousers. Many questions flew through his mind. Not the least of them, why was he helping a man who had tried to kill him? Yes, Frank had prevented Ethel and Cal from being wounded, if not killed. But in Danny's opinion, this wasn't heroism. Rather a case of self-preservation. Frank feared his enemies. And he had reason to, after the years of working as Ferreter's bookie.

Yet this was his brother. No longer the hard man but sick and sorry for himself. The pitiful sight, Danny reflected, should have given him satisfaction. Instead, all he felt was empty.

As the old saying went, Danny was beginning to believe – against the grain – that blood was thicker than water. Even in Frank's case.

Chapter Thirty-Seven

It was well after midnight and the clearing up was finally done. Lizzie was exhausted. Lil had insisted they go into Flo's and sweep the decks clean. Any amount of breakages had yet to be calculated; Lil had threatened to send a list to the Missus and demand replacements.

'I reckon the tea leaves among them have nicked me best cutlery,' Lil was complaining to Doug, as she took a long drag of her cigarette. 'I've six spoons here me mum gave us when we got married. Where are the matching four?'

'We'll find them in the morning, love.' Doug was flaked out in the armchair. 'I need me beauty sleep.'

'Have you looked in on Rosie and Timothy next door?'

'Yes, they're happy to have a bit of space to themselves.'

'I suppose their gran ain't good enough for them now they're getting older. Did you see Timothy with that Miller girl today?'

Doug waved his hand. 'They're growing up fast, love. We'll have to get used to that.'

'All right, all right,' Lil said airily.

'Well, we all think of them as kids.' Doug raised his shoulders on a shrug. 'And anyway, Polly and Tom were happy enough to sleep in the boys' room. I reckon we're all well sorted.'

'God knows how Ethel got a wink with the racket,' Lil persisted; as usual, having the last word.

Doug yawned loudly. 'I'll be asleep before my head hits the pillow.' He gave Lizzie a weary grin. 'You sure you'll be all right sharing with Ethel?'

'Like you, Doug, I'm all in. I could sleep on bare boards if it came to it.'

'You'll never have to do that in this house,' Lil interrupted sharply. 'Now off you go, Doug. I want a word with Lizzie.'

Lizzie's heart sank.

Doug nodded. 'Night, everyone, then. Don't stay up too late.'

When Doug had gone, Lizzie quickly took off her apron, but it was clear Lil wasn't about to let her go. 'Might pour meself a nightcap. Me guts were going over today and need settling. Do you fancy a sherry?'

'No thanks. Is there anything else needs doing?'

Lil took the sherry bottle from the sideboard. 'No. But there is one thing you can do for me.'

'What's that?'

'Ask Ethel about the baby. She'll tell you. I know she will.' Lil sighed tiredly. 'I ain't being nosy, but drawing any information out of Ethel lately is like pulling a tooth. If she's having a kid, I'd like to know about it.' She paused, wrinkling her brow under the turban she'd tied round her head to perform the cleaning. 'You see, if she's worried, I'd like her to talk it over with me, if you see what I mean? I wouldn't like her to do anything silly.'

'What do you mean . . . silly?' Lizzie asked in alarm.

'Well, you know. Get rid of it.'

'Ethel wouldn't do that.'

'But she rowed with Richard, didn't she?' Lil pointed out. 'She might have sprung the news of the baby on him and he didn't want it. You know what Richard is like about money. He would have taken into account there'd be another mouth to feed.'

'Lil, that's jumping to a big conclusion.'

Lil tapped the side of her nose. 'Call it a mum's intuition. Now, off you go, ducks. And thank you for all your help today. I don't know what I'd have done without you.'

Lizzie felt very guilty. She had let Lil believe that Ethel was pregnant and all sorts was going through Lil's mind.

Lil laughed and coughed at the same time as she poured herself a generous measure of sherry. Lizzie wanted to reassure Lil that her worries about Ethel were unfounded. But she was too tired to make the effort.

'Night, Lil,' she said and leaned forward to kiss her on the cheek. 'Thanks for putting us up.'

'It's nice to have your company, love.'

Lizzie left to the sound of a match striking and Lil's indrawn breath as she savoured a cigarette.

Lizzie made her way quietly upstairs. Inside the boys'

room it was hot and stuffy. There was a faint whiff of mothball as Lizzie tiptoed over to the single beds. Tom and Polly didn't stir.

Lizzie knew this room was Lil's favourite and she liked to put company here when they stayed. When her sons Greg and Neil had been killed in the war Lil had kept the room as it was for many months afterwards. Their clothes had stayed in the wardrobe and the heavy green eiderdowns the boys had used had remained in place. All their books and toy soldiers on the shelves hadn't been moved an inch. Lil dusted in there every day until Doug had begun to worry about his wife's refusal to let her sons' memory go.

Lizzie thought of Lil in 1918 as the war had drawn to a close. This house had been a very different place then; dark and gloomy and like a shrine. Although Lizzie had only been twelve she remembered the depression Lil had sunk into. It was thanks to her own mother, Kate Allen, that Lil had finally pulled through. Doug had been at his wits' end and grieving for their sons too. So it was down to Kate to help her best friend through the worst time of Lil's life. Lizzie recalled her mum gradually persuading Lil into packing Neil and Greg's things away. After that, Lil's depression had lifted. She had got on with her life again; her grandchildren soon filled the empty space her sons had left.

Lizzie sighed softly at the memories. She kissed Polly's cheek, then Tom's and left quietly, closing the door behind her. In the next room Ethel was curled up in bed.

Lizzie undressed in the darkness, leaving on her slip. She folded her dress and jacket over the chair.

Lizzie slipped into bed beside Ethel. She waited for sleep to come. But her thoughts churned in her head. Memories came back of childhood; of Vinnie and Bert, and Flo and Babs. They had been a happy family before the war. Bert and Vinnie at ten and eleven had been true boys, always in mischief. But Pa had kept them in line. That was, until he'd left his family to fight for King and Country. It was then Vinnie's mischief had turned to crime. He'd found it was easy to make money as a bookie's runner. If only Pa hadn't gone away.

Lizzie turned over but her thoughts rambled on. Had Syd and his brothers stolen Frank's watch? Could it be Syd and his brothers? Had they tried to kill Frank? And the shop – why had she let Ethel go back to check on Frank? She should have been the one to face Savage's man.

Lizzie shivered. What were Danny and Bert doing now? Would the police find out? Could Ethel keep their secret? Lizzie closed her eyes tightly. But another man floated into her thoughts. This time it was Duncan King, the corpse who Danny had identified as Frank.

'You awake, Lizzie?'

'Yes.'

'I keep drifting off, then waking up with a start. Did all that happen at the shop?'

'Yes, I'm afraid so.'

'I was hoping it was a bad dream. There ain't a breath of air in this room either.'

Lizzie nodded. 'Let's go downstairs.'

Quietly they climbed out of bed. Lizzie put her jacket round her as Ethel went to the window and stared into the night. 'I can't believe it all happened, Lizzie.'

'Neither can I.'

'Was he really dead?'

'I'm afraid so.'

Ethel shivered. 'I've still got this headache.'

'No wonder after all that's happened.'

On tiptoe they left the room.

Ethel stirred her tea, feeling better now. She was sitting with Lizzie at the kitchen table. They were talking in whispers as the pale light of dawn crept through the window. Ethel was ashamed of herself. She had let everyone down. 'My life must have been very boring,' she admitted, fiddling with the handkerchief in her hands. 'Nothing like that has ever happened to me before.'

'That's why I refuse to have a weapon in the shop,' Lizzie said quietly. 'The trigger is pulled and in a split second someone's life can end.'

'Like that man's, whoever he is – was.'

'Yes, after all, he'll have someone who cares about him too, whatever he did.'

Ethel nodded, her fingers clasping together anxiously. 'They're right when they say at the point of death your life flashes before your eyes.'

Lizzie frowned. 'Did that happen to you?'

'It was like going to the cinema. I saw my past go over

the screen, but it took only a few seconds. Mostly I saw the kids when they were born and then growing up through all the ups and downs.' Ethel paused, her eyes growing misty. 'I saw Richard and me on our wedding day. And our first night together.' She smiled wistfully. 'We was just two kids finding out about the world. Perhaps all the years we've been together do count for something after all.'

'I'm sure Richard loves you in his own way.'

'Do you think so?' Ethel said hesitantly. 'He was my first love, though apparently not my last. But what is love anyway? Am I getting it mixed up with lust? It wasn't Cal I thought of. It was my husband.' A tear slithered down her cheek. 'What's happening to me, Lizzie?'

'You've had a big shock.'

Ethel wiped her eyes. 'Why am I thinking about Richard when he couldn't even be bothered to come to Flo's wedding reception with us?' She shook her head in confusion. 'Is it possible to love two men at the same time?'

Lizzie smiled. 'You're asking the wrong person.'

'But you're still with Frank. Yet I know you love Danny.'

'As I said, I'm not the one to give advice.'

Neither spoke for a moment and Ethel lifted the teapot and poured yet another lukewarm cup of tea.

Lizzie sighed. 'I felt a bit guilty last night.'

'Why's that?'

'Your mum's convinced the reason you and Richard

argued was because you're expecting. I didn't stop her from thinking that.'

'You couldn't have. Mum's got a mind of her own. She's sussed me and Cal and won't stop till she finds out the truth.'

'Ethel, what are you going to do?' Lizzie asked.

'I don't know. I really don't. It's like I'm on this train and it's time for me to get off at the next stop. But when the train pulls up at the station I still find myself sitting in my seat, gazing out at the platform.' Ethel thought about the fear she had of being left alone. 'The kids are growing up so quick. Timothy is already hinting about leaving home and finding digs with his mate.'

Ethel thought she'd known what she wanted; the love-making, the passion, the adventure, the feeling of being desired that her affair with Cal provided. She'd thought she'd known right up until yesterday in Lizzie's shop. And in that moment, everything changed. She didn't know *how* it had changed. But it had. She took a long sip of her cold tea. 'You know, I'd liked to have opened that shop with you.'

'We still can, if you want.'

'I don't know about that.'

Lizzie gave a long sigh and nodded. 'I'm sorry. I just meant that if—'

'Lizzie, I'm having a baby.' Ethel looked down at her flat stomach.

'What?'

'I haven't had me monthlies.'

'Are you regular these days?'

'Yes, on the dot.'

Lizzie's green eyes widened. 'Ethel, your mum was right.'

'Yes, funny, ain't it?'

'I didn't give it a thought.'

'Well, why should you? I was surprised myself. After all, me and Richard don't often – you know.'

'Oh Ethel.' Lizzie reached across and grabbed her hand. 'I'm so sorry you had to go through all that at the shop. It was my fault you went there. You might have lost the baby.'

Ethel found herself laughing. 'I might have lost a bloody sight more.'

'Don't joke about that.'

'And before you ask, if I am up the spout, I won't know who the father is.'

Lizzie's mouth fell open. 'You're joking.'

Ethel shook her head. This was her, Ethel Ryde, speaking. She could hardly believe it. This from the woman who until a few months ago had never so much as looked at another man even though Richard never seemed to want her. She'd almost forgotten what it felt like to have a man's arms around her. Then, for no reason she could think of, about two months ago Richard had tried to make love to her. But his clumsy attempts to satisfy himself had ended in disappointment. Needless to say, his ego had been hurt when she hadn't hidden the truth. She knew how important it was for a man to believe he was good in bed. She would have let him continue in blissful ignorance if only he'd considered her too.

The hysterical laughter soon caught in her throat and along with the hot, bittersweet tears she babbled, 'What if it looks like Cal? He's as dark as Richard is fair.' There was a catch in her voice.

Lizzie took a sharp breath. 'You won't know – no one will know – until when?'

'About seven months' time.'

'February,' whispered Lizzie and they stared at each other.

'So do I go on seeing Cal or not?'

'Only you can answer that.'

'If the baby is Richard's, I don't think Cal would forgive me.'

Lizzie was puzzled. 'What do you mean?'

Ethel felt herself blushing. 'I told Cal that Richard and me don't have relations. And it's almost true. But for that one occasion.'

'So why won't Cal accept that? Richard is your husband after all.'

'Cal is a jealous man. And that was what attracted me. I'd never known what it felt like to have someone want me so much.'

They were both silent, looking at each other, until Ethel began to chuckle. Then the laughter erupted and Ethel had to put her hanky over her mouth in order to stop herself from waking the whole household.

'It ain't funny,' Lizzie said, red in the face and wiping the tears of laughter away.

'No. It's not.'

'Then why are we laughing?'

'Because it don't seem like me talking. It seems like someone else.'

'Yes,' Lizzie agreed ruefully. 'Where has my friend gone?'

'Search me.' Ethel blew her nose and pushed away her cup of cold tea. She was a stranger to herself these days.

Chapter Thirty-Eight

Danny pulled the van up slowly to the wharf's edge and killed the engine. He lowered the window and inhaled cautiously. In blew the rawness of Limehouse. The tang of salt on the running tide. The sourness of fish long past its catch. A fragrance of Oriental cooking, not unpleasant in itself, but mixed with the mud and the sewage it hit the bottom of his stomach with a punch.

Opening the door quietly he climbed out. As usual, close to the river, and even in July, a silvery grey mist floated over the mossy stones, growing thicker by the second, until it disappeared and suddenly there was a glimpse of the dark skeletons of cranes and derricks, poking their necks into the night sky.

Where was Bert, he wondered? Had he managed to find the small rowing boat that was kept tied up on the mudflats near the dock walls? Their plan was for Bert to row the boat down to Limehouse. But the wind had sprung up and Danny knew their plans could falter on this alone. The little craft was used by anyone caring to reach the other side of the river. And responsible enough to row it back. He'd never had need of it personally. But it was always there, glued to the muck on which it rested, and from time to time maintained by the water men of the island.

Danny walked to the edge of the mossy stones. He was careful to stop when he heard the water. A whispering breeze could turn easily into a roaring wind in a matter of minutes. His imagination ran ahead of him. Of Bert desperately trying to row against the tide, or even with it. He'd keep to the lights of the shore, but there were few around here. A black void to peer into, the water whipping up and testing with the boat's buoyancy.

And yet, Bert could skull. He'd grown up on the river, played in its mud and swum in its murky depths. He was strong and powerful. And if he could keep his head, he would see the narrow jetty, their landmark, and the appointed place to tie up.

Danny scanned the shadows of the waterside, searching for the sight of the rotting pier. The mist and fog were playing tricks on his eyes. On the one hand, when the muck lifted, he could at least see who might be prowling about in this remote corner. On the other, the breeze shifted things and caused him to start; a can rolling across the cobbles, discarded newspaper billowing eerily over the stones, the rattle of the wind in the rigging of some hidden craft.

Danny took another breath, this time without flinching at the potency. His attention was now fully on the river. He waited expectantly for the sound of oars stroking the water's surface. It was many years since he'd passed this way. And then, it had been in daylight, on the horse and cart as he'd ventured through to the Commercial Road. Limehouse had been part of legend. As a boy he'd listen wide-eyed to the tales of its mystery handed down by his elders. The opium dens and the pukka-poo parlours, the smoking, gambling and drug taking. A subterranean world into which lowly mariners and aristocratic lords alike had been lured.

'Bert, where are you?' Danny whispered into the night, sticking his hands in his pockets and walking a few feet. The mists swirled in folds at his ankles.

In reply, a hooter sounded, and the jangle of a horse's harness somewhere in the distance. Danny stopped still, attuning his hearing to the closer noises. His eyes closed and opened briefly as the swirling yellow cloud in front of him cleared almost instantly. To his utter relief he saw the long outline of the jetty. And something – was it human – bobbing beside it. A head, or perhaps arms, or both?

As the water lapped at his feet, Danny followed the moving outline. At a snail's pace it went, tall and lumbering.

Danny hurried now, making his way with confidence to the rough mud that surrounded the rotting pins of the small pier.

A figure lowered itself into the darkness. Holding his breath Danny went to greet it.

'You been waiting long?' Bert whispered, panting as he

emerged from the shadows. The squelching of his boots in the mud brought up the stink beneath his soles.

'No. Did it go all right?'

'Yeah. I tied the boat up to the jetty as close to the shore as I could.'

'Did you bring the guns?'

'Yeah. I've put 'em in a sack and weighted it down with stones.'

Danny nodded his approval. 'Let's hope the law is otherwise occupied tonight.'

'I'll eat me titfer if we see a rozzer down this way after dark,' Bert assured him. 'Or before it, come to that.'

Danny hoped that was true. Limehouse was, and always had been, a law unto itself. A maze of cheap lodging houses, drug dens and brothels. The Chinese were kings in this long-forgotten area of the East End. From the Tower and Wapping to Limehouse, these slums bred their own variety of criminal. Ripe for smuggling on the water, this stretch of river had always been the Orientals' territory. It would be a brave copper who landed in amongst them.

Danny glanced at Bert, who for a big man moved with agility along the rotting timbers of the jetty. This was the end of the earth, a fitting tomb for evil, Danny thought. But nevertheless felt a moment's pity for the corpse they were about to sink into the river's bowels.

'We'd better get on with it,' he murmured. And together they hauled themselves through the mud and mist, back to the van. Here on land, a cloying air enfolded them. With it came a great wash of sulphur from the coal yards downriver and the stench from ancient drains.

'Blimey, what a corker,' groaned Bert. 'The stink of the dead.'

'Goes with the night,' Danny muttered, eager now to finish the job. They opened the back doors and reached in. Bert pulled out the legs and Danny the shoulders. They had stripped the body of any identification and it was now stiffening with the rigor. They trod carefully, glancing this way and that. Danny heard the water beckoning, the swirling and sucking of the fast-flowing eddies that were whipped by the breeze.

'I'll go first.' Danny stepped into the mud. 'If we strike trouble with the timbers, just let him go and save yourself.'

Bert nodded in the darkness. 'I'll shout if I see an 'ole.'

The murk lifted momentarily a few feet. Danny stepped gingerly onto the pier. The planks creaked and the river lapped at his boots. He took two, then three steps up and tested the way onwards. Bert followed with painful slowness as they crept their way forward.

Then the fog came down again. The rough woollen sweater Danny was wearing clung to his arms. Sweat peeled away from his body and loosened his grip so that he was forced to stop and adjust his hold. Bert did the same. They were puffing and panting by the time they had gone ten yards.

Then the jetty lurched, and they swung sideways. Bert cursed loudly. Danny's footing loosened and he felt his stomach dip. The rotten timbers cracked loudly. Somewhere the structure had broken.

'Gawd, what's that?' Bert demanded as they stood, listening and tense.

'The jetty's given, but where? Can you see?'

'Not a damn thing.'

'Was it behind us or in front?' Danny craned his neck round. But there was no way of knowing. The water was black when the fog lifted, and invisible when covered. A few feet either way and the current was treacherous.

'He's bleeding heavy,' Bert complained. 'We could chuck him in now.'

But Danny knew they must keep to their plan. Their fortune lay with the tide and the flow of the undercurrents mid-stream. They would sweep any living or dead thing into the estuary. And perhaps, with luck, out to sea. He thought fleetingly of Duncan King, bloated, misshapen and disfigured. Mercifully for them all, he hoped the efforts they made tonight would take the remains to a watery grave too far out to return.

'We'll go on as we said,' Danny decided. And with that he moved cautiously, one backward step at a time. He could hear Bert's laboured breathing. And his own. But they continued until the little pier swayed again. A crack here, a creak there. But finally they heard the insistent waves and felt spray on their faces. The wind was at its strongest here and all effluent blown away. There was the smell of rain in the air.

Suddenly heavy drops lashed against them. 'Sod it,' cursed Bert as they paused. 'Rain is all we need.'

'Yes, but it's driven away the fog. We'll make good time into the middle of the river.' Danny saw they were balanced perilously on the last boards. The rope attached to the boat trailed downwards and the tiny craft bobbed at the pier legs, high now as the tide rushed in.

The jetty gave one last rattle and Danny shouted to Bert.

'You go first. He's next.'

There were no rails here, nothing to steady a man. Danny saw Bert reach out. For a moment Bert looked as though he was about to topple forward, but he grasped the slats and slipped with ease into the boat.

Danny pushed the legs over. They dangled stiffly. He saw Bert take the weight and pull, trying to balance himself as he did so.

Fear rose in Danny. The body stretched and swayed. Danny tightened his arms under the lifeless armpits.

The wind took them then and he knew there was no return. 'Now!' he shouted and thrust forward, releasing his grip. Suddenly the weight slithered from his arms. There was a soft thump below and the crunch of wood against wood.

'Have you got him?' he yelled to Bert as he went down on all fours. Sticking out a leg, he tried to find his footing on the slippery stakes of the jetty.

'Yeah, he's in.'

Danny sighed with relief but in the next moment felt

his boot slip. He tried to break his fall, but with a dreadful certainty knew that unless he was lucky his leg was still in mid-air. Unable to stop his momentum, he braced himself for the fall. His hands reached out, clawing at the soaked, slimy struts. But he could find no purchase at all. And before he could cry out, the water was gulping him up; freezing-cold water, even in July. The shock made him gasp and he tasted the river, his arms flailing in the space between the boat and the jetty.

'Christ, Danny, where are you?' he heard Bert yell frantically. But he was too busy swallowing the stinking water to reply. Worse, his boots were filling up and he was being dragged down. There was nothing to hold on to. He'd lost his bearings. He tried to strike out. He was a good swimmer. He'd swum the river to Greenwich many times as a boy. Just for a dare. And he'd survived, though many who'd tried had failed. But now, the inky depths were hauling him downwards. Into the same grave for which the body on the boat was intended.

But it was him that was drowning, not the corpse. Danny cried out in terror. A terror he'd never known before. His panic worsened his plight. His lungs were filling with the flotsam; the putrid waste of the river. He lashed out, reaching for the jetty, but it was gone. He heard Bert calling. But now his voice seemed a long way away.

Where was the river washing him? But the answer to that filled him with dread. In his heavy clothes and boots, it was not out to mid-stream. But under to the bottom.

Another deep gulp of the water and he choked, coughing up debris. He fought hard to resist the pull, just keeping his head above the surface. But it was only for seconds. Then he was pulled down again.

His strength was fading, his arms and legs exhausted from the fight. His chest felt like a leaden weight. The cold ate into him, freezing him from the inside. He was going down, sucked into the belly of the river.

Then, as he took one last gasp of air, his hand hit something. The blow was agony. But in that moment, his mind cleared. Hope replaced despair. He'd found an object to touch, perhaps large enough to hold on to. If he acted quickly, he might find it again. He swam in what he thought was the same direction as the lifeline. But the darkness was deceiving. Was it this way or that? With his last reserves of energy, he struck wildly towards the lights on the shore. A few seconds later, his heart gave a leap. He touched the object once more. Large and splintery, it must be wood, new wood, he thought elatedly. With a final burst of energy, he grabbed it.

'Danny, Danny, where are you?'

'Here! Here!' Danny yelled, his arms now stretched across the raft.

'Where? It's too pitch to see.'

'This way. Follow my voice.'

But the sloshing of the oars and Bert's cries slowly faded. Danny knew Bert was rowing in the opposite direction. He clung to his newly found buoy, grateful for the sharp edges and sweet-smelling timber that roused him back into hope. Beneath him, his boots were full, his trousers like lead weights. But he dared not try to remove them for fear of losing his grip.

The rain began again, softly at first, but then hard enough to rattle on the water. His eyes smarted painfully and the hand he had injured was numb. Even though he was float-ing now, Danny knew his chances of survival were limited. The cold was penetrating his skin. The waves beginning to toss him and the wood into a faster-flowing current. He would arrive in mid-stream very soon.

There was tiredness too. A slow, but insistent lethargy. His mind and body were paralysed. This, not the water, was the real killer. Giving up to the exhaustion, slipping slowly away into unconsciousness.

He tried to yell out for Bert again. But he realized his voice wasn't carrying. It wasn't flying across the surface, but was lost in a mixture of chokes and gasps. He rested his head on the raft's surface, lured by the relief it gave him. If he let go just a little, relaxed his arms . . . the water crept up to his neck, lapped at his chin and gradu-ally entered his mouth.

The next thing Danny knew he was being pulled up fiercely by his collar and out of his slumber. When he found himself fully awake, he was shivering uncontrolla-bly, his teeth were chattering like skittles. But he was no longer in the water.

'Honest to God, Danny, I thought you was a goner.' Bert was slapping his cheeks. In the darkness Danny groaned, then coughed. 'Over you go, mate.' Bert propelled him onto his stomach and landed him a blow between his ribs. 'You've drunk half the Thames, by the sounds of it.'

Danny nodded, spewing up the poisons. 'Thanks,' he mumbled, coughing and spitting again.

'What happened?'

'I . . . missed my footing on the jetty.'

'And you was warning me to be careful!' Bert roared with laughter.

Danny nodded as his body came back to life. But the cold was setting in as the rain continued. He eased himself up onto the wooden seat. He blinked his eyes at the dead man wedged in the boat, startled by the grin of death stretched over his teeth.

Chapter Thirty-Nine

'Can Tom come home with us, Auntie Lizzie?' Polly gulped the last of her doorstep of bread liberally spread with jam. 'Me mates will be out playing.'

Lizzie cleared the breakfast plates from Lil's kitchen table. 'I don't see why not. Would you like that, Tom?'

Tom jumped up, a big grin on his face. 'Are we going in the wedding car?'

'Yes. I expect so.'

'I ain't never seen a lady drive a posh car like that.' He rubbed his freckled nose. 'I bet I could drive it for you.'

Lizzie laughed. 'Yes, but we'd better ask your dad first.'

Just then, Lil walked into the kitchen. 'Blimey, you lot are early birds.'

'We was hungry,' said Polly, as Lil picked up her packet of cigarettes.

'What, after all you scoffed yesterday? If it was up to me I'd starve you for a week.'

They all laughed and Lizzie handed Lil a mug of tea.

'You ain't going, are you?' Lil said, adjusting her floral turban. 'We've got all day yet.'

'I thought we'd get an early start,' Lizzie said, hoping Lil wouldn't take offence. 'That is, if there's nothing I can help you with here.'

'Please yourself.' Lil shrugged. 'Is that daughter of mine still asleep?'

'Yes, so are Timothy and Rosie next door.'

'What happened to Danny last night?'

It was a question Lizzie had been fearing. 'He must have gone back to the garage to finish some work.'

'He works late on Saturdays,' Tom said before Lizzie could answer. Grateful that Tom had spoken up, Lizzie quickly cleared away the dishes.

'I was hoping you'd all stay to dinner,' Lil said, as with a cigarette dangling from her lips she attempted to push a metal curler back into place. 'I've got a nice piece of beef in the larder.'

'You must have had your fill of visitors,' Lizzie replied casually. 'And me and Bert have to get the shop ready for Monday.'

'Talking of which, where did Bert disappear to yesterday?' Lil asked, unwilling to let the subject drop.

'He'd had a few too many.'

'That's not like Bert.'

'No, but it was a special occasion and he let his hair down.'

Lil turned to the two children. 'Go and play in the yard, my loves, till Auntie Lizzie is ready to leave.' Lil watched Polly and Tom bolt out into the fresh air, then, wrapping her dressing gown over her bare knees, she sat down. 'Well, did you ask?'

Lizzie dried her hands on the cloth. 'Ask what?' She knew Lil wanted to know about the baby.

'Is the girl expecting?'

Lizzie shrugged. 'Ethel was asleep when I went to bed.'

'So she didn't tell you anything?' Lil screwed up her eyes in her usual suspicious manner. 'Not even a hint?'

Lizzie pulled on her jacket. 'I only know as much as you, Lil.' It was a white lie, but it had to be Ethel who broke the news.

'As soon as Rosie and Timothy surface, I'll quiz them,' Lil threatened, watching Lizzie's face.

'I wouldn't do that. You might let the cat out of the bag.'

Lil sat up on the edge of her seat. 'So you do think she's pregnant?'

'I didn't say that.'

Lil ground her cigarette into the saucer in the middle of the table. 'Well, you'd better be on your way.'

'Thanks for a lovely time.'

Lil grinned and folded her arms. 'Them Millers are a right handful.'

'Yes. But you and Doug gave Flo a wonderful send-off. Ma couldn't have done better.'

At this, Lil's eyes grew sad. 'I still miss our Kate, you know. And your dad too. But it was your mum who was me best pal. And it was for her, really, that I put me back into giving her youngest a right-royal do. Flo is like family to me, as you all are.'

For all Lil's faults, Lizzie reflected, she had been like a second mother to them after Kate had died. Despite her cutting tongue, she had their best interests at heart. She only hoped Lil would give her daughter enough space this morning to get her thoughts in order. Ethel had to decide what she wanted to do without Lil's interference, as well-meaning as Lil intended to be.

'I'll be off then.' Lizzie slipped her bag over her shoulder and kissed Lil on the cheek. 'Give Doug my love.'

'He's out cold, the lazy date.'

Lizzie laughed. 'I think he's earned his sleep.'

'At least he's not under me feet.' Lil walked with her into the yard where Polly and Tom were playing by the wall.

'Look how many dog-ends we've collected,' Polly called, nudging Tom who held out his pocket for them to see. 'At least over an 'undred. Some of them ain't even much smoked.'

'What are you gonna do with them filthy things?' Lil enquired.

'Give them to Uncle Frank,' Polly said brightly.

'Yeah,' Tom agreed, 'as he can't go out to buy any fags.'

Lizzie saw that even Lil chuckled at this.

Danny was only just beginning to feel warmer. He'd enjoyed the heat of the Primus stove as Cal had cooked them all breakfast. The garage reeked of eggs, bacon and fried bread, supplies that Cal had brought in.

'Grub up.' Cal put the three tin plates and mugs, together with forks, on the old card table in the office. He divided the sizzling fry-up between them.

The vaulted ceiling of the old warehouse trapped the smells as the hot sun baked the metal roofing.

'I ain't sure I can do justice to that, Cal.'

'Come on, mate, it'll put hairs on your chest.'

Danny laughed. 'It's me stomach I'm worried about.' He was still feeling queasy. But he knew he had to get something on board.

'You've got to eat,' Cal urged as he settled himself on the stool, 'or else you'll be farting seaweed.'

They all laughed, though Danny was still chilled to the bone. He'd changed into his overalls, but the stink of sewage was still on his skin.

'Yeah, and you'll have to watch out for webbed feet,' agreed Bert, stuffing his mouth full and swallowing down the hot coffee.

Danny took his fork and toyed with his grub. He was still in the river thrashing the water, his boots dragging him down. The certainty he was about to be sucked under. If that piece of wood hadn't appeared he wouldn't be sitting here now. He'd be alongside the corpse in its silent grave, where finally he and Bert had managed to sink it. Danny saw again that last gruesome act in the murky darkness.

'We're in the clear now.' Cal's cheerful voice startled Danny out of his thoughts. 'There's nothing to tie us in with a floater. Did you get rid of the evidence?'

'You bet,' Bert replied hastily. 'Them shooters sunk like a stone. No one is ever gonna turn them up again.'

With an effort, Danny finished the eggs and returned his plate to the makeshift table. 'We'll have to hope the tide takes him well out.'

'Cheers to that,' Cal agreed as he lifted his mug. 'Anyway, if he washes up, it will take them a month of Sundays to identify him. Even his old lady won't know him. He'll blow up like a balloon within hours. Then the fish'll have their way with him. Just like the John Doe you thought was Frank.'

Danny thought of the day he'd gone to the morgue and identified Duncan King as his brother. Had he wanted it to be Frank? This was the thought that tormented him. He looked hard at Cal. 'You're sure he was Savage's man?'

But Cal only shrugged. 'As sure as I can be.'

'Then Savage will be looking for him.'

'Well, he won't find him, will he?' Bert smacked his greasy lips and, taking Danny's plate, he shovelled the remains into his mouth.

'There is another angle to this.' Cal thrust back his mop of tangled black hair and arched an eyebrow. 'The geezer could have been working on his own.'

'How do you mean?' Danny asked.

'He clocked the till, saw it first time around. And chanced making a return journey. But on his own.'

'Savage would have his balls for that,' grunted Bert.

But Danny nodded. 'You might be right, Cal. Lizzie put a notice on the door, saying about the wedding, that the shop would be closed for the day. He wouldn't have known Frank was there and planned to help himself. But things went wrong when he turned up to find you and Ethel there.'

'But still went ahead,' agreed Bert, nodding. 'What a chump!'

'Do you reckon anyone heard the shots?' Danny asked.

'Don't think so,' Cal replied.

Bert belched and rubbed his stomach. 'That's filled an 'ole.'

Danny stood up. He glanced at the oil-stained wooden clock hanging on the nail by the door. 'We'd better get moving.'

'Yeah, I just need the khazi.' Bert hurried off and clattered down the rickety steps of the office to the lavatory outside.

'You passing Lil's?' Cal asked as he stood with Danny at the top of the stairs.

Danny nodded. 'If the car's not outside I'll know Lizzie's gone back to the shop.'

Cal rubbed his black beard. 'Didn't have a chance to say much to Ethel. You reckon she's all right?'

'Dunno, Cal. She got a big fright.'

'Yeah. Shook her up bad. If it hadn't been for Frank our luck would've run out.'

Danny knew this was true. He should have been relieved that neither Cal nor Ethel was hurt. And he was, of course. But it annoyed him that Bill should have let Frank have the revolver. Frank had broken Lizzie's rule about firearms and all because he feared for his own safety. He'd have to have a serious word with his dad about that.

'I've got to try to see Ethel,' Cal said, but Danny shook his head.

'You ain't thinking of going round Lil's?'

'No, but that's not the only place she'll be.'

Danny wished he could give Cal a piece of advice; stay well away from Ethel for a while. But he only shrugged and muttered, 'You don't want to bump into her old man.'

Cal's flexed his broad shoulders. 'Why, what's he like? Will he be up for aggro?'

'He ain't in your league, mate, if that's what you're thinking. But Richard Ryde ain't just going to stand by and watch his wife walk off with another man.'

'Ethel says he's not bothered.'

Danny seriously doubted Ethel's take on that. Although he didn't know Richard Ryde, at least not more than a few handshakes and that was a long time ago anyway, he couldn't see Ethel just walking out on her husband. She was a good woman, with a conscience. And perhaps that was something that Cal just didn't understand. She wasn't the type to get mixed up in what had turned out to be a cold-blooded killing. It could be argued that Frank topping Savage's man was self-defence. But the long and short of it was, they had all been witnesses – if not accessories to murder.

Chapter Forty

Richard Ryde got off his bike, loosened the clips at his ankles and shook his trouser bottoms free. Carefully pushing the bike into the shed, he slipped his mac from his shoulders and hung it on the peg to dry. The shower had been unexpected, but he always made sure he took his mac rolled up in his saddle bag. Glancing down at his dark suit, he saw no damage had been done. He took off his spectacles, wiped the lenses carefully with his unused, starched white handkerchief and replaced them on his nose. Behind them, his pale hazel eyes searched the garden through the shed window. The grass, which he'd mowed to its shortest this year, was a satisfactory green and for once Timothy and Rosie had observed his rules. There were no tyre marks to be seen on the corners where they took a short cut over the lawn, through laziness, to the shed.

Richard's gaze slewed slowly to the house. He was home early for a Friday. In fact he'd taken the afternoon off. Not something he approved of. But the accounts office where he worked was closed for redecoration.

True, the borough had allotted him a room down the hall, but it was hardly larger than a cupboard. There was no space at all for his ledgers and books. His typewriter, which he insisted he used before handing his work to the typists, was perched on a table two feet by two; his office chair was too large to install in the cupboard and had been removed, along with his effects, to a kind of communal space where there was no privacy at all. Who would believe that a London borough like Greenwich would find themselves in such disarray, just because of a few pots of paint?

Richard took another long look at the back of his detached three-bedroomed house which he was now in the process of buying. Thanks to Mother, they were living in a desirable area, with civil neighbours who worked in professional trades like himself. Blackheath was head and shoulders above Millwall and Poplar. Not that he'd ever consider moving back there. No, what a thought!

He drew his eyebrows together in distaste as he thought of his in-laws, Lil and Doug Sharpe. Mother had been right all those years ago, before his father had died, when she'd warned him that marrying Ethel Sharpe was below his standing. Mother had even upped sticks from Poplar and moved across the water to Lewisham in order to end their courtship.

'The island breeds dockers and costermongers, Richard,' she had warned. 'No refinement at all.'

But had he had the sense to listen?

No, he hadn't planned a future then. Or even given

Mother's words a second thought. He was so besotted with Ethel, he'd cycled miles on end back to the island to court her. Even now, Richard's heart gave a little thump as he thought of Ethel in her school uniform, her blonde wavy hair bouncing over her blazer as he'd cycled beside her, too embarrassed to speak. Well, he'd only been fifteen. And what had he known about women at that tender age?

What did he know about them now? Richard asked himself as he stepped out of the shed and marched towards the house.

Only that women made very little sense at all. He'd given Ethel everything. A decent house in a law-abiding neighbourhood, a holiday in summer in Brighton or Eastbourne and a standard of living that, if Ethel had been thrifty, could have bought them a motor car too. But Ethel had no idea of money. She spent her entire wage on frivolities or spoiling herself and the children.

He should have put his foot down long ago, when she'd first applied for that menial job at Rickard's, the haberdasher's. He'd hoped that, as babies came along, she'd be content to bring up the family and keep house. As women should. But what had she done? Only twisted Mother's arm into having the children while she was at work. Not that Mother ever complained. In fact, he was secretly pleased that Timothy and Rosie were being taught their 'p's and 'q's from someone whose high stand-ards far outreached his wife's.

Richard tugged down his suit jacket and, stiffening his

spine, strode towards the back door. The flower beds needed weeding. The path sweeping. Ethel couldn't even be bothered to spend a few hours out here! And she didn't even have a job at the moment. What was he to make of that?

He rattled the handle, but the door was locked. He tried again and looked up at the bedroom window. There was no movement and so he took out his key and went round to the front of the house. Here the borders were neat and orderly. Ones that he'd seen to himself the weekend before, when Ethel and the children were attending that nightmare of a wedding.

Flo Allen marrying Syd Miller! The notorious Millers of all people! Oh well, like attracted like, he supposed. But there was no way he was getting involved with a lot of ruffians and law-breakers. It had been bad enough to witness the goings-on at Lizzie Allen's wedding to Frank Flowers. Richard had been virtually strong-armed into that one. And look at the mess it turned out to be! With that moron Flowers blatantly drunk and disorderly. Making up to trollops in front of his newly-wed wife's eyes.

Well, no more family weddings after that, Richard had assured himself. If Ethel wanted to associate with these illiterates, she did so with his express disapproval. He'd warned her then that one day she would regret getting so chummy with the Flowerses. They'd had an almighty row over it. He'd stuck to his guns though, even while Ethel had thrown some very unfair accusations his way.

He wasn't gloating now, but his warning to her had

been proved right. Last Sunday afternoon, the day after the Miller wedding, Doug Sharpe had driven Ethel and the children home. Ethel had hardly been able to meet his eyes when she stepped out of the car. And Richard knew why. Predictably, the aftermath had been riotous! He'd got it all out of Rosie in the end. Drunken singing and dancing – and no doubt debauching – into the early hours of Sunday. What was in Ethel's mind to expose herself and their children to such behaviour?

Richard felt a wave of anger wash over him. He'd just about managed to keep a lid on his temper when Doug had informed him that Ethel had been poorly. Well, of course she had, associating with that rabble! She'd been coerced into drinking too much, no doubt, and paid the price for it.

Richard let himself in and stood in the hallway, listening for sounds.

'Ethel!' he shouted. 'I'm home.'

He went into the kitchen and then the front room. The couch cushions were askew. Rosie had left her cardigan on the chair. No doubt in a rush to get out of the house for school this morning. And the breakfast bowls in the kitchen were still piled in the sink. Ethel couldn't even be bothered to wash them up.

'Ethel?' he yelled again, becoming angrier by the minute. Returning to the hall, he leaped the stairs to the landing and stood silently once more.

He dashed into the bedrooms, all three of them empty. Then he hurried downstairs again.

Not a sound. The house was deserted. Well, this time
he was not having it. He was going to cycle over to the
Sharpes' and confront Ethel. This was not the first time
he'd come home to an empty house. When he'd demanded
an explanation, Ethel had told him she was out shopping.
But he knew exactly where she was. At No. 84 Langley
Street, gossiping the day away with her mother. Either
that, or in company with Lizzie Flowers, who he thought
possessed the morals of an alley cat.

A fine way for his wife to carry on!

Forgetting to put on his trouser clips, Richard dragged
his bike from the shed. This kind of behaviour was totally
unacceptable, he told himself as he pedalled furiously
towards Greenwich and the underground tunnel which
would take him to the island. He was going to lay the law
down today. Tell Lil Sharpe to keep her nose out of his
family's business. Ethel was his wife and she should start
behaving like one. She wasn't a child any longer. To be
fawned over and spoilt by parents who had undoubtedly
not been able to sever the apron strings.

She was Mrs Ethel Ryde. And, come hell or high water,
he was going to insist that she started behaving like it!

Chapter Forty-One

Lizzie stared out of the storeroom's dirty window. It was Friday and almost a week since she'd last seen Danny. On Sunday afternoon he'd collected Tom and driven them away in the car. She had tried to take comfort from the news that all had gone according to plan the night before. But Danny's face was tense and his eyes wouldn't quite meet hers. She knew that disposing of a body and keeping that secret was weighing on his mind.

'We'll let the dust settle,' he'd said briefly. 'Just go about your business here. The body might wash up in the next few days. Or, if we're lucky, not for some while. If you need me, send Bert. Make sure Fowler or Elmo are here at all times. Keep your eyes peeled in case Savage shows up.'

Now, at the end of the week, there had been no sign of trouble. She was trying to act as normal. Each day she had scoured the newspapers. There had been nothing about a found body. But every tinkle of the shop bell had jarred her nerves. She couldn't stop looking up and down the road. She didn't really know what for. But she was impelled to do it.

Bert had been unusually quiet. She had tried to ask him
about that night. But he'd only confirmed what Danny
had said. Now, as the morning trade began, Lizzie tried
to revive her spirits. She would tell Fowler to clean these
dirty windows. And Bert could pay serious attention to
the dirty floor.

Walking into the shop, Lizzie saw a pale face coming
towards her. 'Ethel? What are you doing here?'

'I had to come,' she whispered as Lizzie drew her to
one side. 'I've been going round the bend at home, not
knowing anything.'

'We can't talk here.'

'I know. I'm sorry.'

'Frank's upstairs, so we can't go there, either.'

Ethel nodded, looking guilty. 'I shouldn't have come.'

'Listen, we'll drive to the market. I buy all the leftovers
on Fridays. Go and sit in the van parked outside in the
road. I'll only be a few minutes.'

Lizzie gave Bert and Fowler their instructions. Then
she went upstairs to Frank. He was sitting, fully dressed,
in the armchair, reading yesterday's newspaper. Beside
him was the walking stick. He never went anywhere
without it.

'You managed a shave, then?'

He nodded. 'And I made meself a Rosie. All the gas is
off.'

As he was walking around now, Lizzie allowed him to
make a drink. 'I'm going out in the van.'

'What if we get a visit?'

Lizzie knew Frank was obsessed with Savage's return. He feared being unable to defend himself.

'I told you the boys are downstairs.'

'I wish I had me gun.'

'Look what you did with one last time. And we're all suffering the consequences.'

'Would you rather your friends were dead?'

'No, course not. But it might not have come down to that.'

Frank stared silently up at her with his pale blue eyes. He had put on a clean shirt and collar and tie. Was he getting better slowly? Would he be ready to leave soon?

'I'll be back this afternoon.'

'Where're you going?'

Lizzie took her bag and slipped it over her shoulder. 'To Cox Street market, but don't keep asking me what I'm doing, Frank. You make me nervous.'

'Sorry.' He picked the paper up from his knees.

Lizzie hurried downstairs, past Bert and Fowler and the queue of customers lining up on the pavement. She acknowledged them all in her usual friendly way; business had never been so good. The thought nagged at her that she needed to plough back the money they were making into the new shop. But she couldn't concentrate on that now.

'Thanks,' Ethel said as Lizzie climbed in beside her. 'Sorry to be a nuisance.'

Lizzie started the van. It rattled noisily. 'I was coming over to yours anyway.' She drove down Ebondale Street and turned the corner. A fresh whiff of morning air blew in through the window, bringing Lizzie back to the moment. 'Did you tell your mum about the— ?'

'No.'

'You'll have to soon.'

'I'm not showing yet.' Ethel stared at Lizzie. 'So is it – he – gone?'

'If you mean Albert, yes.'

'It's worse when you know a name.'

'Listen, Ethel. You have to put it all out of your mind.'

Ethel gave out a pitiful whine. 'If only!'

Lizzie managed to drive through the morning traffic without getting held up by the inevitable queues to the docks that began around noon. She parked in the alley that led up to the traders' stalls and pointed to the opening through a narrow brick tunnel. 'I'll just pick up my stuff. I won't be long if I can find one of the young lads to help me.'

'Don't worry about asking them. I'll help you.'

'You're in no state to go heaving boxes.' Lizzie looked down at Ethel's stomach.

'I'll take the lighter ones.' Ethel was already climbing out of the van. It was as if she didn't want to be left on her own with her thoughts. And Lizzie could understand why.

Finally they had all the fruit and vegetables stowed in the back of the van. Lizzie felt better for the company of the traders and she knew Ethel did too. From where they

were parked they could hear the welcome noise of the
market, voices echoing through the alley. They could see
the red-and-white-striped awnings and the crowds of
people listening to the patter of the stallholders.

'It was nice to see all your friends,' Ethel said quietly.

'Yes, life goes on as normal.'

'Will it ever be normal for us?' Ethel asked. 'How long
will we have to wait for something to happen?' She
looked depressed again.

'Nothing might ever happen. Not if the body doesn't
turn up.'

'Meanwhile we have to wait.' Ethel pushed her fair
hair from her eyes. 'Last night I had a nightmare again.
This time I was shot. I was afraid the bullet went in the
baby.'

'Oh Ethel, that's awful. No wonder you look pale this
morning.'

'It was like the dream was trying to tell me something.'

'You're not going to be shot, Ethel.'

'I know. But all the same . . .' Ethel's voice tailed off.
She slumped back against the seat. 'I'm fed up with listen-
ing to meself.' She tried to smile. 'Let's talk about you.
Have you seen Flo yet?'

'No, I haven't called round.'

'So you don't know if their honeymoon went all right?'

'Danny said he dropped them off at their hotel near
Marble Arch. It must have cost quite a bit.'

'I didn't know Syd earned a lot.'

'He didn't use to as a porter, but it was regular money.'

Lizzie thought of the watch on Walter's arm. She still didn't know what to do about it. And she couldn't put more troubles on Ethel's shoulders.

'Oh well, I'm sure they had a good time.' Ethel smiled. 'I wouldn't mind a couple of nights up West in a classy hotel.'

Lizzie grinned. 'Me neither.'

Ethel said suddenly, 'Lizzie, I need a favour.'

'What?'

'I'm going to tell Cal it's all over.'

Lizzie gave a soft gasp. 'Are you sure?'

'Yes.'

Lizzie knew this decision was a heartbreaker for Ethel, either way.

'But I'm weak,' Ethel continued. 'If I'm alone, he'll change my mind. But if you're there, he won't be able to say anything. Will you drive me to the garage?'

'What, now?'

'Have you got time?'

'Yes, but are you really sure this is what you want?'

Ethel nodded firmly. 'The kids break up soon. Richard, for the first time ever, said he'd arrange a holiday this year. It wouldn't be easy to get away over the summer even if I wanted to.'

'And you don't?'

'I'm going to try to make my marriage work.'

They sat in silence, each with their own thoughts. Lizzie looked at her friend, then sighed. 'All right, we'll drive over now.'

'Thanks.' Ethel fiddled with her fingers in her lap. 'You'll stay with me, won't you?'

'If that's what you want.'

Lizzie wondered, as she reversed out of the alley, just how strong Ethel's resolution would be when she came face to face with Cal.

Chapter Forty-Two

Richard stared at the long-haired individual wearing a leather apron, and shovelling potatoes from a sack into a woman's open shopping bag. Inside the shop was another man, similarly dressed in working clothes and a dirty cloth cap. Richard studied him closely. Then, with a jolt of recognition, he realized he was looking at Bert Allen, brother to Lizzie Flowers. Time certainly hadn't improved his coarsened features, nor his labouring gait, as he hauled a sack on his shoulders and carried it outside to the pavement.

Richard held fast to his bicycle, deciding to keep his distance. He couldn't see the Flowers woman – or his wife – as his gaze travelled up to the windows above the shop. Could they be there? he wondered. He seemed to remember Ethel mentioning the living quarters above the shop and an airey below. One of those cold, dark basements that were notoriously damp.

Was this where his wife spent her time? he asked himself incredulously. It was unbelievable that she should prefer squalor to the clean and decent middle-class home he had provided for her.

His eyes travelled to the noisy young children playing in the street. Urchins by the looks of them, shabbily dressed and some even without shoes! There wasn't a clean shirt between them and their language was appalling.

Richard smelled something unpleasant. He looked back at the shop as the breeze blew softly in his direction. The long-haired man walked round to a wooden crate on the pavement. He began to strip leaves from the cauliflowers, most of which, Richard noted, were brown and soggy. This problem was solved by a knife shaved over their surfaces. The smell of rot they emitted was overpowering.

Richard pushed his bike a few feet along, craning his neck up to the windows. Was Ethel up there? If so, how was he to attract her attention?

A horse-drawn wagon came clattering up the road. Richard was forced to move aside once more. He positioned himself by the gas lamp opposite, turning his attention to his bicycle clip on his left ankle so that he wouldn't be noticed.

He shuddered at the smell of overripe vegetables. He flinched at the noise and bustle on the street. Appalling, thought Richard. The East End held no attraction for him. He couldn't see how it did for Ethel either. His mother's words sprang to mind. 'The island breeds dockers and costermongers.' And she had never been more right than now.

'You look as if yer just lost a quid and found a tanner,' a deep voice said and Richard nearly jumped out of his skin. He hadn't realized that a figure had approached. He was shocked to find himself looking up into the lantern jaw of Bert Allen.

'What?' Richard stammered, clutching his bike as if it was a life raft in a rough sea.

'Richard, ain't it? Ethel's other half? Saw you at Flo's wedding.'

'Erm . . .' Richard faltered, trying not to make eye contact through his spectacles. He hadn't thought he'd be recognized, at least not by this individual. Stepping back, he positioned his bicycle between him and the towering figure. 'I'm looking for my wife. Is she here?'

'Ethel?' The idiot stared at him as if he'd spoken in a foreign language.

'Yes, Ethel Ryde, my wife,' Richard repeated officiously. 'I called at the Sharpes' in Langley Street and no one is at home. That's why I've come here,' he added as if talking to someone hard of hearing.

'Yer, Ethel called this morning,' Bert Allen replied. 'But she ain't here now.'

'Where is she then?' Richard's annoyance grew.

'With Lizzie. Took the van and gorn to the market.'

'Market?' Richard repeated. 'Where's that?'

The man grinned foolishly. 'Cox Street, up the road. We get our goods cheap for the weekend, see. Caulis, Brussels, beans, spuds, all knock-down prices for Saturday. Bit ripe some of 'em, but with a tidy trim, they do nicely out front.'

Richard didn't doubt that. He'd seen with his own eyes the other man wielding his knife. 'And Ethel went with her?' Richard asked again, making doubly sure.

'Yeah, but that was a good couple of hours back. Lizzie usually ain't gone that long. They must be gassing somewhere.'

'Gassing?' Richard frowned.

'Gorn off for a chat, like women do.'

'But where would they go?' Richard felt like yelling at this numbskull.

'Couldn't tell you, mate.'

'Mr Allen, I really must find my wife. I've tried her family. I've tried here. And I'll try the market. Is there anywhere else on the island they would go?' Richard asked impatiently. 'What about this garage that I've heard Ethel speak of? Would they have driven there?'

Bert Allen frowned vaguely, and scratched his head.

'Never mind,' Richard dismissed. 'I'll find it myself.'

'They wouldn't go there.'

'Why not?'

'It's all motors, ain't it? Nothing that appeals to females. Listen, best way is to come inside and wait. Park yer bike down the side and I'll make you a nice cup of Rosie.'

Appalled at the suggestion, Richard shook his head firmly. 'No thank you. I'll be off now.' He mounted his bike and began to pedal off, feeling extremely put out. There was no way he was going to idle away his valuable time, trying to make conversation with a man who was clearly unhinged. Casting a swift look behind him, he saw Bert Allen still standing gormlessly in the road. With a shudder Richard continued on his way. In his haste to pedal faster he narrowly missed a child not more than two or three years of age who appeared to be urinating in the gutter.

Richard shook his head, puzzled and dismayed. He was relieved to be away from what he could only term a slum. He was simply at a loss to understand Ethel. What on earth could she find to attract her in associating with these people?

He drew in a long breath as he reached Westferry Road. He was still in enemy territory. But the market wasn't far. And if he couldn't find Ethel there, he'd make his own enquiries as to where this garage might be.

Chapter Forty-Three

Lizzie stopped the van on the gravel forecourt and peered out of the window at the garage. For a Friday she thought the place looked very quiet, until she saw the bulbous frame of a lorry emerge from the open doors. Danny sat in the driver's seat. When he saw them he gave a toot of the horn.

'Can you see Cal?' Ethel asked, craning her neck.

'No. He's probably inside.' Lizzie sat back in her seat. 'Ethel, are you sure you want to do this?'

'Yes, but I need your help.'

'What can I do? It's a private matter.'

'Stay with me,' Ethel pleaded, her pale skin going ashen. 'Tell Danny why I'm here.'

Lizzie was afraid Ethel would regret this decision. She would be lonely again without Cal in her life. But she nodded all the same and got out of the van. Danny climbed down from the cab of the lorry as she walked towards him. 'Is everything all right?' he asked, glancing back at the van. 'Has Savage shown up?'

'It's Ethel. She wants to see Cal.'

Danny frowned, slowly nodding. 'So it's finally come to that.'

'She's very upset. But she says she wants to make a go of her marriage.'

'What brought that on?' Danny asked as he wiped his hands on a cloth.

'She hasn't been right since Albert was killed.'

'Cal wasn't responsible for that.'

'I know.'

Danny sighed. 'We'd better make ourselves scarce, then.'

'I think she wants us to stay around. She's worried that Cal won't take no for an answer.'

Danny shrugged. 'There's nothing we can do about that. Cal's my mate. I can't help Ethel with her personal life.'

'I know. But I had to bring her. I didn't know what else to do.'

Danny's blue eyes softened. 'Tell her to come in, then. They can talk in the office. Cal's in the workshop fixing an engine for a motor that the council is using for the new landing stage at Tilbury.' He went to walk away then stopped. 'He thinks a lot of her, you know.'

'Yes, which makes it even harder.' Lizzie went back to the van. Ethel was waiting, her hands held tightly in her lap. 'Is Cal there?'

'Yes, Danny's calling him up from the workshop,' Lizzie replied through the open window. 'You can use the office.'

Ethel pushed back her long wavy fair hair and got out.

She stood, straightening her floral cotton dress and looking uncertain. Tears filled her eyes. 'I don't want to do
this, but I must find the strength.'

When they arrived at the garage, Lizzie stopped. 'I'll
wait here.'

'Can't you come with me?'

'No, that wouldn't be fair on any of us.'

Ethel nodded and slowly made her way up the stairs.

Chapter Forty-Four

Unforeseen circumstances were forcing Leonard Savage to rethink his strategy. The sayings of his deprived childhood were going through his mind. 'When in doubt, do nowt.' Or – and this was more likely in the case of his whore of a mother – 'Strike while the iron's hot.'

Savage shifted restlessly on the lack-lustre back seat of the stolen vehicle. Its battered seats niffed. The engine was rattling like a leper's chest. But there was no sense in using the Daimler. Not for this job anyway. There was a remote chance some nosy river copper might be on the prowl and recognize his motor. Morley's Wharf was a desolate spot, yet not five minutes after his driver had parked by the dock wall a beat-up old van had arrived.

'Do you know who it is, Mr S?' his driver enquired as a female had climbed out and a few minutes later was joined by another.

'One of them is the Flowers woman,' Savage replied irritably.

'Do we go in anyway?'

Savage glared at the back of the man's head. 'No, we sit

tight. Give the thumbs-down to the boys.' He watched as the driver lowered the window and stuck out his hand, giving the signal to the car behind where six of his best men were waiting to follow their lead.

Savage sat back and sighed. He had planned with meticulous care; two men were to go to the rear of the garage, the other four to the front. The takeover of the garage, if performed with the element of surprise as the men worked inside, would be flawless. But now he'd have to wait until the women were gone.

He drummed his fingers impatiently on his knee. Smoothing the material of his trousers beneath his camel-hair coat, he counted the minutes as they ticked by slowly. Then, to his utter dismay, a group of four or five men appeared, ambling along the wharf. They looked like the squatters from the derelict site close by; unshaven, their hair matted as they shifted around aimlessly in their grubby ankle-length greatcoats. If it was one thing he detested, it was the sight of vagrants. They had the gall to occupy premises illegally and pay no rent! Often the law was too lazy to move them on. But not Leonard Savage. No! Later today, after he'd dispatched Flowers, he'd make a return call to these undesirables.

'You want me to move on them drunks?' the new recruit asked over his shoulder.

'No,' Savage replied. 'Not yet.'

'It'd only take a good slap.'

'Don't be so bloody stupid – you'd alert Flowers,' Savage retorted, thinking wistfully of Albert who he'd not seen for some days. 'Come back, Albert,' he murmured softly. 'All is forgiven. After I've given you a good hiding for the bender you've been on, I'll get rid of this idiot and reinstate you.'

'I just thought—'

'You're not paid to think. I've told you a dozen times, we stick to the plan.'

'Yeah, but—'

'Did you hear me?' Savage demanded, cursing the desperation that had caused him to hire such a fool. 'Just watch out for the law. That's your priority.'

'What do I do if I see 'em?'

'What do you think, birdbrain? You don't get out and shake their hands. You drive us out of here, slowly, as if we've taken a wrong turn. That's why I told you to keep the motor running.'

With a groan of frustration, Savage returned his attention to the garage. As soon as the women left, he would give the signal to his men and they'd go in. He'd take possession in under five minutes. Flowers and his pal wouldn't know what hit them with a semi-automatic pointed in their faces.

Savage watched one of the drunks sit down on a pile of rubble. He was soon joined by his friends, smoking and drinking and generally making themselves at home.

Savage groaned again. Should he have them removed? But no doubt they'd put up loud, if useless, resistance. Besides, it wasn't the homeless he was concerned with.

The minutes continued to pass slowly. His frustration

mounted. If Flowers had been a sensible man, he'd have taken his offer for the garage. Saved them all a lot of trouble. But no, he had to stick his heels in and make life complicated!

Ethel stood by the open door of the office. Shock and disbelief were written in Cal's dark eyes. 'Don't make this hard for me, Cal,' she pleaded. 'It's all over.'

'But why? *Why* are you doing this?' he asked in a bewildered voice. 'Is it what happened at Lizzie's?'

Ethel shook her head. Though the truth was, reality had struck home that day in the shop. She had seen herself and her life as it really was. Having an affair with Cal wasn't a game any more. She had shut herself off from the truth, because for the first time in years she had found true happiness. But happiness that was stolen at the cost of her family couldn't last.

'We've been lucky so far,' she continued. 'But Rosie and Timothy need me. And Richard does in his own way.'

'I need you too.'

'No you don't, Cal. Not like them.'

'We've got a good thing going, too good to chuck in.' He pushed his fingers despairingly through his black hair. 'We make each other happy. Ain't that enough?'

'Deceiving Richard is doing my head in. I can't go on telling lies.'

'Then leave him, not me.' He moved towards her but she put up her hand. 'Please don't touch me, Cal. This is over,' she repeated.

'Not for me it isn't. I want to make you happy. I *know* I could make you happy.'

If she didn't leave now, she knew she would weaken. 'I'll go mad if I go on this way,' she tried to explain.

But he only smiled, as if that was nothing. 'There ain't no such thing as sanity, Ethel. Everyone's a little bit mad.'

'Don't make fun of me.'

'I'm not.' He suddenly took her in his arms. 'Here's what we'll do. I'll knock off work and we'll go somewhere and talk it over.'

Ethel stared up into his face, framed by his black hair and ebony eyes. He was such a good-looking man and she loved him. But he was out of reach and had been since the first moment they'd met.

He kissed her lips softly and Ethel shuddered. Just one more kiss, a little voice in her head whispered, a few understanding words, his arms around you to ease the pain and everything will be all right.

'Listen to me . . .' he whispered, lifting a strand of hair from her eyes with his gentle fingers. 'We'll work this out. You ain't on your own.'

She felt herself giving way. 'Don't . . .' she replied weakly.

'We're good together, we—'

'Ethel! Ethel!' A voice called from downstairs.

Cal held her tightly. 'Leave it.'

Ethel heard her name again. Pulling herself free, she stumbled to the landing.

'Come quickly,' Lizzie yelled up from the garage door. 'Richard's here!'

Ethel's mouth opened, but no words came out. Suddenly it hit her. 'Richard?' she breathed, and without looking back she flew down the staircase.

Chapter Forty-Five

Lizzie pointed to the tall, thin man wearing a suit and standing by the dock wall. He was holding the handlebars of his bicycle. 'It is Richard, isn't it?' she asked Ethel who stood with her and Danny.

'Oh my God, it is,' Ethel gasped, her eyes fixed ahead. 'But why is he here?'

'For you, I suppose,' said Danny, his voice cool.

Lizzie watched Richard Ryde shield his eyes against the strong July sunshine and peer towards the garage.

'He should be at work,' Ethel said bewilderedly. 'He would have told me if he was going to come home early so I could have dinner ready.'

'Could your mum have sent him over?' Lizzie thought he may have gone to Langley Street first but Ethel shook her head.

'No, she wouldn't do that.'

'But Lil knows about you and Cal, doesn't she?' Danny said gruffly.

'I've never said anything, but she might have guessed,' Ethel said hesitantly. 'But even if she has she wouldn't send Richard here.'

'Then you'd better go and speak to him,' Danny replied. 'He don't look like he was coming over here.'

'I'll go with you,' said Cal, appearing at Ethel's side. 'We should have told Richard a long time ago.'

But Ethel pulled away, her face shocked. 'No, no!' She stepped back, trying to distance herself. 'Stay away, Cal. Please don't follow me.'

Danny caught his friend's arm, saying softly, 'She's right, leave it alone, mate.'

But Cal only shook his head and hurried after Ethel.

'Can't we do something?' Lizzie said anxiously.

'Like what? We've already got ourselves a headache trying to keep Ethel and Cal's names out of what happened at the shop. They could have been caught any amount of times the way they've carried on.'

'But they're our friends,' Lizzie protested half-heartedly.

'Yeah, and it's their business, not ours.'

Lizzie knew Danny was right but even so her heart ached for Ethel who was trying to escape Cal as he caught up with her, pulled her round and dragged her into his arms.

And all this in full view of Richard.

'Christ! What now!' Leonard Savage exclaimed as he watched the activity.

'A bloke on a bike's turned up,' his man replied.

'I can see that. But what are they doing?' Savage was on the edge of his seat, his heart pumping. It was bedlam here. The mechanic was having a go at the woman and the prune with the bike was just standing there.

His patience exhausted, Savage grabbed the back of the driver's seat. 'Inch forward slowly!' he shouted.

'But you said to stick to the plan.'

'That was before a load of comedians turned up.'

The driver did as he was told. Savage felt the blood pumping at his temples. He was ready for action and wasn't going to wait any longer.

'Nose up close,' Savage demanded as the car's tyres crunched over the gravel.

'We've got an audience, Mr S. There's a geezer and a woman by the garage.'

'We'll see to them after.' His fury was mounting. 'Keep going, keep going!' He sat rigidly, his eyes fixed ahead as he waved his hands. 'Put your foot down, you fool. We'll show Flowers what happens when he turns down a deal with Leonard Savage.'

The big car trembled and picked up speed. Savage smiled in satisfaction as the man and woman, who seemed to be arguing, came into their sights. 'Faster!' he yelled, his small eyes bright with excitement.

'At this speed I'll be sure to hit them,' the driver said nervously.

'They'll move, don't worry.'

But neither Savage nor the man driving the car saw a shape approach. It was only when the windscreen shattered that the vehicle came to a stop.

Chapter Forty-Six

Lizzie saw the car appear out of nowhere. It picked up speed as it headed towards Cal and Ethel, though neither Ethel nor Cal seemed to have seen it. Then suddenly Richard was riding towards Cal and Ethel too, his head bent over the handlebars, his feet flying round on the pedals.

Danny stepped forward waving his arms. 'Stop!' he yelled at the top of his voice. 'Stop!'

But he was too late. Lizzie's knees turned to water as Richard collided with the car. Richard and his bicycle went flying high into the air. She watched in disbelief as Richard seemed to turn a somersault with the bicycle still attached to his legs. Seconds later they were falling, coming down with a heavy clump and a tearing of metal.

Lizzie saw Danny run. He was still waving at the car, but instead of stopping, it reversed, its tyres spinning on the gravel. With a roar, it turned in the opposite direction and was hidden from sight in a cloud of dust.

Lizzie ran after Danny to where Ethel and Cal were standing by Richard's still form.

'What's happened?' Ethel shrieked as Cal held her. 'Why is Richard lying there like that?' Her eyes were wide and dazed as she stared at her husband's distorted body. 'Why doesn't he get up?'

Carefully, Danny lifted the bicycle from Richard's twisted legs. Putting it to one side, he bent over Richard. Then looking up he shook his head. 'I'm sorry, Ethel.'

'What?' Ethel began to shake and tremble. 'Richard, why did you come here?' she began to shout. 'Everything would have been all right if you hadn't.'

Lizzie saw one of Richard's laced shoes lying a few yards away. The other was still on his foot. Blood was flowing into a puddle under his head.

Cal tightened his arms around Ethel. 'Come away, Ethel. You can't do nothing now.' But she pushed him off, her eyes bright with angry tears.

'Leave me alone. Can't you see it was us that caused this?' she sobbed and went to stand over Richard. 'I'm sorry, I'm sorry,' she sobbed, staring down at her husband.

They were all silent, until Danny said quietly, 'Did anyone recognize the driver?'

Cal shook his head and said in a shaken voice, 'No, but there were some blokes over there from the place next door. They might have seen something.'

'Doubt it,' Danny replied, shrugging. 'Even if they did, they've scarpered now.'

Lizzie watched Ethel touch Richard's hair. 'I'm sorry,' she whispered to her dead husband. 'I was going to try to be the wife you wanted.'

Lizzie looked at Danny. In a quiet voice she asked, 'What do we do now?'

'I'll have to call the law. Take Ethel inside the garage and try to calm her down.'

'She's not been right since what happened in the shop. And now this. What are we going to tell the police?'

'You mean what's Ethel going to tell them?'

'I suppose so.'

'Whatever she does decide to say, we'll all back her up, right?'

Lizzie looked at Cal and he nodded. She could see the agony of rejection in his eyes. She knew, as he did, it was over for him and Ethel. Ethel would blame herself for what happened.

Lizzie put her arm around her friend and gently pulled her away. Carefully she guided a sobbing Ethel past Richard's broken spectacles lying crushed on the ground.

Chapter Forty-Seven

Lizzie's head was spinning. The two bobbies had fired questions at them, one after another. Did any of them know who the driver was? Why did the car go off without stopping? Why had Richard come to the garage?

Lizzie's heart had thumped when this question had been directed at Ethel.

'I think Richard wanted to buy a car,' she said in a halting voice.

'Did you know about this?' the policeman asked, looking at Danny.

'No. But I would have helped him out.'

To Lizzie's relief the constables had seemed satisfied with this explanation. But the questioning was very distressing for Ethel. Lizzie knew that what had happened today had changed the course of her life.

When a black van had arrived to take Richard away, Lizzie had taken Ethel upstairs to the office. There were no words of consolation she could find to ease Ethel's grief. Eventually the police had left, taking the bicycle with them.

Now she and Ethel were in the van once more, driving towards Polly's school. Ethel sat with her hands folded together, her face drained of colour and her knuckles white as she twisted her fingers.

'I'll never forgive myself,' she said in a faint voice as she stared vacantly through the windscreen. 'How am I going to live with deceiving Richard? He must have found out about Cal.'

'You don't know for sure.'

'In my heart I do.'

'You told the police the right thing under the circumstances.'

Ethel gave a strangled sob. 'You mean I told more lies to cover up the ones I'd told before.'

When they arrived at the school, Lizzie looked at her sad friend. 'I'll just fetch Polly and then I'll drive you home.'

'How am I going to tell the kids?' Ethel gulped.

'Me and Polly will be with you if that's what you want.'

'What about the shop?'

'Bert and Fowler will take care of that.'

'Only this morning Richard was alive. He asked for cheese sandwiches, cut thin.'

'Stop tormenting yourself.'

'I feel a bad person. But I didn't mean to be.'

'You're not bad, Ethel. None of us sets out to be bad. Things happen that we don't plan for, that's all.'

Ethel fought back the tears. 'I'll have to tell Mum and Dad.'

'Lil and Doug will stand by you.'

'They don't even know about the baby.' Ethel stifled a sob. 'And there's Mrs Ryde. Richard is – *was* – the light of her life. How is she going to take it when the police go round and tell her she's lost her only son?'

'Has she got any other family?'

Ethel nodded. 'A sister who lives in the next road.'

'Well, then, she'll have someone to be with her.'

'I should go over to Lewisham.'

'You've got to put the children first.'

Ethel had shed so many tears, she just stared into space.

Lizzie opened the door and climbed out, running across the playground as she knew she was very late. She dashed in and found Mrs Price sitting with Polly on one of the school's wooden benches. They both stood up when they saw Lizzie.

'I'm sorry I'm late,' Lizzie said as Polly flung herself into her arms.

'Where have you been?' Polly asked anxiously.

'I'm afraid there was an accident.'

'Oh, dear,' Mrs Price said, but, smiling at Polly, she added, 'There you are, Polly. I told you it must be something important to delay your aunt.' Mrs Price looked at Lizzie in concern. 'Are you all right, Mrs Flowers?'

'Yes, but I was worried about Polly. Thank you for looking after her for me.'

'I was going to bring her to the shop. I thought it might be – well, a family upset.'

Lizzie knew Mrs Price was discreet enough not to name

Frank who had been the usual source of trouble. 'My friend's husband was knocked off his bicycle and unfortunately killed,' she explained.

'Oh, how dreadful!'

'A few of us were witnesses and had to wait for the police to take our statements.'

'That's quite understandable,' Mrs Price agreed and patted Polly on the head. 'Off you go now. See you on Monday. And please take care of yourselves.'

'Who was it that was killed, Auntie Lizzie?' Polly asked as they walked across the playground.

Lizzie bent down to her niece. 'I'm afraid it was Auntie Ethel's husband, Rosie and Timothy's dad.'

Polly frowned as she looked into Lizzie's eyes. 'What was his name?'

'Richard.'

'What happened to his bike?'

'It was taken away.'

Polly nodded. 'I ain't never seen him with Rosie and Timothy. Will they be sad?'

'Yes, they will.'

'Is Auntie Ethel sad?'

'Yes, of course. She's sitting in the van over there. Perhaps we can help to cheer her up.'

'I can tell her that he's gone to heaven to be with Jesus,' Polly said slowly. 'Cos that's what Mrs Price says at school.'

As Lizzie took Polly's hand and they walked out of the playground, she thought sadly of the man who had never really shared a closeness with his family. He rarely attended the school functions; it had always been Ethel who supported Timothy's football matches and the nativity plays at Christmas. He had always put his duties as a son first, as though he was still a schoolboy himself. Ethel had always remarked that she felt more like a second mother to him than a wife. He certainly shied away from Lil and Doug and only saw them when they went over at Christmas for Boxing Day tea. But all the same, he was Rosie and Timothy's father and there would be many tears shed in the Ryde household tonight.

'Hello, Auntie Ethel,' Polly said in a whisper, sliding her arms around Ethel's neck.

Ethel hugged her close. 'I'm sorry we were late.'

'Don't matter. Did you know that everyone becomes an angel when they die?'

Lizzie saw the tears rush to Ethel's eyes. She knew they were tears of regret and guilt. But Ethel was going to have to live with what had happened and come to terms with the fact that life just had to go on.

Chapter Forty-Eight

'So we meet again,' the detective said, parading around the garage floor and studying the vehicles. 'Though it ain't much of a surprise,' he added, shrugging his shoulders under his shapeless jacket. 'As you and me have unfinished business.'

'What business is that?' Danny shifted his weight as he leaned casually against the chassis of the truck.

'Unresolved business.' Detective Inspector Bray bared his brown teeth.

'If you say so.'

'This place all yours?'

'Bought and paid for,' Danny replied. 'And in case you're wondering, I've documentation to prove it.'

'Where did the money come from?'

'Hard work, lots of it,' Danny answered, refusing to take the bait that Bray was dangling in front of him. Danny walked slowly over to the Port of London Authority lorry just inside the double doors. He'd given his statement to the police who came that afternoon, confirming Ethel's story that Richard had come to the garage to buy a car.

That seemed to satisfy the cops, and he'd hoped that, at least for today, there would be an end to the interrogations. It was now down to the law to find the driver who was responsible for Richard's death. But to Danny's dismay, just as he was about to lock up, Bray had arrived.

The policeman strolled to the open doors where he nodded to the forecourt beyond. 'Funny how there's a mystery around you,' Bray murmured as he stared at the view. 'A man is killed here today. And nobody knows anything. You sure you didn't recognize the vehicle?'

'No,' said Danny flatly, 'I told the other coppers that.'

'So there was just you and your pal and the two women as witnesses?'

'That's right.'

'Tell me what happened again. Yes, I know you've given a statement, but I'd like to hear your version, if you don't mind.'

Danny frowned, sighing in resignation. 'We saw this motor in the distance. It drove across the forecourt, picked up speed and collided with the bike. Richard was thrown into the air. He didn't stand a chance.'

'So who was to blame?'

'It's your job to work that one out.'

Bray spat the tobacco from his teeth. 'There's glass out there. The windscreen must have broken. So maybe you saw who was driving?'

'I told you, I didn't clock anyone,' Danny replied, smothering the urge to tell Bray to go to hell. But he mustn't lose his temper. Bray was hoping for that.

'So how did the grieving widow take it?' Bray asked callously. 'Her old man being run over in front of her eyes?'

'How do you think?'

'She have any idea who it was?'

'None of us have.'

'So this Mrs Ryde was brought over here by your – er . . .' Bray coughed, raising his eyebrows mockingly. 'Your *friend*, Mrs Flowers?'

Danny was too angry to speak. He'd understood the innuendo, but he wasn't going to react.

'You say you knew the deceased?' Bray continued smoothly.

'I first met Richard years ago.' Danny shrugged. 'Before I went to Australia.'

'When was that?'

'1921,' Danny snapped. 'But you have that down on file from when you was trying to pin Duncan King's death on me.'

Bray leered, wagging his index finger in Danny's face. 'There's still time for a collar, old son.'

Danny stared levelly into Bray's ugly face. 'What's all this got to do with you anyway? The Poplar bobbies are handling it. You're Limehouse nick. This ain't your turf.'

Bray waved his hand. 'I'm always interested in you, Mr Flowers. You was one of my very first cases at Limehouse. Call it a bit of good old-fashioned nostalgia if you like.'

'Well, the sentiment ain't returned,' Danny replied shortly. 'Now, if you've finished, I'm about to shut up shop.'

'Don't mind me having a butcher's around the place

first?' Bray replied, swaggering off towards the vehicles parked at the rear of the garage.

Danny's blue eyes darkened as the copper began to study each motor in turn, making a meal out of the inspection. After a few minutes, Danny couldn't bring himself to watch and walked slowly out into the evening air.

It was a perfect summer's night. The sun was a pale globe of scarlet, slowly disappearing behind a curtain of silvery mist. There were noises over the dock wall, the river men on their way up to the estuary and the barges tying up at the wharf walls. He took out his tobacco and stood with his eyes fixed on the place where Richard had been killed. The car that had hit him had jammed on its brakes too late. Richard hadn't stood a chance.

Poor Ethel. He only hoped she could keep her nerve and stick to the story she'd given the coppers.

And who was the coward who'd snuffed out a life without stopping? As he smoked, his eyes began to adjust to the twilight. Browned tufts of grass and weeds along the dock walls cast long shadows. The gravel half-acre where the car had skidded to a halt and thrown Richard into the air looked eerily lonely.

'So you're claiming this death was an accident?' Bray said, bringing Danny back with a sharp jolt as he arrived at his side.

'I'm saying it's your job to find out.'

'You knew this bloke and suddenly he's brown bread right outside your gaff. You don't think your story's a bit iffy?'

Danny shrugged. 'That's what you said before.'

'And I'm saying it again.'

Danny smiled tightly. 'You're the copper. It's your job to make the deductions, not a blockhead like me.' Squaring his shoulders, he walked back to the big doors and began to pull them across.

'That's not an answer,' Bray shouted.

'It's all you're going to get.'

With narrowed eyes, the policeman stood watching. 'I'll work it out, you know. I'll find out why that poor sod died here. And who did it.'

Danny nodded slowly. 'Be sure to let me know when you do.'

Bray threw his half-smoked cigarette at Danny's feet. Without saying more, he turned and walked across the forecourt, pausing briefly at the glittering shards of bloodied glass on the gravel.

Chapter Forty-Nine

Frank Flowers hobbled into the shop and balanced his stick against the new glass cabinet full of fresh stock. Lizzie had left the prices written on a list by the till; he couldn't go far wrong. Slowly he reached for the leather apron, his fingers fumbling to tie its strings. He was managing better now, though the smallest of careless movements triggered an agonizing back pain. His ribs had mended and so had his shoulder, though there was still a swelling on his chest. He didn't mind that. He was lucky the entry point of the knife had been above his heart. He had a lot to be grateful for, as Lizzie reminded him every day. She kept on at him to exercise, but she didn't really know how much pain he was in. And when the pain came, so did the voices. He hadn't told her that. He didn't want to land back up in the loony bin.

'You all right, Frank?'

It was Fowler, arriving with his usual lack of charm, almost swallowing his roll-up in his haste to drag in the nicotine. But all in all, he wasn't a bad bloke, Frank thought. And far be it from him to wish Elmo and Fowler away. He was all for keeping them close. There were forces out there that were still gunning for him. He was convinced of that. Ever since that night at the hospital, he'd been taunted by the knowledge that, since they hadn't finished him off, they would return to complete the job. But he knew that as long as he had people around him they wouldn't attack. They preferred dark and lonely places to carry out their dirty work. His voices warned him of that. And he believed them. 'Me back is giving me a bit of gyp,' Frank replied with a shrug.

'Then leave all the lugging to me,' Fowler told him, puffing smoke into Frank's eyes as he tied his long hair behind his head with string. One of Fowler's dark, close-set eyes, Frank noticed, had a slight cast to it. It made Frank want to look over his shoulder to see if there was anyone behind him. But he'd done that before and there never was. Still, as Fowler stood at least a foot and a half above him and was wider even than Bert, Frank always felt safe in his company.

'Thanks, mate,' Frank agreed readily. It was his first day in the shop and he wasn't sure he liked it. The two customers he'd served had given him the cold shoulder. No doubt they recalled the old Frank Flowers who'd tried to blow this place sky-high. But, as long as he stayed on his pills, he could crack this. He had a bundle to make up to Lizzie and his dad. And Danny of course. Though he didn't hold out much hope in that direction.

'You ain't going to the funeral, then?' Fowler asked as he began to roll up his shirtsleeves. Frank enjoyed watching the muscle protrude from his arms and the animal strength of his physique. With Fowler around, he didn't have any worries. Or at least, not as many as he would have had if he was alone and back in his rooms in Poplar. The one drawback was that he'd not been able to get himself another shooter. This was the East End. Lizzie was a lone woman, in a tough business. Every trader had hardware stored under the counter. Dad's revolver had looked the business even if it hadn't been used in years. Now, thanks to Danny and Bert chucking it in the Thames, he didn't even have that.

'Didn't know the bloke very well,' Frank replied, relieved that at last, almost three weeks after Richard Ryde's death, the poor sod was being laid to rest. The coppers had called round the shop once or twice to speak to Lizzie. He'd been worried they'd nose around. Not that they'd find anything. Not anything incriminating anyway. Danny had got rid of the bloodstains, done a good job in fact. There was nothing to connect Frank with the dead geezer. There had been no noises about stiffs washing up in the docks either. He'd scoured the newspaper every day. There was nothing, but the cops' presence had made him uneasy.

'Did the law find out who done him?'

'No. Whoever it was has vanished.' Frank returned his attention to the till and pressed a key. A tray sprang out with a tinkle, neatly proportioned into coins and notes. He licked his lips at the enviable sight. Then recalled Lizzie's words to him the night before.

'I've counted every penny in that till, Frank. I know how much there is to the last farthing. And I'll expect to see all your sales written down in the book. So don't try having me over, because you'll be out on your arse if you do.'

Frank smiled. His girl was a real goer. He wouldn't be tempted, no sir. But he could look, couldn't he?

'What's the score then?' Fowler asked as he hoisted a sack of potatoes onto his shoulders. 'The missus giving you the thumbs-up?'

Frank warmed to the fact Fowler had referred to Lizzie as his missus. 'First day in the shop and it's good to be back,' he lied half-heartedly.

'Yeah, this trade ain't a bad lark,' agreed Fowler. 'I never earned a straight wedge before.'

'What's your line, then?' Frank enquired curiously. He'd never had a real conversation with Fowler before.

'This and that.'

Frank nodded knowingly. 'Been around, have you?'

'You could say that.'

'You ever used that iron bar?'

Fowler frowned and lowered the sack carefully. 'Once or twice. Why?'

'No reason, mate. Just wondering. I like something a bit more substantial myself.'

'Like what?'

Frank hesitated, trapped between the impulse to brag that in another life he had been a seasoned villain and admitting those days were over. 'I just wondered,' Frank said, trying to behave himself, 'how it works when the opposition has got an unfair advantage. This Leonard Savage is a maniac. He's tooled his crew up to the eyeballs. You can only swing that bar and no doubt it would do the job. But someone shafting you with a bullet . . .' Frank shrugged, watching the cast turn in Fowler's eye as the big man slowly smiled.

'Yeah, well, a bar's not all I've got.'

Frank felt his insides start to warm. His face took on an expression of anticipation. 'Really?'

Fowler glanced furtively over his shoulder. 'Only don't tell no one.'

'On me life,' vowed Frank, flattening the palm of his hand over his heart. He waited, breath held, as Fowler seemed to pause, weighing up how much he could reveal.

'Your old lady don't want no guns.'

'No. But she's a woman, ain't she?'

'They don't think like men.'

'Too right,' Frank agreed. 'But what was you saying?'

Fowler jerked his head and moved as stealthily as his bulk would allow him into the storeroom. He waited until Frank shuffled to join him. When Fowler was certain they couldn't be overheard, he undid his flies and his leather belt and began to peel down his trousers.

'Hold on a minute, old son,' Frank began, but then stopped, his eyes almost popping out of his head. Strapped to Fowler's muscular left thigh was a small leather pouch. Fowler gently lifted his tackle a few inches to access what was in the pouch.

'Pint-sized but lethal,' Fowler told him as he drew out the small revolver.

'Christ,' breathed Frank. 'What's that?'

Fowler grinned. 'A Smith & Wesson derringer.'

'I've heard the Yanks use them.'

'Yeah, nice bit of hardware, ain't it?'

Frank nodded, unable to tear his eyes away from the unassuming weapon that he'd heard was a favourite of the Mob.

Fowler returned the gun to the holster and did up his trousers. 'Small but lethal and no one sees what you've got strapped to your leg.' Fowler chuckled. 'Takes a bit of practice, mind. When we're quiet one day, I'll show you how it works.'

'I'll take you up on that.'

Frank watched the big man stride into the shop and sling the spuds over his shoulder. He stood for a while mentally reviewing the information he'd just gleaned. That nifty piece of hardware is just up my street, he thought enviously, making a mental note to take Fowler up on his promise.

Chapter Fifty

Lizzie knew from Ethel that the Lewisham church where Mrs Ryde worshipped was only ten minutes' walk away from her house. But Richard's mysterious death with its unanswered questions had required more investigation. Finally, bearing no fruit, it had been referred to the coroner.

So it was on an overcast morning at the end of July that Lizzie sat with Polly, Tom and Bert, together with Danny, Flo and Syd, Doug and Lil at the back of the Lewisham Church of England church. They were watching the solemn procession of mourners file into the pews to the left of the light oak coffin resting in the aisle. On its surface were floral tributes, Mrs Ryde's at the head, a wreath decorated with red ribbons and lilies. The floral spray at the foot was Ethel and the children's. Lizzie's was a small, discreet posy of violets, next to Lil and Doug's white chrysanthemums.

Mrs Ryde, a tall, extremely thin woman, with Richard's gaunt face and slight stoop, sat with her sister in the front pew. Ethel, Rosie and Timothy joined them, but throughout the service, Lizzie watched Mrs Ryde dab a handkerchief at her eyes. Never once did she glance at Ethel who sat with her head bowed.

When the funeral service was over, Richard's coffin was carried by the pall bearers into the hearse waiting outside. Mrs Ryde drew a black lace veil attached to her hat over her face. Together with Ethel, Rosie and Timothy, she was escorted to another black limousine. Lizzie looked for Ethel's and the children's faces as the car drove past, but none were visible.

'Are you going to the cemetery?' Flo asked as they stood in a little group outside the church.

Lizzie nodded. 'I'd like to be there for Ethel and the kids.'

'Yes, course. You don't mind if Syd and me don't go, do you? I've got a doctor's appointment as me ankles are like balloons,' Flo said from under the small black hat she was wearing. She was very big now. Syd stood with his arm supporting her, dressed smartly in his dark suit. He hadn't said much to Lizzie; she couldn't help thinking when she looked at him of Frank's watch on Walter's wrist.

'Thanks for coming,' Lizzie said, giving her sister a hug.

'Poor Ethel, don't know how she's going to cope.' Flo said goodbye to everyone.

As Flo and Syd walked over to their car, parked beside the church, Lizzie thought of her visit to Flo's last week. The house had changed considerably since Syd had started work with his brothers. Flo had everything she wanted. A brand-new pram for the baby. All its white and lemon knitted clothes laid out in a drawer in a chest beside the cot in the small bedroom. Syd had painted the room in rainbow colours. They'd bought an expensive set of cuddly toys from Oxford Street, a journey made in their brand-new Morris. Flo hadn't said how much anything had cost. Nor had she admitted to the price of the three-piece suite in the front room. But it was clear she was very proud of her new lifestyle as she praised Syd's job.

'Are we going to see the coffin go in the ground?' Polly asked as she stood in her dark blue summer dress and two black ribbons tied in her hair. Lizzie had worn dark colours too: a black jacket with a velvet collar and a grey pleated skirt, with a discreet black cloche over her hair.

'Yes, we are.' Lizzie looked at the sombre faces around her. Danny, Bert and Doug all wore dark suits and ties. Tom was wearing his school uniform and Lil had chosen a close-fitting black suit and shoes, attaching a little black lace cap to her up-drawn hair.

'We'd better go then,' Lil said, nudging Doug. 'And get it over and done with.'

'Is Mrs Ryde holding a wake?' Lizzie asked as they walked towards Doug's and Danny's cars parked close by.

'Yes, but me and Doug ain't invited.'

'Why's that?' Lizzie asked as the men and children climbed into the cars.

'Ethel said the old girl wants a word with her and the kids on their own.'

'What does Mrs Ryde mean by that?'

Lil narrowed her eyes. 'It's all about money with Mrs Ryde. And what she's going to do with the house.'

'What house?' Lizzie asked in surprise.

'The house my daughter calls home.'

'But I thought Richard bought it. What's it got to do with his mother?'

'Turns out he borrowed her money and put her name on the deeds, not Ethel's.'

'What!' Lizzie stared at Lil. 'Why did he do that?'

'Probably cos his mother insisted.' Lil gave a mirthless smile. 'If you ask me, that old bat can do anything she pleases now she's got the upper hand. Which, of course, is always what she wanted.' Lil glanced at Danny's car. 'Call back at our place after it's all over for a drink if you like. We can have a bit of a natter.'

'I'm glad that's over,' Lil sighed tiredly as she put on the kettle. 'I feel sorry for Ethel and the kids having to suffer the rest of the day in Lewisham.'

'How's Ethel getting home?' Lizzie asked.

'Doug told Ethel he'd call for her but she said they'd get the bus. She didn't know what time they'd leave. Now take these ham sandwiches in to the men. They'll go down a treat with the beer. Meanwhile I'll give the kids some sponge and lemonade out in the yard. It's a lovely day and they seem happy enough to play out there.'

Once everyone had something to eat and drink, Lil and Lizzie sat down at the kitchen table. Lizzie ran her hands

over its scrubbed wooden surface. She could remember
the times as a child she had sat here next to her mother.
Lil and Kate had shared many secrets over the years. It
was always nudges, winks, and laughter erupting. But
during the war, Neil and Greg had died and it had all
changed. Lil had gone into herself, hiding her grief, even
from Doug. But Kate Allen hadn't been deterred for long.
She'd eventually pulled Lil from the doldrums. Lizzie
realized with a start that, in a strange way, history was
repeating itself. Now it was Ethel who needed help.

Lil sliced the sponge, put down the knife and sat down
with a sigh. 'I know Ethel has been having it off with that
mechanic.'

Lizzie opened her mouth, then shut it.

'I saw them one day,' Lil continued, sipping from the
generous glass of sherry she had poured herself. 'It was
months ago. They were out in that Yankee motor of his.'

'And you didn't tell Ethel?' Lizzie said in surprise. She
didn't think Lil was capable of keeping something like
that to herself.

'No, I didn't.'

'Why not?'

Lil's eyes were distant. 'Because she was happier than
I'd ever seen her.'

'And you thought it was because of Cal?'

'I'd be daft if I didn't,' Lil said, coming sharply back to
the present. 'You've known too, haven't you? You must
have.'

Lizzie nodded slowly.

'Don't worry, I'm not going to have a go,' Lil assured her.

'Ethel found something with Cal she didn't have with Richard,' Lizzie replied. 'I'm not saying it was right or wrong, but it happened. And Ethel must have had a reason.'

Lil nodded. 'I don't like to speak ill of the dead but it was me and Doug who pushed Ethel into marriage. Ethel and Richard was too young to know any better. Nor did we, as grown-ups, it seems.'

'Lil, we all make mistakes. But Ethel has two lovely kids, something she don't regret.'

Lil gave a tight smile. 'She's brought them up nice, too. Given them a bit of freedom. I always kept Ethel on a short leash. Doug said I'd pay the penalty and I have. Ethel don't confide in me. Not the important things.' Lil turned the glass slowly between her fingers. 'And I can see why. I've got strong opinions and I voice them. But losing Greg and Neil together like that – well, I was never the same woman again. It ain't no excuse, but I was always worried that I might lose Ethel.' She gave Lizzie a sad smile. 'I'm still human, though. I need a daughter's love as much as any mother.'

'And you've got it. Ethel thinks the world of you. We all do.'

'Ta, love. You're a pal.' Lil sighed and stood up, going to the sink and staring out into the yard. 'Don't look as if Flo and Syd are back yet.'

Lizzie took her mug to the draining board. She

wondered if she could share with Lil her worries about Syd and the watch. As if reading her thoughts Lil turned and frowned into her face. 'You look a bit peaky, love. Is something wrong?'

'No, not really.'

'You ain't up the spout too, are you?' Lil said with a wry smile.

Lizzie shook her head and smiled. 'I hope Syd and Flo are all right.'

'What do you mean? Cos they had to go today?'

'Well no, not really.'

'Is it Syd and all his new airs and graces?'

Lizzie stared at Lil. 'So you've noticed something?'

Lil rolled her eyes and grinned. 'Come on, it's about time we had a good gas.' She grabbed Lizzie's arm and wheeled her back to the table. 'Now sit down and this time you will have a sherry. It'll lubricate your throat muscles, gel.' She took a clean glass from the cupboard and put it on the table, filling it to the brim.

Chapter Fifty-One

'You know, I'd never have had Syd down for a snob,' Lil said as she lit yet another cigarette. 'But it gets me goat the way that job at the scrapyard has changed him.'

'Have you seen much of him lately?' Lizzie sipped slowly at the sherry.

'I see him drive off in the mornings.' Lil topped up her glass.

'Have his family been round?'

'Yes, they do think a lot of Flo.'

'I'm sure everything's all right, but—' Lizzie said, on the point of telling Lil about the watch when Lil started to cough. She went to the sink and poured a glass of water, drinking it quickly.

'Sorry about that,' Lil said, returning to her chair, wiping her lips with her hanky. 'It's these damn fags, I'll have to cut down. Now where were we?'

'I was saying about Syd—'

'That's right, you was. And I couldn't agree more. Ever since he got that car, it's a case of one-upmanship. He parks it next to Doug's which is half the size and last week he hit our bumper. He said to Doug, could Doug please park up the road a bit, as he didn't have enough room outside his house. I ask you! There's all the street to park in. And we were here first. And have you seen what they've bought on tick? A new three-piece suite and the old one had good wear in it. Flo used to come in for a cuppa every day, but all that's stopped now, as if she hasn't got time for her neighbours. She says she's knackered carrying the baby, but walking ten feet into my front room ain't going to kill her.' Lil stopped, finishing her drink. She blinked at Lizzie. 'Sorry, ducks. I wasn't going to say nothing. But you brought it up.'

Lizzie bit her lip. She decided not to say anything about Syd. She didn't want to make things worse for Flo, who seemed to be getting it in the neck right now.

'I expect it's just the baby,' Lizzie said diplomatically. 'Flo's all at twos and threes and Syd wants to do the best he can. He's a good soul at heart. And when the baby's here, as their best friend and neighbour, you'll be the first person they'll call on.'

Lizzie was relieved to see that she had done the right thing by keeping what she knew about Syd to herself as Lil nodded slowly.

'It'll be nice to hold a baby in my arms again,' Lil agreed on a wistful sigh. 'Especially a boy.'

Lizzie's heart melted. She knew Lil, in her maudlin state, was thinking of her dead sons, Greg and Neil.

*   *   *

It was late afternoon by the time Lizzie thought about leaving. Lil had insisted they all stay for a cheese and pickle late luncheon, washed down by another round of drinks. Lizzie noticed who was doing the best of the drinking; Lil, she realized, must be worried about Ethel's future.

'You ain't leaving, are you?' Flo asked as she walked into the kitchen. She looked at Lizzie who was about to call Polly and Tom. 'Syd's just parking the car. Or have you got to go back to the shop?'

Lizzie smiled. Perhaps this was the opportunity she had been waiting for to get Syd on his own. 'There's no rush.'

'Don't your patient need looking after?' Flo asked in a sarcastic voice.

'If you mean Frank, he's up on his feet and helping in the shop.'

'Helping to fiddle the till, you mean.'

'Now, now, you two,' Lil warned, pushing Flo towards the front room. 'We're toasting the dead here today. Not slagging off the living. Go in, both of you, with the men and I'll bring the refreshment.'

Lizzie followed Flo into the parlour and made herself comfortable on the settee beside Danny, who was in conversation with Doug. Flo sat with Bert at the draw-leaf table that still held the remaining bottles of ale and a saucer of pickles. When Lil brought in a plate of cheese sandwiches and an unopened bottle of port wine, they all helped themselves.

A few minutes later, Syd appeared. The only available seat was next to Lizzie and he took it. Lizzie smiled as he sat beside her, enquiring, 'What did the doctor say about Flo's ankles?'

Without pouring his ale into his glass, Syd drank from the bottle Lil gave him. 'She's doing too much as usual. That's why they swell up.'

'It's not long to go though, now.'

'Just over two months, if she's on her dates.'

'The baby's room looks lovely,' Lizzie said, wondering how she could approach the subject of the watch without offending him. 'Painted in all them lovely colours.'

'It was a quick job. I'm very busy at work, you know.'

'Yes, Flo said. I'm glad it's going well.' Lizzie looked across at Flo who was still talking to Bert as she ate a cheese sandwich. She could hear Danny talking to Doug and Lil was out in the kitchen. 'Syd, do you mind if I ask you a question?'

'Depends what it is,' Syd muttered and gave her a suspicious frown.

'I hope this doesn't offend you as we haven't seen eye to eye of late.'

'You could say that.'

Lizzie gathered her courage. She didn't know what she'd done to offend Syd. But it was clear by his answer that somehow she had. 'Syd, on the day you were married, I saw Walter wearing Frank's watch. I wondered where he got it from.'

Syd's face went a beetroot red. 'Are you accusing my brother of stealing?'

'No, course not, but—'

'It sounds like it.'

'Syd, I recognized the watch. It had a big face with large numbers and it went missing when—'

Syd stood up, spilling his beer over his suit and some over Lizzie. 'Now look what's happened!' He brushed the froth from his jacket. 'If I ruin this suit it will be down to you,' he muttered under his breath, and charging from the room he made a swift exit.

Lizzie sat with her mouth open. When she turned round, the conversation had stopped. Everyone was staring at her.

'Everything all right?' Danny asked.

She nodded.

'What was that all about?' Flo said, struggling to her feet. 'What made him storm off like that?'

'Don't know.' Lizzie felt embarrassed. She couldn't repeat the conversation she'd just had with Syd.

'You must have said something to upset him.'

Lizzie fell silent as Lil came rushing in.

'What the bleeding hell is going on with your husband?' she demanded of Flo. 'Syd just pushed past me, went out the back and slammed the door in my face.'

Flo hurried past Lil. A second later, there was another thump from the back door.

No one commented but, when Lil attempted to refill the glasses, everyone shook their heads.

Now it really was time to leave, Lizzie decided. 'I think it's time me and Pol went.'

'I'll run you back,' Danny said, collecting his jacket

from the chair. As he put it on, there was a knock at the front door. He went to answer it.

When he returned he was with Cal. Cal's face and hands were smeared with dirt. His smelled of smoke and his overalls were black. 'It ain't good news,' Danny said. 'The garage has been torched.'

Chapter Fifty-Two

Danny looked at Cal. 'What happened?'

'I was in the workshop when I heard an explosion. I downed tools and ran up to the garage. The stink of petrol was everywhere. Next the staircase was on fire. I had to think quick, so I chucked the boards back over the cellar. But then the van you brought in for sale – the one we was about to do up, caught light. I had to make a run for it. Before I got a few yards I was blown off me feet.'

'Are you all right, son?' Doug asked in concern. 'Are you hurt?'

'No, just fuming, Doug, that I couldn't get my hands on Savage.'

'How do you know he did it?' Danny asked.

'Robert and Phil, two of the river men, dragged me out of the garage. If it hadn't been for them I wouldn't be here now. They told me they saw Savage parked in his Daimler while his men did the dirty work.'

'Would they swear to that?'

'To you they would. But not the cops.'

'What about the Nissen hut and all our spares?'

Cal just shook his head. 'I left the firemen hosing it down.'

'So what's left?'

'Of the garage? Just a load of muck and mangled iron.'

'And the workshop?'

'It's anyone's guess. We won't know till the firemen have finished.'

'What about your motor?' Doug asked.

Cal shrugged. 'It was parked on the forecourt and I managed to drive it onto the road before it got—' He stopped and began to cough. Lil dragged him into the parlour and pushed him down onto the settee. She went to the kitchen and brought back a glass of water. Cal drank thirstily, looking up at everyone with white-rimmed eyes under the smudges of black. 'We've lost the warehouse, Danny. Savage made sure he did a good job this time.'

Lizzie saw Danny's face fill with anger. He strode towards the door but Doug jumped up and barred his way. 'Danny, where are you going?'

'Over to Aldgate and his so-called office.'

'Don't lose your rag. This is what he wants.'

'Out of me way, Doug.'

'Think, boy! Think!' Doug exclaimed, refusing to let him pass. 'You're walking straight into trouble.'

'You and I know, Doug, I have to settle this once and for all. He's stolen my livelihood. All I worked for in Aussie. And it won't stop with me, will it? He'll move in on all the traders. Someone's got to make a stand.'

'I'm with Danny.' Bert spoke for the first time,

standing up and going to Danny's side. 'We can't let him push us around.'

'He needs sorting,' Cal agreed with Bert. 'There's three of us and we can take them if we're canny.'

'Just hold on!' Lizzie poked Bert in the chest. 'Didn't you listen to what Doug had to say? Leonard Savage is streets ahead of your thinking. He knows you'll go after him. That's just what he's waiting for. What can three of you do, unarmed, against his men?'

Danny smiled without humour. 'I should have done what Frank did, not had a go at him for using Dad's shooter. After today I see he was bang within his rights. The East End is being carved up and us with it if we can't defend ourselves.'

'It's a bit late in the day to side with your brother,' Lizzie retorted angrily. 'Use your brains instead and ask yourself why he torched the garage.'

'Obvious, ain't it, he wanted my gaff.'

'Well, then, why burn it?' Lizzie demanded. 'The truth is he didn't want the garage. If he did he'd never have burned down a place that was of use to him. He lied blatantly to you. The garage isn't the issue. It's the land.'

Danny's frown deepened. 'But it's wasteland. In winter it floods, in summer it's just baked gravel, dust and weeds.'

'Lizzie's right, Danny,' Doug agreed quickly. 'The land must have a value to Savage. He never wanted the garage in the first place.'

'He still torched my property,' Danny said angrily. 'I can't let him get away with that.'

'Playing into his hands won't help.'

'So what's your suggestion?' Danny couldn't hide the contempt in his voice. 'Go back to working a barrow?'

'Course not,' Doug broke in before Lizzie could respond. 'You'll set up again, like Lizzie did. Put your grievance aside for the moment. Go to the garage and suss out the damage. It might not be as bad as you think.'

Lizzie slipped her bag over her shoulder and turned to Lil. 'Can you look after Tom and Polly, till we get back?'

'Where are you off to?'

'I'm going with Danny.'

'I don't need a nursemaid,' Danny said bitterly.

'This ain't just about you, Danny. Like you said, it could be any of us traders next time.'

A fact which, Lizzie knew, no one would argue with.

'No insurance?' the chief repeated as he looped one of the long hoses over his shoulder and paused. 'Then you've got a problem, chum.'

'I ran it as a garage, not a warehouse,' Danny replied as he stared at the remains: heaps of twisted debris lit up every now and then by bursts of flames, to be swiftly doused with water by the firemen.

'You should have thought more seriously about where to open your business.'

'This was my only option.' Danny stared at the blackened steel girders of the warehouse and the empty space where once his office had been. 'The warehouse had height and space enough to service the bigger lorries. Plus a small cellar we used as the workshop.' His gaze travelled slowly to the ash-covered pile under which the cellar was buried. 'Do you know if there's anything salvageable down there?'

'No idea. You can see for yourself there's a mountain of rubbish on top of it.'

'When can I get in there to clear it?'

'Not till tomorrow at the earliest.' The fireman tipped back his helmet. 'Got any idea how it started?'

'That's what I'd like to know.'

'Petrol's lethal. So's rubber. A single match or spark could've done this. Or a dog-end. Your mate didn't seem to have much to say for himself.' He nodded at Cal.

'I can tell you for certain my mechanic's not careless enough to start a fire.'

'He was lucky he wasn't fried down in that cellar.'

Danny was silent, considering his response. Doug and Lizzie had talked some sense into him, but this was hard to swallow. He knew very well it was Savage, but what proof did he have? The river people wouldn't back him. And even if they did, they wouldn't be believed by the coppers who had as much respect for the homeless contingent and their plight as the ex-bargees had for them. But, all the same, this was the time to make his point, if he was going to make it at all.

'Don't go anywhere near the area today,' the fireman warned. 'There's no beams left to fall as the wood went up first with the stairs. But the metals are as hot as a furnace. And one thing more, the Poplar Constabulary was here but another copper came along. Plain–clothes. He's over there.' He nodded to the wharf wall. 'You could take it as a bit of luck you aren't insured and not claiming. Else it all might look a bit iffy to him.'

Danny watched the fireman return to his large red vehicle with its extendable ladders and hoses threaded out through the wet ash. Slowly he turned and fixed his gaze on Detective Inspector Bray.

'What are you doing here?' he demanded as he walked over, noting the detective's smug expression. 'Come to gloat?'

'Couldn't help but notice you had a bit of trouble,' Bray said easily. 'I saw the smoke and wondered if it was you.'

'So now you know.'

'You had a little accident?' Bray said softly, pulling down the brim of his trilby.

'Don't know how it happened,' Danny said shortly.

'Curiouser and curiouser.'

'Sod off, Bray.'

'I can see you have full confidence in the arm of the law.' Bray laughed with genuine amusement. He stood up, squaring his shoulders under his grubby raincoat. 'You've got to admit, it's been busy around here, lately. A hit and run – or an accident – or was it something else? A burning building – a case of arson – or could it be more? Like, how much was you insured for?'

Danny stared into Bray's eyes and smiled. 'I wasn't.'

Bray looked surprised. 'So you're not collecting?'

'No. Sorry to disappoint you.'

Bray's eyes narrowed. 'Oh, you never do that, Flowers. You always come up with a Brahma.'

Danny watched the policeman turn and walk slowly through a small crowd of onlookers. The acrid smell of rubber from the burning tyres hung heavily in the air while a thin plume of smoke twisted above their heads. The heat still radiated from the wreckage and he stared at the firemen hauling in the long hoses that had emptied thousands of gallons of water over the burning warehouse. A lake of evil-smelling grey muck squelched against the firemen's boots. Some still wore their breathing apparatus as they worked to douse the glowing metal remains of the van. Was there anything to be salvaged under that lot? It didn't seem likely.

The only thing he could draw comfort from was that he'd had no Port of London Authority lorries in for repair. The last ten-tonner had been returned yesterday. And his own wheels, the roadster, might well have been incinerated too, if he hadn't stopped by Lil's.

'What did Bray want?' Lizzie asked as she joined him.

'He'd like to nab me for an insurance job.' He turned to look down at her.

'Did you have any?'

'No. I was meaning to shop around. Try to get some cover. But I have to admit the fireman was right. This place was never meant for a garage.'

'Danny, if you need—'

'No, I don't, thanks.' He wasn't about to admit to

being brassic, though God only knew what he was going to do now.

'Is there anything we can salvage?' Bert asked as he and Cal walked slowly towards them.

'Can't go in till tomorrow. But I doubt it.' Danny pushed his hand through his hair. He was trying to put aside his anger, but all he could see was Savage's ugly mug looming up in front of him. 'You'll regret this,' Savage had warned on the day he'd tried to buy him out. 'I'm not finished with you or your poxy garage.'

And the man had been true to his word.

Chapter Fifty-Three

Lizzie sipped the hot tea she had been handed, grateful for the hospitality of the river men who had made them welcome after the fire brigade had left. Danny, Bert and Cal were talking to a poorly dressed man called Robert. They all sat in a semi-circle on upturned wooden boxes inside the derelict building the river men called home.

'You're sure it was Savage?' Danny asked and received a firm nod.

'The same one as come round here and tried to kick us out,' said a woman who had put a battered old kettle on the brazier to boil.

'When was that?' Danny asked.

'A few nights ago. They did us over. Smashed our stuff and, when Robert and Phil tried to stop them, they roughed them up.'

'Told us to get out,' said Phil, who was sitting by Bert. 'Said they'd torch us if we didn't.'

'But it looks like you was first,' said Robert, nodding at what was left of the garage.

'Anything left of your gear?' Phil asked, pushing his straggly dark hair from his face.

Danny shook his head. 'Might be one or two bits in the store. I can't get down in me cellar yet to see if the tools are okay.'

'We'll help if you like,' said Robert.

Danny smiled. 'I'd be much obliged.'

Lizzie noted all the river men still wore their greatcoats, despite the fact it was high summer. But the woman called Mary was sweating as she worked over the brazier. Like the handful of women Lizzie had seen about the encampment, she was dressed in a long skirt, boots and patched blouse with a leather belt. A brightly coloured scarf was wrapped around her head and two black plaits fell out from it. Lizzie thought she must be quite young as there were children playing close by and she appeared to be their mother. But the hard life Mary had lived made her look much older. Her swarthy skin was the same rough texture as the other women's. These were the families of the tough breed of men who, as bargees and boatmen, had made their living on the water. Sadly they had fallen on hard times and their barges were gone. Like Danny, they had lost everything.

Lizzie liked the way Danny and Cal spoke to them, as old friends. He'd told her how much he liked their music and singing and the way the kids played down on the foreshore, digging up bits of coal and timber for their fires. Lizzie thought fondly of the days when, as children, she and Bert and Vinnie had done much the same.

Searching for fuel in the mud, they had been dirty but happy. Just as these children were.

Lizzie smiled at a ragged infant who sat at Mary's feet. Was it a boy or a girl? The child was content as it played with a handful of stones in the dirt.

'Did you tell the copper?' Phil asked.

'That it was Savage?' Danny shook his head.

'Sorry we couldn't chip in, mate,' said Robert, staring into the heat of the brazier. 'But it don't pay us to mix with the bobbies. They'd only try to move us on, so we keep our heads down.'

'Aren't you worried Savage will come back?' asked Lizzie.

'Course,' said Mary. 'But we can't just up sticks. Nowhere to go. We been here a year now, longest we ever been anywhere on land.'

'What happened to your barges?'

'We had to sell 'em as in the depression the dock work dried up.'

'Why is Savage so interested in this land?' Cal asked.

'Dunno.' Robert drank his tea, then looked at Danny. 'With you and us gone, it would leave a big space.'

'Who docs this warehouse belong to?' Lizzie asked.

'Some old geezer up West.'

They all sat silently, until Phil got up and paced around, kicking up dirt as he went. Robert went to talk to him and after a while they both returned.

'There's something else you'd better know,' said Robert, scratching his long beard.

'What's that?' Danny asked.

'That bloke on the bike,' Phil said in almost a whisper. 'What was he to you?'

Danny lifted his shoulders on a shrug. 'A friend's husband.'

'Not family, then?'

'No. But close enough.'

'The coppers ain't found out who done it?'

Lizzie's heart beat faster. 'No, why?'

Robert looked around him, as did Phil. Their bearded faces and dark eyes glowed in the light of the fire. 'It was Savage,' he said, stooping low. 'We was sitting on the wall and got a good butcher's. The geezer on the bike drove under the car's wheels. When the window broke, we saw it was Savage in the back seat.'

'Are you certain it was him?' Danny said.

'Yeah.'

'Savage?' Cal repeated slowly. 'But he didn't even know Richard.'

'Reckon it was just bad luck,' said Phil, 'but only cowards drive off and don't stop to help.'

'We ain't telling the cops, mind.' Robert shook his head fiercely.

Lizzie turned to Mary. 'But Leonard Savage killed my friend's husband, a young man with a wife and a family. He needs to be reported. If we all go to the police together—'

Mary shook her head fiercely. 'You heard the men, love. We don't want nothin' to do with the law. Or with that crook.'

'But if he comes back here as he threatened, you won't have any choice but to defend yourselves.'

'We'll cross that bridge when we come to it,' Robert said flatly. 'Sorry about your friend. Real sorry.'

'Time for us to go,' Danny said, getting to his feet suddenly. 'Thanks for the tea.'

'Remember, no cops,' Robert shouted after them.

Out in the warm evening air, the grey ash skittered around their feet. 'We can't do nothing more tonight,' Cal said, looking at Danny. 'See you here in the morning and we'll start the clearing up.'

Danny nodded but, as Cal went to walk away, Danny took his arm. 'Listen, mate, there's nothing here for you now. No wage and no work.'

Cal grinned. 'Reckon we'll manage somehow. Till we get our lean-to set up.'

'Yeah,' Bert agreed. 'You ain't finished yet.'

Danny made an effort to smile. 'See you in the morning then.'

'Do you think the river men are telling the truth about Richard?' Lizzie asked as they walked to Danny's car.

'Why would they make it up?' Danny said.

'Don't seem like it was intended,' Bert muttered.

Lizzie climbed into the rear. As they drove away, she could see the river men sitting on the wall. She didn't blame them for not wanting to be witnesses. They were as afraid of the law as they were of the underworld.

She could taste the smoke on her lips and feel the dirt on her face. Like Danny, she wanted to vent her anger.

Her best friend had been made a widow because of Savage. Danny had lost his garage because of Savage. The villain had threatened her and her business. What would come next?

'Are we going to tell Ethel?' Bert said quietly.

'Not yet. What good would the knowledge do her, if the man who killed her husband can't be brought to justice?'

'Perhaps not in a court of law,' Danny said, his voice low.

Lizzie waited for him to say more. But he just drove on through the streets, his face set in hard lines as he stared ahead.

Chapter Fifty-Four

'She knows,' Syd said, looking at his brother who was counting out the day's takings. 'I'm telling you, the watch gave us away. I didn't even know you'd nicked it!'

'Fell off in my hand,' said Walter, wetting his thumb as he flicked through the notes. 'Have it, if that makes you happy.'

'It's too late now.' Syd was so frustrated that he wanted to shake Walter. 'She's sussed out that we trounced her old man. I've no liking for him, but you knifed the geezer. He could have died.'

'So? Good riddance to bad rubbish.' Walter sat back in his chair and raised his hands behind his head, locking his fingers together. Putting his feet up on the desk he said with forced patience, 'Do you know, Syd, you're getting on me bleeding wick. All I hear is moans. I ask you to drive my motor, plain and simple. Thanks to Clifford you can now operate four wheels without driving into the back of a bus. But then, all of a sudden, you're on my case, moaning it's nicked.'

'Well, it is,' Syd retorted indignantly. He scraped back

his chair and stood up. Striding up and down the floor of the wooden hut that acted as the scrapyard office, he loosened his tie and stretched his short neck. He hated cheap suits. He hated vulgar ties. And Clifford insisted he wore them every day to impress the clients. Syd was going hot around the collar as he reflected on the duties he performed daily. Most of which were to drive villains from the East End to Soho and back. Not that Walter had ever admitted they were hard men, doing deals that Syd overheard from the back seat and which were having the effect of turning his hair prematurely grey. They weren't your average punter and Syd had recognized the fact from the start. What had possessed him to give up his job as a fish porter? How had it happened that he'd got himself entangled with the escapades of his two brothers? Why had he listened to the Missus when she told him he'd never regret his decision to join the firm? Why had he persuaded Flo that his family might be rough around the edges, but they were legit? If the blagging going on in the back of the motor as he drove Walter's clients up to the city was true, then he was in trouble.

'Your motor's got new plates and a paint job,' Walter was saying as he clipped one end off a cigar and stared innocently at Syd. 'No one knows it was used on a job.'

'But I do,' said Syd, beginning to feel the same hopeless dismay that he'd had each day for weeks now. When he woke up in the morning he tried to convince himself he was looking forward to the day ahead. 'I keep checking over my shoulder, wondering if the coppers are following me.'

At this, Walter lowered his feet and leaned his elbows on the desk in front of him. His smiling round face, benign, now began to turn ugly and Syd recognized that look. In fact he was afraid of it. And he was ashamed of himself for the way he was kowtowing to Walter. 'Syd, you've got all you could ever want in life. A pretty little missus, a kid on the way, a house full of new furniture, a motor and, basically, everything you could want to make your family happy. Yet every day you come in here and chew off me ear. Only six months ago you stank like a bag of shit. And now look at you. All tonsed up to the eyeballs and earning a generous wedge. I tell you, after all the family's done for you, I'm beginning to think you're an ungrateful sod.'

Syd stared into the red-veined eyes that bore down on him, and the fat finger that wagged in his face. He knew in his water that this was a message he wasn't meant to forget. His eyes had been well and truly opened since coming to the scrapyard. There were things he'd seen going on here that made his stomach curl. He tried to turn a blind eye to the violence, blagging and half-inching that went on, but he couldn't any longer. Lizzie had woken him up to the fact that he had a conscience. And conscience didn't mix with the firm's business.

'Look, take the day off,' Walter said easily, his tone immediately softening. He thumbed three large notes from the pile and threw them across at Syd. 'Go home, take the little lady out. Buy her something nice up West. You deserve it.'

Syd stared at the money. He didn't want it, but he was afraid to refuse it. There was threat hidden in Walter's voice, despite the bribe. Or, perhaps, because of it.

'Go on, get out of here.' Walter laughed easily. 'And tomorrow come in with a smile on your face.'

Syd knew he had his family to think of. Every time Walter reminded him of that, he felt the same sick twist in his guts. He was holding a candle to the devil. And the devil was staring right back at him.

It was Rosie who opened the door to greet Lizzie and Polly. 'Hello, Auntie Lizzie. Come in.'

Lizzie kissed Rosie's pale cheek as she entered the house to the smell of a Sunday roast cooking. 'How are you, Rosie?'

'All right, I suppose.'

'Is Mum there?'

'Yes, she's in the kitchen. Hello, Pol.' Rosie smiled. 'Come and see Mum, Pol, then we can go up to my room.'

Lizzie saw Polly nod eagerly as she grabbed Rosie's hand. Last week, when they had called round briefly to tell Ethel about Danny's misfortune, Polly had brought a drawing she'd made of Rosie. It was a very good drawing and Rosie had stuck it on her wall.

As they walked through to the kitchen, Lizzie thought how once Timothy would have been down those stairs in a flash. But Richard's death had affected him. Ethel complained he was going out a lot whereas once he was a home bird. Rosie was reluctant to go out, even giving up her evenings at the local youth club to stay with Ethel.

Ethel shut the stove door quickly. 'I didn't expect to see you two here on a Sunday.'

'We've left Frank to cook the dinner.'

'Uncle Frank said he won't burn it, like last time,' Polly said with a shy grin.

'He'd better not,' Ethel replied. 'Or we'll have the Yorkshire batter him.' It was an old joke and Lizzie was pleased to see a faint smile back on Ethel's face. Last week she had been very down. But it was still early days.

'We're going upstairs, Mum,' said Rosie. 'I'm gonna show Polly me new dress for my job.'

'Your job?' Lizzie asked in surprise.

'Yes. I'm starting work at a dress shop in Greenwich.'

'But you're still only fourteen,' Lizzie said, glancing quickly at Ethel. 'I thought you was staying on at school for your exams?'

'I'm fifteen next month,' Rosie said with a half-hearted smile. 'And I like fashion. I was getting bored at school, anyway.' She looked down at Polly. 'Come on, let's go upstairs.'

'Tell your brother to come and see Lizzie,' Ethel called after them as they ran through the hall and up the stairs.

'How's Timothy?' Lizzie asked as Ethel took the kettle off the stove and poured hot water into the china teapot.

'Distant,' Ethel murmured as she placed two cups and saucers on the table. 'I can't get a word out of him.'

'He misses Richard.'

'Yes, although they were never close.'

'Perhaps it's the shock.'

Ethel glanced up, her blue eyes moistening. 'Richard was too young to die.' She picked up the full cups. 'Let's go and sit in the garden. It's such a lovely day.'

Lizzie followed Ethel out through the open kitchen door and into the bright sunshine. Compared to the yards of the island houses, this was paradise. A green lawn, flowers, a little wooden shed and a proper path. Richard had been very proud of his garden, but it was very much his domain. Now it seemed almost forgotten. The grass was growing high, there were a few weeds in between the paving which Richard would have pulled up immediately. The kids had left their bikes by the coal bunker, the tyres making ridges in the lawn. Richard would have hated that, Lizzie thought, as they made themselves comfortable on the garden bench by the fence.

'Tell me how you really are,' Lizzie said as Ethel sat staring into space.

'Not good, if you want to know the truth.'

'You've got a bit thin, Ethel. You should be eating for two.'

'Yes, but without . . .' She paused, taking a deep breath. 'Even though we'd drifted apart, the house don't feel normal.'

'How are you managing for money?'

'We had some in the Post Office. I've been drawing on that. Richard would have a fit if he knew—' She stopped, shaking her head. 'I keep thinking he's here.'

'It'll take time to get used to things.'

Ethel played with her cup. 'Somehow I've got to make ends meet. Once Mrs Ryde puts the house up for sale—'

'When is that?' Lizzie asked. Ethel had said last week that the house was to be sold but she had been hoping Mrs Ryde would change her mind.

'She wrote and said she has a mortgage to pay. If I can't find the rent then she has to sell it.'

'But can she do that?'

'It's her house, not mine.'

'Can't she wait until you find a job?'

'Where am I going to get a job with a salary to match Richard's? He was earning good money. She's given us a month before she puts the house up for sale. She wants me and the kids to move in with her.'

By the expression on Ethel's face, Lizzie could see that Ethel hated the idea. 'Perhaps this is the right time to buy the leasehold of Mr James's shop,' Lizzie said eagerly.

But Ethel bit her lip. 'I've lost me confidence. I can't seem to think straight. I'd be no good to you right now.'

'I'm sure you'll be fine but I don't want to rush you.'

'We've got to have a home. The kids need security. There's so much to think of.'

'Does that mean you'll accept Mrs Ryde's offer?'

Ethel paused, trying to compose herself. 'It seems the sensible thing to do. She's got a very big house. Four bedrooms of which three are empty, two downstairs rooms, a large parlour and a dining room. There's a sizeable kitchen and scullery and a vast garden, as she reminded me in her letter.'

'Sensible perhaps, but will you be happy?'

Ethel shrugged. 'She is their gran after all.'

'Lil and Doug would have you.'

'How can I, when Mrs Ryde has got such a big house?'

'Does your mother-in-law know about the baby?'

'No. And I'm not telling her, not until I have to.'

Lizzie looked sadly at her miserable friend. 'It sounds like you've made up your mind.'

'What can I expect of life after what I did?'

Lizzie touched her friend's shoulder. 'You've got to stop thinking like that.'

'Richard's death was my fault.'

'It wasn't.'

'I was a married woman and went with another man. If I hadn't, Richard would be here today. We could have got on with our lives as a family.'

'Ethel, you're forgetting how unhappy you were with Richard and why you went with Cal.'

'I wish I'd never laid eyes on him.'

'Don't say that.'

'It's true.'

'You took a chance to be happy. In your eyes it was a mistake, but people make lots of mistakes. You can't spend your life punishing yourself at Mrs Ryde's.'

Ethel turned sharply and said, 'If I have a black baby, what will everyone think? All its life it will be considered not only a bastard but a second-class citizen as well. How am I going to live with that?'

'Ethel, stop this! You'll love your baby and so will everyone else.'

A tear stole its way down Ethel's gaunt cheek. 'I don't know how I'm going to cope.'

'You've got your children to help you.'

'But will they? What will they think of their mother?'

'They love you and will stick by you, no matter what. So will I. So will your mum and dad. And all your friends. You won't be on your own.' Lizzie put her cup down on the grass, along with Ethel's. 'Come here. Give me a hug.'

They embraced and Lizzie said softy, 'Cal is very worried about you.'

'When did you see him?' Ethel pushed her fingers over her wet face.

'The day before yesterday. Though there's no garage now, Danny and Cal have cleaned up all the mess and unearthed the tools. Luckily the fire didn't get to them. All the traders from Cox Street have been taking stuff over. Wood, tarpaulins, and sheet metal to form a temporary shelter. They won't get buses or lorries underneath, but the cellar can still be used as a workshop. And when they have a tall vehicle to mend, they can roll back the tarpaulin.'

'That's good.' Ethel nodded slowly.

'Are you sure you don't want to see Cal? He asked me when I saw you to tell you he's thinking of you.'

'Is that what you've come here for, to run his messages?' Ethel asked, hot colour flooding her cheeks.

'No, course not.'

'Then please don't mention his name again.'

'Sorry. It's no business of mine.'

Ethel didn't reply. Instead, she sat with her hands clasped, her fingers fidgeting again. Just then a tall figure walked from the back door and gave Lizzie a start. It was Timothy, but she had thought for a moment it was Richard. He looked very much like his father.

'Hello, Auntie Lizzie.'

'It's nice to see you, Timothy. How are you?' She wanted to give him a hug, but knew he felt too old for that now.

'Okay, thanks. I'm off out now, Mum.'

'Where are you going?' Ethel asked anxiously. 'Dinner will be ready soon.'

'I'm going out on my bike.'

'Please don't be long.'

Timothy took hold of his bicycle and, wheeling it out through the side gate, he didn't turn round to say goodbye.

'I'm sorry about that,' Ethel said heavily. 'He just won't talk and it's getting on my nerves.'

'He's a teenager,' Lizzie said. 'It's understandable.'

'He wasn't like that once. He was a mummy's boy.' Ethel stared after him. 'He just goes out and I don't see him for hours on end.'

'Grief takes us all in different ways.'

'On top of losing Richard,' Ethel said wearily, 'I'll have to break the news I'm expecting.'

On the drive home from Blackheath, Lizzie thought about what Ethel had said. Timothy had always been close; both mother and son were suffering from the burden of guilt that Richard's death had left them with. But what would happen when the new baby arrived?

It had been over an hour later by the time Lizzie could prise Polly away from Rosie's company. 'I want to be like Rosie when I grow up,' Polly said now as she sat in the van. 'A . . . a mi – minokin.'

'A what?' Lizzie asked with a frown.

'A lady what walks up and down in shops wearing posh clothes.'

'A mannequin, you mean.'

Polly nodded. 'Rosie's pretty, ain't she?'

'Yes, very.'

Polly sat on the edge of her seat. 'Can we go to Uncle Danny's and see the new garage?'

'It won't be finished yet.'

'But Tom will be there. Mrs Williams couldn't look after him today. She had to go and put flowers on the grave.'

'Mrs Williams?' Lizzie repeated with a curious smile.

'The lady that looks after Uncle Danny and Tom.'

'Oh yes, of course.'

'She's got to catch the train to go there as it's a long way away. Tom asked if he could go on a train as he ain't been on one much. And she said next time she went he could go too.'

'That's very kind of her.'

'Tom says Mr Williams is with Jesus, like Mr Ryde.'

'So Mrs Williams travels by train to visit her husband's grave,' Lizzie repeated, realizing that Tom seemed to have told Polly quite a lot about this lady.

'Yes,' answered Polly with a firm nod. 'He used to play football. But he got sick and couldn't run about any more. Tom told her he'd like to be in a team too. So Mrs Williams went up to his school and asked the teacher if he could be.'

'And what happened?'

'They said he could be next term.' Polly sucked in a quick breath. 'So can we go to the garage?'

'All right. But we won't stop long.' Lizzie reflected that Danny rarely spoke about Mrs Williams. When he did, he always referred to her as 'our landlady'. But, by the sound of it, this young widow seemed to mean a great deal more to Tom than Lizzie had realized.

Chapter Fifty-Five

Danny was standing at the top of a ladder when Lizzie
drove up. He'd been working in the fresh air since the
garage had burned down. His forearms were browned by
the sun under his rolled-up shirtsleeves and his hair had
turned to the colour of wheat.

Lizzie saw the shelter had taken shape since she visited
last week. The sheet-metal walls were now nailed to new
timber uprights. A green tarpaulin acted as roof and was
stretched across from one vertical post to the other. The
light breeze was shaking one corner of the rough cloth,
the area that Danny was working on. When Lizzie and
Polly walked up, he let it go and it flapped again, until
taking a nail from between his teeth, he hammered it
home.

'Very nice,' Lizzie said as she stood, looking around.

'It's like the camp me and Tom built in the yard,' Polly
said to Danny, 'only bigger.'

Danny came down the ladder. 'Thanks, Pol. It should
do, as long as we don't have a storm.'

'Where's Tom?' Polly asked.

'Round the back with one of Mary's sons. They've been down on the river.'

'Can I go too?'

'Not dressed in your best clothes you can't,' Lizzie said.

'When can I then?'

'We'll have to see. Now go and find Tom.'

Polly ran off, jumping the newly scrubbed cellar boards laid out in the sun to dry. To the rear of the shelter Lizzie saw the old wooden bench. All the tools on its surface looked clean and oiled. 'We have to pack the tools up each night and take them home,' Danny told her. 'There's no security here now. So we've moved all our spares from the hut to a lock-up under the railway arches. We'll work on the larger vehicles in the open and make the most of the daylight hours. When it rains we'll pull over the tarpaulin.'

'I'm glad to see Leonard Savage hasn't got his way.'

'No,' said Danny with a frown. 'But that don't mean he'll stop trying.'

Just then Tom and Polly and another boy appeared. 'Is that Mary's son?' Lizzie asked.

Danny nodded, grinning. 'Yes, they both like football.'

'Polly told me Mrs Williams went up to the school and Tom's in the team.'

'Yes, he is,' Danny said as he looked at the boys. Turning his attention quickly back to Lizzie, he asked after Ethel.

'She's still very upset.' Lizzie wondered why Danny hadn't said anything about Mrs Williams.

'Has Ethel settled the problem of the house?'

'Mrs Ryde wants it sold. She's offered to have Ethel and the kids.'

He looked surprised. 'Wouldn't Ethel be better off with Lil and Doug?'

'Yes, but their house is too small.'

'So why doesn't Ethel find a job?' Danny asked with a frown. 'She could get a good one after years of experience with Rickard's.'

'It's a home she needs first,' Lizzie said, though she had been thinking the same herself.

Danny rubbed his chin thoughtfully. 'She should talk to Cal. Try to work something out. Richard's dead and buried. Going to live with his mother won't bring him back.'

Or the affection, Lizzie thought sadly, that Ethel once had for Cal.

There were still the odd flurries of ash that blew across the forecourt and Cal watched them now, as he paused, hidden behind the tarpaulin. He could hear Lizzie and Danny clearly and had been going to go round to greet her. But when Ethel's name was mentioned, he came to an abrupt halt. It was a quiet day, on the whole, and a sweltering one. He could see the heat rising up on the horizon in a wavy mist. Even the noises from the river traffic and the whirring and clanking of cranes seemed softened in the high temperatures.

He wiped the sweat that beaded his forehead with the

back of his arm. Then, unable to listen to the conversation any longer, he turned away. If what Lizzie said was true, and he didn't doubt it, then Ethel really was lost to him. He'd still held out hope for them on that fateful day she'd come to the garage. He'd wanted to face Richard and tell him that he was in love with his wife. Even though Ethel was trying to end their affair, he'd been sure she would change her mind, once she was away from her husband.

She was the only woman he'd ever loved. He wanted to look after her and protect her. To give her what he'd never had in his own life, true commitment to another person. Then Savage came along. Everything had changed from the day Leonard Savage walked into Lizzie's shop and scared the hell out of Ethel.

Cal shook his head as he walked slowly to the wharf wall, his broad shoulders slumped. The words that Lizzie had said taunted him. Ethel blamed him for Richard's death. He'd lost her to something that had never got started. And he couldn't deny it had been just a fling at first. But he'd soon begun to know it was more. He'd realized he was jealous of Richard. Of every moment he spent with Ethel. Of the afternoons she'd had to hurry away to get her husband's meals. Even of the tidy little suburban house that once, when he'd first come to England, would have seemed like a prison.

Suddenly he'd wanted all that. And more. For the first time in his life he'd thought about kids. A woman to go home to. And bricks and mortar to live in. Not a dingy room over a stinking café. And any female he could pay for when the need arose. No, there was no woman for him. Only Ethel.

A tap on his shoulder made him start. 'You need some help today, mate?'

Cal turned to find Phil and Robert standing there. He tried to draw his thoughts back to the present. But all he could think of was Leonard Savage.

Cal nodded. 'Yeah. Danny could do with a hand. I'm off now.'

'Good day to skive,' Robert agreed with a grin under his beard.

'Oh, this ain't skiving, it's something I've got to do,' Cal said, his voice threaded with anger.

'What's that, then?' Robert enquired uncertainly.

But Cal only shook his head and turned away. He knew what he was going to do. Retribution had been a long time in coming.

But he was taking it now.

Chapter Fifty-Six

Through the shop window Lizzie was watching Polly and her friends in the street. Her long, skinny legs were going ten to the dozen as she jumped the chalked lines on the pavement. It was a hot August Monday. There was no keeping the kids in the back yard now. There were too many in the school holidays to accommodate. But she supposed there was safety in numbers. Polly knew if any unfamiliar vehicles appeared, she was to come in straight away.

As Lizzie listened to Fowler and Bert stack the vegetable crates in the storeroom, she saw a cab draw up. The kids all scattered, though when Gertie climbed out, Polly ran to her. Gertie was soon followed by Bill, the three of them walking slowly across the street to the shop.

'It's Granda and Gertie,' Polly announced excitedly. 'Look what they give me. A quarter of bull's-eyes!'

'That's nice.'

'Hello, ducks.' Gertie kissed Lizzie's cheek, carefully moving her shopping bag from one arm to the other. 'And here's some sherbet dabs, Pol. Now scram and play with your friends.'

'It's lovely to see you,' Lizzie said as Polly raced back to Georgie March who, having spotted the sweets, was waiting outside. Gertie's old black coat smelled of mothballs. Her frizzy grey hair was tucked under a brown beret.

'Yer, we thought we'd pay a visit.'

Bill greeted Lizzie with a warm smile. Lizzie saw he was wearing his old coster's coat, tieless shirt and cloth cap. But Gertie must have insisted he wore his pressed suit trousers and polished black shoes for the outing.

'You're looking better, Bill.'

'I am,' he replied wheezily. 'Sorry to land on you like this.' It had been all of six weeks since she'd last called by Gap End, a fleeting visit after school to tell them how Frank was. Danny had broken the news about the garage, she knew. But it was rare that Bill and Gertie ever caught a cab and she looked at them uncertainly. 'I expect you've come to see Frank.'

'That would be nice,' Gertie said vaguely. 'Up and about, is he?'

Lizzie nodded. Bill and Gertie glanced at each other.

'Is something wrong?'

'We don't know. But we wouldn't trouble you if it wasn't important.'

'I've got something you need to see.' Gertie opened the straw bag and closed it again as two customers walked in. 'Can we go upstairs?'

'Yes, course. Frank will be pleased to see you. Get him to put the kettle on. When I've finished serving I'll leave Bert and Fowler in the shop and join you.'

As Lizzie watched Bill and Gertie make their way over the shop's freshly swept floor, she remembered the days when Bill, of a Monday morning, at the crack of dawn, would be heaving the sacks in from the traders' carts. It was no mean feat to haul them in at break-neck speed and arrange them in neat rows around the shop. Now she saw two small figures, stooped and slow-moving.

What was important enough for them to make the journey over here by cab, she wondered?

By the time Lizzie got upstairs, Frank had made the tea. He was talking with Bill and Gertie as they all sat round the kitchen table.

'You've done a fine job on this boy,' said Bill with a rueful grin at Frank. 'He's never looked so good. What you been giving him?'

For the first time Lizzie took a long, studied look at her husband, who she suddenly realized had put on weight during his convalescence. He was wearing his vest and braces and the exercise in the shop had broadened his shoulders and rounded the muscles in his arms. His skin had lost the yellow pallor that had made him look jaundiced. And his blue eyes were clear, rid of the dark, puffy pouches that had added years to his appearance.

'I been living a healthy life, Dad,' Frank replied as Lizzie took the chair beside Gertie.

'I'll say it again,' Bill continued, 'you owe your recovery to this girl.'

'Never a truer word,' Frank agreed solemnly, glancing at Lizzie.

'So you'll be having your marching orders soon.' Bill looked Frank up and down. 'Going back to your rooms?'

'I had to give 'em up as they was costing a fortune.'

'What about your job at the hospital?' Bill persisted.

'Dunno. I ain't gone out anywhere yet. Got to find me sea legs first.'

'Well, you won't find 'em under Lizzie's feet, that's for sure.'

Lizzie knew Bill was only trying to help. The old man hadn't forgotten his son's true nature. And neither had she.

Everyone fell silent and it was Gertie who spoke next as she opened her bag and drew out a parcel. She placed it carefully on the table.

'What is it?' Lizzie looked at the newspapers tied with string.

'Don't know.' Bill shook his grey head. 'It was delivered this morning by a gent who said he was a friend of yours and could we give it to you.'

'When I asked why he didn't deliver it himself,' Gertie continued, 'he said he was passing our way and knew where we lived. Then he shook my hand and Bill's as we stood on the doorstep. Said what a nice little gaff we had and rode off in his posh car.'

'What did he look like?' Lizzie managed to ask, despite the start of a sinking sensation in her tummy.

Gertie shrugged. 'I'd have said, for all his finery, he was up to no good.'

'Have you looked inside?' Frank asked, reaching across and drawing the parcel towards him.

'No, course not.'

'Shall I open it?'

Lizzie stopped him. 'We don't know what's in it.'

Frank pulled back his hands.

'Whatever it is,' Gertie sensibly commented, 'it's been up and down in me bag more times than a whore's drawers. And it ain't done me no damage.'

Bill pushed it around the table. 'It only feels like papers.'

With unsteady fingers, Lizzie pulled on the string.

'Christ almighty, what's that!' Bill exclaimed.

Lizzie stared at the opened sheets of newspaper revealing two buff-coloured envelopes. One held a letter, as yet to be read. The other, a handful of black hair.

'Is it an 'orse's?' asked Gertie.

Lizzie picked up the long, silky strands. 'I don't think so.'

'Then what is it?' Frank said nervously.

'It's human hair.' Lizzie dropped the hair as though she'd been burned. Even as she said the words, she realized her suspicions were true. The feeling of apprehension when she'd seen Gertie and Bill arrive was now turning to dread. 'There's only one person I know with hair that colour, Cal Bronga.'

'What, Danny's mechanic?' Bill said in surprise.

'The Aussie?' Gertie repeated. 'Are you sure?'

They inspected the hair again. 'The man who delivered this was Leonard Savage,' Lizzie explained. 'The villain who came to the shop and threatened me. The same man who burned down Danny's garage and killed Richard Ryde.'

'So you think Savage has got Cal?' Frank said in a whisper.

'If this is Cal's hair, he must have.' Lizzie picked up the second envelope. '*For Danny Flowers,*' she read aloud and, replacing it on the table, added, 'and we'll only know for certain when Danny opens this letter.'

Once again they all sat in silence, until Lizzie left the kitchen and went to the top of the stairs. 'Bert, are you there?' she shouted down. When Bert's head appeared, she lowered her voice. 'Drive over to Danny's. Tell him I need to see him straight away.'

'But this is the busiest time of the morning,' Bert protested.

'Leave Fowler to serve the customers.'

Bert scratched his head, looking puzzled. 'What's all the rush?'

'Just go, Bert. And on your way out, tell Pol to come in and bring Georgie March with her. They can play out in the yard.'

Bert reluctantly began to peel off his apron. 'Don't know what all this fuss is about,' he muttered under his breath.

'The quicker you go, the sooner you'll find out.'

Lizzie walked slowly back to the kitchen. There was no murmur of voices or smiles from the assembled. It was finally dawning on everyone that Leonard Savage had something unpleasant in store for them.

Chapter Fifty-Seven

'It looks like Cal's,' Danny confirmed, staring down at the hair.

'But what's it doing in them newspapers?' Bert said with a frown.

'Ain't it obvious, you dumb cluck?' Gertie snapped. 'It's come off his head.'

'It'd take a bit of manpower to nobble a strong bloke like Cal,' Bill pointed out.

'When did you last see Cal?' Lizzie asked Danny.

'Yesterday morning, before you arrived. Then, after you left, Phil and Robert turned up to help. Robert said he saw Cal who told them he was pushing off early cos he had something to do. I was so busy I didn't think much of it at the time. But God help him if he was off to confront Savage.'

'Not on his own, he wouldn't, would he?' Frank said doubtfully. 'I mean he'd have to be an idiot not to take muscle.'

Danny stared at his brother. 'Cal ain't an idiot. He's a proud man, a brave one. If he had a grudge to settle he would square it himself.'

'I'd like to know how this villain found my place,' Gertie said curiously.

'He said he knew everything about us,' Lizzie replied. 'And that must have meant you and Bill too.'

'But I've never seen the geezer before.' Bill offered round the wafer-thin cigarettes he'd made. 'Or that posh motor of his with the cracked windscreen.'

'Cracked windscreen?' Danny repeated.

'Yeah. Like it had been clobbered with a hammer.'

'When the car hit Richard, its windscreen broke,' Lizzie said quietly, staring around at the startled faces.

'Look, this is getting us nowhere.' Bill waved his hand impatiently. 'Danny, read the letter, son, and put us all out of our misery.'

Danny opened the buff-coloured envelope. Inside were two sheets of paper. He read from the first . '*Flowers, this is my final offer. If you want to see your man again, accept my price and bring the deeds of your property to my office tonight at ten. Leonard Savage.*'

'What does he mean by that?' Bert asked.

Danny unfolded the second sheet. After reading it, he raised his eyes slowly. 'It's a contract of sale for the garage. He's offering me three hundred pounds.'

'Three hundred!' everyone repeated.

'Twice what he offered before.'

'But you ain't got no garage now,' said Bert. 'He burned the bloody thing down.'

'He doesn't want my garage. Like Lizzie says, it's the land.'

'He writes it's his final offer,' Bill said slowly, 'and you have to admit, boy, it's a generous one.'

'Oh, it's generous all right. But he could double it or treble it for all I care. I'm not selling.'

'But he's got Cal,' Bert said through the smoke that was polluting the air.

'That's blackmail,' Bill said indignantly. 'He's trying to force your hand.'

Danny stared at the paper in front of him, then dropped it to the table. He leaned back against the chair and said, 'He's trying all right. That's why he knocked on your door and asked you to give the parcel to Lizzie. He wanted to let me know that you and Gertie and Lizzie are in as much danger as Cal. It's blackmail and he has all the cards.'

'We can't let him do this, Danny.' Lizzie was fighting the anger that, after the shock, had begun to fill her.

Danny stood up and slowly paced the kitchen. Then suddenly he stopped. 'I'm going to meet him tonight.'

'What?' Bill stared up at his son in surprise. 'You're selling?'

'No, Dad. Not if I can help it.'

'Then what's your plan?' Frank asked.

'I'll say I want double that figure.'

'What, six hundred quid!' Bill exclaimed. 'That's a fortune.'

'If he wants it that bad, he'll pay up. Remember, he knows quite well that with my signature on that document his ownership can't be contested. I'll tell him to come over to the shelter tomorrow night with Cal and the cash. We'll make the exchange and he gets what he wants – or so he thinks.'

Once again, no one spoke.

'So what happens then?' Lizzie finally asked.

'I'll be waiting, but not on my own. First thing tomorrow I'm going to Limehouse to see my friend Bray.'

'What? You're going to the law?' Bill said disbelievingly.

'I've got evidence now, Dad. Hard evidence.' Danny waved the letters in the air. 'Savage made a big mistake. He's admitting in writing to extortion and blackmail. And the cash in his pocket will be the icing on the cake.'

'Do you reckon the copper will listen?' Bill asked doubtfully. 'He ain't been no friend to you.'

'No, but when he knows I can give him Savage on a plate and provide the proof for a long stretch, he'd be a fool to refuse.'

'Don't like it,' Bill said, shaking his head.

'Neither do I, Dad. But I like the thought even less of Savage taking my property, even if he says he'll pay for it. Where's it all going to end? Next thing we know he'll own every man Jack of us.'

'He's right, Bill,' agreed Lizzie, 'it could be the shop next. Me and Bert are going with Danny too.'

'No way,' said Danny at once, shaking his head fiercely. 'I'm going on my own.'

'Savage would like that, wouldn't he?' said Lizzie, refusing to take no for an answer. 'United we stand and united we fall.' She smiled. 'But we ain't going to fall, are we?'

Chapter Fifty-Eight

Danny hurried up the creaking iron staircase to Cal's lodgings. The smell of fried food from the café beneath was strong. He paused, staring at the open door in front of him. Shoving it cautiously with the tip of his boot, he peered inside. The room was dark and, though Danny had visited once or twice before, he felt wary of entering. There was no noise and he called out Cal's name.

'He ain't been home, mate,' a voice yelled and Danny took a sharp step back. Looking down, a man stood beneath staring up at him. The cook wore a dirty white apron and was wiping his hands on a towel, one foot wedged in the café door in order to keep it open.

'How do you know that?' Danny asked.

'Cos I always save him a pie and chips. Even on Sunday he gives me a knock.'

'So he didn't come back last night?'

'No and he wouldn't miss his grub. Are you the geezer with the garage?'

Danny nodded. 'Any idea where he might be?'

'Dunno. He ain't a drinker, so he won't be down the

boozer. Quiet sort, but I've took to him. Pays me the rent every Friday on the dot. And regularity ain't something a landlord favours these days.'

Danny raised his hand. 'Thanks, anyway.'

The café door slammed shut and Danny walked into Cal's rooms. He looked around, adjusting his eyes to the gloom, smelling the absence of his friend. From previous visits he'd seen that Cal had never put much effort into making the place comfortable. He had a sneaking suspicion that Cal would have lived just as well in an open field, or on one of the river barges, gazing up into the night sky. His friend had never settled in Aussie and it was down to the garage that he had stayed put for almost a year. The man loved motors as much as he did. Many an early morning Danny had walked in to find the big doors open, the motors out on the forecourt and Cal down in the workshop smoking a fag, up to his eyes in grease and oil and relishing it.

Now as he stared around, it was evident that Cal had rarely spent time in the old armchair by the unlit grate. Or eaten from a plate at the worn table, or even bothered to sweep the dried and cracked linoleum.

Slowly Danny walked over to the door that led to the bedroom. Curiously it felt a little less abandoned here. The faded net curtain at the window blew softly in the breeze. The bed was made, though it looked as though it hadn't been slept in for a while. His eyes caught the chipped mirror on the dressing table. A dog-eared photograph was tucked into a rusting clip securing the glass.

He went over to look closer. The photograph was of

Lil and Doug Sharpe, with three young kids. Must be Ethel with the plaits, he thought, and Greg and Neil, not yet grown into teenagers. All tousled fair hair, smiling, unaware of the tragedy that lay ahead when both boys would embark on their fatal journey.

Ethel must have given this to Cal, Danny reflected as he thought of Cal and Ethel, as unlikely a couple as you could wish to find. Ethel, as straight as a die, a traditional housewife and mother, kids she worshipped and a nine-to-five husband. Who'd have put her down as the type to go off with a wild Aussie loner?

But as Danny considered the photograph, he knew that Cal would have seen in Ethel the things he had never had himself. The close-knit family, parents like Doug and Lil who raised their children in love, not war.

But when his gaze lifted to the faded wallpaper above the mirror, his heart sank. He saw a pale indentation in the shape of a long stick. Cal's grandfather's club was gone.

The hair prickled on the back of Danny's neck as he remembered the only story Cal had ever told him about his past. A drunken youth creeping into his grandfather's house one night had stolen without shame. The old man woke and in trying to stop him had perished in the effort. After burying the old man, Cal, at barely fourteen, sought out the thief. He'd taken a life for a life, and never returned to his grandfather's home again.

Danny stared at the vacant space on the wall. Then he gazed back at the photograph. Cal had taken the club and gone to seek justice, just as he had for his grandfather.

Chapter Fifty-Nine

After Danny had gone, Lizzie looked at her brother. 'Do you know where Chancel Lane is?'

'The back of Aldgate. Use to be liveries up there in the old days.'

'Bill, will you and Gertie stay the night, give an eye to Polly?'

'Course,' Bill said slowly, 'but you know I don't like it.'

'Let's hope his mate is all in one piece,' said Frank, lifting the hair and staring at it.

Lizzie didn't want to think of the alternative. 'Cal is all Savage has to bargain with.'

'Yer, but like Bill said, they wouldn't have taken him easy.'

'And they've got more than a broom,' said Frank, looking accusingly at Lizzie. 'We should have kept Dad's gun.'

'What's that?' Bill asked, sitting up. 'Where've you put it?'

'Didn't put it anywhere.' Frank lowered his eyes.

'I got rid of it, Bill,' Lizzie said with a shrug. 'I don't hold with guns, as you know.'

'I've had it years,' Bill said indignantly. 'It was a life-saver in the trenches.'

'About time it went, then,' said Gertie, nudging Bill in the arm.

'Don't you start.' Bill looked offended. 'The way villains like Savage are taking over the East End, every bent Tom, Dick and Harry will carry them. What's an ordinary man like Danny got left to defend himself with?'

'It certainly ain't brooms,' Bert nodded, looking at Lizzie.

'If only I was a few years younger,' Bill began, but Gertie waved her hand in his face.

'And what would you do, Bill Flowers? Go off half-cocked, no doubt, and shoot yourself in the foot.'

Bill looked up sharply. 'I'm a coster, Gertie. Not a ruddy criminal. But I wouldn't let a thug like Savage carve me up. I tell you, I'd—'

'You'd what?' Gertie challenged, raising her eyebrows.

'Steady on there,' Bert said, holding out his arms to separate them. 'We've got enough trouble without fighting each other.'

Lizzie saw Bill's lips tighten and she knew he was angry over his lost revolver. But how could she disclose the fact that Frank had killed a man with it? Bill and Gertie had worry enough to contend with.

Lizzie looked at the people sitting in her kitchen; her family, her kith and kin, who were at their wits' end to try to resolve an impossible situation. They were all well aware that Danny was walking into danger, even if it hadn't been said in so many words. Was she wrong in objecting so fiercely to firearms?

'Even if we had a weapon,' she said reluctantly, 'we wouldn't know how to use it.'

'I would,' said Frank and drew everyone's attention.

'What do you mean?'

'I've been practising.' He looked around, his tone boastful as he added, 'Well, I've had a lot of time on me hands. And it was only on the sacks of rotted spuds in the yard.'

'You've got another gun?' Lizzie demanded. 'After what I told you?'

Frank shook his head quickly. 'No, gel, I wouldn't do that. But it's—' He paused, chewing on his lip. 'Well, it's Fowler's.'

'What!'

'It's only a small one, a Smith & Wesson derringer.'

Lizzie walked over to him and pointed a finger at his chest. 'After all that's gone on, you didn't tell me?'

'Cos I knew you wouldn't like it,' he replied trucu-lently. 'And you'd probably get rid of him.'

'Too right I would,' Lizzie said angrily.

'See, you're wrong there, gel,' Frank replied. 'Fowler is all the muscle we've got. If you get rid of him, Bert would be on his jacksie.'

'Yes, and so would you.'

'I've still got me bad back. How can I help anyone, like this? Else I'd be right alongside Danny tonight.'

'Well, now you've got your chance.' Lizzie stared into

her husband's face and nodded slowly. 'Since you're such a good shot, you can bring the gun and come with us.'

Frank jerked his head up. A look of fear spread across his face. 'But what about my back?'

'Your back don't pull the trigger, does it?'

'No, b-but . . .' Frank stammered, his eyes moving fast in their sockets. 'It's Fowler's. Take him.'

Lizzie shook her head in disgust. 'Not on your Nelly. Fowler stays here to do the job I pay him for. Look after my property.'

Four faces gazed silently up at her. She couldn't believe that Frank had gone against her wishes again. Even after the escapade with Albert and the risk it had posed to Bert and Danny in disposing of the body he hadn't learned his lesson.

'You should have kept your mouth shut, Frank.' She stepped back and swept her hand in front of her. 'You'd better go downstairs and find yourself another sack of potatoes to practise on.'

'Goodnight and God bless, monkey.' Lizzie pulled the sheet up to Polly's chin as she sat on the bed. 'I love you all the tables and chairs in the world.'

'That ain't much,' answered the sleepy voice. Two blue eyes flickered tiredly.

'Add all the beds and pillows, then.' This was what they always said at night. Lizzie looked over to where her bed stood. Sleeping in the same room as Polly was not an encumbrance but a joy. Polly was good company, a ray of sunshine every morning when she woke. But Polly was growing fast. She would need somewhere soon to put all her clothes, books and treasures that were now packed away in a box.

'You ain't going away, are you?'

'No, whatever made you think that?'

'Cos you're all dressed up. You've got your new coat on.'

'Come here, silly.' She hugged the tiny little figure and stroked Polly's hair. 'I'm driving Uncle Frank and Uncle Bert to see some people on business.'

'You're all staying up late, ain't you?'

Lizzie laughed, settling Polly down again. 'Yes, but I'll be here when you wake in the morning.'

'Will Granda and Gertie look after me?'

'Yes, course they will.'

'I ain't tired yet.'

'You should be.' Lizzie tucked Polly's hair over her ear. 'You've been out playing all day.'

'I wish Tom could come and stay.'

'He's probably with Mrs Williams.' Lizzie thought of Danny, preparing to set out tonight, leaving Tom to be cared for by his faithful landlady. She knew she was jealous and she hated herself for it. If she'd taken steps to free herself of Frank, which, it seemed, she had not been able to bring herself to do, perhaps she wouldn't be in fear of another woman catching Danny's eye. Frank was still in her life and it was as much of a puzzle and regret to her as it was to Danny. Perhaps it was pity that kept Frank under her roof. But she was slowly hardening her heart.

Polly forced her eyes to stay open. 'They was nice sweets Gertie brought me. Georgie says he don't have a Granda or an auntie. Why not?'

'Some children don't.'

Polly grinned. 'I'm lucky ain't I? Even though my mum don't come round, I've got you.'

Tears were suddenly close. Polly was such a beautiful child, as sweet on the inside as she was on the outside. How Babs could ever stay away from her daughter, Lizzie didn't understand. She kissed Polly's forehead and whispered, 'Your mum will come back to see you one day.'

The next moment, Polly fell asleep.

As Lizzie left the room, she gazed back at her niece. Her heart tightened as she thought of the little baby she'd held in her arms over six years ago, staring up at her with sea-blue eyes. Babs had rejected her child from the off. But Polly didn't know that. She just accepted that Babs had gone away. As time had gone on, Polly had even stopped asking about her. But Lizzie still prayed for Babs to return. Frank was now a reformed character. Or so he claimed. So why not hold out hope for Babs? Even though Lizzie loved Polly as her own, she knew the bond between mother and daughter was unbreakable.

Chapter Sixty

'This ain't my idea of comfort,' Frank complained from the rear of the van where he sat shoulder to shoulder with Bert. 'It's killing me back.'

'For goodness' sake, give it a rest, Frank,' said Lizzie from her seat at the front next to Danny who was driving.

'Dunno why we couldn't go in Danny's motor,' he continued to complain.

'Because the van is bigger,' Bert explained patiently, 'even though it's an old bone-shaker. You'd be surprised at the speed it kicks up.'

'Yeah, I would be,' said Frank miserably. 'It reminds me of the day you brought me over from Dad's. I thought you was taking me up the crem before my time.'

'There's still a chance of that,' Danny threatened as they drove along the Commercial Road towards Aldgate. 'Remember you are the only one with a gun.'

Lizzie knew that none of them had any sympathy for Frank. Even though he had saved Cal and Ethel's lives by a fluke, cowardice was natural to Frank's character.

Trying to remain calm, Lizzie stared out of the window

at the passing shops and darkened buildings of the East End. At this time of night, only the street vendors and taverns were still trading. With the pub cellar doors shut at pavement level, their windows above were enticingly lit, drawing in thirsty customers. The trams sailed by like ships in the night, running towards Aldgate and Bloomsbury. Buses made their way east to Wanstead and Dagenham, west to Paddington and Marylebone, and to Brixton and Blackheath, where Ethel lived, south of the river.

She sighed, bringing her thoughts back to the present and the narrow, twisting streets Danny was driving them through. Who was to say what would happen at Chancel Street? Would Danny's plan succeed?

The horse-drawn vehicle in front of them caused Danny to drive painfully slowly. Lizzie recognized it as one of the costermonger carts that always made their way to Covent Garden in the late and early hours, serving the traders who would be preparing for the break of dawn.

She glanced at Danny, his face set, his eyes trained ahead. She hoped, for all their sakes, that this gamble tonight would bring them success. For if it did not, what would the outcome be?

Danny drew the van to a halt. Chancel Lane could have been any back street of the capital, had it not been for the rows of rooming houses and their stable yards, used in days gone by for the liveries of the wealthy and accommodation for their lowly servants. Savage had chosen well, Danny thought as he narrowed his eyes along the gloomy lane. Unlit and likely to be unpatrolled by the law, it felt menacing. In the middle of summer there was still a paleness in the sky to give the atmosphere a little light relief. But a multitude of shadows streamed out across their path, distorted and strange-shaped. The air was mild for August and still. They sat quietly, listening to the squabble of cats and the chimes from a nearby clock tower.

'Which belongs to Savage?' Lizzie said and Danny leaned forward, his heart beginning to thud in apprehension. With Lizzie to protect, he had to be careful. He wasn't afraid for himself or even Cal. His friend had walked of his own choice into Savage's lair. Cal must have known what awaited him. As for himself, he'd been in tight corners before. Push come to shove, he would have felt much easier on his own, but he knew Lizzie would have come, with or without his nod. As for Bert, he was grateful that he would keep an eye on Lizzie. Frank would be certain to watch out for number one. But perhaps Savage would be surprised by their number. Danny had given a great deal of thought to this moment. But there was no guarantee of success.

'Look, up there, on the bend.' Bert leaned forward and pointed to a dull light shining from a set of bow windows. 'Someone's at home.'

'Must be the place then.'

Danny nodded. 'Bert, stay here with your sister until you get my signal.'

'We'll all go together,' Lizzie argued as Danny knew she would.

'I'll go first,' Danny told her. 'I need you to watch the lane.' He indicated the length of the street. 'If you see anything untoward, then squeeze the horn.'

'How long do we wait?'

'Give me fifteen minutes. The deal should be done by then.'

Lizzie nodded doubtfully. 'Bert and me are coming after you if you're not out by then.'

'Don't worry. I'll have Frank with me.'

'Me?' Frank said from the rear of the van. 'You've got to be kidding. I'll only hold you up.'

'Then I'll go slowly, just for your benefit.' Danny turned to look at Frank hidden in the darkness. A pale, frightened face stared back at him.

'Why don't you take Bert?' Frank objected, clapping Bert on the shoulder. 'He's twice my size and fit as a fiddle.'

'You're a Flowers, Frank. I want Savage to clock you bringing up the rear, like Lizzie said, a united front. He won't be expecting that.' Danny went to the back of the van and unlatched the double doors.

Frank climbed out, still protesting. 'This ain't a good idea, Danny.'

'It's the best one I've had tonight.'

Frank hesitated and reached for his stick.

Danny grabbed his arm. 'You won't need that.' If there was trouble, Danny knew Frank would be about as much use as a pork pie at a Jewish wedding, as Bill always said. But that was old news. His brother had been a liability for years and he wasn't going to lay odds that Frank would change now. But it was time Frank earned himself some respect.

'What about the gun?' Frank looked pale and stooped as he stood up. He put his hand on the bulge of his suit pocket. 'I don't feel safe with the only shooter. What if someone spots it?'

'They won't be asking for a character reference. So get your head up and if you don't try any death-defying stunts, you'll survive.'

Frank pulled his shoulders back an inch. He glanced warily behind him. 'Don't mind admitting that—'

'Yeah, I know, your back hurts.' Danny set off down the lane. He was wearing his best suit and tie for the occasion. He wanted Savage to know he was taking this deal seriously. He had to make an impression; convince Savage to come to the wharf tomorrow. Indicate that his demand for six hundred pounds would bring a result.

'Blimey, where's the fire?' Frank muttered as he tried to keep up.

'When we get inside, don't say a word,' Danny threw over his shoulder. 'Let me do the talking.'

'You can say that again,' Frank mumbled, puffing.

Danny came to an abrupt halt as he reached the lit window. He looked up at the old hostelry, its weathered boards and oak timbers in need of repair. There were figures inside, but the dirty, sagging curtain drawn across the glass gave no clue as to how many.

'There it is,' said Frank nervously, pointing up at the sign.

Danny read aloud, '*Leonard Savage & Co. Security and Credit Brokers.*' He saw with satisfaction that someone had thrown paint at the grubby black lettering, some of which had trickled down to the window, running into a lake on the ledge. 'A popular man by all accounts,' sneered Danny, and pushed the door open.

Chapter Sixty-One

Lizzie turned to Bert, wiping the sweat from her fore-head. The van felt like an oven. It was only a short while since Danny and Frank had gone, but she was anxious to follow them. 'Can you see anyone suspicious?' she said, narrowing her eyes at the deserted lane.

'Yeah, over there.' Bert clamped a hand on her shoul-der. 'There's some old sort on the other side of the road.'

'It's only a woman.'

'Looks like a dock dolly,' Bert agreed. 'She might have her minder in tow.'

'We'll wait till she goes by, then.'

But the figure lingered and was, as Bert suggested, joined by a man. 'It's a knocking shop,' Bert said. 'They could be busy all night—'

Lizzie didn't wait for him to finish. She opened the van door. Bert jumped out from the back and joined her. They stood under the moonlight in the balmy summer air, look-ing back and forth along the lane. 'There's another geezer coming up,' Bert warned softly. 'On his own, see?'

Lizzie nodded at the stumbling figure. The drunk seemed

to pose no danger. 'Let's take a look in the window.' She hurried towards the light. Her summer dress was damp and clung to her. Even her hair, tied behind her head, felt sticky on her neck. She went a little faster.

Bert pulled her back. 'Hang on there, gel.'

Lizzie knew her nerves were getting the better of her. She tried to quell the unsettled feeling in her stomach. Danny knew what he was doing. What could go wrong? She tried to take a deep breath. But she was so anxious, she couldn't. The moon and its light cast even more shadows; they seemed to move around the two people on the other side of the road.

She stood still. The sweat was ice cold on her forehead. The door opened and a dull light flowed out. Before Bert could grab her, someone roughly pulled her in.

A sack was over her head; her hands were tied behind her back. It had all happened so quickly. She was being pushed along, stumbling her way forward. What had happened to Bert?

Suddenly she was made to stop. The sack was pulled from her head; she blinked at the sudden light.

'We meet again, Mrs Flowers.' Leonard Savage was standing in front of her. Behind him were his men, positioned around the old inn in a dim light. Gone was the polished bar and welcoming hearth with horse brasses, tongs and scuttle. Now the room looked neglected, abandoned, with cobwebs strung across the narrow wooden staircase leading to the upper floor.

'Where's my brother? Where's Danny?' she managed to croak.

'All in good time.' Savage was smiling, looking every inch the gangster surrounded by his mob. It was as if he had dressed especially for the occasion: a blue pinstripe suit, a white tie folded into a huge knot beneath his chin, a dark-coloured Homburg on his head and a cigar poised between his fingers.

'So what have you to say for yourself, my dear?' Savage said, his smile false. 'You come here with your friend, a greedy fool who should have accepted my money when first offered . . .' Savage shook his head and slowly walked towards her. 'Did he really expect me to bargain? Did you?' She flinched as, folding his hand into a fist, he drew his knuckle down her cheek. 'Now, let's you and me be sensible, shall we? I'm certain we can come to an arrangement.' His fingers went over her hair.

'Wh-what sort of arrangement?' she stammered.

'I hear you're thinking of expanding.'

She turned her head sharply. 'How do you know that?'

'I told you, I know everything.'

'It's no business of yours what I do.' Lizzie tried to stop her voice from shaking. How did he know about Mr James's shop? He must have followed her there.

'How very short-sighted,' he snapped, blowing thick grey smoke in her face. 'Meet your new partner, Mrs Flowers. We'll be working closely together. Very closely.' He smiled as he looked into her eyes. 'You'll run the shops for me, and receive a small percentage. I'm certain we'll get along — after a fashion. In fact, I'm looking forward to our close acquaintanceship.'

How could I have been so blind? Lizzie thought as she stared at him. This man intends to take everything, including me.

'As I say, such a pity this hasn't ended in a more civilized way.' Savage drew an envelope from his pocket. 'You'll watch and learn as you see Mr Flowers sign this. After which, I'm sure you'll be ready to meet my — er — terms.'

'Danny will never sign his land over.'

'Not without encouragement, I agree. I hope you have a strong stomach, my dear.'

Lizzie drew in a breath. Danny had underestimated this man. They all had.

Savage leaned forward and murmured, 'You have beautiful skin, by the way.'

Lizzie closed her eyes as he touched her; he made her skin crawl.

'Did you really think — the both of you — that I didn't anticipate resistance? Why, I know every trick in the book and believe me, he *will* sign the papers.' Savage added slowly, 'And you'll encourage him, as neither of you would want those pretty children to be orphaned so early in their young lives, now, would you?'

Lizzie stared at him in disbelief. It was as if someone had stuck a knife into her ribs. Her mouth dried and she couldn't move. It was Polly and Tom he was threatening.

'And of course there's the mechanic,' Savage continued

easily. 'A man who has caused me a great deal of inconvenience. He took out two of my men only yesterday. Now, I wonder what his fate will be?'

Lizzie was very afraid. But she was also very angry. If Savage was going to kill them all, why hadn't he done so already? It must be because he wanted those papers signed. And he was using her to do it. But if she refused to help him, what about the children?

'I miss Albert, you know,' Savage told her. 'He washed up with the tide at Gravesend a week ago . . .' He raised his hairless eyebrows. 'Albert had many good points but he was always a tea leaf. I can only assume he was caught in the act by someone. I wonder who that someone could be.'

Lizzie looked into his eyes. 'You'll never know, will you?'

'Sadly not.'

'You knocked my brother-in-law off his bike,' she said without shifting her gaze, 'and drove away.'

'Ah, the man with the bicycle!' Savage dismissed with a wave of his hand. 'He should have looked where he was going.'

'You killed him,' Lizzie accused, her green eyes glinting.

Savage began to laugh. He wiped the tears of amusement from his eyes, until suddenly he stopped. 'Enough of this! I was prepared to be fair. Who wouldn't consider my proposition as reasonable? Only a fool would refuse.'

'Did you really expect Danny to agree after what you've

done to us?' Lizzie said helplessly, her wrists painful behind her back. 'One day, the law will catch up with you.'

Savage came close to her, his breath on her face and his smile fading. 'The law is in my pocket, where it should be, Mrs Flowers. The only effective law in the East End is mine. As you are about to discover.'

Chapter Sixty-Two

Bert was slowly recovering from the clout to his head; he counted himself lucky he had a thick skull. But in the few moments he was out he'd been parted from Lizzie and that was worrying him. Though as it was now very dark, he couldn't see exactly where he was, but there was movement in the animal's straw he could smell and feel around him. It must be a stable and, from what he could gauge, listening carefully, there weren't any horses. With his hands and feet bound together, he tried to roll over.

'Is that you, Bert?' It was Frank's voice.

'Yeah, what's going on?'

'Dunno. My hands and feet are tied.'

'It's as black as the ace of spades in here.' Bert tried to wriggle his hands but they were clamped at his backside. 'Someone's trussed us up like turkeys. We've got to get out.'

'Easier said than done,' Frank replied, 'I can't move without giving meself gyp.'

Bert sighed heavily, gazing into the dark. 'What happened to you and Danny?'

'It was a set-up. The moment we walked in, they nabbed us. Savage never intended to deal. They shoved me out here – in the stable – and I heard them knocking Danny about. Then it went quiet and I've been lying here, till they brought you.'

'Savage was waiting for us,' Bert said, trying to see into the pitch black. 'Must have been.'

'Where's Lizzie?'

'Wish I knew.'

'Danny should have kept her out of it.'

'If she makes her mind up, nothing ain't gonna stop her.' Bert moved agitatedly, trying to kick his legs free from the ropes round his ankles. 'Somehow we've got to get free.'

'Yeah, and what do we do then? These characters are tooled up to the eyeballs. I saw enough shooters to stock an army. Let's face it, we're well out of our league here. Danny should have sold to Savage when the garage was burned down. Now we're all going to pay a penalty.'

'Don't you ever stop moaning?'

'Not when I've something to moan about.'

'Have you got the gun?' Bert asked hopefully, thinking perhaps he could reach Frank's pocket.

'What do you think?' Frank huffed. 'They found it and laughed at it. Said it was a kid's toy.'

Bert suddenly sat up. 'What's that?'

'What?'

'That breathing sound.'

'It's probably a horse.'

Bert squinted, listening. 'There's someone in here with us.'

'Wh-who?' stammered Frank.

Bert strained his chin forward. 'Danny, Cal, are you there?' He cricked his neck upwards to a shaft of light in the roof. Now his eyes were accustomed to the darkness, he could see the twinkle of stars. As he looked down he could make out a shape, a motionless shape. It didn't look like a horse. 'Danny? Is that you?' he called, his heart thrusting hopefully against his ribs.

'Bert?' said a voice. It was Danny's.

'Blimey, Danny are you—'

'Someone's coming,' Frank interrupted.

Bert lay still. He listened to the march of boots across a yard. He heard voices and then a rattle and a clink. Suddenly the stable door swung open, shedding a gloomy light onto two figures. One of them was holding an oil lamp, the other a shotgun. Bert swallowed hard, feeling the prickle of fear on his neck. The lamp swung and the man with the gun stepped forward.

'Don't shoot!' Frank shrieked. 'We ain't done nothing!'

The men looked at one another, smiling, enjoying their captives' terror. Bert licked the sour taste from his lips. Shot on his back, like a defenceless animal, wasn't the way he planned to go. His mind flashed to the night he and Danny ditched Albert in the Thames. The poor sod hadn't thought that he'd meet his end that way either. No doubt about it, life was a bugger.

★   ★   ★

'But why us, why me and Danny? I'm just a small trader and Danny's land can't be worth that much, can it?' Lizzie demanded as she stood in front of Savage. She knew he was trying to intimidate her, but she'd be damned if she let her fear show.

Savage continued to look at her in amusement. 'Wrong on both counts, my dear,' he said slowly, enjoying the surprise on her face. 'You are the only woman in the East End who has survived a bombing and brought her business back from the dead. An example to us all, of course, and someone I want working for me, rather than against me.'

Lizzie suddenly began to understand this man's mind and the strategy he had planned to pursue his racketeering. Once she and those like her who flatly refused his demands had fallen, he would have no argument with others, like the stallholders who had resisted in the past and failed.

'As for your friend, Flowers,' Savage continued as he casually blew smoke into the air, 'he's just not willing to see sense, is he? I was prepared to give him a generous price for his land, a sum many men would have grabbed with both hands.'

'But why do you want Morley's Wharf so much?' Lizzie said in confusion. 'It doesn't make sense.'

'Oh, wrong again, Mrs Flowers. For I have it on good authority from friends in high places that some of London's wharfs are to be expanded and developed. A very rich and lucrative transaction for godforsaken pieces of marshland, like Morley's Wharf.' He paused, tilted his head to one side and murmured, 'But perhaps a vision too far for your eyes, my dear?'

'You'll never get away with it,' Lizzie breathed on a choked whisper. 'The law won't let you. You can't force a person to sell their property.'

At this, Savage's mouth fell open and with a sickening belly laugh he clapped his hand on his chest. 'Oh, from the mouths of babes!' he derided, laughing until the tears glistened in his eyes and he swept them away with a fat finger.

Lizzie stood there feeling humiliated as he slowly recovered, his smile turning to a frightening grimace.

'The first rule of good business,' he told her in a menacing voice, 'is planning. To plan well, you must know everything. How many times have I told you this?' He stopped, staring into her gaze as if he despaired of her. 'The law – you say – won't let me do as I wish? My dear Mrs Flowers, the law has *helped* me. A bent copper of some influence on the payroll together with his minions allows me to work in complete freedom. And Charlie Bray met the criteria.'

'Bray?' Lizzie repeated. 'He works for you?'

'Of course.'

'So it was you who had Danny pulled in for the Limehouse corpse?'

'Indeed.' Savage moved closer. 'As was Duncan King.'

'But – Duncan King was a—'

'A low-life and expendable,' Savage completed for her.

'He was also the same build and same hair colour as your husband. With a little imaginative clothing, King finally served a purpose.'

'You killed him?' Lizzie gasped.

'Not personally, but yes, he met with an accident and ended up as we all know at the bottom of the river.'

'So you meant Danny to misidentify him?'

'Of course. Your husband had disappeared, and I have to admit that I didn't know or care where he was at the time. I suspected my predecessor, Ferreter, had got rid of him and it was the perfect opportunity to pull in his brother who had the motive for murder.' Savage pointed his cigar in her face. 'You, my dear. He intended to have you, come what may. And put an end to his own brother to achieve it.'

'Danny would never have done such a thing,' Lizzie burst out. 'No one who knew Danny would believe it—'

'The law would,' Savage broke in calmly. 'And all would have gone according to plan if that fool Bray had managed to make the charge stick. God knows why he didn't. But it's a mistake that I shan't forget in a great hurry.' He sighed, walking away from her, only to turn suddenly, his expression bland. 'Now all your questions are answered—'

'And Richard Ryde?' Lizzie interrupted, feeling sick at the thought of what Savage was capable of. 'Did you mean to kill him?'

'That little hiccup was unfortunate.'

'How can you be so heartless?' Lizzie said, appalled.

'Richard was a young man in his prime, with a family to support, and now Ethel is a widow!'

Savage stared at her contemptuously. 'I'm sure her recovery will be swift. I'm acquainted with Mrs Ryde's little intrigue of the heart, confirming my opinion yet again that human nature is both devious and fickle.'

Lizzie was speechless. He knew about Cal and Ethel! He knew about everything, just as he had said he did. They had all been dancing to his tune, ever since Duncan King's body had been found.

'You can't kill us all,' Lizzie croaked. 'Not even you could get away with that.'

'You would be very surprised at what I can do,' he snarled, walking slowly towards her. 'First, I want the deeds to the land on Morley's Wharf and a contract of sale signed and sealed. And on that, your futures depend.'

Lizzie lifted her chin. 'Danny will never sell.'

'In that case, you will persuade him for me.' He reached out and lifted the hair from her shoulders, putting his face close to hers. '*Think* about what you love most in life, and imagine it being taken away. So that you will never see it – or hold it – again, and then you'll know exactly what you are capable of.'

Lizzie closed her eyes. Tears pushed themselves from under her lids. She knew he was talking about Polly.

Chapter Sixty-Three

'Please no!' Frank screamed again, wriggling back against Bert, groaning and yelping.

'You stinking bastards,' Bert cursed, looking into their faces. 'Murderers, the lot of you.'

The click of metal on metal gave Bert his reply. He waited for the bullet to reach him, plunge into his brain or his heart, rip at the delicate organs that had served him so well in his short lifespan. He wondered if the pain would be unbearable, his body racked by the spasms of death. And not a flicker of compassion in their killers' eyes, but perhaps another shot to confirm the kill. His only hope was that someone would find their bodies. That justice would be done in some shape or form.

But neither the pain nor the blackness arrived. Instead the lantern swung violently and in its precarious light he saw another figure. The glint of a blade slipped silently across the night and two bodies sank slowly to the ground. Bert stared at the heap. The gun that had been pointed towards him lay on the ground.

'What's happening? Who are you?' Bert strained his

eyes to see. He tensed, ready for a delayed shot, something he had failed to identify.

The figure came closer. Bert saw the brief flash of white teeth in the lamplight. Features lean as a whippet's, dark eyes shrewd and keen.

'Who are you?' Bert repeated as the ropes at his hands and feet were loosened.

'I'm the answer to your prayer, Mr Allen,' said the man in a rich, throaty accent.

'How do you know my name?' Bert asked, his eyes fixed on the quick-moving stranger.

'I'm a friend of your brother's.'

In the light of the lamp, Danny took the hip flask from the man he recognized as Murphy.

'Drink up, my friend,' Murphy told him as he held the lamp aloft. 'I think you're in need of sustenance.'

Danny gulped hard and the pain at his ribs soon eased. Savage had never intended to bargain. He'd hardly stepped inside the hostelry before he was downed, bound hand and foot and given a solid booting. But as he eased himself into an upright position, Danny smiled. 'Thanks,' he said gratefully and he spat the blood from his mouth.

'Would you look at that now,' Murphy said with a wry smile. 'Didn't I warn you that you might be out of your depth?'

Danny spat again, glancing up at the Irishman. 'You were right, Murphy. I'll give you that. Now get me up.'

It was Bert who took his arm. 'You all right, Danny?'

'I'll do. Are you?'

'A moment later and we'd have been dead ducks.' Frank brushed the straw from his clothes. 'But this geezer—'

'His name is Murphy,' Danny said, staring the Irishman in the eye. 'And I owe him a favour.'

'I'll call it in one day,' Murphy acknowledged.

Danny frowned, staring curiously at the man who had just freed them. 'How did you know we were here in Aldgate tonight?'

Murphy shrugged easily. 'My soldiers never leave me, Danny boy. Not even for a woman.'

Danny suddenly understood. 'Fowler? He's still your man?'

'Indeed.'

'*Our* Fowler – he's one of *your* men?' Bert said in alarm.

'Sure, you can't trust a soul these days, can you?' Murphy laughed, his eyes dancing in the glow of the light.

'And Lizzie?' Danny said anxiously, his heart racing at the thought of what might be happening to her.

'She's inside the hostel, my friend, safe enough for the moment,' Murphy replied calmly. 'And the Australian—'

'Cal?' Danny feared the worst. 'Is he alive?'

To his relief, Murphy nodded. 'But he's in no shape to join us. I've had my men take him across the road to my people where he'll be cared for.'

'Your people?' Bert repeated. 'But there's only a brothel.'

'That's right,' Murphy agreed. 'And a fine one it is too.'

'But me and Lizzie thought—'

'That the two in the street were conducting business?' Murphy twisted his lips in a mirthless smile. 'They were in a sense, my friend. My business, lookouts posted to watch the scum who stole this inn from me.'

'This was yours?' Danny said in startled surprise.

'It was,' Murphy replied, drawing in a slow breath. 'I'd not a penny in my pocket when I left Ireland, but I shed honest sweat to make this a fine and upstanding business. Then one day, Savage paid me a visit, as he did to you. Of course I refused him – as you did.'

'What happened?' Frank said in a whisper.

'He did with me as he did to your friend. And to others, I suspect, who opposed him. I was thrown into the well.'

'Christ,' said Bert, taking a sharp breath. 'He tried to drown you.'

Murphy nodded. 'But I paddled on the surface, like a drowning dog. I went under several times, but his face appeared to me. The thought of revenge kept me alive. My lungs were bursting, my knuckles bruised and bloody from clinging to the sides. Nothing has ever felt so good as the touch of the bucket to my fingers. I clung to it and the rope that was my lifeline. By morning I was near my last breath. But I saw daylight again and survived.' Murphy heaved in a sigh and glanced at Danny. 'Since then, I've learned patience and how to keep what is mine, by the strength of my wit and good and true soldiers about me.'

Frank leaned into the light and broke the silence. 'So you must know a way we can get out of here?'

For a moment Murphy was silent, then threw back his head and laughed. 'And here's me thinking you'd want to save your lady first!'

Frank looked embarrassed. 'I only meant—'

'Ah, sure, I know what you meant.' Murphy turned to Danny. 'How many did you count when they took you?'

'Two handfuls of men, maybe more.' Danny paused. 'How many do you have?'

'Enough,' was all Murphy answered.

'He has Lizzie, remember. There can't be any shooting—' Danny began but Murphy was already shaking his head.

'We've other ways, quieter ways,' he said softly, his hand slipping to the knife in his belt. 'There will be no shooting match, no chance of her being harmed.'

'You could be outnumbered,' Danny warned, thinking but not saying that knives were no match for guns.

'I've people I can trust,' Murphy assured him. 'Strong men, as you yourself know.'

'But they'll see us coming,' said Frank apprehensively. 'They've guards at the back and front.'

A hush filled the stable. Murphy passed the lamp to Danny. 'Hold this, my friend, while I show you.' Murphy found a spade and began to clear the straw. He scooped away the fetid earth and paused. It was then Danny saw the boards beneath.

A trapdoor.

Chapter Sixty-Four

'Bring the Daimler round,' Savage told one of his men. 'Mrs Flowers and I are leaving.'

'Where are we going?' Lizzie tried to pull away but he held her fast.

'Somewhere a little more comfortable. Time to get to know one another.'

'Let me go.' Lizzie pulled her arm again but, with her hands tied, she knew resistance was useless. Where was he going to take her?

Lizzie knew there was no escape. She stumbled as he pushed her towards the door. It was opened by one of his men carrying a gun. 'You know what you have to do,' Savage instructed. 'Flowers will cooperate when he knows we have her – and should it be necessary, his boy. Then, when he's signed – tidy up.' Savage pushed Lizzie into the warm, dark night.

She looked along the street for help. It was deserted. The van stood to one side, but it was empty. If she screamed would the people in the brothel hear her?

But before she could think what to do, a limousine she

recognized as Savage's drew up. The driver, wearing a peaked cap, got out and opened the back door. Savage roughly thrust her in. She stayed still, trying to get her breath, looking out of the window, wondering, if she yelled out, would anyone come to help her?

Savage climbed in beside her. He waved to the driver. 'Carry on.'

Lizzie closed her eyes. When she opened them the car was going smoothly along the lane. She glared at Savage with hatred in her eyes.

He laughed aloud, shaking his head. 'My dear, if you could see your face!'

'What are you going to do to Danny and the others?'

'Do you really want to know?' he spluttered, sliding his hat from his bald head and balancing it on his knee. 'Why, of course you do. Curiosity gets the cat, and women are feline, are they not?' He laughed again at his own joke. 'Sadly, there isn't much to tell. They will be dispatched – I have a system, a rather clever one. Tried and tested many times. Crude, cold and wet. But very effective.'

'What do you mean?' Lizzie whispered, her breath caught in her throat.

Savage's smile left his face. 'Just remember, my dear, I've warned you. And if you and your Polly want to survive, then behave!' He placed his fingers over her thigh.

'Such beauty. You would do well to try to preserve it.' He pulled her face round to him, squeezing hard. 'Mrs Flowers.'

Just then, the car swerved. Flowers let go of her and leaned forward. 'What the hell do you think you're doing?' he yelled at the driver.

There was no reply as the driver brought the Daimler to a sharp halt. Lizzie heard Leonard Savage's growl of anger as the back door was thrust open.

'Why have you stopped, you idiot?' he demanded, staring up.

'Because this is the end of your journey,' replied a voice in a throaty drawl. Lizzie watched in breathless silence as the driver doffed his hat and made a low sweep of his arm. 'This way – sir.'

'Who are you?' Savage said, a thread of fear in his voice.

'Why now, would you believe it? Such wit in this fellow,' laughed the Irishman. 'A grand man like yourself should recognize the stench of his own turf. The same place as not a few minutes ago you were describing to the lady beside you.'

Savage recoiled. 'Murphy!'

'As ever was.'

'But you're dead!'

'And truly resurrected,' Murphy said, reaching in and grasping Savage by the throat. 'Did you think this day would never come?' Murphy spat into Savage's face. 'Well, here I am to haunt you. And to see you surely on your way to hell.'

Lizzie heard Savage scream as Murphy dragged him from the car and Danny stepped forward to help.

★   ★   ★

'I'll give you everything, every penny I have,' pleaded Savage on his knees.

In the light of the many Tilleys now lit in the stable yard, held aloft by Murphy's men, Lizzie could see the Irishman clearly. He was younger than she had first thought and slim, with a proud bearing, his features chiselled and lean. His brown hair was razored at the sides and his leather waistcoat hung loosely across his bare chest. His soldiers, as he called them, stood watching silently.

'There's nothing you can give me,' Murphy said, 'that wasn't mine already.'

'Don't kill me,' Savage begged, squirming on his knees towards Danny, Bert and Frank. 'Tell him to give me another chance. I promise you'll never see me again. You'll have your land—'

'I already have it,' Danny said coldly. 'You've nothing to bargain with. As I had nothing. Your time's up in the East End.'

'No!' Savage shrieked as Murphy signalled to two of his men. 'Take him to the well.'

'What?' Savage bleated as they pulled him to his feet. 'You're putting me down there? But you can't!' Savage stared around him, sweat pouring from his bald head. He looked at Lizzie. 'Don't let him do it! Please, I beg you!'

'Is there no other way?' Lizzie asked Murphy.

'So the dog can bite again?' Murphy smiled. 'What's more important to you? This man or your family?'

'I wouldn't harm anyone, I promise,' Savage screamed. 'I'll change. Just give me the chance—'

'I'm giving you a chance,' Murphy said, his voice thick with emotion. 'The same chance as you gave me and the friend of this man, who fell foul of you.' He narrowed his eyes, pushing his face into Savage's. 'But I warn you, fight hard to stay afloat down there in the dark. Grasp at the wet stone until your knuckles bleed and your heart is bursting out from your ribs. Fight, or else you'll be sucked down, into the bowels of the Thames. Keep that in mind as the freezing water fills your mouth and enters your lungs.'

At the sound of Savage's screams, Lizzie turned away. She had heard and seen enough of violence and madness. Leonard Savage didn't deserve a chance. But Murphy was giving him one; a chance in a million perhaps, but it was more than Richard had had.

More than Savage would have given any of them, if he had won the day.

Chapter Sixty-Five

One month later

It was six o'clock on an unseasonably hot September morning and Lizzie was trying to fight off the effects of the dramatic arrival of her brother-in-law on her doorstep, just over an hour before. She'd been making breakfast for Polly and Bert when they'd heard a car screech to a halt outside. Next, there had been an almighty banging on the shop window. They'd rushed downstairs to find Syd outside, tearing his fingers through his uncombed hair.

'You've got to come with me,' he'd implored when Lizzie had unlocked the door. 'Flo's had pains all night. She won't let me drive her to hospital.'

'You mean the baby's on its way?' Lizzie had asked.

'Dunno.' Syd had looked desperate. 'You've got to come and see.'

It had taken Lizzie only a few moments to gather her things and leave Polly in the care of her uncle before Syd drove them wildly to Langley Street.

But when they'd arrived at the house and rushed

upstairs to the bedroom, they'd found Flo fast asleep in bed. Just where Syd had left her.

Now Lizzie gazed at her sister, who had woken at the disturbance. 'What's going on?' she demanded sleepily, surprised to see Lizzie. 'Syd, I told you it was a false alarm.'

'What do I know about having babies?' Syd groaned, glancing sheepishly at Lizzie and collapsing in the chair.

Flo struggled to sit up, pushing her damp fringe from her forehead. 'Whatever it was has stopped now.'

Lizzie sat down on the bed and smiled. 'Are you sure?'

Flo nodded and pointed to her bump. 'I reckon he was having a lark inside there.' She grinned at Syd. 'Trust a man to panic.'

Red-faced, Syd stood up and wrung out the flannel in the enamel bowl. 'What else was I to do? Stand around twiddling me fingers?'

Flo chuckled. 'He was hopping around in the early hours trying to find his trousers. I couldn't help seeing the funny side.'

'Trust me, there's nothing funny about seeing your wife in agony,' Syd protested, thrusting his hands in his pockets.

'I had a few pains yesterday, but they weren't very strong.'

'You didn't tell me,' Syd replied shortly.

'No, because you would have fussed. And me waters ain't broke yet and there's almost three weeks to go.'

'Syd did right,' Lizzie said as she looked at her down-cast brother-in-law. 'Dr Shaw said because of your near miscarriage he wanted you back the minute you started labour. By rights you should be in the hospital by now.'

'Not likely!' Flo exclaimed. 'You won't ever catch me near that place again.'

'What?' Lizzie said in surprise, staring at Flo.

'Precisely my point,' Syd interrupted. 'You'd better tell your sister what you told me.'

Flo shrugged, looking guilty. 'I want you to deliver the baby, Lizzie.'

'Me?' Lizzie half laughed. 'Flo, don't joke at a time like this.'

'I'm not. You helped to bring Polly into the world. She came out all right, didn't she?'

'I had no choice,' Lizzie protested. 'Babs was in a terrible state and there wasn't anyone to help, just you and me. If Frank hadn't gone to get Dr Tapper, I dread to think what would have happened.'

Lizzie still had nightmares about the day Polly was born. Babs had been in a terrible state, sick and undernourished and very distressed. Frank, who was thought to be the father, had been drinking heavily with Vinnie, their brother. Lizzie would never forgive Vinnie for running off and leaving them. At least Frank had eventually gone for help.

'Babs had a breech birth,' Flo reminded her calmly, 'but this baby is coming out the normal way. And I guarantee you I won't need no hospital.'

'How do you know that?'

'I just do, that's all.' Flo's face crumpled as she held her stomach.

Syd sprang forward. 'Have the pains started again?'

Flo looked up and grinned. 'No, you silly, I just want to wee.'

Syd sighed, passing his hand across his forehead. 'Christ, I'm having kittens here.'

'You're lucky it's only kittens and not a baby.' Flo threw back the sheet. 'Go and make a cuppa, love, while I use the commode.'

When Syd had gone and they had taken care of nature's demands, Lizzie helped Flo back to bed. Her sister was breathless at the effort it cost her and flopped back heavily against the pillow. 'Sorry Syd caused a fuss,' she apologized, glancing across to the empty landing. 'But now he's out of the way, I've got something to tell you.'

'And I've got something to tell you,' Lizzie interrupted as she plumped Flo's pillows. 'I ain't delivering this baby, no matter how hard you try to get round me.'

'Just listen first.' Flo pulled her down on the bed again. 'Do you believe in ghosts?'

'Ghosts?' Lizzie repeated, a half-smile on her face. 'What sort of ghosts?'

'Real ones, like spirits returned from the dead. Do you think there are such things?'

Realizing Flo was serious, Lizzie considered the question before replying. 'As I haven't met one, I don't know. I suppose I might if I did. Why?'

'Well, I've seen a real-life ghost.'

Lizzie grinned. 'You ain't delirious again, are you?'

'No, course not. Do you want to know when?'

Lizzie rolled her eyes. 'You're going to tell me, anyway.'

Flo nodded, her eyes beginning to sparkle. 'It was in hospital, the night you and Frank took me there. I was in a sort of twilight world, wondering what me chances were of ever getting out of that place again.'

'Flo, the hospital wasn't so bad.'

'To me it was. I couldn't sleep and was listening to all the moans and groans going on around me and you know, I thought, if I die here in this hospital bed, would me and my baby come back to haunt this place?'

'Flo, what a thing to think!'

'Couldn't help it. I was frightened out of me wits. I knew I had to stay for my baby's sake. But I kept thinking about those nurses at the sanatorium when I had scarlet fever and how, when someone died, like the girl in the bed next to me, there was those white figures that drifted silently in during the night and took her away. Next morning her bed was empty. I never saw her again.'

'That girl was very ill, Flo.'

'Yes, but I was very scared. I thought it might be me next.'

Lizzie touched Flo's hand. 'I'm sorry, love, it must have been awful.'

'You see, my very worst fear in life – the fear of dying in hospital – started when I had scarlet fever and had to stay at the sanatorium.'

'They wouldn't let me stay with you,' Lizzie said sadly. 'I could have spread the infection.'

A soft smile touched Flo's lips. 'Someone *was* with me this time.'

'Someone? Who?'

'Ma,' Flo whispered, her brown eyes very wide. 'She was suddenly standing by the bed as real as you are now sitting there. It felt so normal, like I was a kid again. I just said, "Ma, I don't want to lose my baby. And I don't want to die, neither." And you know what she said in reply? She said, "You won't die, nor will the baby, because your sister is going to bring it into this world." That was all. That was just what she said, word for word. And then she went away.'

Lizzie shook her head slowly. 'Couldn't it have been a dream?'

'It wasn't. She was real.'

'How do you know that?'

'Because last night, when I started to have pains, and before I woke Syd up, Ma came into my mind again. She wasn't there, this time. But I heard her saying you would bring my child into the world and not to be afraid. Then the pains went away, by which time Syd was up and on his feet. I didn't realize the bugger would rush off at a tangent and wake you up.'

'He didn't. We were up already.'

'That's good.'

'Syd has every right to be worried. So am I.'

'You needn't be. It's all in hand.'

Lizzie looked at her sister and a slow smile formed on her lips. 'I don't know what I'm going to do with you, Florence Allen. No, sorry, Florence Miller.'

Flo smiled, sliding her hanky over her damp brow. 'I think I'll just have another forty winks. Them pains fagged me out last night. Can you go downstairs and cheer up my other half before you go?'

'Are you sure you're all right?'

'Course I am.' Flo's eyes began to close. Very soon she had drifted off and Lizzie tucked the sheet over her hand. What had happened to Flo in the hospital, she wondered? She was frightened and alone with memories of the sanatorium tormenting her, so it was not surprising Flo had hated her stay there. But could Ma really have come to visit her little sister or was the dream so clear it seemed as if Ma was standing by the bed? Had fear or love, whichever had been the greatest, bridged the gap between life and what everyone thought of as death?

Chapter Sixty-Six

Syd's skin was the colour of parchment and his hands were shaking as he made the tea. Even though they were not on good terms and hadn't spoken properly since the day of Richard's funeral, Lizzie couldn't help but feel sorry for him.

'Shall I do that?' she asked softly.

'No, I'm better on the move.'

'Syd, I know we haven't seen eye to eye lately but—'

He looked up quickly and his face flushed. Tears filled his eyes and he sank down at the table, dropping his head to his hands.

Lizzie sat down too, waiting for him to speak. When he didn't she asked quietly, 'Syd, something's wrong, isn't it?'

Her brother-in-law nodded. 'I – I done something bad. Very bad.'

'Do you want to tell me what it is?' Lizzie stared at the top of Syd's bowed head. Why wouldn't he look at her?

'Everything started to go wrong when – when – Walter took Frank's watch.'

'What?' Lizzie felt the breath knocked out of her. 'It's true then? You and Walter did beat Frank up.'

'No, it wasn't me,' insisted Syd mournfully. 'It was Walter and Clifford. I tried to stop them, but they just laid in to Frank. I didn't even know Walter took the watch till you pointed it out.'

'But why?' Lizzie demanded. 'Frank didn't do anything to harm them or hurt your family.'

'I asked for their help. I wanted to frighten Frank off so he wouldn't come sniffing around again. But Walter and Clifford, well, they just went berserk.'

'They almost killed him,' Lizzie said angrily. 'How could you let them?'

Syd gave a smothered sob. 'I tried to pull them off, but I couldn't. I just wanted to help you, but it all went wrong.'

'I told you I would take care of things in my own way. It wasn't up to you to get involved with my affairs.'

'I know. And I should have listened.'

Lizzie shook her head in despair. 'Why didn't you?'

'It's down to a bloke to provide for his family,' Syd said in a bewildered voice. 'And there was me. I couldn't give Flo a nice house, or nice things. I couldn't even drive a car.'

'No one is blaming you for that.'

'I blamed myself. I was just a fish porter.'

'Oh stop it, Syd. You had a good job and you could have done very well if you'd stuck to it.'

'Walter said fish portering was a waste of time. If I went into the scrapyard they'd teach me to drive and I'd soon be earning big money.' He gulped. 'And I am.'

'Yes, and has it made you happy?'

Syd shook his head silently.

'You don't want to go to prison, do you?'

'No, course not.'

'If the law had followed up Frank's case properly, all three of you could have been charged with attempted murder.'

Syd gave a low howl of pain. Once more he held his head in his hands.

'Does Flo know what your brothers did?' Lizzie demanded, though she was dreading his answer. She wouldn't like to think that Flo had known about the beating, even agreed to it.

'No,' Syd said heavily. 'She hates Frank, but she'd never go along with what Walter and Clifford did.'

'So why did you lie to me about the watch?'

He shrugged, his slumped shoulders making him look a beaten man. 'I was ashamed. I knew Flo would go bananas if she found out. She didn't want me to chuck in my job, but I convinced her we needed the money. I've made a big mistake there. Walter and Clifford don't have no scruples and are mixing with very dubious types up in Soho. I don't like what I hear and see when I'm around them. But I can't turn the clock back now.'

'So what are you going to do?'

'Dunno.' Syd stared bleakly into her eyes. 'But I do know I'll never let you down again.'

'No you won't,' Lizzie agreed firmly, 'because if your brothers ever wrong-foot Flo in any way, I shall hold you personally responsible. Everyone makes mistakes and you deserve a second chance. You're a good man at heart. You stood by Flo and me through those troubled years and I'm grateful for it. But you've put yourself in a bad position and it's up to you to think of a way out of it.'

'I will. I promise.' Syd nodded, but Lizzie could see the fear in his eyes. Though he was a loyal husband and good son to the Missus, he was weak when it came to his brothers. Walter and Clifford were dangerous and, reading the expression on Syd's face, she knew that he was thinking the same.

Just then they heard a cry from upstairs. Syd shot to his feet and chased out of the kitchen. They both ran up the stairs and, when they entered the bedroom, Flo was sitting on the edge of the bed. 'Me waters have broken,' she gasped, staring down at her wet nightdress.

'Is it the baby this time?' Syd breathed, standing stock still.

Flo nodded, clutching her stomach.

Lizzie hurried to her sister and, after removing the nightdress as Flo fought the pains that were coming hard and strong, she shouted over her shoulder to Syd.

'There's a nurse who lives in March Street. Mabel Cranfield her name is, I think. Mum used to know her and she helped a lot of women round here. Go through the alley to No. 54 at the end of the terrace.'

There was no reply, just a crash of the door downstairs and the sound of Syd's running footsteps through the open window.

Chapter Sixty-Seven

Nelson Sydney Miller arrived in the world just thirty minutes later, slipping out from between his mother's legs into Lizzie's hands with an effortless cry. The little boy was not so little, Lizzie saw delightedly, as she wiped the blood and mucus from his well-formed limbs and wrapped him in a towel.

'You were right, love,' Lizzie said as, after hugging the baby to herself for a few precious seconds, she laid him gently in Flo's arms. 'He's perfect. And I'll bet he's no less than a ten-pounder.'

Flo clasped the bundle to her breast, tears of joy escaping down her cheeks. 'My baby, my beautiful son,' she whispered over and over again.

Just then the baby opened his dark eyes and let out a yell at the same time as Syd entered the room. Close behind him, Lizzie saw a plump young woman wearing a blue uniform, carrying with her a small brown case.

'I'm Nurse Edith Cranfield.' The nurse introduced herself breathlessly. 'Not a midwife, although I've done my training of course. Mrs Miller, your husband says you've had pains all night?'

Flo nodded, then smiled up at Syd. 'It's a boy, love. Nelson Sydney Miller. Just like we planned.'

Syd stepped slowly forward, his mouth hanging open. Lizzie slid her finger from the infant's grasp, a strong, healthy grip together with a scream to match.

'Well, we'll leave you and your son for a couple of minutes,' the nurse said, sounding a little put out. 'But I must see to the cord. Your husband will have plenty of time with the baby when you're tidied up.' Catching hold of Lizzie's arm, the nurse ushered her out onto the landing.

'From what Mr Miller tells me, his wife started labour yesterday,' she said in an offended whisper. 'Isn't she booked in with Dr Shaw at the maternity ward of Poplar Hospital?'

Lizzie shrugged. 'You'll have to ask my sister about that.'

'Your sister?'

'I'm Lizzie Allen, but you're not Mabel Cranfield, are you?'

'She was my aunt.'

Lizzie could see the resemblance. Edith was a smaller, younger version of Mabel. 'We – that is, the Allens – used to live in this house and I remembered a nurse living in March Street. So I sent Syd round to see if she was still there.'

'My aunt wasn't a real nurse, you know.' Nurse Edith

Cranfield frowned as she folded her hands under her ample bosom. 'No, no, not at all.'

'I didn't know,' Lizzie admitted. 'But she did help a lot of people.'

'She would be very old by now, if she had lived. I'm one of her many nieces and my husband and I took over the house after she died. Auntie was a bit of an eccentric. But I have to admit, she did help many babies into this world, though her practices would be very frowned on now and, I assure you, we do things very differently these days.' She paused, looking Lizzie up and down. 'Have you had any formal nursing training?'

Lizzie shook her head.

'I see. Mr Miller told me his wife had problems during her pregnancy. In fact she almost miscarried.'

'Yes, that's true.'

Nurse Cranfield eyed Lizzie with suspicion. 'The couple have a car, so he could have driven his wife to the hospital when she first started having contractions. Any complications that might have arisen could have been avoided.'

Lizzie just smiled. Tell that to my sister, she thought.

'Well, no time to lose.' The nurse pulled back her shoulders. 'If we have to ask the doctor to visit I'm sure Mrs Miller wouldn't object to that!'

'I'm sure she wouldn't,' Lizzie agreed, hiding her amusement.

The nurse sighed and glanced back into the bedroom. She gave Lizzie a little shove towards the stairs. 'Now, be a dear and fetch me some boiled water, clean towels and sheets.'

As Lizzie hurried off to the kitchen, she thought of Flo's prediction, that Nelson Sydney would be born safely and into Lizzie's own hands. A dream or a visitation, it had certainly come to pass.

Much to Lizzie's own surprise.

Chapter Sixty-Eight

Lizzie rolled up the waste in the newspaper and placed it in the bin outside. Returning to the kitchen she washed the china cups that just before Nurse Cranfield had left she had filled with hot, sweet tea, to celebrate Nelson's arrival. With her business concluded, the nurse had promised to call early the next morning, bringing the midwife and doctor with her.

Relieved that all major decisions were now being taken by those who knew best, Lizzie returned the china to the cupboard. The stew she had prepared was cooking on the stove and the house was quiet. Lizzie glanced around the kitchen, satisfied all was in order. She couldn't wait to go home and tell Polly she had a new cousin. Syd, the proud father, was eager to let the Missus know, but Flo had been reluctant to have visitors just yet.

With a sense of exhausted relief, Lizzie gazed out of the kitchen window to Flo's and Lil's back yards. Lil's washing was drying in the bright September sunshine, a clothes prop in the middle where the tails of Doug's shirts flapped in the breeze. Very soon, mused Lizzie, there would be rows of fluffy white nappies pegged to Flo's line and Lil and Flo would join each other at the fence, indulging in a few moments' peace as the baby slept in the pram.

Lizzie's thoughts inevitably drifted to Ethel. Her friend had moved to her mother-in-law's in Lewisham, so Bert had said after his visit to Danny's last week. Not that he'd found Danny very talkative, but more distressed at Cal's imminent departure from Tilbury to Australia. Cal had recovered now from his ordeal at the hostelry, but had given up hope of a future with Ethel. Lizzie knew that Danny would be very sorry to see his close friend leave for such distant shores.

A soft rumble met Lizzie's ears and, following it, she found Syd in the front room, sprawled out on the armchair, snoring loudly. She smiled at the prone figure. His sleepless night and the excitement of the day were catching up with him.

Quietly, Lizzie went upstairs. She fully expected Flo to be sleeping too as Nelson had been fed before Nurse Cranfield had left. But Flo was sitting up, her dark hair drawn behind her ears and her eyes fixed wistfully on the crib beside the bed. Flo beckoned her and Lizzie tiptoed in, to sit in contented silence, gazing at the new arrival: a chubby pink face, ebony half-moon eyelashes and a head full of dark fluff. Miniature fists peeping out from a white-knitted shawl.

'Ain't he handsome,' Flo whispered. 'A real boy.'

'Just as Ma said,' Lizzie replied softly.

'Now do you believe it wasn't a dream?'

Lizzie nodded, but so much had happened that she

didn't really know what to think. What was important was that the baby had arrived safely in this world.

'Talking of which, where is Syd?'

'Taking a cat-nap downstairs.'

Flo chuckled. 'Poor sod didn't get much sleep last night.'

'And he won't tonight. Not if Nelson has anything to do with it.'

'Lizzie,' Flo said quietly, 'I don't know what I'd have done without you.'

'Just don't ask me to deliver the next one.'

'Sorry, gel.' Flo looked down. 'I shouldn't have sprung that on you like I did. You've had enough on your plate without me to worry about.' Flo's eyes suddenly had a mischievous glint. 'Can't wait to tell Nelson when he's old enough that it was his Auntie Lizzie who brought him into this world, the same auntie who faced up to a rotten crook who got his just deserts at the bottom of a well.'

'Shh!' Lizzie put her finger to her mouth. 'I promised Murphy I'd never repeat to anyone what happened at the inn.'

Flo pouted. 'I can keep a secret. Do you think Murphy left Leonard Savage in the well?'

Lizzie shivered at the thought. 'I haven't asked him.'

'Have you seen him, then?' Flo's eyebrows shot up.

'Who, Murphy?' Lizzie shrugged. 'He's called by the shop a few times.'

Flo's mouth opened on an indrawn breath. 'Oh, I see!'

'No you don't. He was just seeing we was all right, that's all.'

'If you say so.'

Lizzie sat up straight, eager to change the subject. 'Flo, all I want now is to forget the past and for us to get on with our lives.'

'Does that mean you're ready to move in with Danny?'

'It means,' said Lizzie firmly, determined to avoid any more leading questions, 'that I'm going to open Mr James's old shop as a cooperative for women.'

Flo's frown deepened. 'A cooperative?'

'A shop where women can bring their goods and put them on sale. We'll take a percentage, or buy from them immediately if they're hard up.'

'No one does that around here.'

'Well, I'm going to.'

'You might lose a lot of money.'

Lizzie nodded. 'Or I could make us all some too.'

'But what about your love life?' replied Flo reproachfully, unwilling to be sidetracked. 'You could lose Danny if you're not careful. According to Polly, he's well in with his landlady, Mrs Williams.'

'When did Polly say that?' Lizzie felt her heart jump.

'Oh, you'd be surprised what our Pol tells us. She don't miss a trick, that kid. Me and Lil think this Mrs Williams is after Danny.'

'So you and Lil are on speaking terms again?' Lizzie tried to divert the conversation.

'Yes, course we are. Now about this Mrs Williams—'

'I don't know anything about her,' Lizzie said abruptly. 'Except that she seems a very nice person.'

Flo shook her head despairingly. 'Don't you see Danny's pride is hurt? Bloody Frank's still in the picture and then this Irishman turns up on the scene.'

Lizzie closed her eyes and sighed. When she opened them, she said slowly and clearly, 'I'm grateful to Murphy for what he did, but that's where it ends. As for Frank, you'll be pleased to hear that he's had his marching orders.'

Now it was Flo's turn to sit up, a look of disbelief on her face. 'You have? When?'

Lizzie took another patient breath. 'I went to the hospital and asked them if they would give him his job back. And they agreed.'

Flo gasped. 'I can't believe you did that. What did Frank say?'

'He didn't like the idea but I reminded him of our arrangement. That he was to leave as soon as he was well.' Lizzie put up her hand as Flo was about to interrupt. 'I also pointed out that Polly needs to know he's a decent, hard-working person and, as Bill and Gertie are prepared to put him up, on the understanding he'll be bringing in a wage, she can see him as often as she likes.'

Flo's jaw fell open. 'Well, I'm blowed!' She flopped back on the pillow, shaking her head. 'I'll never stop being surprised at you, Lizzie.'

'Nor me at you.' Lizzie gazed at her sister with pride. Then slowly her gaze fell on the baby. Nelson was fast asleep blowing bubbles that popped out from his tiny Cupid lips. Despite all her talk of independence, there was an unsettling tug deep inside her. When she'd held Nelson in her arms, with his new-baby smell on her skin, she hadn't wanted to let him go. She hadn't thought about shops, or fighting her corner. Instead, she'd envied the warmth and contentment of motherhood that Flo had accomplished.

'We'll always be here for you. Me, Syd and Nelson, whatever you do in life,' Flo said, and Lizzie nodded.

'Thanks, little sister.' Lizzie gently fussed with the pillows, trying to stem the tears that now felt so close. 'I've put a stew on to simmer and left a suet pudding that Syd can steam. I couldn't find any currants, but I've made the custard and—'

Flo caught hold of her wrist. 'You've done more than enough. Wake Syd and tell him to drive you home. Off you go to Polly, and that's an order.'

'All right,' Lizzie agreed doubtfully. 'But I'll leave Syd to sleep. I could do with some fresh air.'

Flo smiled, her liquid brown eyes shining. 'You've brought my baby into this world and I'll never forget that. You and Ma.'

As Lizzie left Langley Street that afternoon, with the soft breeze on her face, she felt very different. She wondered if what Flo had said was true and Ma had been with them at Nelson's birth.

All the Allens had been born at No. 82; Vinnie, Bert, Lizzie, Babs and Flo. Langley Street was the Allens' turf. And perhaps one day, Babs and Vinnie would return to the East End and old wounds would be healed with the help of the new generation.

Lizzie liked to think so. She wouldn't give up hope.

Chapter Sixty-Nine

Autumn, 1933

The smell of newly applied distemper stung her nose as Lizzie slid the key into the lock and opened the door. In just one week, the decorators had painted all the walls in a soft cream colour and the carpenter had built shelves on either side of the floor space. The dark brown linoleum, her greatest expense and perhaps extravagance, had yet to be laid.

She could see at a glance where she would position the greengrocery and the shining new glass cabinet. No more browned caulis or wilted greens; this time, she was buying from Covent Garden, choice merchandise, together with fresh flowers, a welcome splash of colour.

As Bill followed her in, they stood together in the middle of the room. In silent admiration of what was now a transformed selling space, complete with two storerooms at the rear and rooms above, Lizzie surveyed her new kingdom.

Her heart raced a little as she thought of the investment she was making, the risks she was taking.

'You've ideas above yourself, Lizzie girl,' Bill said as he leaned heavily on his walking stick, shrugging his shoulders under his old navy-blue greatcoat. 'And I like 'em.'

Lizzie laughed with relief. 'I was afraid you wouldn't.' Lizzie anxiously pulled the soft curves of her jacket around her, her long black hair falling across the delicate cloth. 'Every halfpenny counts, don't it?'

'You're a pioneer, girl,' Bill said thoughtfully. 'Breaking the mould, that's what you're doing. You're giving the power back to the people. Letting the women think and bake for themselves. That's how we'll survive the next depression.'

'I hope that's a long way off.'

'You was with me in '28 when all the small shops went under. But you kept us afloat, gel, you was canny.'

She smiled gratefully at the elderly man. They had survived the roughest of times together, celebrated the best, and today was no different. 'Do you really think I can do this, Bill?'

For a moment he paused and Lizzie's heart stood still as she waited for his reply. 'I wouldn't be standing here now if I didn't,' he told her. 'I only wish I was young again and could join you.'

'You've taught me everything. You'll always be in my head, telling me which way to go.'

Bill nodded contentedly. 'That's good enough for me, Lizzie girl.' He shuffled slowly across the floor to frown out of the window. Saying over his shoulder, 'You'll be interested to know Frank's toeing the line. He's started at the hospital, Gawd help the patients. Doing his bit about the house. Gertie fusses over him like an old mother hen. I reckon she deserves a bit of consideration after all these years.'

'So do you, Bill.'

He laughed softly, turning slowly to gaze at her. 'We'll see how long it lasts. And then when he buggers everything up, Danny can have the satisfaction of saying I told you so.'

Lizzie shook her head. 'He wouldn't do that.'

'My young 'un still in the picture?' The question came unexpectedly and Lizzie felt her cheeks grow warm.

'I ain't seen him, Bill.'

'Won't take ten minutes to drive over to there.'

'He could come to me.' Lizzie lifted her chin and continued to look steadily at the old man.

He nodded again, his shoulders sagging even more as a horse-drawn cart arrived outside. The young driver pulled hard on the reins and then, frowning in, raised his cloth cap to Bill.

'That's my ride,' he puffed, indicating the cart. 'The kid next door said he'd call and take me home.'

'I'd like to drive you, Bill.'

'Good excuse to get some air.' With a wry smile, he nodded. 'Take care of yourself, girl. And show the world your mettle.'

'I will,' she said, trying to hide the catch in her voice.

A moment later, the young man was helping Bill to climb aboard the cart. Settled under a blanket, Bill looked happy as he took the leather reins in his hands. The cart clattered off and, in silence, Lizzie gazed about her.

Could she believe it? This shop was hers. In a month's time its doors would open and a new chapter of her life would begin. Unbidden, her thoughts flew to Ethel, from whom she'd not heard in many weeks. 'It's time you were here with me, Ethel. We've work to do,' she told the cloudy grey sky that stretched over the roofs of the terraced houses on the opposite side of the street. 'There's a future here for you, making our dreams come true.'

In answer, the sun burst out from the clouds, lighting up the interior of the shop. 'Small steps,' she whispered knowingly. 'And today is the first of many.'

Taking the key from her pocket she glanced one more time around the spacious room, a smile of confidence on her lips. Then, pulling her shoulders back determinedly, she left the shop, eager to embark on the next step of her journey, beginning with the drive to Lewisham.